BEYOND POWER

CONNIE MANN

D1056808

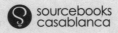

sourcebooks
casablanca

Published by Sourcebooks Casablanca, an imprint of Sourcebooks
P.O. Box 4410, Naperville, Illinois 60567-4410
(630) 961-3900
sourcebooks.com

Printed and bound in Canada.
MBP 10 9 8 7 6 5 4 3 2 1

For Leslie Santamaria, incredibly talented writer, amazing human, and priceless friend, who always knows what I meant to say. Cheering you on every step of the way and thanking God we get to ride the roller coaster together!

CHAPTER 1

IF ONLY HUMANS WERE AS PREDICTABLE AS THE MONKEYS she'd come back to Ocala to study. Delilah Paige Atwood took a sip of her coffee and sighed. Expression carefully bland, she studied the patrons at the Corner Café while she uploaded her latest batch of photos and research notes using the free Wi-Fi. At least part of her plan had worked. No one appeared to have seen through her disguise or questioned the name Delilah Paige. Equally noteworthy, no one from her antigovernment, paranoid family had burst through the door with guns blazing, furious that she'd dared to come back to town.

It was the other part that worried her. She'd spent every morning of the past two weeks eavesdropping on the locals, and she still had no idea how to find her family. Her sister would be sixteen in two weeks, which meant Delilah was running out of time.

She shut down her laptop and had just tucked her field journals into their zippered compartment when the bell above the door jangled merrily. The whisper of awareness that slid down her spine told her without looking that Josh Tanner—"Hollywood" to his friends—had just walked in.

His eyes lit up when he spotted her, and that breath-stealing grin flustered her, just as it did. Every. Single. Time. While he ordered coffee, she reorganized her backpack, hoping he didn't notice her ridiculous blush. After her isolated childhood, she'd spent years studying people's social interactions like a research project, desperate to learn how to behave, what to say, how to relate to others. She'd learned to look people in the eye, go on dates, and even thought herself in love once, but every shred of her hard-won poise vanished whenever he walked in.

He…unsettled her. And intrigued her in equal measure.

Something about his kind eyes, his sometimes-sad eyes, whispered to a part of her she hadn't known existed. To say nothing of his movie-star good looks and the intimate smile that made her fumble and stammer. Still, she kept showing up at the café, hoping for more of his fun, flirty banter, despite the uncomfortable fact that he was FWC, a Florida Fish & Wildlife Conservation Commission officer. His uniform alone should have sent her running, but somehow, the man wearing it had snuck under her defenses and tempted her to linger over her coffee cup.

You have more important things to do, her mind chided.

Five minutes won't change anything, her heart countered.

It was selfish, she knew, to put her wants above Mary for even a second, but she couldn't make herself leave. Not yet. Ten minutes. No more.

"Good morning. How's my favorite monkey researcher today?" Josh asked as he strolled to her table and turned a chair around. He straddled it, sipping the coffee he'd just purchased and eyeing her over the rim.

She raised a brow and sent him a cheeky grin. "I'm pretty sure I'm the *only* monkey researcher you know." Was that really her voice, sounding all low and sultry?

"True, but you're still my favorite."

She laughed and gripped her coffee cup as she tried to think of something witty to say. He'd propped his sunglasses on top of his head, and she couldn't help studying the khaki uniform that molded to him like a second skin. She dragged her gaze away from his chest in time to realize he'd been studying her, too.

"You have paint on your fingers." He pointed.

Delilah glanced down at the traces of dark green she'd missed when she'd scrubbed her hands. "Thankfully, most of it's on the camper." She sent him what she hoped was a casual smile. "It's done and it looks good, if I do say so myself." Getting the camper habitable had been step one, so she and Mary would have a place to stay.

"I'm sure it looks great. Can't wait to see it. So where are you headed today?"

Her stomach did a little flip. Did he really want to see her camper and spend time with her away from here? Or was that just Josh being a nice guy and making conversation? She'd never seen him flirt with anyone—except her. And he always seemed to end up sitting at her table. But chatting over coffee and inviting him into her home were two very different things.

She couldn't begin to think about all that right now. "I figured I'd swing by Tanner's Outpost and rent a kayak from your sister, see if I can track down one of the other monkey troops today. Babies are starting to arrive," she added, grinning. She would also scout out the area, check if anyone had seen the Atwoods recently. She wasn't overly optimistic they would tell her even if they knew, but she had to try. And she'd keep trying until she found them. "The other troop I've been watching this week has been hanging out just south of the Silver River, near one of the trails in the state park. Lots of people have gathered out there, watching them."

He straightened, suddenly serious. "Have you found anyone feeding them?"

Frustration washed over her. "Unfortunately, yes. I tried to educate the family. They're from Michigan, so I likened feeding the monkeys to what happens if you feed bears. I think I got through." She hoped. This was why her research mattered so much. She wanted to prove that instances of so-called aggression toward humans would be severely lessened, if not eliminated, if people quit offering them food.

"Did I hear you say monkeys?" another voice asked.

Delilah looked up, and all her instincts went on alert as a tall, thirtysomething man with thinning hair pulled out a chair and sat down at the table. Not as tall as Josh, his pale skin and doughy shape said he spent most of his time at a desk somewhere. He extended a hand across the table, and Delilah hesitated before she shook it, instantly recoiling from his damp palm. He didn't seem to notice her reaction, but Josh did. He grinned and sent her a flirty wink that made butterflies swoop in her stomach.

"Casey Wells, with the local paper." He hitched a thumb over his shoulder. "Folks say you're from Florida State University, studying our Silver Springs monkeys this summer."

Wary, Delilah nodded. "It's part of my master's program in anthropology." She didn't tell him her grant was from the National Geographic Society or exactly what her study of the rhesus macaques entailed. She'd earned her disdain of the media the old-fashioned way—she'd inherited it from her government-fearing family.

Wells nodded. "Good for you." He glanced between the two of them, smirked. "I'm just curious. After yesterday's incident, do you agree with the Florida Fish & Wildlife Conservation Commission that the monkeys should be removed because they're not indigenous?"

Delilah froze, and a chill slid down her back. "What incident?"

Wells smiled smugly. "There's a video online that has gone viral, showing the monkeys charging a family of tourists in the state park."

Was that the same family she'd spoken to? She narrowed her gaze. "And did they feed the monkeys?"

Wells shrugged. "I couldn't say. I'm just going by what I saw online, like everyone else." He paused. "But getting back to my earlier question, will your study be for or against the monkeys' removal?"

"Since rhesus macaques have been here longer than many of the human families in this area, I believe we should leave them alone. How are they different from the Cracker cows originally brought here by the Spanish? Or the wild pigs, descended from those DeSoto brought with him? When do we stop calling a species 'non-native'?" She felt her voice rising, so she swallowed whatever else she might have said. Yes, she was passionate about the monkeys, determined to protect them, but she was a logical researcher representing prestigious organizations, not a nutty radical spouting emotion.

Casey Wells smiled widely. "Well said, Ms. Paige." He turned to Josh. "Care to comment on that, Officer Tanner?"

Josh sent her a look that said *I'm sorry* before turning to Wells. "While I agree that the monkeys have been here a very long time, they are not without issues. Managing the growing population is complicated. Non-native species like these can have a negative impact on the native populations already in this area. There is also concern about the herpes B virus they carry." When Delilah opened her mouth to argue, he added, "Though there is no documented evidence of the virus being transmitted from monkeys to humans. Right now, though, the biggest concern centers around signs of aggression toward humans."

Delilah stiffened at his political-sounding response, and all her childhood warnings about law enforcement, about how cops said one thing and did another, came rushing back. She should never have let her guard down around someone in uniform, no matter how nice he seemed or how fast her heart beat whenever he was around. She took a breath and deliberately kept her tone even. "So-called aggression toward humans is a growing concern because people think 'don't feed the monkeys' doesn't apply to them."

Despite her carefully modulated tone, the café suddenly went quiet, all eyes turned their way. Josh glanced around before he looked back at her. "On that, we agree. Many of the issues would resolve themselves if people stopped feeding the monkeys—or any other wildlife."

Delilah stood and finished loading her backpack. She felt far too exposed with everyone watching them, too disappointed in Josh. Hearing him spout the official FWC party line completely threw her, since tourists came to Tanner's Outpost from all over to see the monkeys. Add her increasing worry for Mary, and she could easily say things she'd regret. Besides, none of this mattered right now.

"Look, Delilah," Josh began, just as his cell chirped. He checked the screen and muttered, "I need to go." When he looked up, his eyes held apology. "I want us to finish this conversation." He glanced at Wells, then back at her. "Alone." His phone chirped again. "I'm sorry." He stepped closer and squeezed her hand, sending a little zing up her arm. "We'll talk later. Be safe out there today." And then he was gone.

Delilah blinked in surprise that he'd touched her and again when she realized how much she'd liked it. As he walked away, his clean scent lingered in her nostrils, and she wondered what else he'd wanted to say.

Wells shot to his feet. "He makes a valid point. Aren't you worried about being out in the forest alone?"

Delilah slung her backpack over her shoulder, irritated that Wells was still probing for information. "Can't think of a reason to be." She knew what he meant, but she wouldn't encourage further conversation.

"Well, after that other researcher was beaten so badly last year…" He let the statement trail off. "They never found out who did it, did they?"

Delilah figured he knew the answer to that as well as she did. But she had tracked down Vanessa Camden, who hinted that the media had exaggerated what happened. She had wanted to go home—Vanessa hated being in the forest—so that had been the perfect excuse. Delilah didn't tell Wells any of that.

"The other study was aimed at the dangers associated with the rhesus macaques remaining in the area and strongly supported their removal. I view the situation from a different perspective and have no desire to see that happen. People who support them staying would have no problem with my study." She hitched up her chin. "So, no, I'm not worried."

"I hope you're right," Wells said before he tucked his notebook into his shirt pocket and walked away.

Delilah headed outside, scanning the parking lot before she climbed into her pickup. Josh had said he had to go, but a little part of her had hoped he'd wait for her. She wanted to hear what he had to say.

She hit the highway and forced herself to take several deep breaths to settle the emotional stew churning in her gut. She couldn't think about Josh and the butterflies he unleashed in her stomach or her disappointment that he didn't share her opinion on the monkeys.

There were only two weeks left until Mary's birthday.

━━━━━━━━

An hour later, Delilah sat in her rented kayak on the Ocklawaha River, using her camera's zoom to pan the trees on both sides of the waterway. As she did, she mentally ran through her list of options. Tracking her father down for a confrontation and shouting, "How could you have done that?!" would make her feel better, maybe, but wouldn't faze him in the least, not even if she pointed her Glock at him as she did so. It wouldn't convince him to let Mary go, either. Not a "mere" woman, acting out of emotion.

John Henry was all about control. He was harsh and ruthless and took deliberate action, believing he had absolute power. He feared no one. She'd bet her camper that he would dismiss her without a word, just as he had before. Unless she found a way to level the playing field.

Dark memories of his cold indifference to pain—both physical and emotional—chilled her, a stark contrast to the calm of a quiet summer morning. She pushed it aside and looked around at the beautiful scenery while she considered and discarded various next steps. The sun beat down, and humidity shimmered in the still air. There was no breeze, so the river was smooth as glass.

Liberally coated in essential oils to keep the mosquitos away, Delilah lowered her camera and listened. *There.* Was that them? She could usually hear the rhesus macaques chattering in the tree-tops long before she could see them.

Several quick strokes toward the opposite shoreline and she raised her camera again, listened. *Yes.* Now she heard them, though she still couldn't locate them in her viewfinder. They were too far back in the trees to see from her vantage point.

Knowing how sound traveled over the water, she quietly pad-dled toward shore and beached her kayak between two cypress stumps, carefully securing the rope to a tree, lest the current tug it free. She slung her backpack over her shoulder and gingerly stepped onto the bank, using the cypress knees to avoid the muddy spots.

She slowly walked inland, following their chatter and search-ing for telltale movements high up in the tree canopy, but she also studied the ground. Monkey sign, or as she and Mary called it, "monkey poo," indicated she was in the right area.

The chattering stopped.

After she checked a fallen log for snakes and bugs, she sat down to wait. Sometimes, the quiet meant they'd moved on, but other times, it meant they were watching.

She tried to ignore the twitchy feel of unknown eyes study-ing her by taking slow, deep breaths. Within two minutes, her damp shirt stuck to her skin, so she pulled it away and flapped the fabric to create a breeze. She remembered the way Josh's apprecia-tive glance had run over her this morning, just as she'd run hers over him. The way his uniform shirt hugged his torso had made her throat go dry. But it was more than his looks that turned her from intelligent, well-spoken researcher into stammering idiot. His slow, thorough perusal made her acutely aware of herself as a woman, and that flustered her. She'd never been the pretty one. She was the smart one, the one voted "most likely to be in the library on a Friday night" by her classmates.

He never seemed to notice her social awkwardness, though, engaging her in flirty conversation and sending her a lazy, dimpled smile that always made heat wash over her body.

Why couldn't she stop thinking about him?

The monkeys started chattering again, and seconds later, she heard a noise behind her. She jumped to her feet, spun around.

It took a few beats to recognize what sounded like teenage voices, male and female. She caught a flash of movement and started in that direction. Maybe they could tell her about any nearby campsites.

"Excuse me! Hello?"

Instead of stopping, they took off into the trees. Hadn't they heard her? Delilah ran faster, trying to keep them in sight. Another glimpse and she spotted two mountain bikes. "Wait!"

The girl sent a quick glance over her shoulder as she followed the young man. Late teens, she'd been wearing a long cotton dress, her hair in a braid down her back, similar to what Delilah had worn as a child.

When they disappeared, Delilah slowed to a stop, defeated. But then she saw their tire tracks and smiled. She could follow a trail like that blindfolded. They were probably camping in the area, and given the girl's dress, she'd bet money they knew her family. She wasn't sure they'd say anything about the Atwoods, but as this was the first lead she'd found, she set out to track them down.

The scent of a smoldering campfire made her quicken her steps as a wave of memories crashed over her. She was close.

She ran into the small clearing and stopped short, surprised there was no one there. She didn't see any bicycle tracks, either, so the teens must have veered off earlier and she'd missed it. So much for her great tracking skills.

Pushing her disappointment aside, she looked around. Someone had been here recently. Her eyes caught the small grooves high up on two tree trunks, and the hair on the back of her neck stood up. They looked just like the ones her father carved to secure Mama's laundry line.

Don't jump to conclusions.

She backed up, and the ground beneath her right heel gave way. Arms flailing, she lunged forward and landed on all fours. She stayed that way for a moment, breath heaving, before she carefully climbed to her feet and studied the leaves and branches that had camouflaged a deep hole in the ground. Dread and elation warred inside her as the truth dawned. Above her was a tall tree, the kind her father always used to raise their tarp-covered food overnight to keep it safe from foraging animals. The pit below—the one she'd almost fallen into—was designed to net another meal when an unwary critter followed the scent and found itself trapped in the hole.

She'd found her family's campsite. They hadn't left the area.

The smoldering embers meant they'd abandoned this site in a hurry, though. Otherwise, her father would have smothered the fire more thoroughly. He'd never risk starting a forest fire.

Delilah stepped closer and crouched down. Something poked out of the dirt and ashes at the fire's edge. She studied it, and her heart almost stopped.

No. That couldn't be. Could it?

She grabbed a branch and used it to poke at the object, then dragged it to the edge of the fire ring. Her hand shook when she reached down and then held it up with two fingers, blinking rapidly, convinced her eyes were deceiving her.

Her heartbeat pulsed in her ears as she ran her fingers over the charred remains of a homemade doll. The brown fabric dress was mostly intact, as was the soot-covered cloth face. Embroidered eyes stared at her like childhood memories and tried to yank her back in time, but she pushed them aside.

Focus. Make sure.

She swallowed hard and slowly turned the doll over. There, on the back of the neck, was a small heart, embroidered in red thread. It was identical to the one Mama had embroidered on Delilah's doll. She'd later added one to Mary's, saying it was a kiss from their Mama. Memories of Mary playing with both dolls, setting them side by side for a tea party, flashed through Delilah's mind. This belonged to her sister. There was no question.

Time stood still and then shot backward before it flipped her world upside down with a speed that made her dizzy.

Her father had burned Mary's doll.

Dear Sweet Jesus. It's happening again.

Delilah turned her head and threw up, heaving until there was nothing left in her stomach.

She wiped the back of a trembling hand over her mouth, then pulled a plastic bag from her backpack and carefully placed the doll inside.

With a last look around, she ran back to her kayak, feet pounding in time to her heart, and paddled back to Tanner's Outpost as fast as she could. She needed her truck.

Forty-five minutes later, hands clutching the steering wheel, Delilah sped through the forest, the truck fishtailing and her mind spinning. She finally looked around and realized she'd blindly headed toward the campsite where she'd last seen her family eight years ago. Her heart still knew these woods, knew the trees and abandoned cabins and all the various landmarks that guided those who lived off the grid and under the radar. She'd checked here once before and found nothing, but maybe now, they'd come back.

She stopped a half mile before she reached the campsite and tucked her truck behind a clump of scrub palm. She went the rest of the way on foot, dodging sandy spots that would leave footprints. The closer she got, the faster her heart pounded. The anger she'd locked in a sturdy metal box roared up and threatened to choke her. How could her father do the same thing to Mary that he'd done to her? She stopped, hands on her knees as she breathed deeply to steady herself. If she didn't handle this right, she'd never get Mary out of there. *Control your emotions and you control the situation.*

Head high, she marched into the small clearing and stopped short. They weren't there. Since she'd been drawn back to the place her world had completely changed, she'd foolishly imagined it would bring them back, too. She snorted. Her father didn't have a sentimental bone in his body. He forced the family to move their campsite regularly simply to keep anyone from snooping around.

She took a steadying breath. There was one place they always returned to, though. Maybe they'd left a clue at the storage bunker her father had built when they'd first come to Florida. You couldn't dig too deeply out here before things got muddy, but John Henry had found a small depression in the earth, what appeared to be the remnants of a sinkhole, and had used it to conceal some of their supplies. Her family wasn't what people called "preppers," so they didn't hoard piles of food and nonperishables. Instead, they were survivalists who knew how to live off the land.

As she headed toward the nearby bunker, the smell hit her first. She covered her nose and tried to pinpoint where it was coming from. Once you'd smelled a dead animal, you never forgot the stench. Out here, decomposition didn't take long.

She moved closer, scanning the area, realizing whatever it was, it must be a larger animal. Possibly a deer, maybe even a hog. She eased around a stand of trees and almost tripped over the body.

And it wasn't an animal.

She breathed in through her mouth and forced herself to squat down and look closer. He'd obviously been a hunter, given the bright orange vest. She squeezed her eyes shut. Half his face was missing, as were huge chunks of his chest. He was clearly dead.

Her head snapped up as she felt a vibration in the ground followed by a low rumble. An icy chill slid down her back. She knew that sound. "Stay calm," she muttered to herself as she slowly eased to a standing position.

Moving nothing but her eyes, she scanned the area and spotted the black bear heading in her direction. Male probably, based on its size. Normally, she'd make a racket to let the bear know she was here, but if he'd picked up the scent of the hunter, she didn't want him seeing her as competition.

She couldn't run, either. *If you run, you're prey*, her father's voice reminded her. She slowly backed up, one quiet step at a time, and eased behind a tree, out of the bear's line of sight. She forced herself to take quiet breaths as she melted farther and farther into the trees. She didn't take off running until she was confident the bear couldn't hear—or smell—her anymore.

She burst into the clearing and skidded to a stop when she spotted two white pickups parked by the bunker. *Crap!*

She slipped behind a tree and tried to catch her breath while she studied the scene. Two men were transferring a stack of wooden crates from one pickup's bed into her family's bunker while two others watched. Next to them sat an open black satchel with what looked like stacks of money inside.

One of the men grabbed an automatic rifle and put it to his shoulder. She jerked back behind the tree and then ducked at the sound of gunfire. Bark flew just above her head. She peeked out again, and when a second man raised his rifle and took aim, she realized they were using the tree next to her as target practice. She had to get out of here. She must have made a noise, because the first man's head snapped up like a deer scenting danger. Delilah froze as their eyes met and held.

Her brother Aaron had aged in the past eight years and now sported a full beard. But his eyes were still the same, not just the color but the harshness in them.

She started to call his name before it dawned on her that he didn't recognize her. The last time he'd laid eyes on her, her hair reached her backside and she'd been wearing an ankle-length dress. Now, here, with short hair, wearing "worldly" clothes, a ball cap, and sunglasses, he'd have no reason to suspect it was her.

One of the other men turned slightly, and Delilah gasped at the sight of her father. John Henry had aged, too, but still held himself ramrod straight, no softening anywhere. She'd seen the third man at the café but didn't recognize the fourth. While her mind scrambled for what to do, Aaron seemed to have no such trouble. He lifted the gun and continued firing, as did the other man. When her father sighted a weapon, Delilah scrambled backward and dove behind the nearest tree, then leaped behind another and another, desperate to stay out of their line of sight. She crouched low and tore off into the forest, zigzagging the way she'd been taught. Bark rained down and sand spit up as she ran, the sound of gunfire in her wake.

CHAPTER 2

IF AARON HAD BEEN TRYING TO KILL HER, SHE'D BE DEAD, Delilah told herself as she ran, though that did little to calm her racing heart. Same went for her father. Both were excellent marksmen. When she finally made it back to her truck, winded and shaken, more of her childhood training kicked in. She grabbed a palm frond and used it to wipe out her tracks. As she backed toward her vehicle, she heard the buzz of an airplane.

She finished erasing her trail and then hopped into the truck and sat quietly, waiting for it to pass overhead. When she glanced up through the trees and saw the Fish & Wildlife logo, her heart pounded harder.

Once the sound of the plane receded, she put the truck in gear and drove around in circles to be sure she wasn't followed back to the tiny 1970s vintage camper she'd picked up for almost nothing. She'd set it in a thick stand of trees ten miles from where she'd grown up so she wouldn't run across any family members unless she meant to and had painted the outside dark green to camouflage it further. The whole thing was barely big enough to turn around in, but given the size of the camper their family had lived in, it was plenty big.

Right now, it was the only safe place she could think to go. Her hands shook as she cranked open all the windows to let out the old, musty smell common to anything in Florida that was closed up awhile. Afterward, she still felt like the walls were closing in, and she couldn't seem to catch her breath. She debated firing up the generator so she could run the small window air conditioner, but both made a racket, which could carry through the forest. Plus, the generator was almost out of fuel, and she didn't want to have to carry more gas cans out here.

She poured a glass of water and shook her head at her racing, dis-jointed thoughts. She had to calm down, think logically. She looked around the interior, wondering what Josh would think when he saw it. Assuming, of course, she decided to invite him. She was inor-dinately proud of the way it had turned out. The brown paneling was now a crisp white, and the green-and-gold curtains had been replaced with pretty flowered sheets she'd tossed over the rods. Until Josh, she'd never considered inviting anyone to see where she lived—a lifetime's training and all that—never mind a handsome man who made her palms sweat and her stomach do backflips.

What was wrong with her? She sank down on the sofa and dropped her head in her hands. She couldn't use Josh to avoid what she'd seen. She should call him right now, report the man's death. She squeezed her eyes shut to block out the images.

But was the man's death somehow connected to her family? They had never been part of a formal militia group, but they had definitely made alliances with other like-minded families and pro-cured weapons when asked. She'd started going along on deliver-ies when she was twelve years old, providing cover. But the stacks of crates she'd seen earlier took things to a whole different level. What were they up to? Had they recognized her? If so, would they take off again? Maybe leave the area for good? She swallowed hard. She couldn't let that happen, or she might never find Mary and Mama again.

She picked up her cell phone, then set it down, indecision gnawing at her.

Memories of the man's mangled body made her stomach lurch, but she forced her sorrow and revulsion aside so her scientist's brain could look at the situation from a clinical distance. Why had the bear attacked? Had the hunter provoked him in some way? She'd studied enough animals to know this behavior was unusual. Unless they had a very good reason, bears did not attack humans.

Mind racing, she grabbed her phone again. She should call

Josh, let him know what she'd seen. Despite her ingrained mistrust of law enforcement, everything she'd learned about him said he was a good man. Right now, though, calling him would mean questions, so many questions she didn't want to answer.

She hopped up and paced the tiny space, trying to decide what to do.

———

Florida Fish & Wildlife officer Josh Tanner looked out the window of the Cessna 182 and scanned the section of the Ocala National Forest below him, fighting his irritation. Normally, he enjoyed taking the FWC plane up for special assignments or search and rescue, a nice change from his usual patrol by truck, boat, or ATV. Today, though, when Hunter Boudreau, his lieutenant and friend, had asked him to follow up on a hot tip about a significant new marijuana grow in the northwest section, Josh had almost growled at the timing. He'd wanted to finish his conversation with Delilah, answer all those questions he'd seen in her pretty blue eyes after Wells questioned him about the monkeys. He wished he had her number, but the way she sometimes froze when the door to the café opened, like a rabbit poised to run, had made him cautious. Hopefully, she'd be at the café tomorrow morning so he could explain. Her opinion of him mattered, more than he was comfortable with, but there it was.

He checked his divers' watch and figured he could make a few more passes and still get to the Forest Community Center for basketball practice. He never wanted the boys to think he was blowing them off.

Josh's frustration grew as he scanned both sides of the river. He couldn't find the location their anonymous caller had described. Given the dense foliage and vegetation, unless FWC or some other law enforcement agency happened to fly directly overhead, no one would ever know the grow was there.

He had just made another pass near where the Atwoods used to camp when he heard several bursts of gunfire. His eyes flicked over the ground, trying to locate where the shots were coming from. Were they aiming at him? John Henry Atwood's radical leanings kept him on law enforcement's radar, but this wasn't like him or his son.

This also wasn't anywhere near the gun range, nor was it private property or hunting season, when target practice was allowed with a proper backstop. Maybe he'd found the marijuana grow and someone wasn't happy.

He called dispatch and searched for a dirt road wide enough to land the Cessna.

His radio crackled. "Backup en route, 413. Lieutenant Boudreau said not to do anything stupid, Hollywood."

"10-4. I'm putting her down just off Forest Road 11." He rattled off the GPS coordinates and then focused on landing the plane.

Once on the ground, he grabbed his rifle and stayed low as he ran into the trees bordering the road. The gunfire had stopped, which would make it hard to locate the shooter or shooters.

Josh made his way toward the Atwoods' former campsite, stopping to listen every few yards. To date, his dealings with the family had been brief but cordial, nodded greetings at the local bait shop. John Henry treated his wife as though she were invisible. She kept her head down, never made eye contact, and walked in her husband's shadow. Their grown son, Aaron, was on the cocky side, and their teenage daughter, Mary, mimicked her mother's body language. Josh didn't like it, but it wasn't his job to evaluate people's relationships unless he suspected abuse. He'd made a casual survey of both mother and daughter and saw no obvious signs.

He wasn't really surprised to find their campsite empty. He studied the area for a moment and then noticed two sets of tire tracks that appeared to have been made recently. Very recently, since it had rained yesterday afternoon.

He stood, sniffed the air. The smell hit him at the same moment the noise registered. He quietly headed in that direction, careful not to step on twigs or make any sudden noises. He ducked from tree to tree until he saw the flash of black and realized it was a bear, not a human. Whereas he might sneak up on a human, noise was the way to go when confronting a bear. He shouted and threw rocks until the bear stopped, turned, and stood on its hind legs to assess the danger. "Get! Go on! Get on out of here! Scram!"

When the bear hesitated, Josh put his rifle to his shoulder just in case.

The silence lengthened while the bear made a decision. It looked over its shoulder at what had captured its attention, then back at Josh, and finally lumbered off into the forest.

Josh waited a bit, then headed toward whatever the bear had found. Though they were mainly vegetarians and loved berries, they were not above eating carrion for the protein, so Josh expected a dead animal, perhaps a deer or maybe a possum or a raccoon. He stopped, stared, and it took him a minute to process that he was seeing human remains instead.

He forced himself to take a deep breath and push his emotions aside. He scanned the body, noticing the bright orange hunter's vest and the rifle clutched in the man's hand. He'd have to check if it had been fired, if perhaps the hunter had tried to protect himself and that was what caused the bear to charge.

But first, he used his shoulder radio to call dispatch. "This is 413-Ocala, and I've got a code 7 at my location. Victim appears to have been mauled by a bear. Better call the biologist, too. Have him bring a bear trap. Bear is still in the area."

"Are you safe, Tanner?"

"As far as I know. I chased him away so I could get close to the body."

"Backup should be there in ten, Hollywood. Sit tight."

"10-4, thank you."

While he waited, Josh studied the body, one ear cocked for sounds of the bear, since it wouldn't give up its food unless it had to. Flies were already present, but no maggots yet that he could see, so he didn't think the man had been dead very long, but the medical examiner would determine time of death. Josh pulled on latex gloves and reached for the man's rifle, sniffed. He checked the barrel. Fully loaded.

Next, he checked the pockets of the bright orange vest. No wallet, but he found a can of bear spray. If you had bear spray in your pocket and a rifle in your hand, why the hell wouldn't you fight back? It made no sense.

The man's vest also held a digital camera and a small notebook. No cell phone. Josh clicked through the photos, surprised to find nothing but pictures of the monkeys. Page after page of the notebook was filled with notes on monkey behavior, along with several references to locations.

He bagged the items and then forced himself to study what was left of the man's face. He didn't recognize him, which wasn't surprising. He certainly didn't know every hunter who roamed the six hundred thousand acres of the Ocala National Forest every year.

Before long, he heard approaching vehicles. FWC officers generally worked alone, but thanks to their computer-aided dispatch system, when he called in, every officer in the area had heard about it and would have headed in his direction.

Hunter Boudreau arrived first in his FWC F-150 pickup. He took one look at the body and muttered, "Holy crap, that's a tough way to go."

"I was thinking the same thing, but it's weird. The guy had a rifle in his hand and bear spray in his pocket. Why did he let the bear get that close? And why aren't there any defensive wounds?"

Hunter crouched beside the body and studied it as well as the surrounding area for several minutes, fairly vibrating with

BEYOND POWER 21

intensity. Josh could see him working his way down his mental checklist. "He have any ID on him?"

"Not that I've been able to find."

Marco Sanchez, another FWC officer, reacted to the body with the same shock as both Josh and Hunter. "What the heck happened out here? We've never had a bear kill somebody."

Hunter stood, nodded. "True. Let's try to ID this guy so we can notify next of kin."

Josh noticed a set of footprints leading away from the body and followed them into the tree line. As he walked back to the others, he held up a black object. "I found his wallet. Twenty-five dollars in cash, but no ID and no hunting license." He raised a brow. "Can't imagine the bear taking his driver's license." Josh hitched a thumb over his shoulder. "There are footprints leading away from the body. I'll go see where they lead."

Hunter's eyes narrowed. "Maybe he was with a friend and his buddy escaped. But right now, that's all speculation. Sanchez and I will wait for the medical examiner and the biologist and see what else we can find."

Josh held up the evidence bags. "He also had a camera with nothing but pictures of the monkeys and a notebook filled with notes about them in his pocket."

The three men looked at one another. "Is this guy another monkey researcher?" Sanchez asked.

They all remembered the female PhD student from the University of Florida who had been beaten severely last year and had eventually called off her research project due to death threats.

"Be careful, Hollywood," Hunter added as Josh started tracking the footprints.

They were smaller than his own, so he figured whoever they belonged to wasn't quite as tall as his own six feet.

He'd gone a quarter of a mile when the footprints ended abruptly. It took him a few minutes before he discovered a set of tire tracks several yards away. Someone had tried to erase their footprints. What were they hiding?

Resigned to a hot, sweaty walk, he followed the tracks as they headed into the sand, then looped back to the road several times, further raising his suspicions.

The trail ended in front of an aging green GMC Sierra, parked in front of an even older camper. As he studied the fresh coat of dark-green paint, he flashed back to Delilah's paint-stained fingers, and his heart sank. She'd gone to a lot of trouble to disguise her presence. Dozens of questions and possibilities sprang to mind, but he refused to speculate.

He walked up the camper's rickety metal step and knocked. No curtains twitched at the small windows on either side, but he kept his hand on his weapon in case she wasn't alone. Besides enjoying their morning flirtation over coffee, he knew nothing about her personal life or living situation. "FWC. Open the door, please."

No sound came from within, so he knocked again. "Officer Tanner. FWC. Open up, please. I need to ask you a few questions."

Josh was ready to circle around back when the door eased open several inches. Delilah stood behind the partially open door, arms crossed over her chest, chin up at a defensive angle, both surprise and alarm in her expression. "Officer Tanner. What brings you all the way out here?" Her frosty tone suggested she was still ticked off about their earlier conversation.

He studied her a moment. Outwardly, she looked tough and intimidating, but then he glimpsed that flicker of worry again, the hint of vulnerability that always hit him like a one-two punch to the gut and tempted him to wrap her in his arms and tell her everything would be okay. There were deep currents in Delilah he wanted to explore, but right now, he needed answers. He kept his smile friendly, casual. "Hello, Delilah. May I come in?"

She nodded once, and he followed her into the tiny but immac-ulate camper and sat down across from her at the dinette. Their knees bumped, and he muttered "Sorry," but his eyes never left her face.

Just as he opened his mouth to ask what she'd been doing near a dead body, she leaned forward, frustration—and a hint of confusion—in her gaze. "Your family runs an outfitter. You and I have talked about the monkeys. Now you're telling Wells you support FWC removing them? What does that mean exactly? Have they hired a trapper?"

He held his hands up, palms out, and decided to roll with the conversation. He'd learned to let witnesses talk, get whatever was on their minds said, since they often told him what he needed to know without prompting. If not, he could always redirect. He also wanted to clear the air and reestablish the trust they had been building. "First of all, I wasn't going to give Wells my personal opinion and have him quote it as an official FWC statement."

She raised her brows and nodded, waiting.

"And second, nothing official has been decided. There is no timeline or management plan in place, but after yesterday's incident, I'm sure it's coming."

"Would you stop it if you could?"

He looked away, then back at her. "I don't know. I tend to think we'd be better off without them."

For an instant, she looked like he'd stabbed her in the heart, but then her temper flared. Dang, she was beautiful with her cheeks flushed and her blue eyes flashing.

"You said yourself most of the problems would resolve themselves if people quit feeding them."

"I did. I also think they're fun to watch, and I am well aware they bring money to the Outpost." He sighed. "It's complicated. But that doesn't mean we can't be friends, does it?" The words popped out without warning, and he froze, waiting for her answer.

"No. Yes. Okay, maybe." She huffed out a breath. "You're making me crazy," she muttered, but a smile escaped as she looked at him.

He grinned like an idiot but then sobered. *What the hell are you doing, Tanner?* He cleared his throat and turned the conversation to official business. "Tell me what happened in the forest today."

Delilah's faced paled, and wariness crept into her eyes. Her chin came up, and she asked, "What do you mean?"

He raised a brow, waited, but she said nothing. "I followed your trail from where we found a deceased individual. Who is he?"

Delilah squeezed her eyes shut as though blocking the image, then she shrugged and shook her head. When she looked up, her eyes were sad. "I don't know."

"Based on some evidence we found, it looks like he was here to study the monkeys, just like you. You haven't run into him since you've been here?"

She shook her head no.

"Okay, walk me through it. Where did you go after you left the café?"

Delilah glanced away, and Josh couldn't help admiring her profile. Between her high cheekbones and full lips, she really was beautiful, but he had the sense she didn't realize it. *Focus, Tanner.*

She tucked a strand of dark hair behind her ear and tugged on it as though surprised at how short it was. "I rented a kayak and went to study the monkeys like I'd planned, and afterward, I tried to connect with some friends. But they weren't where I thought they'd be."

"You mean the Atwoods?"

Her eyes flew to his, then darted away again. "Yes. Do you know them?"

"I know their campsite used to be in that general vicinity. But they moved on a couple of months ago."

"Do you know where they—" She cut herself off. "Never mind."

He folded his arms and leaned on the table, trying to figure out what she wasn't saying. "What happened after you got to the campsite?"

She stared down at the table, fiddled with a napkin. "Since it was obvious they weren't there, I headed back to my truck. That's when I came across the, uh, the dead man."

"He was already dead when you got there?"

"Definitely, as far as I could tell. The smell was terrible. When I heard the bear, I backed up slowly and slipped into the trees."

"What did the bear do? Did he see you?"

Delilah squeezed her eyes shut again as though to block the memory. Josh couldn't blame her. "I don't think so. When he leaned over the man, I took off." She wrapped her arms tightly around her middle, and he couldn't help noticing they were toned and tan. "That's all I can tell you. Do you know who the man was?"

"Not yet." Josh studied her body language and all the things she hadn't said. "Why didn't you report a body?"

She blanched and chewed her lower lip, and he ignored the flare of heat that shot through him.

"I was pretty rattled. I hadn't quite worked my way up to it yet."

Delilah forced herself to meet Josh's questioning gaze as shame washed over her. For the sake of the dead man, she should have called immediately. She'd been so worried about what to say, she'd hesitated. That wasn't the kind of person she wanted to be.

When he'd shown up, she'd thought he wanted to finish their earlier conversation about the monkeys. The fact that he was FWC and would logically be investigating a bear attack hadn't even crossed her mind.

She took a slow, calming breath, then another, until her brain got a tight grip on her panic so she could think. She couldn't tell him who she was. Certainly not while she was trying to get Mary away from her family. Her identity would raise questions that would only muddy the waters.

Her imagination was running away with her, and she was behaving like her paranoid father. A bear attacking a man near where her family was transferring guns and money had to be an unfortunate coincidence. But in Delilah's experience, things were never quite that simple. Though for her, like for the dead man, they were often that sad.

Josh was watching her, eyes intense. "Are you okay?"

She nodded and bit her lip again. When his eyes tracked the movement, she became acutely aware that her nervous tell had become something else. The familiar zip of attraction flared in her belly, but she ignored it. Those green eyes of his missed nothing, and she couldn't risk him looking too closely, probing too deeply. She should have remembered John Henry's number one rule: keep to yourself.

"I'm sorry. Seeing him really threw me. But I should have called someone." She'd been equally shaken by seeing her brother. And father. And having them aim guns in her direction. She couldn't conceal a shudder and jerked in surprise when Josh laid a comforting hand on her arm.

Delilah looked from his hand to his face and saw the concern there, the interest. For a moment, she wished they'd met at some other time, in another place. Josh Tanner seemed like every girl's dream. But despite her research, she was here to rescue her sister. She couldn't lose sight of that, not for a single minute.

"Besides the bear and the hunter, did you see anyone else in the area?"

Delilah kept her expression bland. She had been raised that it was none of the government's business what she did, but her family had also been strict adherents to the Ten Commandments. The only exception to "Thou shalt not lie" was when it involved any kind of police or government authority. She couldn't lie to Josh, but she couldn't tell the whole truth, either. "Those two pretty much kept my attention."

The thrift-shop clock ticked loudly while he studied her. She wouldn't look away.

Finally, he said, "Is there anything at all you can tell me that will help us figure out who this man was? We need to notify his family."

Delilah straightened her spine and met his eyes. "I'm sorry. I wish I could help you, but I didn't know him."

"Did you hear gunfire about the time you found the body?"

"I did, but that's certainly not unusual out here."

"Why did you try to hide your tracks?"

A trained investigator lived behind that easy smile, and she'd be a fool to forget it. She attempted a casual shrug. "Habit, I guess. I was raised to fly under the radar, not get involved in things that aren't my business." *Lame, Delilah.* More words wanted to tumble out, so she clamped her mouth shut.

"You know that makes it look like you have something to hide."

She hated the disappointment in his expression.

"You sure you didn't know him? Haven't seen him around anywhere?"

"I've never seen him before. Truly. And I have absolutely no idea why a bear attacked him. It doesn't make any sense." Given all she was hiding, needing him to believe her on this point wasn't logical, but there it was.

He nodded once and stood, his large frame taking up way too much space in her tiny camper. He pulled out a business card, wrote something on it before he handed it to her. "My cell number is on the back. If you think of anything, please call me. Day or night. In the meantime, avoid that area while we trap the bear."

"I will." She glanced down at the card, then back up at his face, not sure what else to say.

"Be extra cautious when you're out doing your research, okay?" He touched a finger to the brim of his official FWC ball cap and said, "Delilah," in a low tone that curled her toes.

She didn't draw a full breath until she peeked through the curtains and saw him disappear into the forest.

———————————

Josh headed back the way he'd come, his odd conversation with Delilah running through his mind. Her words had been straightforward enough, but her eyes said there was quite a bit she wasn't saying. Since she was normally warm and friendly, even a bit flirty on occasion, her response today was way off, and that made his cop antenna twitch.

Given her passionate position on leaving the monkeys alone, if the victim was a researcher with an opposing viewpoint, had there been a professional disagreement she was embarrassed to mention? He couldn't quite see it, but he couldn't ignore the connection, either.

By the time he arrived back at the scene, Sanchez was bagging evidence, and the medical examiner was on-site, preparing the body for transport. Hunter had been taking photographs and stepped away when Josh arrived. "Did you find whoever those footprints belonged to?"

"I did. I followed them to a truck, which led me to a camper, which led me to Delilah Paige." At Hunter's questioning look, he added, "The monkey researcher we've seen at the Corner Café."

A quick grin flashed over Hunter's face as he and Sanchez exchanged a look, but then he sobered. "Two monkey researchers in the same place? What was she doing out here?"

"She said she'd come to see the Atwoods, claims she's a friend of theirs, only they weren't there. On her way back, she ran across the body. Says she has no idea who he is. Has never seen him before."

"Why didn't she call it in?" Sanchez asked.

"I asked the same question. She said when she got back to her camper, she was pretty shaken up."

Hunter studied him for a moment. "What's bothering you?"

He had worked homicide in New Orleans before joining FWC and had great instincts. He also had great faith in his men's instincts.

Josh narrowed his eyes as he scanned the area, trying to pinpoint what it was about his conversation with Delilah that nagged at him. "It's nothing concrete. I just got the distinct feeling that there was more to the story than what she was saying."

Which grated like sand in his shoes. Delilah had been trying to deflect his attention from something, not realizing that'd only made him more curious. And determined to get answers. His late fiancée, Elaine, hadn't even told him she had cancer, let alone that she had refused treatment. He still hadn't completely worked his way through the quagmire of guilt, fury, hurt, and frustration she'd left behind, but one thing was for sure. He'd never again let things slide when he wasn't getting the whole story.

"You figure out where the gunfire came from earlier? Did she hear anything?" Hunter asked.

Josh rubbed a hand over the back of his neck. "She said she heard it but didn't seem to find it unusual. I didn't see the Atwoods or anyone else in the vicinity. I couldn't find the marijuana grow either, but maybe I got close and someone wanted to keep me away."

Hunter studied him. "Keep digging until you get answers that make sense. Might not hurt to keep an eye on her, too, while we figure out what's going on here."

Before long, the medical examiner left with the body, and Sanchez and the biologist set up the trap and started tracking the bear. Hunter checked in with their captain, but Josh was only half listening. His mind was focused on the mystery of Delilah Paige.

CHAPTER 3

AFTER JOSH LEFT, DELILAH PACED THE SMALL SPACE. HE WAS clearly suspicious because she'd acted guilty. The last thing she needed was a cop dogging her heels. Especially a gorgeous, funny, tempting cop who seemed to see past all her carefully constructed defenses. If John Henry suspected official heat of any kind, he'd pack up the family and disappear. Again.

She pulled Mary's burned doll from her backpack, and the sight of it galvanized her. Here was proof of John Henry's plan. She could no longer coast along with a vague hope that things would be different this time. She had to take action. Fast.

Once she checked her camera battery, she repacked her backpack. She had to think, and the forest had always been the best place to do it. She threw on a clean T-shirt, coated herself with more essential oil against the bugs, and set off on foot.

There were four documented troops of rhesus macaque monkeys that roamed the area near the Silver and Ocklawaha Rivers, and she'd been fascinated by them since childhood. So had her sister. When John Henry wasn't around, Mama had let her take Mary and follow them for hours. Right now, she needed that sense of connection to her sister.

She also needed to burn off the antsy feelings inspired by Josh's questions and piercing gaze. Delilah heard the monkeys chattering before she saw them and smiled. This was just what she needed, a distraction while her subconscious mind worked on a plan. She approached slowly but didn't make eye contact, as they saw that as a sign of aggression.

She settled on a log and watched the alpha male approach from the corner of her eye. She tucked her backpack down between her knees and fiddled with her camera, head down as she waited. She heard rustling in the trees all around and knew the other monkeys were moving closer, waiting for his signal that there was food to be had. Doggone it. Why wouldn't people follow the rules and quit feeding them?

She kept her breathing slow and even, though her heart rate picked up as the troop inched closer. She slid the air horn from her backpack, just in case she had to scare them away. Humans only used about 15 percent of their strength, but she'd read that a monkey used 85 percent. They were not only incredibly strong, they could be mean when thwarted. She wasn't far from a walking trail, and based on the way the monkeys were watching her every move, they were obviously used to getting a handout.

The goal of her research—and her most fervent hope—was to convince people to leave the monkeys alone and stop feeding them. But she wasn't naïve. People did what they wanted, especially when cute, furry creatures were involved. Slowly, she aimed the camera in the male's direction and took several pictures of his expression before ducking her head again. Most of the current research outlined the dangers posed by the monkeys' continued presence in the area. The viral video Wells had mentioned only added weight to that argument. But she'd watched the entire clip— not just what the news media showed in an endless loop—and sure enough, the family she'd spoken to had not only fed the monkeys, they'd started taunting them, too. That was what proponents for their removal didn't want to talk about: the so-called signs of aggression could almost always be directly linked to people feeding the monkeys.

If her research could persuade people to leave them alone already and follow the rules, the safety barrier between humans and monkeys could be restored and the problem of "aggression" would resolve itself. Just thinking about that video sent enough fury racing through her veins that her hands shook. She took a deep breath and forced herself to relax. Even with no one around, she was poised to fight, ready to defend her beloved monkeys to anyone who would listen.

Which immediately brought Josh Tanner to mind. How could he not agree with her on this? His family owned a local outfitter. Tourists came from all over the country hoping to catch a glimpse of the rhesus macaques playing in the trees, and who could blame them?

The alpha male gave an angry screech, and she quickly captured his furious expression before she grabbed the air horn and braced for an attack. She chanced another peek. He still looked ready to charge, so she waited, motionless, as sweat beaded the back of her neck and mosquitos buzzed around her head.

After what seemed like hours, he sent her one more annoyed hiss and then turned and leaped up into the nearest tree. As soon as he moved, the tension dissolved as all the monkeys went back to whatever they'd been doing, completely ignoring her as they chattered among themselves, eating leaves and grooming one another.

Delilah let out a sigh of relief and then slowly raised her camera again. From what she could tell, there were at least four pregnant mothers. She couldn't wait for the little ones to be born. Several mothers had already given birth, and she watched two young monkeys race up and down branches, leaping from one to the next, making her smile. One launched himself onto a sapling, and the branch bent almost to the ground. Looking panicked, he leaped into another tree, his little friend right behind him. She snapped dozens of photos, grinning. This was why her research mattered. Why they should be left in peace. She wanted the next generation to be able to see what she was seeing.

She'd bet old Colonel Tooey had no idea the firestorm of public opinion his marketing plan would launch. He had run a tour boat on the Silver River in the 1930s and imported a troop of rhesus macaques from India and set them on an island in the river, figuring they were a great way to get more customers aboard his jungle cruise. Imagine his surprise when he returned with his boatload of guest to find them gone. He hadn't known the monkeys could swim. Decades later, the descendants of those monkeys still roamed the area while lawmakers and environmentalists debated their future.

The monkeys suddenly started chattering again. At the same time, Delilah heard a noise and snapped her head around, scanning the area. Had the alpha male snuck in behind her?

She waited, air horn gripped in her hand. When she didn't spot him or any other creature, she used her zoom to scan the area but found nothing. "Mary?" she called quietly. She knew her sister showing up here was an eight-year long shot, but she still hoped.

The rustling came again, but there was no response. She stood, the prickly feeling at the base of her neck telling her someone was definitely watching. She just didn't know if they were human or animal. "It's okay, Mary," she said, but there was no answer.

She waited until long after the adult monkeys went back to grooming one another and the babies returned to their play before she headed back to her camper. She walked in roundabout loops, all her senses on alert.

She hadn't been able to spot anyone, but that twitchy feeling between her shoulder blades convinced her someone was still out there.

She just didn't know who.

Or why.

Josh pulled up to the community center with five minutes to spare. He'd assumed he'd have to cancel practice tonight, but Hunter insisted he go. All the guys in the Ocala FWC squad had gotten involved with the kids at the center in one way or another since so many didn't have strong male role models. Just an hour of basketball practice several times a week was making a difference in their attitudes, their schoolwork, and how they carried themselves.

When he walked into the large steel-framed building, several of the boys were engrossed in an impromptu pickup game. "Hey, guys! How's it going?"

Donny Thomas separated from the group and hurried over. The twelve-year-old had had a traumatic couple of weeks. "I didn't think you were going to come today," Donny said, just as he did every time Josh appeared.

He winced. After Elaine died, he'd been too angry to show up. His brother, Pete, and sister Charlee had pointed out none too gently that his anger was only hurting the boys. That got through, and now he never missed a practice if he could help it. He reached over and ruffled Donny's hair. "Why wouldn't I? Unless you didn't want me to show because you know I'm still going to beat you."

Donny snorted and sent him a lopsided grin. "You wish, old man. I've been practicing, and we're going to whip your old butts."

Josh laughed and grabbed a basketball from the box nearby. He tossed it to Donny, who caught it in both hands. "Big talk, boyo. Show me what you've got."

For the next thirty minutes, he took the team through drills, relays, and other team-building activities to sharpen their skills. But everyone liked the end of practice best, when they divided into teams, kids against grown-ups.

As Josh raced up and down the court, he wished he could block everything from his mind as he usually did. But today, a pair of blue-gray eyes haunted him.

He'd bet his badge Delilah was in some kind of trouble. He didn't know what kind yet, but he planned to find out.

Secrets destroyed people and relationships. He knew it wasn't fair to compare the woman he'd planned to marry with someone he'd just met, but the fact that Elaine had hidden her illness from him still smoldered like a burning coal deep in his gut. He wanted to blame it all on her, certainly had for months, but he couldn't lie to himself anymore. The truth was, he'd been a coward. He hadn't pushed her for answers, even when his gut had told him something was very wrong. It'd been easier to back off when she refused to talk, to take her claims of being tired and overworked at face value. That was what gnawed at him in the dead of night. If he'd confronted her, would it have made a difference? He'd never know. Delilah and Elaine were not the same, and certainly the situations were completely different, but he was done with secrets and evasions.

It didn't matter that Delilah hadn't asked for his help and whatever she was involved with was none of his business, except as it involved his investigation.

He wouldn't quit until he uncovered her secrets.

CHAPTER 4

JOSH GROANED WHEN THE ALARM CLOCK JOLTED HIM AWAKE the next morning. He and the rest of the scrub squad had been out in the forest until almost two in the morning. While Sanchez, Hunter, and the biologist had tracked the bear and coaxed him into the trap for transport, Josh had installed a trail camera and then watched over the scene, just in case. While swatting mosquitos, he spotted a bobcat, three raccoons, and a couple of opossums, but no critters of the two-legged variety had passed his way.

Something about the whole scenario didn't sit right. The fact that the victim had no defensive wounds and hadn't fired his rifle was a huge red flag. Then there was the gunfire he'd heard. What happened out there?

He checked his watch and decided he'd swing by the Corner Café before meeting the squad at the Outpost. Never mind that his little cottage sat on Outpost property. He'd just go get a quick cup of coffee first, see if Delilah was there.

The moment he walked through the door, he wished he hadn't. All conversation came to a halt, then chairs scraped the wooden floor as people hurried in his direction to bombard him with questions.

"Hey, Tanner, what's this we hear about a bear attack in the forest yesterday?" Marion County commissioner Rory Kilpatrick asked as he stepped in front of Josh. Built like a lumberjack with a voice to match, Kilpatrick was a force of nature, and all eyes focused on the two men. Behind Kilpatrick, Josh saw Dwight Benson, another commissioner, and Bill Peterson, the mayor of Ocala, sitting at the table where Kilpatrick had been.

He raised his voice to be sure everyone heard him. "Come on

now, Rory. You know as well as I do that I can't comment on an ongoing investigation." Out of the corner of his eye, he saw reporter Casey Wells reach for his cell phone. "Lieutenant Boudreau will keep everyone apprised of the progress of the investigation as information becomes available."

No way would he give Wells any other info. Hunter would have his hands full dealing with the arrogant reporter as it was.

Movement in his peripheral vision caught his eye, and Josh couldn't help smiling as he spotted Delilah at the counter chatting with Charlee, who had just handed over one of her amazing cupcakes along with a cup of coffee.

"I heard that poor tenderfoot was all tore up by that bear," Bill Peterson said, blocking Josh's path.

He returned his attention to Bill and the rest of the crowd, frustrated as ever by the speed at which gossip traveled. "All I can say is that there was a fatality and there was evidence of a bear in the vicinity. FWC, in conjunction with the sheriff's office, is investigating."

"Have you caught the bear yet?" This from Wells.

"Lieutenant Boudreau will update the media at the press conference later today."

He ignored the additional questions and pushed his way through to the small table in the back where Delilah sat sipping coffee.

He knew all eyes were on him as he approached her table. "Mind if I join you?" He didn't wait for an answer, just slid into a chair and leaned forward slightly, voice low. "Are you okay this morning?"

The dark circles under her eyes said she hadn't slept well, but her half smile was genuine if not at full power. "Doing okay, considering." She cocked her head in that adorable way she had and ran her blue eyes over him. "You look like you've been rode hard and put away wet, Hollywood."

He snorted at the expression and rubbed a hand over the back of his neck. "Sounds about right." He paused, capturing her gaze. "Have you thought of anything else that might help the investigation?"

Her eyes slid over his uniform, and then her gaze caught on something behind him. Her expression suddenly cooled, and her hands tightened on her coffee cup. "I believe I answered all your questions yesterday, Officer Tanner. I have no new information."

The chair next to him scraped the floor as Wells slid into it. "Since that other monkey researcher was attacked in the forest last year, is there a chance these two cases are connected?"

Irritation flared at the man's untimely arrival and choice of questions. Lucky guess or had someone at the medical examiner's office or FWC leaked word of the monkey photos found on the dead man's camera?

Without waiting for an answer, Wells turned to Delilah. "Miss Paige, did you know the victim?"

Delilah's face went carefully blank. "Why would I know him?"

"There is some speculation that he was also studying the monkeys. And last year, that researcher from UF was almost beaten to death." Wells shrugged. "Just thought maybe you researcher types all know each other."

Josh watched Delilah swallow hard and tug on her chin-length hair, like she was reaching for a ponytail that wasn't there anymore. He'd seen the same nervous gesture yesterday. "No. I'd never met the man."

"Where are you getting your information, Wells?" Josh demanded.

"I have my sources. You know how it is, Officer." He shrugged, and Josh fought the urge to snatch him by the shirtfront and demand he spill, but he knew that wouldn't work. He also knew he'd never get a moment alone with Delilah now.

Josh glanced at his watch, pushed his chair back. "I'm sure you have other things to do this morning, Wells."

The reporter leaned back in his chair, smile wide. "Actually, I have plenty of time to—"

The bell above the door jangled, and Delilah looked up. All the color leached out of her face, and she shoved her chair back, grabbed her coffee. "I need to go."

Josh glanced over his shoulder and spotted Aaron and John Henry Atwood with another man he didn't recognize standing near the county commissioners. Casey Wells was still talking as Josh grabbed his coffee and followed her out the door. "Delilah, wait up," he called as he hurried over to her truck. "I thought you knew the Atwoods." Hadn't she said she'd gone to their campsite to talk with them?

The question seemed to surprise her. "I do. But with that reporter there, now isn't a good time." She opened the door to her truck.

"Did something happen with them yesterday?" he asked, putting a gentle hand on her arm.

She froze, swallowed hard. "I've told you everything I can." Her eyes darted to the door of the café. "I really need to go."

She climbed into her truck and never glanced his way as she roared out of the parking lot. She would have run over his boots if he hadn't jumped back in time. Why had the sight of the Atwoods spooked her?

He climbed into his official F-150 and headed to the Outpost, trying to make sense of their conversation. The Atwoods' former campsite wasn't far from where the body had been found. What was she hiding? And what, if anything, did it have to do with the Atwoods?

―――――――

Delilah couldn't believe she'd been dumb enough to show up at the café this morning. The stupid, girly part of her had hoped Josh would show up and smile and banter with her and everything would go back to normal between them, even as the logical part of her warned that spending another minute with him was something to avoid at all costs. But after a night spent tossing and turning on her too-thin mattress and nightmares featuring her brother, her father, guns, and Nate, she had to escape the turmoil of her own thoughts. If nothing else, she figured she could chat with Charlee or Liz and try to shake off the aftereffects of her near-sleepless night.

Clearly, that had been a mistake. She clenched her hands on the steering wheel and replayed her conversation with Josh. From the way he'd beelined it to her table, he'd been looking for her. But why? Was he worried about her, as he'd said? Or was there more to it? Had FWC already figured out who she was?

A chill raced over her skin despite the muggy air blasting through the open window. Would he have said anything?

In the midst of her frantic thoughts, a realization struck like lightning. Why was she running—still—like the scared little girl she used to be? She wasn't that woman any longer. She hadn't done anything wrong, and Josh wasn't her enemy. Yes, she'd panicked when she locked eyes with Aaron. She still wasn't sure if he'd recognized her, but either way, she wouldn't risk a public confrontation with him or her father. Not with unarmed, innocent people around.

But she could follow them and have it out in private.

A quick U-turn on the highway, tires squealing, and she raced back to the café.

She had all the power here. She'd seen John Henry and Aaron with guns and money. Both had always pretended not to care about law enforcement and governmental laws and rules, but they'd been very careful to stay under the radar. She could offer them a trade: her silence for Mary.

She pulled back into the parking lot, took a calming breath as she headed inside, then stood a moment, waiting for her eyes to adjust.

She scanned the patrons once, then again, and her anticipation seeped away like a deflated balloon. She was too late. They were gone.

Delilah waved to Liz before she marched back to her truck, annoyed with herself. Why hadn't she thought of this earlier? Opportunity had just slipped right through her fingers.

Someone had to know how to find them. But who? She tapped a finger on the wheel and smiled as the answer occurred to her.

Thirty minutes later, she approached the Forest Community Center, glad someone had finally invested money in the people who lived in the forest. The jumbled collection of old mobile homes, tarps covering the walkways, had been replaced by a big steel-framed building.

When she spotted RN Kimberly Gaines's antique powder-blue VW parked in its usual spot, something settled inside her.

"Hey, Ms. Gaines," Delilah said from the doorway to Kimberly's office.

It took a moment before Kimberly's eyes widened behind her wire-rimmed glasses. Her blond hair was streaked with gray now, but the curls still bounced when she leaped out of her chair and wrapped Delilah in a breath-stealing hug, murmuring, "Oh, sweet girl, it's so good to see you."

Though it shamed Delilah to admit it, Kimberly Gaines had always been the mother she'd wished her own had been. Her love was exuberant and noisy and unconditionally accepting.

She cupped both Delilah's cheeks. "How are you? I almost didn't recognize you with the short hair." She grinned. "Though I'm guessing that's the point." She paused. "What brings you back here after all this time?"

Delilah's jaw clenched, but she kept her fury tightly leashed. "Mary. John Henry burned her doll."

A mix of horror and worry flared in Kimberly's gray eyes. "Oh my sweet Lord. When is it?"

"I don't know yet. But her sixteenth birthday is in less than two weeks."

"I imagine John Henry won't let a little thing like a change in the law making seventeen the legal marriage age affect his plans." Kimberly grabbed her hands. "How can I help?"

Delilah smiled. This was exactly why she'd come. Kimberly would dive headlong into trouble for those she cared about. Hadn't she done the same when Delilah showed up at the clinic, bloody and terrified, all those years ago?

"I need to find Mary. I went to the family's campsite, but they're gone. Do you know where they've moved to?"

"I might be able to find out. I wormed a bit of information out of your mama the last few times she's come in."

Delilah sighed. "Is she all right? Another miscarriage?"

"Sadly, yes. Two this year. I've warned Sarah that she needs to stop trying. But she just looks away and says that John Henry wants more children."

Delilah rubbed the ache in her heart that never quite went away. She understood why her mother wouldn't stand up to her father. Hadn't she spent her whole childhood "going along to get along," as the saying went? It was safer. Because when her father was displeased, his carefully meted out fury was terrifying, and her mother often bore the brunt of it.

"What about you?" Kimberly asked. "Have you met a nice young man to settle down with yet?"

Delilah merely raised a brow.

Kimberly cupped her shoulders, forced her to meet her eyes. "What that man did, and what your family allowed, was wrong. On every level. But don't put all men in the same category. The right man is out there, and he'll treat you like a princess."

"Maybe. But so far, I've only met frogs," Delilah quipped, though that wasn't entirely true. When she and Andy became best friends in college and later drifted into bed together, she'd thought they'd eventually get married. He was comfortable, familiar. But after he left for a research project in Peru, she realized she missed his friendship more than anything else. None of the casual dates she'd had since had ever made her think about princes. Or the future.

When Kimberly opened her mouth to argue, Delilah held up a hand. "I know what you're saying, I do. But I'm not interested." *Liar*, her heart said as Josh's handsome face and dimpled grin popped into her mind. Just the way he looked at her made little shivers pass over her skin.

"How is your schooling going?"

"I got a grant from the National Geographic Society to do a study on the monkeys this summer."

Kimberly raised one eyebrow. "Smart girl. It also gives you the perfect excuse to be here. But you still haven't told me your plan regarding Mary."

The less anyone knew, the less they would have to deny. "I need to get her away from the family. Will you help me?"

"You don't even have to ask. What do you need?"

"Will you get a message to Mary and ask her to meet me?"

"Of course. I'll set up the meeting for tonight. Will that be soon enough?"

Delilah swallowed the lump in her throat at such unquestioning support. "Yes, thank you." Before she finished the sentence, she was wrapped in Kimberly's arms yet again.

"She'll be okay, sweet girl. We'll make sure of it."

Delilah straightened, eyes hard. "Yes, we will. I won't quit until she's safe."

———

When Josh arrived at the covered pavilion next to Tanner's Outpost, the rest of the squad was already there.

His brother, Pete, in his Marion County Sheriff's Office uniform, nodded toward the to-go cup in Josh's hand. "You show up late without bringing coffee for everyone? No cupcakes, either?" He shook his head in disgust.

"If you'd wanted me to bring stuff, you should have said so." Josh ignored the comments and groans. "Actually, I went by the café to see if I could pick up any helpful local scuttlebutt."

Hunter raised an eyebrow and glanced at the rest of the squad, the teasing gleam in his eyes a contrast to his usual serious demeanor. "That's not what I heard. Charlee said he went to chat up the sexy little monkey researcher."

Josh pictured Delilah chewing on her lower lip and ignored the flash of heat. He had to stop thinking about her. "Wells from the paper was there, too, fishing for information. He asked if I thought this was related to the attack on the monkey researcher last year."

"Where did he come up with that?" Pete asked. "That's not public information."

"He claimed 'sources' and clammed up." He nodded to Hunter. "I said you'd make a statement later, Lieutenant." He couldn't help chuckling as Hunter bit back a curse. They all hated dealing with the media.

"What were you thinking, man?" fellow officer Marco Sanchez asked.

"He wasn't thinking," Pete said, batting his eyelashes. "He was looking into Ms. Paige's pretty blue eyes and got distracted."

Everyone laughed, and Josh ignored the way his heart sped up whenever anyone mentioned her name.

Hunter narrowed his eyes. "This might work to our advantage. I'll come up with a statement that will keep folks out of our way." He pulled out his phone. "The medical examiner knew we were waiting on preliminaries, so he sent me what he had so far."

At that, Pete whistled appreciatively. "How many dozens of Charlee's cupcakes did you have to promise to get to the front of his line?"

Hunter sighed. "Let's just say your sister and I will be doing a lot of baking in the near future." After the laughter subsided, he continued, "We ran the victim's prints through AFIS and every other database we can think of and did not get any hits. The ME sent a picture of a tattoo, but that's about all we have right now as far as ID goes." He looked up and folded his arms across his chest. "Here's where it gets really interesting. The ME says he found honey on the victim's face and chest."

Josh straightened, his mind spinning. He glanced at Pete and Marco, then back at Hunter. "Are you saying someone tried to lure the bear to the body?"

"That's what we need to find out. I told the biologist to hold off putting that bear down. It may not have killed anyone."

If what they suspected was true, this had just gone from an unfortunate wildlife encounter to murder.

"I'm waiting for more information from the ME. In the meantime, let's check in with folks, see who saw this hunter around. Somebody has to know who he was. Hollywood, widen the circle, and see if you can find some more trail cameras in that area."

Josh nodded. "I'll swing by the Atwoods' new campsite, too, see if they know the guy—or will admit to knowing him."

"Right. Take a close look at Miss Paige, too," Hunter said. "See if we can figure out how she ties into all this. Let's make sure she isn't next on someone's list."

Josh froze. He'd been so hung up on wondering about Delilah's possible involvement—or, more likely, knowledge of what happened—that he hadn't really considered her research making *her* a target. *Idiot.* He blew out a breath as he climbed into his truck.

He decided not to mention Delilah's reaction to Aaron and John Henry's arrival at the Corner Café. He wasn't sure why he didn't, except for this protective streak she unleashed in him. If anyone was keeping an eye on her and looking into her background, it would be him.

And if someone had targeted her because of her research, they'd have to go through him first.

CHAPTER 5

DELILAH DIDN'T LIKE THE FOREST AT NIGHT. SHE NEVER HAD. There were too many unidentified noises, too much evil that could happen under cover of darkness. In daylight, you could see who was stalking you, and could gauge how fast and how far you would have to run. Once the sun set, it got a lot harder. She hoped she remembered enough of her father's lessons to get Mary safely away tonight.

Kimberly had given her landmark-based directions to an old homestead that had been reduced to a tumbledown chimney and some barely visible rotting logs. Delilah sat on a rock she'd carefully checked for snakes and waited, a prepaid smartphone in one hand, her gun in the other. She remembered her father proclaiming that women didn't need technology—though he and Aaron carried cell phones—and shook off her irritation. The past wasn't her priority tonight. If she couldn't convince Mary to come with her, a possibility she'd be foolish not to consider, at least Mary could call until Delilah blackmailed John Henry into letting her go.

She stared at the night sky, visible only in small patches above the trees. Since Kimberly had set the meeting for 10:00 p.m., the family's new campsite had to be fairly close. Otherwise, how would Mary get here alone at night? Sneaking out of the camper was nearly impossible.

But her biggest worry was that her sister wouldn't show. Except for glimpses across the farmers market and the birthday and Christmas cards Delilah secretly left for her there, they hadn't spent any time together since Delilah left. Would Mary still trust her? Or did she feel her big sister had abandoned her?

She glanced at her watch and her heart sank. It was 10:45. Mary wasn't coming. Maybe she couldn't. If their father had gotten wind of their plan, he would have put a stop to it. Delilah wouldn't think about how he might have done that.

A slight rustling sound came from behind her. She froze. There it was again. Nothing more than the whisper of a breeze. Even so, her heart leaped.

"I'm here," Delilah whispered.

The shadow stopped, and Delilah held her breath, afraid Mary would turn and run. "Delilah?" Mary whispered.

She slowly rose to her feet but didn't move toward her sister. Not yet. "Yes, I'm right here."

Mary ran toward her and crashed into Delilah with enough force that she almost tumbled backward over the rock. She reached out to wrap her arms around her sister, but instead of the hug she hoped for, Mary started pounding on her chest. "You left me and you didn't come back. You said you'd never abandon me, but you did. You did."

Delilah's heart shattered into jagged pieces. After a few minutes, Mary stopped pounding and burst into tears. Delilah held her while she cried, murmuring, "I'm sorry, Mary Lou Who, I'm so sorry. I never meant to leave you." Over and over, she said the words, hoping the silly nickname Delilah had coined from the Dr. Seuss Grinch movie they'd seen at the community center years ago would somehow get through.

Eventually, Mary's sobs turned to hiccups, and as they pulled back, Delilah was surprised they were at eye level. It was eerie how much Mary resembled her at that age. Long brown hair in a braid to her waist, no makeup, the long-sleeved blouse and ankle-length denim skirt paired with hiking boots underneath.

"Why did you want to meet?"

"It's almost your birthday," Delilah said quietly, then waited for a reaction.

Mary hung her head, nodded. "Yes, sweet sixteen and all that." The sarcasm was unmistakable. But it gave Delilah hope.

"I found your doll." She reached into her backpack, handed her the plastic bag.

Mary took it, crossed her arms over it. "He burned her, said it was time to grow up." Her voice dropped to a desperate whisper. "But I don't want to get married. I want to go to college and live somewhere besides the camper. But Papa won't listen."

"That's why I'm here. I've come to take you away."

Mary froze. "To live with you?" The hope in her voice was unmistakable.

"Yes. I'm working on a research project with the monkeys, and you can help me. But we have to go now, tonight."

Worry filled Mary's face. "Now? But what about Mama?"

What will Papa do to her if I disappear? She didn't say the words aloud, but Delilah heard them anyway. Guilt clamped her heart like a vise, and she wanted to rail against the terrible choice Mary faced. It was the same one Delilah had faced eight years ago.

Tonight, she could save Mary or protect Mama from John Henry's fury. She couldn't do both, and the knowledge tore at her. She gripped Mary's trembling shoulders, anger at her father burning her from the inside out. Nobody should have to make choices like this.

"We'll get a message to her so she knows you're safe." That wasn't what Mary meant, but it was all she could offer. "But we have to go right now."

"I-I don't know if I can—"

Gunfire shattered the night.

Mary glanced over her shoulder, eyes wild with fear.

Delilah reached for her. "Come with me."

"I can't just leave Mama." Mary slipped through her grasp and disappeared into the woods.

Delilah didn't give the shooter a single thought. She raced after her sister.

Josh had been wandering in ever-widening circles for hours, using his night-vision goggles to locate trail cameras in the area. If they could track down the owners and get a look at the SD cards, they might show someone coming or going around the time of the hunter's death. After he texted Hunter that he was calling it a night, he decided to swing by Delilah's camper. He'd had plenty of time to think, and every cop instinct he possessed said she hadn't killed anyone. Or spread honey to lure a bear.

But that was where his certainty ended. Though she denied a connection to the dead hunter, there was still something off about her response. Same with her reaction to the Atwoods, whom she'd claimed were friends.

Still, he had a need to see her, make sure she was okay. Finding a dead body rattled a person, no matter who you were. Hopefully, they could get past whatever had spooked her and made her shut him out. He wanted things to go back to the easy, flirty way they were before. He missed their spirited conversations, the way her eyes lit up when she saw him, and the low, husky laugh that made him say ridiculous things just so he could hear it again.

And from a purely practical stance, he wanted to make sure no one was hanging around her camper who didn't belong. Her remote spot and dark-green paint hadn't escaped his notice. He just wasn't sure if that was to keep her safely inside or to keep other people out.

As he reached her campsite, he watched her leave, flashlight in hand, but it wasn't turned on. All his senses went on alert. Where was she going?

He followed her deeper and deeper into the forest. She stopped every so often to turn the flashlight on, scan the area, then turn it back off. She was obviously looking for something.

When she finally stopped and sat down on a rock, he positioned himself behind a tree so he could keep an eye on her and the small clearing around her.

Mosquitoes buzzed around his head, and sweat trickled down his back by the time a young woman stepped out of the shadows.

The teen was wearing the long skirt and boots typical of the ultraconservative, fundamentalist families who lived here in the forest. When she launched herself at Delilah, he was shocked. Who was she? And how did Delilah know her?

Before he could make sense of that, rifle fire erupted, and the dirt at their feet exploded. The young woman disappeared, Delilah hot on her heels.

Josh took off after them, gun at the ready.

———————

Delilah raced after Mary, ignoring the gunshots spitting sand up at her. She'd pulled her weapon from her waistband, but she didn't fire, wouldn't risk hitting Mary by mistake. She just had to find her, fast.

If Mary disappeared now, Delilah might never see her again. Her family would disappear, and their like-minded friends would make sure no one could find them. She couldn't bear the idea of her sister going through what she had.

She ran despite the bullets that just kept coming. Some part of her brain was surprised she wasn't down on the ground, bleeding, but whoever it was knew exactly where they were placing those shots. They were trying to keep her away, not kill her.

The moon slid behind some clouds, and Delilah momentarily lost sight of her sister. One minute, Mary was ahead of her, and the next, she'd disappeared.

Delilah ran farther, heart pounding, until the gunshots stopped and the silence told her Mary was gone. Panting, defeated, she collapsed against a live oak tree and slid down to the ground. Bark scraped her back, but she didn't notice. "Oh God. Mary."

She'd hoped once her sister knew she'd come to rescue her, she'd meekly follow and they'd get the heck out of Dodge. Easy-peasy. She snorted at her own naïveté. What had made perfect sense in her Tallahassee apartment she now saw for the same childlike thinking that had gotten her trapped eight years ago.

Frustrated, she climbed to her feet. She wasn't that scared girl anymore, but she understood Mary's thinking. Her sister had no doubt been rigorously indoctrinated into the importance of family and sticking together against the outside world. Her reaction tonight said she'd also seen enough to want to protect Mama.

But given the gunshots, Mary's cooperation was only part of the equation. Either Aaron or John Henry obviously didn't want her to leave. They didn't go to that much trouble for a "mere woman" without good reason.

Which meant she not only had to find them, she had to find out exactly what they were planning so she could use that as leverage, too.

———————

When Delilah stopped behind a tree, Josh deliberately made noise as he approached so as not to startle her. He was shocked to his toes when she stepped into view, Glock held in front of her, hands rock steady on the grip, eyes hard. "Hands up and move closer so I can see you," she ordered.

He froze, stunned. Her confidence hit him square in the gut and made the attraction he felt for her burn even hotter. Damn, she looked good like that.

"It's Josh Tanner, Fish and Wildlife. Please put down the gun, Delilah, for my safety and yours."

Through his night-vision goggles, he saw her eyes narrow in surprise and suspicion, but she immediately holstered the gun.

He stepped into the small clearing, hands on his utility belt, in reach of his own weapon.

She gave his uniform a quick once-over, then fisted both hands on her hips. "What are you doing here?"

"I was going to ask you the same question," he responded, her attitude fueling his own. He pulled off his goggles. "Why are you sneaking around out here in the middle of the night?"

She huffed out a breath. "Seriously? Since when can't people go outside at night without being interrogated by Fish and Wildlife?"

He almost laughed at her belligerent tone. Almost. But then he noticed the pain shadowing her features. He softened his voice. "Who were you meeting with?"

Her chin came up, lips pursed. "I'm not sure that's any of your concern."

She was dressed in black from head to toe, the fabric of her T-shirt clinging to her curves, her hands propped on a utility belt that looked a lot like his own. He'd thought her beautiful when she was sipping coffee. But whoever the girl was, she'd sent Delilah into full-on protective mode, reminding him of Xena, the warrior princess. He felt the jolt all the way to his toes.

He took a step closer, and she stilled. When he reached out and plucked a leaf from her hair, she captured his wrist, questions swirling in her huge blue eyes. Seconds ticked by as they watched each other, her mix of strength and vulnerability drawing him closer. He ran his thumb along her jaw, and her grip on his arm tightened. He studied her lips, lush and full, and the urge to taste had him inclining his head. Inches before their mouths touched, their eyes met, held. She blinked, effectively breaking the spell as she eased out of reach.

He shook his head to clear his muddled thoughts. *Focus, Tanner.* "Who was the girl?"

She crossed her arms over her chest and regarded him steadily. "And if I said, again, that it was none of your business?"

"I would say I was making it my business, since you are considered a person of interest in a recent death here in the forest."

Her eyes narrowed right before she huffed out a laugh and called his bluff. "Seriously? You and your FWC buddies have declared me a person of interest because some poor hunter got killed by a bear?"

Josh had to tread lightly. He couldn't discuss an active investigation, but that death scene wasn't right, which was why he was out here in the middle of the night to begin with.

"Who is she?"

"I don't like being backed into a corner, Officer Tanner."

She scanned the forest as though looking for answers, and he wondered again where her obvious distrust of law enforcement came from. Finally, she turned and glanced at him over her shoulder. Moonlight slid over her short dark hair and left her eyes in shadow. Tension vibrated off her in waves. "Her name is Mary."

Josh propped his fists on his hips. "Are you going to make me drag this information out of you one word at a time?"

"Never answer a question you haven't been asked. And never offer more information than what is required." She tossed the words out in a way that made Josh think they had been drilled into her from childhood.

He pulled back his irritation. There was something else at play here, something that clearly worried her. "I am not your enemy, Delilah. But I do need answers." He paused. "How about a last name, if that won't offend your sensibilities too much?"

He watched one side of her mouth kick up in a half smile. Then she sighed. "Atwood."

"Any relation to John Henry Atwood?"

She looked away. "She's his daughter."

His mind spun as everything he knew about the Atwoods raced through his mind. "How do you know her? There's quite an age gap between you two."

The silence went on so long, he thought she wouldn't answer. Finally, she seemed to come to some decision and let out a breath. The eyes that met his held challenge. "She's my sister."

The word hit Josh like a slap. Delilah was John Henry Atwood's daughter? He searched his memory and found no mention of her anywhere. How had they managed to hide a daughter? Of course, he was gone for a few years after college, flying for a small commuter airline in Alabama. And given the way the Atwoods kept to themselves and avoided law enforcement and local government officials, it wasn't really surprising. Especially since they moved their campsite regularly. The sheriff's office and the Ocala FWC squad kept an eye on all the militia and survivalist types who lived in the area, but they usually went no further than that. Not without good reason.

He studied the woman in front of him, trying to reconcile all the bits and pieces that were Delilah Atwood. There were far too many gaps for him to see her clearly. But by the light of the moon shining down on the clearing, two things became abundantly clear. Delilah Atwood was not only worried; she was spitting mad.

"Do you know who was shooting at you?"

"Not definitively, no. Though I have a couple guesses." Flames practically shot from her eyes.

Josh suddenly realized the shooter had taken great care *not* to hit either woman. "John Henry or Aaron?"

She spared him a glance before she spun on her heel and walked toward the edge of the clearing.

Josh hurried after her as she melted into the forest. She retraced her steps to where she and her sister had been talking and scooped up a cell phone and a plastic bag with what looked like a bundle of fabric inside it.

"Talk to me, Delilah. Please. Let me help."

She stopped and stared at him. By the light of the moon, he saw myriad emotions cross her face. Besides the anger, he caught a flash of longing, layered with worry and a plea for understanding, all swirling in her big blue eyes. But then she looked away and clenched her jaw as though holding words back. "I appreciate that, but you can't. This is a family matter, something I have to deal with myself." She squared her shoulders and set off again.

He easily caught up to her and matched his steps to hers. "You don't have to say a word to me if you don't want to, but if you're heading back toward your camper"—he hitched a thumb over his shoulder—"you're heading in the wrong direction."

———————

Delilah glanced up to see Josh grinning at her in the moonlight. Part of her wanted to throw her arms around him and laugh at his absolute audacity. And the other part wanted to shove him away with both hands because he kept turning up, kept looking at her like he wanted to kiss her senseless, and seemed completely impervious to all her attempts to push him away. "Since you're about as hard to get rid of as a deer tick, you might as well lead the way. The faster we get there, the faster I'll be rid of you." She couldn't help smiling as she said it.

But then her smile faded. Delilah was discovering that under Josh's laid-back exterior and sexy grin, he had a stubborn streak.

And therein lay the danger. No matter how affable he seemed, he was still FWC. She'd been a fool to tell him as much as she had. She couldn't risk him or anyone else digging around in her family's business. Not before she had Mary with her. If they connected the Atwoods to the guns she'd seen and started making arrests… No. She couldn't allow that. No matter how tempted she was to explore the heat that flared whenever she was around Josh, she had to keep him at arm's length.

Her focus had to stay on Mary.

———————

Josh considered Delilah's acquiescence a small victory. He threw his left arm out with an "after you" motion and then put a casual hand at the small of her back. He expected her to step away, but eventually, she loosened up enough that they walked in companionable silence.

Questions crowded his tongue. He wanted to know why she was meeting her sister alone in the forest at night, why he'd never heard of another Atwood daughter, why she called herself Delilah Paige, why shadows crossed her eyes when she didn't think anyone was looking. The sadness especially called to him, something they had in common, and he wanted to know its cause.

But the woman wore her secrets like a winter coat. What was she hiding? He had to assume part of it was being raised under John Henry's iron control and mistrust of law enforcement, but what was the rest? Why had John Henry or Aaron been trying to scare the two women?

By the time her small camper came into view, Josh hadn't voiced a single one of his questions. The fact that she'd allowed him to walk her home seemed a major victory. If he pushed hard right now, he had no doubt that the next time he came by, her camper would have disappeared.

He walked her to the rickety steps that led inside.

She paused, hand on the door latch. "I know you want to help, and I appreciate it, but what you saw tonight has nothing to do with the dead man I found in the forest. I can't help your investigation."

He studied her. Interesting. Who was she protecting? Her sister?

"Thank you for walking me home, Officer Tanner."

The blatant attempt to keep distance between them made him grin. He picked up one of her hands and raised it to his lips, watching her eyes widen. "When I'm with you, I'm just Josh, okay?"

Their eyes met and held, attraction sizzling like a live wire, pulling them closer. She looked down at his thumb rubbing the back of her hand, then met his eyes and tightened her grip. She took a step toward him, their chests a hairsbreadth from touching. "Can you separate the two?" Her voice was low, husky.

He swallowed hard, then opened his mouth to insist that of course he could, but the lie wouldn't come. Josh the man and Josh the cop were one and the same. "I'll do my very best." He deliberately stepped back before he blurred the lines even further. "Lock up behind me, Delilah," he said and walked back into the forest.

CHAPTER 6

JOSH STOPPED BY THE CORNER CAFÉ EARLY THE NEXT MORN-ing on the off chance Delilah would be there. He should have known she'd avoid him, since she'd basically told him to butt out of her business, but he'd hoped for a few minutes with her just the same.

Liz greeted him with a smile as he came through the door. This early, it wasn't too crowded yet. "How you doing this morning, Hollywood?" She eyed him up and down. "Hate to say it, but you look rough." She smiled to take the sting out of her words.

"I'm fine." He looked at the display of cupcakes behind her. "How about a dozen of those chocolate ones with the white frosting?" He didn't want to take all the inventory before the regulars arrived.

She grinned as she reached below the counter for a box. "Squad meeting this morning?"

He raised a brow. "Trying to break the donut stereotype."

"Good thinking." She boxed them up, opened the register to make change.

He turned to go, but Liz leaned closer and asked, "Have they found out who that poor hunter was yet?" She shuddered. "I can't imagine being attacked by a bear."

"No matter how good your coffee, Liz, you know I can't talk about an investigation."

She grinned. "Figured it couldn't hurt to ask, Hollywood."

The bell above the door jangled merrily as Commissioner Dwight Benson and his good buddy Mayor Bill Peterson saun-tered in, Commissioner Rory Kilpatrick hot on their heels. Even though Ocala had grown over the years, at heart it was still a very small town, with all the political power in the hands of a few. These three assumed that meant them and no one else.

Josh nodded as he passed. "Gentlemen."

"Not so fast, Tanner," Benson said, stepping in his path. "You have any more news about that poor hunter?"

Josh kept his expression neutral. "Now, Dwight," he began, making sure his look encompassed all of them, "you know you'll get whatever information we have just as soon as we get it."

The bell jangled again, and Josh stepped aside to let the next customer in. Aaron Atwood strolled through the door. He stiffened momentarily when he spotted Josh, but then his expression cleared, and he touched the brim of his hat as he passed.

Josh turned to go but happened to glance up just as Aaron and Dwight made eye contact. The look Benson aimed Atwood's way could have blistered paint. The one Atwood shot back was equally lethal looking. Atwood didn't say a word, simply stalked to the counter and ordered coffee.

As Josh headed toward the meeting Hunter had called at the Outpost, his mind spun. For a guy who came from such a tightly closed community, what was Aaron doing at the café two mornings in a row? And what was that look between him and Benson all about?

———————

Delilah stumbled into the tiny bathroom of her camper the next morning and squinted at her reflection. She shoved her hair back and groaned at the ever-darkening circles under her eyes. If she didn't get some sleep and soon, she wouldn't be able to help anyone.

As she'd tossed and turned, she'd berated herself for blurting out Mary's name. Why did she keep letting herself get sidetracked by Josh's great smile, sad eyes, and caring personality? He was FWC, for crying out loud.

She wished she'd kept quiet, but he would have found out anyway. Maybe now he'd think the mystery was solved and leave her alone. Which was what she wanted, right?

By 2:00 a.m., she'd given up all attempts to sleep. Only two people could have taken those shots last night: either her father or Aaron. It wasn't her own dumb luck or skill in running away. Which meant one of them had followed Mary. What would they have done when they realized Mary had spoken to her?

That question haunted her the rest of the night. She'd pulled out her laptop and focused on typing her research notes, because every time she stopped, her mind flashed back to her childhood, times she had either innocently or deliberately broken one of her father's rules. As punishment, John Henry regularly locked her out of the camper, forcing her to spend the night in the woods. She shivered, remembering. Had they done the same to Mary?

Other times, though, he'd punished Mama. And those memories were even worse.

After last night, sneaking Mary away before her family figured out she was back was no longer an option. All right, then. She'd track them down and confront her father. She reached under the dinette cushions and pulled out the envelope of cash she'd hidden inside a sweatshirt. John Henry had always acted as though feeding Delilah was an added burden, so she'd offer money in exchange for Mary. She checked her Glock, added an extra magazine, and stashed that in her backpack, too, under her camera. If money didn't convince him, she'd threaten to tell FWC what she knew about the guns and cash. She had options. When the scared sixteen-year-old she'd been urged her to find another way, to avoid a confrontation, the new Delilah gently told her to let her handle it. This wasn't about her old fears. Or the past. It was about Mary's future.

The counselor Kimberly Gaines had sent her to years ago had taught Delilah that courage wasn't the absence of fear. Courage meant looking fear in the eye and doing the right thing anyway.

On the way to the Corner Café, she called Kimberly, who promised a map and directions. She told herself she needed a serious shot of caffeine, but as she slowed to make the turn into the parking lot, she admitted that was a lie. She wanted to see Josh. When the man himself stepped onto the porch in his khaki uniform, looking like he belonged on a magazine cover, Delilah turned her blinker on and slowed to a crawl, eyes following him as he walked to his truck.

What was she doing?

She pressed the accelerator and kept going, eliciting a honk from the annoyed driver behind her.

No matter how much he tempted her to curl up against his hard chest or how much she'd started imagining what it'd be like if they gave in to the attraction between them, she couldn't afford to get distracted or involved in any way, not when she planned to leave town as soon as she had Mary with her. Grant, or no grant.

The scrub squad was already seated at one of the picnic tables in the Outpost's pavilion when Josh arrived.

"Wondered if you were going to grace us with your presence, Hollywood," Lieutenant Boudreau drawled.

Josh raised the box of cupcakes bearing the Corner Café logo. "Y'all quit ragging me, or I'll eat these myself." He set the box on the table, and they descended like locusts.

Once everyone had a cupcake in their hands, Hunter said, "I heard from the ME right before I texted everyone."

The good-natured ribbing stopped as everyone froze, cupcakes suspended midair.

"Cause of death was a stab wound to the heart."

There was a beat of silence. "We were right. This was murder." Josh glanced at Pete, who was brushing cupcake crumbs off his green sheriff's office uniform.

"Looks to be," Hunter confirmed.

"So the killer spread the honey around to draw the bear and cover the murder." Josh shook his head as he spoke. "That's pretty ballsy. And implies some clear thinking in crisis. Did he kill the guy and then think, oh, crap, now how do I cover it up?"

"Or was it premeditated, and he brought the honey with him?" Sanchez asked. "Otherwise, who carries that much of the stuff in their vehicle?"

"And those, ladies and gentlemen, are among the many questions we have yet to answer."

"What do we know about the knife? Anything?" Lisa Bass, aka Fish, asked.

Josh glanced over and saw Pete eyeing Fish with what could only be called interest. Their gazes collided, and she ducked her head and looked away, uncomfortable. What was up with that? Those two were forever sniping at each other over something.

"Not much," Hunter said. "Based on the length and width of the blade and its smooth edge, it's the same size and shape as the knives every hunter around here wears on their belt."

"Do we know who the victim is yet?" Pete asked.

Hunter nodded. "Byte emailed me late last night. He tracked the guy's tattoo to a particular tattoo artist, who keeps a record of all the ink he does. Our victim is Robert Black. He was born in Ocala but lived near Tallahassee and came back here regularly to go hunting, according to his social media."

"Any ties to…ah…anyone local?" Josh caught himself before he blurted out Delilah's name.

Hunter merely raised a brow. "Why don't you go talk to our neighborhood monkey researcher again, see if his name rings a bell? Byte found nothing that suggests he's a researcher—he works in banking—but maybe he and Ms. Paige crossed paths some other way. Find out what she's not saying."

Josh nodded, mind racing. Oh, he'd bet his left arm there was worlds of stuff she wasn't saying. "I'll let you know."

"Before I forget," Hunter continued, "we need to start thinking about who's wearing the tux and schmoozing the locals at the Mayor's Ball this year."

"I'll work security, as always," Sanchez said.

"Maybe," Hunter replied, nipping the evasive maneuver in the bud.

Josh caught Pete eyeing Fish, who sighed as she scanned their faces. "I suppose you're expecting me to get all dolled up again this year and act like one of you is my date." She rolled her eyes and made air quotes around the last word.

Hunter nodded. "Appreciate it. It'd look weird if this year's tux lottery winner had to go stag."

Everyone groaned.

"You have a better idea on how to choose who puts on the monkey suit?" he asked. No one responded.

"I'll let you know who's going." He handed out more assignments, but Josh's mind had turned back to Delilah. Since this was now a murder investigation, he'd definitely have to check into her background, which would tick her off.

But it also gave him the perfect excuse to talk to her in person again.

He grinned in anticipation.

———————

Later, Delilah headed into the forest, Kimberly's directions beside her. Her stomach clenched as she thought about confronting an angry John Henry. What had he done when he realized Mary had met with her? She shoved that aside, because she couldn't change it. She had to focus on the future. *Speak calmly and lay out your position in a logical fashion. Offer money. Then threaten if needed. You have the power here.*

The aching knowledge that Mama would pay the price no matter what she did, same as when Delilah escaped years ago, sent pain knifing through her. *I'm sorry, Mama.*

Keep your focus on Mary, she told herself.

This far into the forest, the tree canopy blocked much of the sunlight, and Delilah gripped the wheel tighter, afraid the shifting shadows would make her miss the barely there dirt track Kimberly said led to their campsite.

Maybe, just maybe, she could get Aaron alone and get him on her side. At one time, her brother had been just as frustrated with John Henry as Delilah was. Maybe she could still reach him.

As she drove farther and farther into the forest, the sky darkened and the wind picked up, indicating a storm was brewing. She squinted through the dusty windshield, determined to find the campsite. There, that was the turnoff Kimberly had mentioned. She hooked a right past the huge live oak tree that had been scarred by lightning and kept going, her confidence increasing with every landmark she found.

Heart pounding, she made the final turn into the clearing and stopped.

The campers were gone.

She was obviously in the right place, since signs of habitation were all around, but she was too late. She leaned over the steering wheel and studied the clearing as the reality sank in. Rather than deal with her, her family had packed up and moved.

Just like eight years ago.

Only that time, she'd found the burned remains of all her clothes in the fire, a clear message that they'd completely turned their backs on her.

The past threatened, but she pushed it away and focused on today. With Mary's wedding coming up, they wouldn't have gone far. She'd find them.

Delilah slid out of the truck and scanned the area. She walked to the fire ring, held her hand over it. It was cold, so they had probably left last night. A few steps farther, she picked up a clothespin that had fallen underneath where the clothesline had been.

She stood, hands on her hips. "I won't go away quietly this time, John Henry," she shouted. "I let you bully me, but I won't let you bully Mary. I won't let you do it, either, Aaron."

Feeling marginally better, she walked the perimeter to be sure she hadn't missed anything. She was ready to climb into her truck when she noticed a small pile of rocks. She stepped closer, curious, as they appeared to have been stacked on purpose. She pushed them aside and found a folded piece of notebook paper.

> *Delilah, I hope you find this. I'm sorry I ran away. Papa has gone completely crazy since you showed up. Aaron, too, and they won't stop fighting. I'm scared. Please find me.*

Her breath caught at the fear that bled through the note. "Be strong, my Mary Lou Who. I will find you. Make no mistake."

Determination shot through her as she roared back toward the main road. John Henry was a live grenade on a good day, and Delilah had inadvertently pulled the pin.

She was driving too fast, bouncing over dirt roads, sliding around sandy corners, fear for her sister keeping her foot on the accelerator. "Slow down, you idiot," she muttered, "or you're going to crash."

She had to think smart. And that meant a more concrete plan than careening around the forest.

By the time she pulled up to the camper, she'd realized that no matter how careful her family was, somebody would know where they'd gone. She just had to figure out who and then get them to tell her. Easier said than done, but she wouldn't stop until she did.

Hang on, Mary. I'll find you.

CHAPTER 7

Josh sat in his official FWC truck outside Delilah's trailer and stewed. Where was she? He'd been sitting here long enough that mosquitoes buzzed through the open windows and humidity coated his skin like glue. The more minutes that ticked by, the more irritated he became, which was ridiculous, since they hadn't planned to meet and she certainly had no obligation to keep him apprised of her whereabouts. The fact that he'd been looking forward to seeing her just made him more annoyed.

He opened his truck-mounted laptop and typed *Delilah Atwood* into the database. He found a birth certificate, which surprised him, given that she had probably been born at home and John Henry would have seen no reason to deal with government documents. Perhaps the midwife had filed it.

He also learned that Paige, the last name she'd been using here, was actually her middle name.

He found her listed on the university website and on one social media site. There were only a few dozen posts, mostly regarding the monkeys or the latest anthropology research or nature photos. Clearly, she wasn't someone who lived her life online. He focused on the few personal photos, which showed Delilah with several other women in various locations. She always looked slightly uncomfortable and held herself stiffly, like she wasn't sure how to act or where to look from that side of the camera.

The short bob was new. Given what he knew about the Atwoods, maybe it was part of her break from her family. All the online pictures showed shoulder-length, deep-brown hair with hints of red. Either way, she had an unconscious sensuality that tempted a man to get closer, to want to touch.

He also checked the background of any group photos, looking for Robert Black. She claimed she didn't know him, but maybe he'd known her? Followed her? It was a long shot, but he had to check, though he wasn't really surprised when he found nothing. No sign of her in any of Black's social media accounts, either.

Her truck roared up, and she hopped out and hurried toward the camper almost before the vehicle came to a complete stop. He intercepted her before she disappeared inside. "Delilah. I need to ask you a few more questions."

She tried to rush past him, head down. "Sorry, now is not a good time."

He stepped in front of her. "It won't take long."

She bristled but stopped. When she finally aimed a quick glance his way, his questions vanished. "What's wrong? What happened?"

She shook her head, but he saw the devastation in her face. Something, or someone, had upset her. Badly. "Talk to me, Delilah. I can help."

"I wish you could. Please. It's better if you just leave me alone." She marched up the steps.

After she unlocked the door, she turned and stopped him with a hand on his chest. He automatically gripped her upper arms, and attraction crackled in the air as they studied each other. His heart pounded, and he wondered if she could feel it under her palm. She snatched her hand away as though she'd been burned. "I can't spar with you right now." Her voice was a desperate whisper.

"I won't take much of your time, but I have to insist." And maybe, afterward, he could get her to tell him what happened.

Her blue eyes shot sparks, but he wouldn't look away. Finally, she sighed and stepped into the camper. He followed and waited while she cranked the windows open, which didn't help much, since there was no breeze.

When she perched on the edge of the futon, he sat at the small dinette across the room, unwilling to crowd her any more than necessary.

"We were able to ID the victim you found on Saturday."

When she looked up, her expression held nothing more than polite curiosity and a flash of pity.

"His name was Robert Black, and he lived in Tallahassee."

"I'm very sorry for him and his family. Do they know yet?"

"Yes, his parents have been notified. He wasn't married." He waited a beat, then asked, "You sure you didn't know him?"

Her head shot up in surprise. "I've never seen him before in my life. Except, you know, the other day."

He leaned forward and braced his forearms on the table. "As Wells alluded to, we found notes and photos that suggest he was also studying the monkeys."

"I've never met him. I didn't know there was another researcher out here."

Josh rubbed a hand over the back of his neck. "Delilah, it wasn't a bear that killed him. He was murdered."

All the color drained from her face. "Why would somebody kill him? Wait. Does that mean the bear just showed up to investigate?"

"We don't have those answers yet, but we're working on it."

She narrowed her eyes. "And since I am also studying the monkeys and happened to find him, you think I had something to do with this."

It sounded as far-fetched coming out of her mouth as it had when he'd thought about it earlier. But he had to tug on the string, however thin, that connected Delilah to the victim and see where it led. "All I know is that your paths intersected in the forest. Had you met him in a class somewhere maybe? A coffee shop on campus?" When she simply shook her head no, he asked, "Do you own a hunting knife?"

Indignation flashed across her features before she reached into the backpack she never seemed to be without. She pulled out a knife, its sheath the kind typically worn on a belt. "This is the only one I have."

It was about the right length, but the murder weapon had a smooth edge. He scanned it anyway, checking crevices for signs of blood, but knew he wouldn't find any. "Mind if I take this with me? I'll see that you get it back."

Delilah sighed and then waved a hand. "Fine."

He blew out a breath, frustrated by the distance she seemed determined to keep between them. "You know I'm just doing my job, right?"

"I know. But it doesn't make me like you very much." She smiled slightly when she said it, and he smiled back.

She'd picked up his business card and was turning it over in her hands.

"You should keep that with you. You never know when you might need an annoying cop."

They both stood, and the space suddenly seemed too small. She took a step back, and her hips hit the dinette table. He reached out to tuck a lock of hair behind her ear but pulled his hand back at the last second. Their gazes collided, and he watched her eyes dart to his mouth and back again before she looked away. The fact that she was as attracted to him as he was to her did not help. He stuck his hands in his pockets to ensure he didn't do something dumb like yanking her into his arms. He was working a case. Still, he couldn't help asking, "Are you okay?"

She sent him a rueful smile. "I will be. My day did not go at all the way I had hoped."

"Something to do with your sister?" He had no idea what was going on in her family, but he'd bet money Aaron or John Henry had fired those shots last night, though he'd be hard-pressed to prove it.

"I needed to speak to my father today. And my brother," she added. "But apparently, they wanted no part of that."

"Why didn't they want you talking to your sister last night?"

The silence lengthened. Finally, she said, "I want Mary to come live with me. Based on the less-than-enthusiastic response, I guess John Henry doesn't like the idea."

Which confirmed the shooter had been one of the two men. What kind of crazy family was this, where people discussed things with weapons instead of words? "I'm sorry. Is there anything I can do to help?"

She cocked her head as though he was some sort of unfamiliar species and then shook her head and sent him a sad half smile. "No, but thank you for asking."

His cell phone buzzed with an incoming text from Hunter. "I have to go. If you can think of any connection at all between you and Robert Black, I hope you give me a call. Day or night." He looked over his shoulder from the doorway. "I don't know what's happening here, Delilah, but I hope you'll decide to trust me enough to let me help."

She opened her mouth, closed it, a battle raging in her eyes.

He had no idea if what was going on with her family was connected to Robert Black's murder, but he planned to find out.

Which meant he was sticking close. She clearly wasn't used to anyone helping her or standing beside her, but that was about to change.

Nobody was showing up with a gun again while he was around to prevent it.

CHAPTER 8

DELILAH WONDERED IF JOSH HAD ANY IDEA HOW CLOSE SHE'D come to telling him everything. Or how tempted she'd been to run her hands all over his chest instead of backing away. Every time he showed up, it was harder to keep her distance. But for Mary's sake, she had to.

The camper walls were closing in on her, so she grabbed her gear and headed out, intent on finding the same troop of monkeys she'd studied the other day. Nothing reset her equilibrium like watching the little ones play while the adults interacted. Their predictable behavior settled her, especially on days like today, when her own family acted in ways she couldn't begin to comprehend.

She was in luck, because the troop was high in the treetops, in the same area as before. She pulled out her camera and smiled as she watched several females grooming one another, others eating.

A flash of movement in a small tree caught her eye. "Oh, there you are, babies," she crooned, grinning like mad. The infants had crossed the three-week mark, and several of them were sitting on branches, munching leaves. The first few weeks, they stayed with their mothers, nursing exclusively. She panned the area with her camera and found the mothers nearby, keeping a watchful eye on their offspring while they ate and groomed one another.

She snapped photo after photo, relieved that the little ones all looked healthy. She caught a few "aunties" inching closer, which concerned her. These young females, often from the same mother, would sometimes try to take the little ones to practice mothering. But if the auntie wasn't lactating, unless the mother took the infant back, things could quickly become life-threatening.

She waited and watched, relieved that all seemed well with

both the mothers and their offspring. The tiny male she'd nick-named Oscar caught her eye, and she snapped photo after photo of his adorable face as he scampered and played. As she studied him, she took her first deep breath in hours, finally letting herself relax. At least out here, things made sense.

But then that same twitchy feeling that she was being watched started between her shoulder blades. Annoyed that her fragile peace had been shattered, she packed her camera and headed home.

Time crawled by as the clock neared midnight and she paced her tiny camper. Why had John Henry moved the family? The only thing that made sense was that he and Aaron were worried she might cause trouble, which convinced her Aaron had recognized her that night. She smiled a little at the idea that she'd made them nervous.

Over the past eight years, she'd told herself she was okay without family, but tonight, a wave of loneliness swept over her, followed by the familiar wash of guilt. How bad had things gotten for Mama after Delilah ran away?

She couldn't undo the past, so she had to focus on getting Mary out of there. Which meant thinking like her father. There were two possibilities to prompt a move: the guns she'd seen or the dead hunter was somehow connected to the family.

Which brought her back to Josh and his earlier questions. She had no doubt his offer of help was genuine. He was that kind of guy. But until she knew what her family was into—and how it could affect Mary—she had to keep steeling herself against the growing temptation to curl up in his arms and tell him everything.

Wait. Who was Mary supposed to marry? Once she had a name, she'd talk to the creep and get him to cancel—she'd threaten, even pay him off if necessary. She pulled out her camera and studied the photos she'd taken earlier, trying to organize her thoughts. She'd bet Kimberly would help her track down this model citizen.

When she finally fell asleep with the camera still in her hands, the images she'd worked so hard to forget came back to torment her. Suddenly, it was two weeks before her wedding, and Nate had taken her out to dinner and a movie. He'd been funny and solicitous and treated her like a fairy-tale princess. The way he looked at her and things he said had made Delilah feel beautiful and cherished, and she thought again that maybe being married wouldn't be such a terrible thing after all.

They were in the truck, headed back to her family's campsite, when he suddenly pulled off the dirt road and into the woods. Delilah looked around at the darkened forest, and a little shiver passed over her skin. Nate turned toward her with a smile. "Slide over here by me. You're too far away."

Delilah returned the smile and inched her way toward him, unsure what to do. He'd kissed her a few times, and it had been very nice, but now, there was something different about him. He had a predatory gleam in his eyes that set off warning bells in her head. He must have noticed, for his grin widened. "Relax, little girl. I love you. I won't hurt you."

Delilah wasn't sure how to respond. She liked hearing he loved her but stiffened at being called "little girl." Before she came up with a response, though, he yanked her into his arms and covered her mouth with his, trapping her against the truck's bench seat. Startled and uncomfortable, she put her hands on his chest, trying to push him away, but it only seemed to make things worse. He tightened his grip and glared at her. "You've been teasing me long enough. That ends tonight."

Delilah wasn't sure exactly what he meant, but what little she knew and the possessive, angry look in his eyes scared her. "I think we should go home now," she whispered.

He laughed as he pulled her close again. "We'll go when I say we go. And I'm just getting started."

His hands seemed to be everywhere at once, and the more

she struggled, the more aggressive he got. Terrified, she twisted and turned, biting back her cries, since any sound she made just seemed to excite him further.

Tears leaked out of Delilah's eyes as she realized she couldn't escape. He was bigger and stronger, and soon, she'd be his wife, so he could do what he wanted, whenever he wanted. Her life would be just like this, all the time. She was trapped. Forever.

When he held her down with one hand and unfastened his pants with the other, a new wave of terror jolted through her, and her mind rebelled against everything she'd been taught. No. She didn't want this, wouldn't let him do this to her. She had to stop him. Had to get away.

Get out of the truck, her mind screamed, and she fought harder.

Between one heartbeat and the next, a knife appeared in his hand. She planted her feet on the seat, but the knife connected with her thigh, and she screamed in pain as it sliced into her skin.

As she looked up at the angry face looming above her, she spotted his rifle in the gun rack above her head. She lunged upward, throwing him momentarily off balance, and grabbed the rifle. There wasn't much room in the cab, but she put all her weight behind it and slammed the butt into his forehead.

He screamed and grabbed his head as blood spurted, then tried to reach for the gun. "You'll pay for this, bitch!" He couldn't see past the blood, so she hit him again and again until he stopped fighting. Then she scrambled out of the truck and took off running.

She ran, half hobbling, one hand clamped over the gash in her thigh, until she reached the clinic.

Breath heaving, she leaned against a tree. Kimberly Gaines had always been kind to her. Delilah pulled the door open with the last of her strength, took two steps inside, and collapsed on the floor.

Gentle hands touched her face. "You're safe now, sweet girl. You're going to be just fine."

After she bandaged her up, Kimberly tried to get Delilah to report what had happened. "No, please. I just want to go home."

Kimberly studied her for a long moment, then nodded once. She drove her to the campsite and held Delilah tight as they studied the empty clearing, the remnants of Delilah's burned clothing smoldering in the fire pit. The message was clear as day, and Delilah's heart broke as she realized her family had turned their backs on her. Without a word, Kimberly took Delilah home with her. The next day, she helped Delilah disappear.

A noise outside the camper brought Delilah sharply awake, and her head shot up like a forest animal scenting danger. Breathing hard as she shook off the last remnants of the nightmare, she eased over to the tiny window and peeked out. The camper was dark, so no one could see her. A mama raccoon and her babies walked past, but the sense that there were other eyes watching wouldn't go away.

She knew she wouldn't sleep anymore tonight, so she turned on a lamp and powered up her laptop. She would transfer the photos from her camera and then sort, crop, and save the best of the best for her next progress report.

At the sound of a vehicle approaching, she froze.

Again, she crept to the window and peeked out. An official FWC pickup pulled up at the edge of the clearing, and Josh climbed out. She braced for his knock at her door, but it didn't come. Instead, she heard him make a careful circuit around her camper. When she looked out again, he lifted his hand in a two-fingered salute before he climbed back into his truck.

After thirty minutes had gone by and he still hadn't left, Delilah realized he was keeping watch. She went back to the window, squinted through the blinds, and saw him in the cab of the truck, head back against the headrest, as though he planned to stay.

Why? Was he worried she was going to run away? Annoyance shot through her, followed immediately by another thought. Maybe it was the opposite. Maybe he was trying to keep her safe.

Which threw her completely off balance. She always felt like he could see right past her defenses. She was used to being alone and taking care of herself, but he kept trying to walk beside her, to help, and she wasn't sure how to react. His clean scent, hard body, and twinkly eyes also made her acutely aware of the differences between male and female.

Just thinking about his laser-sharp focus directed at her started a delicious heat in her belly. The contrast between him and her nightmares of Nate was like the difference between heaven and hell.

She peeked out the window again, oh so tempted to walk to his truck and run her hand along that hard jaw, let her palm slide over the stubble of his beard. Images of the two of them, wrapped around each other on her little futon, hands caressing bare skin, scorched her. But she couldn't let that happen. He'd stirred something inside her, something that went far deeper than a casual relationship, and that was a risk she couldn't take.

Her focus had to stay on Mary.

Tomorrow, she'd figure out who they were marrying her sister to, and she'd go from there. Nothing else mattered.

She'd have to keep her distance from her self-appointed protector. She turned off the lamp and opened the blinds. Josh turned toward the camper as though he could see her. His teeth flashed white in the moonlight and he nodded. Knowing he was there, she curled up on her lonely futon and slept.

———————

The next morning, Josh headed for the Corner Café after a quick stop at home to shave and shower. He'd caught a few z's in his truck and had made sure he was gone well before dawn. He figured Delilah wouldn't appreciate the fact that he'd been there all night, but he hadn't been able to leave. He couldn't shake the sensation that danger hovered around her. He'd learned not to ignore that instinct.

Liz greeted him with a smile, then studied his face and frowned. "Officer Tanner, they're going to start calling you Hangdog instead of Hollywood if you don't get some sleep."

Josh sent her a lopsided grin. "I knew there was a reason I stopped in here for coffee. Who else would say such nice things to me this early in the morning?"

She laughed, then pointed to a copy of today's paper lying on the counter. "I'm guessing this is what's causing those dark circles under your eyes?"

Josh glanced at the headline. HUNTER MURDERED IN FOREST MADE TO LOOK LIKE BEAR ATTACK. FWC was hoping the information would get people talking.

It wouldn't be long before the barrage of questions started. He heard the bell above the door jangle behind him and turned slowly, counting down as he went. Three. Two. One.

"Is this for real?" Mayor Bill Peterson waved a copy of the paper around.

"That's what I hear," Josh said noncommittally.

"Don't you know? Isn't FWC investigating?"

Josh looked from Peterson to Commissioner Benson to the other regulars scattered around the room. He raised his voice to be sure everyone heard it the first time. "What you read in the paper is correct. According to the ME's report, Robert Black was not killed by a bear but by a stab wound to the chest. It looks like someone deliberately tried to draw the bear to the body to conceal the crime."

Josh heard the bell and turned to see Delilah striding through the doorway.

The moment she spotted him, she marched in his direction. "I need to talk to you." She'd tried to lower her voice, but the tone carried.

Josh looked over his shoulder, aware that all conversation had stopped as people openly eavesdropped. "Let's take this outside."

He led them to the other side of his truck, out of view of the café windows.

She propped her hands on her hips, drawing his gaze. She wore form-fitting khaki pants today, with a white button-down shirt tucked inside. With her dark hair, she looked amazing. "Why were you outside my camper all night, Josh? Did you think I was going to run away?"

He pulled his attention back to her words. "What? No." He blew out a breath, rubbed a hand over the back of his neck. Suddenly, what made perfect sense in the middle of the night seemed less clear-cut in the light of day. "Look. Besides Black being murdered and the monkey researcher last year who was beaten almost to death, there is also the matter of guns being fired around the time you found the body. And let's not forget either your father or brother firing shots, in the dark no less, to keep you away from your sister."

She raised a brow. "It still doesn't explain what you were doing outside my camper."

"I was trying to protect you." The words came out a low growl.

She studied him as though judging the truth of his words, and then a slow smile spread over her face. Seconds later, it vanished. "Were you there all night?"

"Most of it. I left just before dawn. Why?"

She held out a plastic bag with a piece of paper inside. "I'm guessing you didn't leave this on the hood of my truck."

He snatched the bag from her hand and read the note. Someone had written "You don't belong here," in thick black marker.

"Why would I leave you a note? Makes no sense." He shook his head. "And just for the record, I don't think that. I think this is home for you, even if you've been gone a long time."

He watched surprise flash across her face before she reached into her pants pocket and pulled out another baggie. This one held a shotgun shell. "Then I guess you didn't leave this next to the note."

He froze. A note was one thing. The implied threat of the shot-gun shell was something else. Someone must have shown up after he'd left this morning. Had they been watching her, too? His mind raced through possibilities, but he kept his voice calm. "You guess right." He studied the shell, then looked up. "Good thinking, bag-ging both. Did you touch them?"

"The note, yes. For a second, I thought you'd left it, and I was ticked off." She shrugged, embarrassed. "I didn't touch the shell."

He propped his arm on the cab of the truck and leaned closer, catching a whiff of something soft and citrusy that suited her perfectly. "Just so we're clear. If I have something to say, I'll say it straight out. I won't leave a note on your truck."

The silence stretched, and he thought he just might drown in the pull of her deep blue eyes. She surprised him by reaching up and cupping his jaw. "I can take care of myself, you know." Her voice was low, almost a whisper.

He shrugged, smiled. "Call me old-fashioned."

Her smile curved her lips and drew his attention. His mouth was inches from hers when he remembered he was in uniform and they were standing outside the café, in full view of anyone who drove by.

He eased back and cleared his throat. A wash of color flooded her cheeks, and she looked away. At least he wasn't the only one affected. *Focus, Tanner.* "I'll take these and have them run for prints. Any idea who might have left them?" He had a few ideas but wanted her opinion.

"I know some people don't want me out here studying the monkeys. They're convinced they're a threat to the environment and should be removed." Her chin came up, but she smiled as she added, "Guys like you."

He smiled back, then blew out a breath. "Right. People get a little nuts about the monkeys, on both sides of the issue." He paused, kept his eyes on her face as he held up the shotgun shell. "Is this something John Henry or Aaron would do?"

She glanced away. "I'm not sure. Possibly."

He considered. "Doesn't seem like their style. They seem more like shoot-first-ask-questions-later types."

A rueful smile touched her lips. "You're probably right about that."

"Are they the same people responsible for the gunfire I heard the day you found Robert Black?"

She stiffened in surprise, then tried to hide her reaction. She looked away, then back at him, conflicting emotions warring in her expression. Worry, fear, uncertainty. Finally, she seemed to come to a decision. "Yes."

He'd suspected as much, and it raised a whole host of other questions. "Tell me what you left out of your story before, Delilah. I need to know."

She went instantly back in warrior mode. "My priority, my only priority, is to find Mary, get her safely with me."

"You've said that before. But what does that have to do with the gunfire? Was she there, too?"

"No! Neither was Mama. And John Henry and Aaron weren't trying to hit anyone. They were just practicing."

"The gun range is nowhere near there. Target practice any-where else is only allowed during hunting season, which this is not." He kept his voice neutral to keep her talking. "Did you see them before or after you found the victim?"

"After. I wanted to avoid the bear, so I took off running. I stum-bled across their target practice."

"Where?"

She hesitated for a long moment, then said, "There's a spot my family has always stored stuff in."

Crap. Was there a whole arsenal nobody knew about? Then a whole other worry occurred to him. "Did they see you?"

She swallowed hard. "Yes. But I'm not sure they recognized me. Aaron might have."

"Which would explain him trying to keep you away from Mary, to keep you out of the family's business."

She sighed. "That's what I'm thinking, yes."

It also put a chat with Aaron and John Henry at the top of his list. Provided he could find them. "What else did you see?"

The question sent her into full-blown panic. She gripped his arms with both hands, her hold fierce, eyes frantic. "You can't arrest them. Not until Mary is with me. Promise me, or I won't tell you a thing."

"Easy. Take a breath. Right now, we're just talking. That's it. Tell me what else you saw."

"No. You know that's not it. You're FWC. You'll investigate. You have to!" She spun away from him, clenched her fists. "You'll burst in, and Mary and Mama will—"

He stepped in front of her, cupped her shoulders. "Delilah. Stop. Breathe." Her eyes darted around and finally landed on him. He waited while she took several calming breaths. "You're jumping way ahead. Just tell me what you saw, and we'll go from there."

She swallowed hard, and he stilled, waiting. *Come on. Tell me all of it. You can trust me*, he wanted to say. Which was absolutely true. But they both also knew he'd have to follow up on whatever she told him. He held perfectly still while she wrestled with herself.

"There were long wooden crates, several of them. And a bag with a whole lot of cash in it."

Damn. That wasn't good. "Do you know what was in the crates?"

She heaved a resigned sigh. "Since they took the rifles out of one, I'm guessing the others contained more of the same."

Neither John Henry nor Aaron Atwood were licensed gun dealers. He wasn't even sure they had driver's licenses, what with their distrust of all things government, but he'd make it his business to find out. "How many crates were there?"

"Four."

His mind was clicking through his next steps when she faced

him again, arms akimbo, back in warrior stance. "I answered your questions, now I want that promise. You won't arrest John Henry or Aaron until after I get Mary out of there. She's not even sixteen yet, and her birthday's in less than two weeks, which means I need to get her out of there. Fast."

He wanted to ask what exactly Mary's birthday had to do with anything, but he didn't. Knowing Delilah was John Henry's daughter, her distrust of law enforcement made perfect sense. He was surprised she'd told him as much as she had. "You have anything else to add to your story?"

She bristled. "Still waiting on that promise, Hollywood."

He chose his words carefully, thinking through every angle. "You know I have to look into this"—*huge understatement*—"but you have my word that I'll do everything in my power to give you time to get your sister away before we issue any warrants, if it comes to that. Right now, all we have is an 'anonymous tip' from a concerned citizen."

It was the best he could do. He wouldn't make promises he couldn't keep.

She studied him carefully before she nodded. "I suppose I'll have to take what I can get."

He couldn't prevent a smile at her disgruntled tone. "Right back at you, Madam Researcher." There were more questions he wanted to ask, more secrets he sensed she was hiding—maybe not about the investigation but about her family. He'd have to earn her trust before he heard the rest.

But that didn't mean he wouldn't do what he could to protect her. He glanced at her outfit. "You heading out into the forest today? By yourself?"

"I always go by myself. Besides, I have a report due, which means meeting those pesky deadlines."

He mock shuddered. "Paperwork, the bane of law enforcement everywhere."

She grinned, and this time, it lit up her whole face. "Call me a nerd, but I love taking all this information and compiling it into something useful, something that can make a difference." She rubbed her hands together in anticipation. "Nothing I like better than a good research paper."

He shook his head "Are you sure you weren't abducted by aliens? You can't possibly be a regular human."

"We all have our gifts, Hollywood. Not all of us can get by on good looks alone."

"Why, Miss Atwood, whatever do you mean?" He tried to bat his eyelashes and managed to cross his eyes.

She burst out laughing, and suddenly they were standing too close again, yet not close enough. He got another whiff of her citrusy shampoo and fought the urge to nuzzle her neck.

Nearby, a car door slammed, and someone called, "Morning, Hollywood, ma'am," as they walked by.

He stepped away, cleared his throat. "Sure I can't convince you to take someone with you today?"

She rolled her eyes. "I'll be fine, Hollywood. I have my Glock, too." She held up a hand. "Properly documented, in case you were wondering."

He smirked, looked down at her feet. "At least you have snake boots on."

She sent him an arch look. "This girl's not stupid. I grew up in the woods, remember?"

He smiled. "I remember. You have my number in your phone?"

Another lovely flush spread over her skin. "Yes, though there's not much signal out there."

"Text often works when calls won't go through. Don't hesitate if you run into any, shall we say, unwelcoming folks."

"Thanks, but I'll be fine."

He wanted to argue, the offer to go with her on the tip of his tongue, when his cell buzzed with a text from Sanchez. "I have to go. Be careful out there, Delilah."

"Yes, Officer," she quipped.

"Josh," he corrected and climbed into his truck.

He backed out, met her eyes in the rearview mirror, and smiled. Her answering grin sent a wash of heat through his body.

But as he drove away, his smile faded. Someone had her in his sights.

CHAPTER 9

DELILAH HIKED INTO THE FOREST AND TRACKED DOWN ONE OF the troops of monkeys she'd been studying, but she couldn't focus. She went through the motions of taking photos and scribbling notes, but she wasn't sure she'd be able to read her own writing, her mind still focused on her conversation with Josh. But her advisor didn't care about personal issues. She expected a report, on time and well written, neither of which Delilah felt capable of today.

She still couldn't believe she'd told him about the guns. Had she completely lost her mind? She knew he'd have to investigate. He'd said as much. But would he give her the chance to get Mary away first?

She'd have to trust that his word meant something. Meanwhile, she'd keep looking for her sister. Somebody had to know who they were marrying her to.

As she stood behind a tree taking photographs, her mind circled back to the note and shotgun shell. That didn't seem like something her brother would do. Certainly not her father. So who was trying to scare her away? Why? To stop her research?

She shook her head and raised her camera again, determined to corral her thoughts. The sooner she got her work done today, the sooner she could search for her sister.

She watched three of the tiny young monkeys scamper around on a tree branch, jumping back and forth over one another, cavorting like rambunctious toddlers. She zoomed in, searching for the mamas. Where were they? Usually, they were close by.

In a nearby tree, she found another infant crawling over and around his mother, generally making a total pest of himself in the way of children everywhere. After a few minutes, Mama had enough and gave him a quick swat to the rump, along with a scolding that clearly implied, "Settle down." He chattered back and scrambled onto another branch, safely out of her reach.

Delilah grinned as she slid down the tree trunk and leaned against it while she looked through her photos. These were some great shots. The few minutes of video she'd captured would round out her assignment nicely.

She raised her camera again and zoomed in on the first trio of infants. Then she slowly, carefully panned the tree, looking for the mamas in case she'd missed them earlier. They weren't there. Uneasiness crept up her spine. This wasn't good. *Come on, mamas. Where did you go?*

One of the young monkeys suddenly started looking around, frantic, and she realized it was Oscar. His little cry wrenched Delilah's heart as he scampered back and forth, obviously looking for his mother. She tightened her grip on the camera, following him as he searched, climbing first one branch, then another, crying all the while.

Delilah stood, ready to spring into action—though what she'd do, she had no idea—when a monkey leaped out of a nearby tree and grabbed him. But instead of cuddling him close to nurse, the mother turned, and he climbed on her back. Delilah zoomed in, her relief changing to worry when she realized that wasn't his mother. It was one of the aunties. She was too young, and she wasn't lactating.

So where was Oscar's mother? Had the auntie run her off so she could kidnap him? Delilah took a breath. Sometimes, like human moms, the mothers needed a break and let the younger females babysit. But as she continued searching, she couldn't find the mothers anywhere. Where were they?

The alpha male suddenly screeched in alarm. Within seconds, the whole troop disappeared into the forest as though they'd never been there. Delilah rose slowly, scanning the area, trying to pinpoint what had set them off. She heard faint rustling behind her and froze, the hair on the back of her neck standing at attention. Man or beast?

She pulled out her weapon and kept it at her side, heart pounding. Sweat trickled down her back as she stood motionless, listening. She didn't move a muscle until the sound faded into the distance and the squirrels around her resumed their activity. But the sense that someone was still watching persisted.

The researcher in her wanted to follow the troop, but this morning's warning made her cautious. When several mosquitos found her, meaning her essential oil had worn off, she called it a day. She tucked her camera into her backpack but kept her gun handy as she hurried toward her truck, all her senses on alert.

She glanced over her shoulder every couple of steps on her roundabout path. She couldn't spot anyone, but instinct told her someone kept pace behind her.

———————

"Hi, Delilah. It's good to see you," Charlee Tanner said when Delilah walked into Tanner's Outpost a while later. "How's that essential oil mixture working?"

Delilah smiled. "You read my mind. That stuff is amazing, and I need more."

"Told you. Best stuff ever." She came from behind the counter and handed Delilah a bottle. "This one is bigger and should last a bit longer. How's the research going? Josh said you grew up around here, but I don't remember you from school."

Normally, Delilah would've stiffened at such obvious probing. But coming from Josh's sister, it just seemed like friendly interest. Delilah figured she could do a little probing in return. "Our family didn't socialize with the outside world very much. I was homeschooled."

"That explains it, then." Delilah expected a pitying look or the raised eyebrow that often accompanied the word *homeschooled*, but Charlee simply cocked her head. "Does it feel weird to be back in town? You've been gone a long time, right?"

"Right. And we weren't really part of the community, so I felt like I grew up in a parallel universe. In some ways, coming home feels like coming for the first time, if that makes sense." Delilah snapped her jaw shut to keep from spewing more personal information. Charlee's openness made the words pour out. Sort of like what happened whenever she was around Josh.

Charlee looked her up and down. "I'm thinking you were out in the forest this morning."

Delilah decided not to mention her worry that she was being watched or her concern about the mama monkeys. A good researcher didn't jump to premature conclusions; they documented facts. "I was. And I got some great shots of several of the infants." She hesitated. "Want to see?"

"Absolutely." Charlee stepped closer as Delilah scrolled through the morning's photos.

"So you must know everyone around here, right? Keep an ear to the ground on all the locals?"

Charlee looked at her oddly, and Delilah winced. She'd come on too strong.

"Sure. Comes from working in two places the locals hang out. Why do you ask?"

"I'm trying to figure out who—"

The door swung open, and none other than Josh Tanner strolled in. He'd been in his FWC uniform this morning, but now he was sporting swim trunks, a T-shirt, and flip-flops, dark shades propped on his head. "Hey, Sis. Hey, Delilah. What are you girls up to?"

"I thought you were working today," Charlee said.

"I am. I'm just doing a little, shall we say, incognito work this afternoon. You have a group coming in a little while, right?"

Some kind of look Delilah didn't understand passed between the siblings before Charlee said, "I do. You coming along?"

Josh nodded. "I thought I would if you've got room for one more." He turned to Delilah. "You coming too?"

Delilah looked between the two, unsure. The invitation in Josh's movie-star grin made warning signs flash in her brain, reminding her how easily she opened up to him, this morning's unexpected truth-fest case in point. The fact that he wasn't chasing down her family this instant reassured her. If she went along, she could keep an eye on whatever "incognito" work he was doing and might get what she needed from Charlee, too, if she phrased the questions just right. "Um, sure. Maybe the monkeys will be around, too, which would be perfect. Do you have room?"

Charlee grinned. "Of course. This will be fun. The new college kid we hired will be here in just a bit to mind the store while we're gone."

Delilah returned her smile and then made the mistake of glancing in Josh's direction. His gaze had heated, and the look he shot her before he jerked his eyes away—like he wanted to run his hands over every inch of her skin—made all the reasons she should keep her distance seem murky and foolish.

They were two consenting adults who clearly had chemistry on their side. And they liked each other. Why not indulge while she was here? Even as the thought registered, she knew why. Josh Tanner didn't just turn her on. It was much more than that. He made her feel things she'd never felt before and inspired thoughts of children and picket fences and all the things she thought she'd never have. That was scarier than looking down the barrel of a loaded shotgun. She could never fall for a man who lived in Ocala of all places, because she wasn't staying. Ever. Distance was safer.

For today, she was looking for information. Period. No longing looks, no smoldering glances, no flirting.

If only her body could remember that.

Josh returned Delilah's smile, and guilt smacked him like a base-ball bat to the head. She had an amazing smile, the kind you could get lost in, and that was what brought him up short. He'd vowed not to get lost in anyone's smile. Not after Elaine and her secrets. But somehow, the need to make Delilah feel safe, to coax her to let down her guard, had made him careless with her.

He'd been acting like a jerk, sending mixed signals, and that wasn't fair. Until he was ready to risk his heart fully in another relationship, he needed to back away from the flirting and keep things firmly in the friend zone. Never mind that she was connected to an active investigation. Everything about Delilah said she wasn't a casual-relationship kind of girl, and he never wanted to hurt her or lead her on in any way. So what if she was hot enough to melt pavement and seemed to want him as much as he wanted her?

He would keep things casual while making sure whoever had left that note and bullet wasn't dumb enough to do anything more serious than that. He agreed with Delilah that it probably hadn't been her brother or father—wasn't their style—but that raised the question, who then?

He'd stay close.

As Delilah filled out paperwork, he checked his phone for updates from Byte and Sanchez, who were in Tallahassee search-ing Black's house. Delilah changed clothes in the restroom, and when she reappeared in board shorts, a tank top, and flip-flops, he glanced up and sucked in an audible breath before he could stop himself. *Damn, she was beautiful.*

Charlee walked past him and hissed, "Quit drooling, Hollywood."

Embarrassed, he shot her a cocky grin, but she didn't smile back.

Her expression turned serious. "I think she's been hurt, Josh. Be careful."

"I don't have any intention of hurting anyone. I just—"

Charlee held up a hand. "Stop. This is me you're talking to. I know you loved Elaine—I did, too—but I'm still pissed off about what she did, and I'm pretty sure you are too. She hurt all of us. Until you've sorted it out in your head, don't go starting something with Delilah. That's not fair to either one of you."

Even though he'd just told himself the same thing, being chastised by his sister rankled. Before he could insist that he simply planned to be her friend, Delilah rejoined them, and the door swung open as the afternoon tour trooped in.

There were two families, each with a couple of younger children, but it was the tall, bearded dad Josh was interested in. Phone records confirmed that the last communication Robert Black had sent before he died was a text to this man, Oren Hughes, that said, "Meet me at the Outpost, Tuesday, 1 p.m."

His phone chimed with an incoming email from Byte to the squad. He'd found a flyer in Black's email about a meeting of "those interested in keeping themselves and their families safe from government oppression."

That sounded like someone was organizing a group, possibly a militia. This trip would be the perfect opportunity to get more information.

━━━━━━━━━

His heart hadn't stopped racing since the moment he saw the headline in today's paper. He rubbed a hand over his chest as he hurried in from the parking lot. His blood pressure was through the roof, and based on the odd looks people sent his way as he rushed by, he figured his face was flushed and he didn't look so good. Several colleagues tried to engage him in conversation, but he brushed pass them as though he hadn't heard. He had to get to the safety of his office.

He opened the door, and his secretary stood up from her desk, a sheaf of messages in her hand. "Sir, these are for you."

He held up his hand. "Not right now. I'll get them in a little bit. Thank you." He forced himself to close the door calmly behind him, though he wanted nothing more than to slam it shut. But that would arouse suspicions he couldn't afford.

He collapsed into the leather chair behind his desk and buried his face in his hands. He pulled the newspaper out of his briefcase and set it down on the desk blotter. How on earth had it come to this? His plan had seemed foolproof. If that bear had done its job, there should've been no way anyone could have figured out the guy died any other way.

"What were you doing out there anyway?" he muttered, looking at the photo. He shook his head. He was losing it. The guy had been dressed in camo and carrying a rifle. Obviously, he'd been out hunting. Or maybe he hadn't been. Maybe that was all for show, and he'd really been there spying on the operation. With the man dead, there was no way to tell. But when their eyes had locked, he'd panicked, especially when the man said his name. If he'd taken the time to think about it, he would've tied him up and questioned him first, figured out how much he knew.

He leaped up from the chair and started pacing his office. None of that mattered now. The man was dead, and FWC was calling it murder. Could they trace it back to him? He didn't think so. He'd been so careful. Then again, he hadn't expected them to figure out it hadn't been a bear attack either.

His hands shook, and he curled them into fists and then released them again and again, hoping it would help him calm down.

What should he do? Mind racing, he considered and discarded various options. But in the end, he decided to wait and watch. He'd go on as usual, try not to draw any undue attention to himself, and deny everything if it came down to it.

He picked up his phone. Just in case, he'd make sure he had an airtight alibi. And cover all his bases.

If he went down, there was no way he was going alone.

He sat, drummed his fingers on his desk as he thought. Actually, there was a way to make sure he didn't go down at all.

He just had to tie up a few loose ends.

Oren Hughes hung back as their group paddled the river. Josh didn't blame him, given the enthusiasm and volume at which his family attacked the trip. He figured this was the perfect opportunity to deliver bad news and ask some important questions, since Hughes couldn't walk away.

Ahead of them, Charlee and Delilah were laughing and talking like old friends while the other two families paddled in front of them. As he watched, he realized that here, finally, was the real Delilah, the woman he'd been getting to know at the café. So different from the guarded woman she became whenever he was in uniform. Though given what he was learning about her family, he couldn't really blame her. Still, the transformation was amazing, and he couldn't take his eyes off her.

"Do you live around here?" Hughes asked from beside him.

Josh glanced at the man and jerked his thoughts back to his assignment. "This is home. Except for college and a few years as a pilot, I've never lived anywhere else. How about you?"

The man shrugged. "Lived here all my life." He hitched his chin toward his family. "I usually kayak alone, but I was supposed to meet an old friend of mine today." He shrugged. "He didn't show."

"His name's Robert Black, right?"

Hughes's head snapped around. "How do you know that?"

Josh raised the hem of his T-shirt so Hughes could see his badge. "I'm FWC, and I'm very sorry to tell you that your friend is dead."

"What? When?" There was a long moment of stunned silence as Hughes processed the news. Then he said, "Wait a minute. The hunter that was, uh, killed. Was that Robert?"

"Sadly, yes, it was. I'm very sorry for your loss."

Horror crossed the other man's face, and he was silent for several moments. "The paper said he was murdered. Why would somebody do that?"

"That's what we're trying to figure out. How long did you know Robert?"

"Seems like most of my life. We grew up together."

"Do you know why Robert wanted to meet with you?"

Hughes shook his head, then smiled sadly. "I have no idea, but if I know Robert, it had something to do with money. He always had a scheme going to make a buck. Some panned out, some didn't, but he was always working an angle."

Josh kept his eyes steady on Hughes's face. "Do you have any ties to a local militia group, Mr. Hughes?"

The other man stiffened, and his eyes narrowed. "Why? What does that have to do with Robert's death?"

"Maybe nothing, but he had a flyer in his inbox about a meeting, something that sounds like a militia organizing maybe. Do you know anything about that?"

Hughes looked around, muttered under his breath. "This has gotten out of hand."

"What's gotten out of hand?"

"Some of these young guys, they get themselves all stirred up, don't think before they act."

"You mean young militia guys? Which guys?"

Hughes's jaw snapped shut. "Sorry, Officer. I couldn't say. That's just an opinion." He shook his head. "I can't believe Robert's dead. He was a good guy."

"Again, I'm sorry for your loss." Josh pulled a card out of his pocket, handed it over. "If you think of anything, any detail that might help us figure out who killed your friend, I'd sure appreciate a call."

Hughes tucked the card into a waterproof bag, and Josh looked up just as one of the boys flicked his paddle over the water and soaked Delilah. She sputtered and said, "Oh, it's like that, is it?" and sent a wall of water flying back at the boy.

A water fight erupted, and Josh paddled over and joined in. He came up behind Delilah and used his paddle to soak her. She deftly spun her kayak around and faced him, laughing and swiping water out of her eyes as she prepared for battle. "You'll pay for that, Hollywood!"

Her wet tank top clung to her skin, and he was too busy enjoying the view to see her launch an equally large splash over him. He sputtered and realized he was laughing and enjoying himself as he hadn't in a very long time. "This means war, Xena!"

They shot water back and forth, grinning like fools, until one of the boys nailed her with another wall of water from behind, laughing in triumph. "Oh, you've got it coming now," she growled. She tried to spin her kayak and splash the boy at the same time, only she stuck her paddle in too far and tipped her kayak over.

Josh was beside her in two strokes, just in case. She popped up and was treading water, laughing as she swiped her hair out of her eyes.

Charlee and the boy's mother paddled over. "Are you okay, Delilah? Oh, goodness, I'm so sorry." She turned on the boy. "What were you thinking?"

While the boy stammered an apology, Delilah waved it away. "It's fine. We were just playing."

Josh maneuvered next to Delilah's kayak and flipped it over. "You okay?" When she nodded, he said, "I'll steady it while you climb back in."

"Thanks." She flashed him a quick grin and then pushed herself up and into the kayak in one smooth move.

He saw the cocky grin she sent over her shoulder and smiled back. "You've obviously done this before."

"Yes, but I hadn't been kayaking in years until I came back

here." Something sad flickered in her eyes before it disappeared. "Thanks for the help." She caught up to the boys and continued the water fight.

He watched her, the way her clothes molded to her wet skin and her carefree abandon as she played, and an odd stirring of hope passed through him. Maybe it was time to lay Elaine's ghost to rest and think about the future.

A bang echoed across the water, and Delilah ducked as though from gunfire. A large tree limb fell on shore across from them, but that didn't ease the tension in her shoulders. From that moment on, her playful demeanor disappeared. Though she talked with Charlee and occasionally teased the children, she kept her eyes along the bank, watchful, as though she were looking for someone.

CHAPTER 10

WHEN DELILAH LEFT THE OUTPOST, SHE WAS TIRED, HOT, AND A little sunburned. And except for her overreaction to the falling limb at the end, she also felt alive in a way she hadn't in years. Spending time with the Tanner family opened doors to places in her heart she had firmly locked a long time ago. With them, she could break out of the tidy box in which she existed, free to laugh and play without guarding every word and gesture. They made her feel welcome and wanted and like she was a person worth being around. The muscles in her arms ached from overuse, but it felt good.

The Tanners were apparently huggers, because first Charlee and then Josh wrapped her in exuberant embraces before she left. Josh's hug was tighter and lasted significantly longer than Charlee's and came with a chaste kiss on her cheek, followed by a killer grin and sexy wink. She winked right back and enjoyed the flash of surprise in his eyes and then shivered when it turned to a smoldering look that promised...more.

She and Charlee were becoming friends, which was very different from spending time with fellow students or other teaching assistants, which were more circumstantial acquaintances. Delilah hadn't had a close friend since Andy left for Peru, so the possibilities today opened up made her smile.

On the downside, she still didn't know who Mary was supposed to marry, despite her careful questions. Charlee had never met her mother or sister, though she'd seen her father and brother at the Corner Café a time or two over the years. Which didn't help.

She hadn't been able to head home until she'd checked her family's campsite again, even though she'd known it was a long shot. They weren't there, though a foolish part of her had hoped. She consoled herself by thinking through additional places to check as she drove. When she approached a sharp turn with lots of sand, she eased her foot off the accelerator and tapped the brakes. She knew if you didn't do it right, you got bogged down and sank, truck or no truck.

Her foot went straight to the floor. "Doggone it. Now is not the time for the brakes to quit." She pumped the pedal, hoping that would help, but nothing happened. No pressure.

Because of that, she went into the turn much too fast and had to use the handbrake to slow the truck. It helped a little but not enough to combat the sand. The truck stopped, and she gave it a little gas, but as she expected, the tires spun and she sank deeper.

After a few more tries, she accepted defeat and turned the ignition off. It wasn't going anywhere tonight, so she'd better get moving. She took a minute to coat herself with mosquito repellent, grabbed her Maglite, and tried to figure out where her camper was in relation to her current location.

She looked up through the trees, saw the thick clouds, and laughed out loud. "Of course. It would be too much to ask that there be moonlight tonight, right?"

A rustling off in the bushes made her jump, and she shook her head at her own foolishness when a raccoon lumbered into view. Time to pull out all the lessons her father had taught her growing up. The irony did not escape her. The fact that those skills could help her now upped her confidence. She wasn't a helpless, scared sixteen-year-old anymore.

Lesson one was to make a plan before rushing into action. She pulled out her phone, hoping to use the GPS, not really surprised at the little "no signal" bar at the top of the screen. "Alrighty then, moving on to plan B." She scanned the area and decided to head toward the main road, where she should be able to get a signal. Once there, she could pull up a map or call somebody for a ride. Josh's face immediately popped into her head, but she decided he'd be her last resort. Hadn't she just told herself to keep her distance?

If she triangulated her location in her head, the main road would put her closer to her camper, so she headed in that direction. At least she thought she did.

When she came upon the same huge, lightning-damaged, downed tree for the third time, she admitted defeat. Somehow, she'd managed to wander around in circles. It was humiliating. She sank down on the log and pulled out her phone, still no signal. She tapped Josh's name in the message app, and her finger hovered over the phone. What would she tell him? She figured "near the downed tree" wouldn't be terribly helpful.

Her brain went around in circles, unsure, until she finally put the phone back in her pocket.

From the time they were little, her father had instilled in his children that if they ever got lost, to stay put. Wait for someone to come find them. But that was then, and this was now.

She stood and kept moving.

———————

Today had been illuminating in more ways than one. Josh tapped a finger on the steering wheel of his official FWC F-150 as he left the main road and turned onto one of the many dirt roads that crisscrossed the forest. After Delilah left the café this morning, he'd called Hunter, told him what she'd said, and filled him in on the note and shotgun shell. He'd been prepared to argue long and loud for keeping his word to Delilah, but Hunter had simply said, "We'll consider her an informant. You keep her safe and try to figure out what the deal is with her sister while we follow up on the guns and cash and see how that figures—or not—into Black's murder."

Something Oren had said earlier about Black and money nagged at him. But it was his evasion on the question of militias in the area that had brought Josh here. He figured John Henry Atwood had the answers he needed, but whether he'd be willing to share them with a government man like him was another story. He and Hunter had decided Josh would follow up on the militia angle, see how or if it fit.

When he arrived at the Atwood family's campsite, he wasn't surprised that they had cleared out and moved on. John Henry was one of the more rigid survivalist types who lived out here, convinced the government was just waiting to pounce and get into his business. Guys like him never stayed in one place for long and dragged their families from pillar to post on a regular basis.

He shone his Maglite around the campsite in case they had left any clues behind, but except the fire ring, there was no evidence anyone had been there. He climbed into the truck and headed back a different way, thinking he'd swing by Delilah's camper, just to make sure she got home safely.

He hadn't gone far when he ran across what looked like Delilah's truck, stuck in the sand. He hopped out and ran over, concerned she was hurt, but the vehicle was empty. He shone his light around the area, but there was no sign of her. "Delilah? Are you here?"

He studied the ground, trying to figure out which direction she had gone. He only found one footprint but decided it was better than nothing and headed in that general direction, calling her name as he went. What had she been doing out here?

Probably the same thing you are. Trying to find her parents. And her sister.

What would it have been like to grow up with John Henry? The things she hadn't said, combined with her worry for Mary, painted an ominous picture. He hoped she'd trust him enough to tell him the whole story soon. He really did want to help.

"Delilah? Where are you?" He kept calling her name as he walked, scanning the area with his flashlight.

He thought he heard a sound and hurried in that direction.

Even late at night, humidity hung like spiderwebs in the forest, sticking to your skin and weighing you down as you walked. The essential oil Delilah had gotten from Charlee had long since soaked into her skin, and she walked along waving a hand in front of her face, trying to keep the pesky bugs from gnawing on every bit of exposed skin. *Dang, I hate the forest at night.* Something rustled in the underbrush to her right, and she stopped, held herself motionless as she'd been taught, and waited until she could identify what she was hearing. She debated turning on her flashlight but didn't want to scare whatever it was. Based on the sound, it was either an opossum, raccoon, or some other small mammal. If it had been something larger, it would have made more noise.

Images of the bear flashed through her mind, and she kept going. She sensed movement behind her and spun around. As she did, she caught her left ankle in a small hole and fell down with a startled cry. She glanced up just in time to see a white-tailed deer bounding away.

Shifting to a sitting position, she let out a small groan when she tried to move her ankle. She turned her flashlight on, relieved that there were no bones sticking out of the skin. She lightly ran her fingers over the area and decided it was probably sprained, not broken. Hopefully. Her snake boots probably kept it from twisting worse than it had.

She got up onto all fours and then pushed herself upright. The moment she tried to put weight on that ankle, it buckled, and she sank back down to the ground.

Frustrated, she scooted backward until she could lean back against a tree. She sat for a while, heart pounding, ankle throbbing, and tried to sort out the sounds of the night critters. Despite all her childhood drills, she felt like a complete and utter failure because the world around her seemed completely foreign and unknown and scary. So much for all her lofty thinking about how far she'd risen above her humble beginnings. She was lost in the forest in the dead of night, hurt, and she had no idea what to do next.

Except call Josh.

She pulled out the phone and sighed. Still no signal. She swallowed her pride and texted: Truck stuck in sand. Somewhere near my folks' old campsite. Ankle sprained. Can you help?

She hit Send, watched the screen for a moment, and hoped it went through. Then she leaned her head back against the tree trunk and settled in to wait, determined not to jump at every rustle and chirp.

A different noise, one that seemed more stealthy, made the hair on the back of her neck stand up. She carefully looked around but didn't see anything. Or anyone. Still, she was sure eyes were watching her. There probably were, she reminded herself. Animal eyes.

She refused to consider any other possibility.

———

Delilah must have gotten a ride with someone or walked home, because she wasn't nearby. He stopped at another small clearing, called her name again, and shone his Maglite all around, hoping for a glimpse of her. What if she'd fallen? Hit her head or couldn't answer? He took a breath, annoyed with himself. He didn't normally overreact, but his concern for Delilah was making him act like a mama wood duck with only one chick left.

When his phone buzzed, he pulled it out of his pocket and read her text. Maybe it wasn't worry so much as intuition where she was concerned. He texted back: I think I'm nearby. Shine a flashlight, call my name, I'll find you.

He cupped his hands around his mouth and shouted, "Delilah! Delilah, where are you?"

He called several more times and then stopped to listen. When he heard a faint response, he took off running in that direction.

Josh's text sent a surge of relief through Delilah, and she sagged against the tree, eyes closed. "Oh thank God." Seconds later, panic hit. Worried he would give up and leave before he found her, she scrambled to her feet, wincing as she accidentally put weight on her left foot. One hand braced against the tree trunk, she shouted his name, waving her flashlight over her head like a shipwreck survivor who'd finally spotted a Coast Guard vessel.

When he raced into the clearing, Delilah launched herself into his arms. He stumbled back a few steps before he caught his balance, wrapping her tightly in his arms, murmuring, "I've got you. I've got you."

She pulled back to see his face, and suddenly, her lips met his—or his met hers, she couldn't tell which—and they were kissing with the kind of desperation reserved for real shipwreck survivors. The kiss went on and on, sensations rushing over her faster than she could sort them out. She wrapped her arms around his neck and pulled him closer still, nuzzling his neck, sighing as he murmured in her hair and placed soft kisses along her jaw. His grip shifted, and she realized her legs were wrapped around his waist after she'd climbed him like a tree. His hands cupped her bottom, and when she crossed her ankles to get closer still, she winced in pain.

The moment shattered, and he slowly pulled back. She blinked, dazed and not at all sure she wanted the kiss to end. His eyes said he felt the same, but even so, reason had reasserted itself. He brushed her lips once more, then steadied her as she unwrapped her legs and lowered them to the ground. She winced again when her injured ankle touched down. His grip on her waist tightened. "Easy. Go slow."

With infinite care, he maneuvered her down against the tree, then crouched beside her. He ran his flashlight over her with crisp efficiency before he set it off to the side so it wouldn't blind them. His touch was gentle as he tipped her head up so he could see her face. "Are you okay? Which ankle?"

She met his concerned gaze. "Left one. And I'm fine. Nothing much injured except my pride." She couldn't believe she'd launched herself at him. "Sorry I, ah, overreacted."

One side of his mouth curved upward. "The forest can be unsettling at night." Then his grin widened. "But feel free to over-react anytime you want."

They grinned at each other like idiots for a minute before she remembered she had to keep her distance. But dang, the man could kiss. He removed her boot, and the sharp pain jerked her back to the present. He ran his big hands from her calf all the way to her toes, then carefully rotated her ankle, and she bit her lip to keep from crying out. When he was done, he gently slid her foot back into the boot, tucking the laces inside rather than tying them, since it was already starting to swell.

"The good news is I don't think it's broken." He sent her the lopsided smile that turned her insides to mush. "The bad news is that I don't think you're going to be able to walk on it."

"How far away is your truck?" she asked.

"Not too far if you have two good legs." He stood and held out his hands to help her to her feet. The moment she was upright, he pulled her into his arms and wrapped her securely against his hard chest again. "I'm so glad you weren't hurt worse."

He kissed her again, gently this time, and Delilah slid into the kiss like a warm bath. She absorbed the strength of his arms around her and the beat of his heart thundering against her chest, feeling cherished and protected in a way she never had before. Slowly, reluctantly, she pulled back, and their eyes met and held, awareness buzzing between them like an electrical current. The heat in his eyes sent a low hum through her body. It buzzed through her a split second before he slapped at a mosquito on her cheek. She yelped in surprise, and he grinned. "Sorry. Bloodthirsty little buggers. Let's get out of here."

Keeping one of her hands in his, he turned his back and crouched. "Climb on. I'll carry you back to my truck."

Delilah was shaking her head no before he finished speaking. "You can't carry me. I'm way too heavy."

He raised an eyebrow. "Are you doubting my manly strength?"

The absurdity surprised a laugh out of her. "I would never doubt your manly strength, Officer Tanner."

"Then climb on, and let's get out of here already." He crouched lower. "And stop calling me Officer Tanner."

Since she didn't have much choice at this point, Delilah gingerly climbed on. He scooped her up, piggyback style, and set off into the forest. He spun her around a few times as he walked, singing an off-key version of the seven dwarves song. "Heigh-ho, heigh-ho, it's through the woods we go," then he whistled the rest, making up words here and there.

Delilah laughed and attempted, badly, to sing along, appreciating his attempt to distract her from her throbbing ankle. She took her cue from him and decided to enjoy the ride, the feel of her arms wrapped around his neck, his rock-hard arms supporting her as he strolled through the forest as though she weighed nothing. She was used to thinking her way through life, but with Josh, she was learning to simply enjoy the moment.

After a few minutes, he asked, "What were you doing out here so late? Looking for your family?"

"That was the plan, but they're gone. What about you?"

Delilah could feel him smile. "Great minds and all that. I was here to talk to them, too, but they've obviously moved on again."

"They don't usually stay in one place for very long. At least they didn't when I was growing up."

"From the little I know of them, that seems to be their typical pattern."

She held her breath after she asked, "Any ideas about where they might've gone?"

Josh thought for a moment. "There's no set pattern that I can see."

"There wasn't when I was a child, either. At least not one I noticed."

He scooted her up a little higher when she started slipping, and he asked, "So what happened to your truck?"

"The brakes quit. They were fine on the way here, but as I was leaving, they gave out."

They found her truck, with his beside it. He gently set her on the passenger seat, then climbed in behind the wheel.

"What do you mean by 'gave out'? Did they go soft on you?"

Delilah shook her head. "No. Gave out as in my foot went all the way to the floor."

"That's not good. Let me take a quick look before I drive you home so I have an idea what we're looking at."

"You don't have to—"

Josh sent her a look. "Take the help that's offered, Delilah." He cranked the engine and turned on the AC, then maneuvered his pickup so the headlights illuminated her hood.

He drove her truck a few hundred yards before coasting to a stop. She let out a relieved sigh. Nothing was more annoying than a vehicle issue that magically disappeared when someone tested it. Josh climbed out of her truck, and next thing she knew, he was lying half under it, flashlight in hand.

When he brushed the sand off his back and returned to his truck several minutes later, his expression was grim. "You said the brakes were fine on the way out here, right?"

"Yes. I haven't had any problems. Why?"

Josh tapped a finger on the steering wheel, then turned to face her, eyes hard, looking every inch a cop. "Someone cut your brake lines. I took a picture with my phone, but from what I can see, this was definitely deliberate."

A chill slithered down her back. Would Aaron or John Henry have done that? Or was this the work of whoever had left the bullet and note? After a lifetime of living under the radar, being singled out like this made her feel naked and vulnerable. Why was someone doing this?

She swallowed hard before she asked, "What happens now?"

"Hunter and Pete and I will take the truck to the Outpost, document what was done, and I'll fix the brake lines for you. It will be quicker and definitely cheaper." He grinned as he said that last bit.

"I can't ask you to do that." Indecision swamped her. She wasn't comfortable asking for help, but she needed a vehicle to search for Mary.

"You didn't ask, Delilah. I offered. Big difference."

She couldn't find words, so she simply said, "Thank you." The man continually surprised her with his kindness.

The truck's motion must have lulled her to sleep, because next thing she knew, Josh had scooped her into his arms and carried her into her camper. He laid her down on the futon and propped several pillows under her ankle before he rooted around in her tiny bathroom for supplies. After he carefully wrapped her ankle, he tucked an instant ice pack around it. "You have some ibuprofen?"

Delilah told him where they were and dutifully swallowed several with the water he handed her. "I don't know how to thank you."

Josh didn't answer, just covered her with an afghan and sat down at her tiny dinette. "Get some rest. We'll sort it all out tomorrow."

When it dawned on her that he wasn't leaving, she pushed herself up on her elbows. "I'm fine, really. There is no reason for you to sit at my kitchen table all night. Go home."

Josh glanced up from his phone. "I'll feel better if I keep an eye on you."

"I'd rather you leave," she shot back, then sucked in a breath and added, "please." They faced off across the small space. She was perfectly capable of caring for herself, thank you very much, and besides, he needed sleep. Therein lay her dilemma. Her futon was the only bed, and if he climbed in here with her, there was no way she'd be able to keep her hands off him. Josh Tanner stirred feelings in her she didn't know what to do with and that, frankly, scared her spitless. If she slept with him, instinct said her heart would be tied to his in ways that wouldn't be fair. Not to her or to him, since her days here were limited. But she couldn't put any of that into words, so keeping her physical distance seemed the safest choice.

Josh didn't argue. He simply stood, kissed her on the forehead, and said, "Sleep well. I'll be outside if you need me."

"You don't need to—"

He walked out and shut the door before she finished her sentence. Delilah flopped back down on the pillow and pulled the afghan up under her chin. It was too hot for it, but it made her feel safe. Before she could muster up the energy to go tell Josh he was free to leave, she fell asleep.

CHAPTER 11

THE DULL ACHE IN HER ANKLE KEPT DELILAH TOSSING AND turning most of the night, trying to get comfortable. After another dose of ibuprofen, she finally fell into a deep sleep just before dawn.

Pounding on her front door jolted her awake. Then Josh's voice. "Delilah? Are you up? I brought breakfast."

She shoved her hair out of her face and realized she must look a fright, but there was no hope for it now. She hobbled to the door, and he shouldered his way in, filling the space with his big body and clean male scent. He set a cup and bakery bag on the table. "I brought coffee, cupcakes, and a dose of sympathy from Liz at no extra charge. She hopes you feel better ASAP." He glanced around her small kitchen, started opening cupboards. "How do you take your coffee? Cream and sugar?"

Delilah struggled to keep up. She was never at her best when she first opened her eyes, but apparently, Josh had no such trouble. She sank down at the dinette and then squinted at the clock. "Ten o'clock? Oh wow."

"How's the ankle this morning?" He nudged the bakery bag in her direction.

Delilah wasn't sure which question to answer first, so she said, "Cream and sugar please. Too soon to tell on the ankle." She stirred both into her cup, then added, "Thank you for breakfast."

He sat down across from her, handed her keys back. "Hunter, Pete, and I checked out the truck this morning and towed it to the Outpost. We got it fixed, and Pete's outside, ready to give me a ride back to town." He paused, and in the blink of an eye, easygoing Josh morphed into Officer Tanner. "I'm concerned for your safety, Delilah. Leaving a note that says *you're not welcome here* is one thing. Shooting at you and cutting the brake lines on your truck are something else entirely." He crossed his arms over his chest. "Charlee said you could stay with her until we figure this out." His tone made it sound like a command.

Delilah sipped her coffee, stunned by his family's kindness. His concern also proved she wasn't simply exaggerating things in her own mind. But had a random stranger targeted her? Or was this her family's doing?

She'd have to think about that when he wasn't watching her like a bug under a microscope. "Please tell Charlee I appreciate the offer very much, but I'll be fine. And I never expected you to fix my truck. Thank you. How much do I owe you?" He rattled off a number and as she handed him the bills, a horn outside gave one short blast.

He ignored it and took her free hand, his thumb rubbing circles on the back. "I wish you'd stay with Charlee. But since you won't, if anything weird happens or you feel like something is off, you call me. Day or night. Understood?"

"I'll be fine, but I appreciate the concern, truly."

Just before he left, he sent a look over his shoulder that made her want to grab him and yank him close, but she smiled instead. Then she plopped down on the futon, mind whirling. If Aaron had cut the brake lines on her truck—because she couldn't see her father doing it—it still came back to why? Was this about Mary's wedding or about what she'd seen the day Black died? If she tracked her brother down and confronted him, would he tell her the truth?

The idea circled as she finished breakfast.

She drove straight to the community center and found Kimberly in an empty exam room. Her eyes narrowed at Delilah's uneven gait. "Why are you limping?"

"I twisted my ankle. Doesn't hurt too badly this morning, so I'm pretty sure it's not sprained." She hopped up on the exam table.

Kimberly folded her arms across her chest and raised an eyebrow. "What happened?"

"I tried to find my family, but they've moved again. Any guesses where they've gone this time?"

"Sweetie, you know they've never followed a pattern. That would defeat the whole purpose."

"I know, but I was hoping maybe you'd heard something."

Kimberly made a "go on" gesture, and Delilah huffed out a breath. "Someone cut the brake lines on my truck, and when I tried to walk home, I twisted my ankle. Officer Tanner was in the area, so he took me home. Then he and a couple of other FWC officers fixed the truck this morning."

Kimberly's eyebrows rose to her hairline, and a slow grin spread across her face. "Really?" she said, drawing out the word. "You could do worse than having a hunky FWC officer looking out for you, girl." She sobered abruptly. "Do you think Aaron cut the brake lines?"

"It's the less scary of the two possibilities." She hesitated before she told Kimberly about the threatening note and bullet left on the truck.

Kimberly planted both hands on her hips. "And what exactly is Officer Tanner doing about all this?"

"He offered to have me stay with his sister. And told me to be really careful. Which means..." She shook her head. "I have no idea what that means."

"It means he's concerned about you. So am I." Kimberly started pacing. "I think you need to track Aaron down and get the truth out of him." She stopped. "Have you checked all the hidey-holes your family has used in the past?"

"That's my next move." She slid off the table, gratified her ankle barely caused a wince. "You don't have another forest map handy, do you?"

Kimberly rooted around in a file drawer, then handed her one. "Where do you plan to start?"

"I thought I'd run out to the old quarry. I often babysat Mary when Mama was delivering babies or visiting the sick. She and I spent a lot of time in those caves. John Henry and Aaron used to store supplies in there, too."

"You know it's been turned into a zip-line park? They've done a really nice job on it, but it's pricey."

She'd have to figure out how to get in there to look around. There was a quick knock, and then another nurse poked her head in. "Oh, sorry, I didn't realize you had a patient."

"Delilah's not really a patient. She's family. Sarah Dutton, home health nurse, meet Delilah, ah, Paige. Sarah also just moved back to the area."

Sarah's smile was open and friendly, her handshake firm. "Nice to meet you, Delilah. Any friend of Kimberly's is a friend of mine."

"Sarah's also dating FWC officer Marco Sanchez." Kimberly winked at Delilah. "Delilah just met Josh Tanner a while back."

Sarah's smile widened. "The Tanners are a great family." She glanced over her shoulder. "I'll stop back by later. Nice to meet you, Delilah."

"I think you two would be good friends. And I think, like you, she could use a few of those."

Unsure what to say, Delilah simply nodded. "You've done far more than I can ever repay, but I need your help with one more thing. Can you find out who Mary is supposed to marry?"

"No guarantees, but I'll do my best."

"Ms. Gaines, I can't thank you enough for everyth—"

"When are you going to start calling me Kimberly?" she asked as she wrapped Delilah in her arms.

"Old habits are hard to break."

"Do it anyway," Kimberly said and patted Delilah's cheek.

As Delilah headed for her truck, the warmth of Kimberly's love and acceptance made her throat tight. When unflattering comparisons to her own mother surfaced, she focused on the next moves in her search.

Her phone chirped with a text from Josh: Be careful today.

Will do, she sent back as an entirely different kind of warmth filled her. He'd left her camper last night without argument and had kept watch in his truck, two nights in a row. And fixed her truck at the crack of dawn this morning.

She didn't know what to do with a man who put others' needs ahead of his own, who showed up for the people he cared about. Much as she wanted to protect her foolish heart, it was getting harder and harder to keep him at arm's length.

No time to daydream about sexy FWC officers. She had a quick stop to make before she started scouring the forest for Mary. She'd swing by the location she'd last seen the monkeys and make sure little Oscar was safely back with his mama.

Thankfully, they were hanging out in the same general area today, so it didn't take long to find them. As usual, she used the zoom on her camera to identify specific monkeys. Where was Oscar?

Several minutes later, she finally heard his little cry, and all the hair on her arms stood straight up. It sounded weaker than before. She panned the trees but couldn't find him in the canopy above. The other monkeys chattered and played, and no one seemed the least bit concerned.

His cry sounded again, closer, and she swung her camera in that direction. Her heart almost stopped when she found him. He was down on the ground not twenty feet away, climbing on cypress roots and crying with a pitiful little sound that shredded her heart.

Where was his mother? Had she died? Usually, one of the other mothers would step in and adopt the little one. But Oscar was all alone.

He spotted her and suddenly turned and walked toward her.

The closer he got, the more Delilah could see that he was too thin. Even though he'd started eating regular food, his primary source of nutrition should still be mother's milk.

When he stopped in front of her and cocked his head to study her, Delilah quickly scanned the trees above her, hoping his mother was hiding above, prepared to dive into action to save him. But there was no one there.

Watching him watch her, Delilah's heart and head went to war. Feeding the monkeys was wrong, illegal even. And ultimately, not in their best interests. She knew that and believed it with every fiber of her being. Wasn't her study all about the dangers of feeding them?

And yet. He was hungry. And he was staring at her with a trusting expression, little ribs way too prominent. Sometimes, mothers didn't care for their male offspring like they did females. Was that what happened here? Had he been abandoned?

Delilah reached into her backpack and withdrew her snack mix. Telling her conscience to hush, she took a handful of nuts and dried fruit and tossed them his way.

He leaped on the food and sat watching her as he gobbled up every bite. She tossed him another handful. And another until the package was empty. He scarfed it down like he hadn't eaten in a month.

A sound nearby startled them both, and she looked up. The other monkeys had seen what she was doing and were moving in her direction. Too late, she remembered that there was a food hierarchy, and he might get beaten up for what she'd given him, so she now had a new worry. But he turned and disappeared almost before she could blink.

"Be safe, little Oscar. I hope you find your mother."

She grabbed her gear and left before they descended and demanded more food, which she didn't have.

But the whole way back, she worried, hoping she hadn't made things worse for him by trying to help.

CHAPTER 12

DELILAH WALKED INTO TANNER'S OUTPOST THE NEXT MORN-ing, relieved that her ankle barely twinged. She was ready to dive back into Rescue Mission Mary, especially after yesterday's wild-goose chase. She'd driven to every place she could remember her family setting up camp, but they weren't at any of them. Thanks to Kimberly's map, she'd even found a few of their more recent camp-sites, but there was still no sign of them. She didn't know the exact date of Mary's wedding, but her sixteenth birthday was coming quick, the days ticking away like a giant clock in her head.

About four this morning, she'd decided to poke around the old quarry today. She figured Charlee might know something about the layout now that it was an attraction.

She'd noticed several pickups in the Outpost's parking area but hadn't realized who they belonged to until she crossed the thresh-old and found herself face-to-face with a smiling Josh.

Charlee waved from behind the counter. "Hey, Delilah. Heard you had an adventure the other night."

It took Delilah a minute to decide which adventure she meant. Right. Josh. Brakes. "Yeah, that definitely wasn't what I had planned. But I sure did appreciate the help from Officer Tanner here."

Josh stepped up beside her, a twinkle in his green eyes. "If you don't stop calling me Officer Tanner, I'm going to have to take dras-tic measures." He raised both eyebrows in a mock dramatic gesture that made her laugh. Then he turned and indicated the others in the room. "In case everyone hasn't been properly introduced, that big lug over there is my older brother and sheriff's deputy, Pete, and the smooth-talking Cajun with his tongue down my sister's throat is FWC Lieutenant Hunter Boudreau. The lovely lady next to Pete is FWC officer Lisa Bass, otherwise known as Fish. Everyone, this is Delilah Paige."

She relaxed when he left the Atwood off her name. After a flurry of greetings, Josh put his back to everyone and asked quietly, "How's the ankle today?"

The words barely registered as she studied his mouth, reliving their dizzying kiss. He raised an eyebrow, a knowing grin on his face, and she realized she'd made a humming sound low in her throat. What was the question again? "As long as there isn't a marathon on the agenda, I should be good to go."

"Glad to hear it. So what brings you here?"

Delilah glanced behind him, uncomfortably aware that everyone was awaiting her answer. "I thought I'd go exploring. I heard the old quarry has been turned into a zip-line adventure place."

"What a coincidence. We were all heading out there this morning, too," Josh said.

Over Josh's shoulder, Delilah saw confusion cross Pete's features. "I thought we were doing that this aftern—"

She pretended not to notice when Fish elbowed him sharply in the ribs.

"Why not come with us?" Charlee asked. "It'll be fun."

Delilah suddenly registered that none of them were in uniform. They were all wearing shorts, T-shirts, and tennis shoes. Josh's aftershave teased her nostrils, and the muscled arms rippling beneath his T-shirt brought back memories of him carrying her as though she weighed nothing.

He bent down slightly so she had to meet his eyes. "Come with us. Please?"

Between that coaxing smile and those twinkling green eyes, Delilah was lost. All logical arguments flew right out of her head as that oh-so-tempting fluttering started in her belly. *You don't have time to get sidetracked*, her brain warned. Right. "Actually, I wasn't planning to do the zip line. I just wanted to look around the place."

A challenging glint came into his eyes. "You're not afraid of a little zip line, are you?" Delilah shook her head, and he sobered instantly. "It's fine if you are. I'm just teasing."

"It isn't that." She bit her lip. "Mary and I used to play in some of those caves years ago. I wanted to go check them out, see if maybe..." She let the thought trail off.

"We aren't just going to have fun, either. We're scoping out a tip from an informant. His info isn't always terribly accurate, but since we were going to try the zip line anyway, we decided to check things out while we were there." He gave her shoulder a friendly bump. "What do you say about coming with us? Make it an even six."

Delilah looked from Josh's expression to the friendly faces smiling at her and found herself saying, "Why not? It sounds like fun." The group had an easy camaraderie she envied, and they'd opened the circle and invited her in. How could she refuse? She'd let herself enjoy something she'd always wanted to try while keeping her eyes peeled for any sign of Mary and their family. Spending time with the mouthwatering Josh Tanner was simply an unexpected bonus.

———

Josh tucked Delilah into the passenger seat and turned, not really surprised when Pete stepped up behind him.

"You sure you know what you're doing, Little Brother?" Pete asked.

Josh kept his voice low so Delilah wouldn't overhear. "What's that supposed to mean?"

"Elaine hasn't been gone that long. I don't think you should rush into anything."

Josh quelled his irritation. That was the second time this week one of his siblings had offered opinions on his personal life. "When I need your advice, Bulldog, I'll be sure to ask for it. As for today, by taking her with us, we'll be able to keep an eye on her, make sure nobody tries anything stupid. And if they do, we're here, so it's a win-win."

Pete digested that. "Makes sense. I think she knows more than she thinks she does."

Or more than she's been willing to say so far, Josh thought as he climbed into the truck. And that gnawed at the cop in him. He wasn't sure how to get her to open up about whatever else she knew, but he wouldn't give up until she did. He couldn't help it if he didn't know the problem.

"Did you spend lots of time out here when you were a kid?" he asked.

What was now the Ocala Zip Line Adventure Park had been a limestone quarry in the 1800s. Several years ago, an enterprising family had purchased it, and the once-gaping holes were now filled with water, giving visitors the impression they were somewhere in the mountains, not Florida. The change was startling.

"We did. Whenever we camped in this area, Aaron, Mary, and I would sneak over to explore the caves. I think my mother would have had heart failure if she had realized what we were doing." Delilah smiled at the memory and then shook her head. "After a while, Aaron stopped coming, but I still brought Mary whenever I was babysitting."

"Are you hoping to find a clue in the caves as to where they've gone?"

"Hopefully. But sneaking under rusting fences and poking around is different from exploring a public attraction."

"If you find evidence that she's been there, how will that help you find her?"

"I'm not sure yet, but I have to try. I can't just…"

Josh waited, but she didn't say anything else. "Why is it so important that you find her?"

Her look implied he was not the brightest bulb in the chandelier. "She's my sister."

When they pulled into the parking area, he turned to her. "If you don't want to tell me, that's fine. Let's go have some fun. And maybe you can find the clues you're looking for."

She narrowed her eyes at him. "You need to quit being so nice. Makes me feel like a jerk when I snap and snarl."

"There is a cure for that, you know." He raised an eyebrow, smiled. "You could always be nice."

"Now where's the fun in that?" She tossed a saucy grin over her shoulder and hurried toward Charlee.

Five minutes later, she wished she hadn't caved to that dimpled grin. Josh had told her he wouldn't push, but he was FWC, and cops pushed. It was what they did, part of their DNA or something. And she'd just agreed to spend time with not one but four cops. Together.

She took a deep breath, gathered her resolve. She could do this. She'd take Josh at his word and enjoy herself. She'd also try to find the caves she and Mary had played in. With water in the quarries, she wasn't sure she'd recognize anything, but there was only one way to find out, and that meant riding all nine zip lines. Uneasiness slid through her. Everything would be fine as long as she didn't let Josh's nearness lull her into blabbing things better left unsaid.

"Okay, folks, if your waivers are signed, we need to get your harnesses on. My name is Curly, and yes, that's either from the Three Stooges or maybe just the hair." The guide pointed to his curly brown mop. He looked to be in his early twenties, tattooed, and fit, with the kind of easygoing personality that put customers at ease. "This guy next to me is Mo, also from Three Stooges fame. Though I hear his mother calls him Maurice."

Mo appeared to be in his early thirties, with a bushy, dark mustache and twinkling brown eyes. "Nice to meet you folks. Curly and I will be your guides for the zip lines. Soon as we get you outfitted, we'll do a little practice run to make sure you're comfortable before we head up to the first of the towers."

They shuffled to an outdoor area, and Delilah studied the other groups, trying to calm the sudden butterflies in her stomach.

Josh stepped up beside her, voice low. "You can still change your mind."

"And have you brand me a coward? I don't think so." At his skeptical look, she added, "I'm always a little nervous at first, but it doesn't keep me from trying new things."

He looked her up and down, eyes twinkling, "Why, Madam Researcher, who knew an adventurer lurked inside your scholarly"—his eyes paused on her chest—"heart?"

She didn't let him see her smile, since he looked far too pleased with himself as it was. Curly stepped up just then and instructed her to step into the harness. She dutifully tightened clasps and listened to instructions, but she wasn't sure she could repeat any of them. She shook her head, annoyed with herself. All she needed was to do something stupid because she couldn't think when Josh was nearby.

Within a few minutes, they were heading up a dirt path on an extra-long golf cart. Delilah found herself beside Josh, with Hunter and Charlee behind them, and Pete and Fish bickering in the last seat. Mo drove while Curly made jokes and recited the quarry's history. Delilah tuned him out as she studied the scenery, trying to reconcile it with what she remembered. She didn't think she had ever been on this side of the quarry.

Josh stretched his arm along the back of the seat and leaned closer. "Beautiful, isn't it?"

His scent blended with the trees around them—woodsy and fresh—and she inhaled deeply as she looked around. Sunlight filtered through the trees, making her think of an enchanted forest. "I keep expecting to see Hansel and Gretel's cottage."

They stopped at what Curly called the "practice zip." As Delilah went through the process, she let her earlier anxiety give way to excitement. Doing things just for fun, without guilt, was something she was still learning. Her family had believed in hard work and being prepared, which left little time for anything else.

That was why she and Mary had loved the caves. Here, they could laugh and be themselves without censoring their every thought and action. She wanted Mary to have that freedom always.

After the practice zip, they climbed onto a large platform for the rest of the instructions. "Are you guys ready?" Curly asked with a grin. "Mo will always go first to meet you on the other end, and I'll bring up the rear." He checked each harness and explained the whole clipping and unclipping thing before Mo jumped off the platform and zipped across the canyon, yelling "Yahoo!" as he flew. Curly checked Charlee's gear, and she leaped off the platform behind him with a loud yell. Hunter went next, and Curly scolded him for trying to clip his own carabiner. "Let me take care of that, sir."

Hunter scowled. "I'm pretty sure I can attach my line unassisted."

Curly was unfazed. "I'm sure you can, sir, but this is our policy." He shot him a grin. "Safety first and all that. I'm sure you understand." He finished checking all the harnesses and then said, "You're good to go."

Josh and Pete held off laughing until after Hunter pushed off the platform and flew across the canyon after Charlee. Delilah was next, and as Curly deftly checked her gear, she focused on the canyon below, looking for anything remotely familiar.

Nothing did, but maybe it would when she went over.

"Show them how it's done, Delilah," Fish said.

Josh's eyes sparkled with excitement but also with concern. "You ready?"

Delilah looked at Curly, who nodded. "See you on the other side," she quipped and pushed off.

She kept her legs straight out in front of her, gloved hands ready to slow her speed, and gazed out over the quarry as she zipped along. The warm breeze blew into her face, and she felt like she was flying. It was exhilarating, and she wondered why she'd never done this before. She thought this must be what the monkeys felt like, swinging through the trees—anyway, it was as close as she was going to get to experiencing what they did. She finally remembered to scan the lower sections to see if she could find the caves, but nothing jumped out at her. Before she knew it, Mo was yelling, "Coming in hot! Slow it down, Delilah, slow it down."

It took her a beat to realize he was reminding her to use her gloves to slow her speed. She did as instructed and managed, barely, not to plow into Mo when she reached the platform. He deftly grabbed her harness and steadied her as she found her footing. Charlee and Hunter stood beaming, and each offered a high five as soon as she joined them.

"Isn't this awesome?" Charlee asked.

Delilah couldn't help beaming back. "Totally awesome."

She might have said more, but beside her, Mo started flapping his arms like a great big bird, yelling, "Coming in hot. Slow it down—slow it down."

Josh was flying high when he reached the platform. Delilah watched him with such a look of longing on her face, everything in him tightened, and he almost forgot to slow down. He would've crashed headlong into the support beams if Mo's arm flapping hadn't caught his attention at the last second. He found his footing and waited impatiently while Mo detached him from one zip line and clipped him to the next. He turned to Delilah, and before he thought it through, he grabbed her around the waist and tried to spin her around. Which would have been fine anywhere else, except that it got their harnesses all tangled up and made Mo shout.

"Whoa there, cowboy," he scolded. "Set the lady on her feet, and let's get you two untangled." Mo grabbed his radio and muttered into it, then deftly got them unclipped and reconnected to the proper lines. He picked up the radio again. "Send the next one. We're ready."

"Wasn't that incredible?" Josh asked, still beaming.

Mo grinned as he wagged a finger in his face. "Don't be doing that again."

"Sorry, man, just got caught up in the moment." He glanced at Delilah and saw an embarrassed flush race over her cheeks, but he wasn't sorry. He'd never seen her look so unguarded and happy.

"Pretty awesome, isn't it?" he asked.

"Definitely," Delilah agreed, eyes sparkling. Josh took another step closer, wanting to prolong the moment as long as possible. But just as he reached out to touch her, Pete came flying toward them, and she stepped aside to make room.

As before, Mo made flapping gestures with his arms to slow him down, but Pete completely ignored him. If not for Mo's quick grab, he might have knocked them all over like bowling pins. Mo scolded good-naturedly, and the rest of them laughed as Pete tried to regain his footing and act cool.

"Good thing you're not a girl, Pete," Charlee said. "We sure wouldn't have called you Grace." She rolled her eyes, and they all laughed.

A minute later, Fish came flying toward them. She slowed down and stepped onto the platform, dainty as you please. They all applauded, and she bowed. "And that, my friends, is how it's done."

"Beginner's luck," Pete mumbled.

"Luck had nothing to do with it. It's called following instructions," Fish shot back, wearing a cocky grin. "All I had to do was follow Charlee's and Delilah's examples."

While they waited for Curly to join them, Hunter stepped over to Pete and Josh. "You guys see anything?"

Josh shook his head and winced. He'd seen quite a bit, but none of it had anything to do with the investigation. He'd gotten completely sidetracked by Delilah and her wide smile and obvious enjoyment.

Their informant had mentioned vague rumors about some stuff possibly moving through the caves but hadn't known what. Which could mean anything from drugs to guns to animal skins to teens looking for a make-out spot. It wasn't a lot to go on.

"Nothing yet," Pete said. "But this is just the first line. We still have eight to go."

As they prepared for the next run, Josh forced his mind to the task at hand. But he couldn't stop watching Delilah, more fascinated by the minute by the way she was slowly relaxing and becoming part of the group.

He decided to live in the moment and enjoy the day.

Her secrets could wait.

Time lost all meaning. With each zip line they flew down, Delilah reveled in the feeling of flying while she scanned the nooks and crannies below, searching for signs of the caves she knew. But it all looked so different from above. For all she knew, they were going right over them. Her frustration increased, but she'd known it was a long shot. She decided her best bet was to come back at the end of the day, after the place closed and before it was full dark, to see if she could find the caves then.

In the meantime, she let herself enjoy being part of the group. They were very different personalities but obviously liked and respected each other, despite the teasing. After years of nothing more than surface interactions with classmates and colleagues, she'd been welcomed into something much deeper and infinitely more comfortable. They all seemed to like her for herself and that made her feel...free. And part of something. It was such a new sensation, she wanted to take time to sort it all out in her mind. She heard Kimberly say, "Don't overthink it, girl. Just live it."

So she did.

Too soon, they reached the last and longest of the zip lines, which stretched fifteen hundred feet across the canyon. "Okay, campers," Curly said. "This is the big one. Take a second to look around, enjoy the view, because it doesn't get any better than this." He scanned the group, and his eyes landed on the women. "I'm not saying these guys are great big lugs, but you ladies are quite a bit lighter. For this one, their weight will work to their advantage. Those who weigh less sometimes don't make it all the way to the end. If you come to a stop, immediately spin around and propel yourself hand over hand to get to the platform. Otherwise, you may start going backward, and you'll have a much longer distance to pull yourself back. Make sense?"

Charlee went first as always. She put her hands in position and glanced over her shoulder. "Okay, ladies, let's show these guys how it's done." They all cheered as she stepped off and flew through the air.

Delilah studied the canyon ahead, the rock walls and trees, the platform way off in the distance, and felt just a little bit sad. She didn't want this day to end.

When it was her turn, Josh said, "Go get 'em, Delilah." She grinned and pushed off the platform. Her speed picked up as she flew downhill, her eyes scanning the area below. The water in the canyon sparkled in the sunlight, a bright greenish color that seemed out of place with the terrain. She knew some of the kids from the high school used to dive into these lakes, but she and Mary had never had the guts to try.

As she scanned the ground below, something caught her eye. A reflection. A flash. She tried to keep her eyes on the spot, but she was moving too fast. She whipped her neck around to see if she could find it again but couldn't.

Just as Curly had predicted, she started slowing down. Seconds before she started sliding back the way she'd come, she reached up with her gloved hands to spin herself around.

But before she connected with the wire above her, she heard a crack and felt her harness give way. It separated from the zip line, and suddenly, she was falling, the water rushing up to meet her. She dimly heard shouts from the others as she plunged downward.

Time seemed to slow down and speed up at the same time, but she managed a quick lungful of air just before she hit with a huge splash. The water closed over her head, and the rays of sunlight disappeared as she sank.

Her harness was heavy and awkward and pulled her down, the water rushing by faster and faster with every passing second. She fought against it with everything she had, kicking with her legs and using her arms to push against the wall of water. She'd never been a strong swimmer, but she knew if she didn't stop her downward trajectory and find a way to get back to the surface, and fast, she'd be in serious trouble.

Her lungs screamed for air, and she fought the harness with every bit of her strength. But she didn't feel like she was making any progress. Which way was up? Her strength was almost gone, and when she stopped fighting for a split second, she sank faster. She wanted to scream but fought the urge to open her mouth. Her heart pounded. She couldn't do this much longer.

Suddenly, one thought broke free and sent a burst of adrenaline surging through her body. She was not going to drown, not today. Not when her sister needed her.

She kicked harder.

CHAPTER 13

Josh stood on the platform watching Delilah, waiting for the signal that it was his turn. He saw her scan the canyons, just as he and the others had been doing on every zip line. At the same second that she did, he saw a flash of…something…from down near the water's edge. He looked again, but it disappeared.

Pete stepped up beside him. "What are you seeing?"

"I'm not sure. A flash of something." He was about to say more when suddenly, they heard a crack, Delilah's harness broke free, and she plunged toward the water.

"No!" He launched himself off the platform while Curly shouted for him to wait.

He flew toward the place where her wheel was attached to the zip line, marking the spot. He used his gloved hands to slow himself down and stopped directly above the place where she'd fallen. He wiggled out of his harness, frustrated by the time it took, and glanced down, watching for her head to break the surface. The last thing he wanted was to land on top of her.

She still hadn't reappeared, and his heart pounded. Did she know how to swim? He flipped around and dove into the water, making sure he went in on an angle to avoid hitting her.

As he plunged down, he was grateful the sun was shining, its rays penetrating quite a depth. But not far enough to spot her. He reversed direction and burst up again. He spun in a circle and sucked in air, prepared to dive again. "Delilah! Where are you?"

She surfaced with a gasp, arms flailing as she fought against her waterlogged harness.

His arms were around her in two quick strokes. "I've got you. I've got you. Just breathe."

It took a few seconds before her wide, panicked eyes recognized him and she stopped fighting.

"You're okay, Delilah. I'm here."

She gripped his shoulders, struggling against the weight of the harness. "Heavy," she gasped, spitting out water. "Need...off."

He gripped the straps, lifting the weight off her as best he could. "I know, but we need to leave it on for a minute." They would need it to try to figure out what happened. He heard a shout and looked up to see Pete above them, preparing to jump in, too. "It's okay. I've got her. Which shore?"

Pete pointed toward the nearest shoreline, and Josh sent him a thumbs-up, then turned back toward Delilah. "Let's get out of here, okay? Hold on to me."

Delilah nodded, and together, they started swimming, his arm around her, grip tight on her harness, determined not to let her go. She tried to help, but it was tough going with the heavy gear.

A quick glance over his shoulder showed Pete heading for the other platform hand over hand.

He and Delilah were both breathing hard by the time they reached the shore. He boosted her out of the water and onto the limestone ledge before he heaved himself up beside her. Her eyes darted around, her chest heaving. He yanked her into his arms, pulling her as close as possible with her harness between them. She started shaking from the adrenaline crash, and he tightened his hold further, murmuring, "It's okay, you're safe, I've got you," over and over as he rubbed her back.

His heart pounded in time with hers, and the knowledge of how close she'd come to dying ripped through him. He gripped the back of her head and covered her mouth with his, needing to feel her breath, the reassurance she was alive. Her lips were cold and trembling, and she kissed him back with the same desperation he felt. Her citrusy scent surrounded him, and the feel of her soft lips under his made him pull her closer still. *She's alive. She's okay.*

Gradually, the edges of his panic softened, and the kiss slowed from frantic to a warm welcome. He sighed into her mouth, and his hands cupped her cheeks. She felt so right in his arms, something in his heart whispered, *Home.* The thought startled him so much that he went completely still, shocked to his toes. Where had that come from? He hardly knew her, this studious, fiercely protective woman with secrets. But he wanted to know more.

His surprise must have communicated to her, because she froze, too. He eased back and read the same desperate longing in her face, the same surprise.

She brushed one more kiss across his lips, then burrowed her face into the crook of his neck.

He wanted to kiss her again, but Charlee's warning echoed in his mind. Was he ready to go all in on another relationship? Was she? Until he sorted through his own crap where Elaine was concerned, he had no business starting something with anyone else.

When their breathing finally slowed, he eased away and looked around, cleared his throat. "With all this gear, we're about as graceful as a couple of elephant seals." The joke fell flat, but he desperately wanted to ease the awkwardness. "Are you okay?" He leaned over and brushed a soggy strand of hair off her face.

Delilah looked around, swallowed hard. "Yeah. I think so." She straightened her legs, moved her arms, rotated her shoulders. "Everything seems to be working."

He studied the water again, looked up at the zip line, then turned and inspected her harness, which appeared intact except for the connecting wire.

"There was someone out there," Delilah said, then shook her head. "Maybe that's not right. But I saw a flash of something just before I fell."

"I saw it, too. And heard it," Josh said, banking his fury. He couldn't let emotion cloud his thinking. They'd send the harness to a lab, but given Mo and Curly's care and safety consciousness, his gut said it wasn't faulty equipment. Someone had deliberately shot out the wire. Whoever it was had either been aiming for Delilah and missed, or they had deliberately shot out the wire so she would fall.

Neither scenario calmed the anger racing through his veins.

"You don't think my gear just malfunctioned, do you?" Delilah asked after a few minutes. Her breathing had returned to something approaching normal, but she was still much too pale.

"Do you?"

He watched her scan the area again before she shook her head no. "If I hadn't seen something down there just before, I might buy it. But Mo and Curly have been harping on the whole safety thing all day, so this doesn't make sense. They checked everything before every zip line. If something was fraying or coming apart, I'm pretty sure they would've noticed."

"I agree, but we'll need to ask them about it anyway."

"Was that a gunshot I heard?"

"That's my guess." Her ability to think clearly and logically despite the circumstances upped his growing admiration. But the fact that she wasn't frantically asking who would do such a thing told him she thought her family was behind it. He thought so, too, which meant he was going to find the Atwoods if he had to uproot every damn tree in the forest to do it. And if it turned out they weren't responsible, he'd keep searching until he found whoever was.

They heard tires on gravel and spotted an ATV racing toward them. Within seconds, a representative of the company ran over, face pinched, a first-aid kit in hand.

"Are you both okay?" In his forties, he wore a collared shirt, and his doughy physique said he spent more time behind a desk than he did on the course. One of the owners maybe?

The man immediately tried to help Delilah out of her harness, but Josh stopped him. "I think we're going to wait here for just a few minutes until the rest of our group can get down here and take photos."

The man's eyes widened. "Oh no, sir, this area is not open to the public. We're getting your party back to the office now. You can reunite there. Unless we need to get EMTs down here?"

"I'm Officer Josh Tanner with FWC. I need to use your cell phone."

CHAPTER 14

DELILAH STOOD OFF TO THE SIDE AND LET THE CONVERSA-tions in the office swirl around her. By the time Hunter and Pete reached her and Josh, all three men were in full-on cop mode. Gone were the friendly, fun-loving guys who'd been joking and laughing all morning. In their place were focused, questioning officers of the law. Fish had also gone straight into cop mode, but on her, it didn't sit quite as tightly. It was such a dramatic change, Delilah was having trouble figuring out which were the real people. But as she watched them interviewing staff, talking on cell phones, demanding answers, she realized they were two sides of the same coin. She couldn't let herself forget that.

Sometime later, Josh walked over. "I think we're about done here. I'll have you ride with me, and Charlee will follow us in your truck."

"That's not necessary. You guys are heading back to the quarry once you drop me off, correct? To find the cave the flash came from."

His jaw hardened. "This was no accident. We need to figure out what happened. That means police work, no civilians."

Delilah straightened, irritated by his sudden distance and frosty tone. "I understand that. But I was the one who fell in the water." She cocked her head and watched his expression. "Aren't you worried for my safety?"

He froze as though she'd slapped him and stepped close, hands clenched, his green eyes blazing fire. "I am nothing but concerned for your safety. Which is why I'm trying to figure out who tried to kill you today." When heads turned in their direction, he lowered his voice. "Work with me, Delilah. Not against me."

His words reduced more of the bricks protecting her heart to rubble. It was a good thing she was leaving soon, or she could totally fall in love with this guy. Had any man ever looked at her like he did? Like she was precious and important and deserved protection? It made her want to toss responsibility aside and curl up in his arms for a good long while. But she couldn't lose focus. Not with Mary still trapped. "Take me with you. Once you've collected evidence, I need to look around. Please." Before he could say no, she added, "Otherwise, I'll just come back on my own later."

He shook his head in disbelief, blew out a breath, and then turned back toward her. "Fine. But you stay in the truck until I tell you."

She wanted to grin in triumph but understood the fine line he was walking by taking her along. "Thank you."

One side of his mouth tilted up in a grin. "Tread lightly, Miss Atwood. I don't want to have to arrest you for interfering in an FWC investigation."

She sent back a saucy smile. "Then don't try to shut me out, Officer Tanner." She raised her chin and marched out ahead of him.

Josh shook his head at her audacity. She was accusing him of shutting her out? The woman had chutzpah, he'd give her that. He admired her tenacity, even as he cursed her stubbornness. But he also understood.

Hunter stepped up beside him. "We're heading back to the quarry. Meet us there after you drop Delilah off."

Josh didn't mention Delilah's plan, figuring the old adage about it being easier to ask forgiveness than permission applied here.

Delilah was quiet as they wound around the dirt road. As soon as he parked the truck and climbed out, both Hunter and Pete were in his face. Fish stood behind Hunter, also scowling.

"What is she doing here, Hollywood?" Hunter demanded. "You know better than that."

Josh didn't deny it. "She wants answers, too. Besides, this way, we can keep an eye on her."

Pete's jaw clenched. "I hope you told her to stay in the truck. We don't need a civilian mucking up evidence."

Irritation flared at his brother's tone. "Yes, Deputy Tanner, I am well aware of the rules of evidence."

Pete huffed out a breath. "Right. Just a little touchy. What if the shooter missed or one of us was the real target?"

Josh knew they were all thinking along the same lines. Whoever shot out Delilah's connecting wire either had great aim, or they meant to shoot her and missed. The second possibility sent a chill down his spine. He couldn't discount Pete's idea of a third possibility—one of them as the target—but it didn't ring true. His gut said Delilah was at the center of whatever was going on.

"One step at a time, Pete," Hunter said. "Let's see if we can figure out who was back here. If we're really lucky, there will be some spent shells." He looked over at Fish. "You have your camera handy?"

She held it up. "Always in my car, LT." She led the way, taking pictures of everything as they approached the limestone cave cut out of the hillside.

Josh glanced over his shoulder, relieved to see Delilah sitting in the truck. He scanned the area, his eyes following the cable far above them. From this distance, you'd need a rifle with a scope to see exactly who was riding the zip line. So if Delilah was the target, how did someone know she would be there and which one she was? In his mind, that meant the shooter had gotten inside information from Mo or Curly or some other zip line employee.

Fish stepped up beside him and lowered her camera. "Whoever took out that cable is one hell of a good shot." Since she regularly beat the pants off everyone in their squad on the firing range, he didn't argue.

"That's what I was thinking," Josh said as they followed Hunter and Pete into the mouth of the cave. Everyone had grabbed flashlights out of their trucks, SOP even if they weren't driving official vehicles, and four matching beams clicked on. They swept their lights over the limestone floor, careful to stay just inside the mouth so as not to obliterate any footprints. "Yes!" Fish shouted and carefully stepped closer with her camera. "We've got boot prints," she said.

Pete panned his light all the way around one side of the cave while Josh slid his over the other. "No brass that I can see. How about you Hollywood?"

"Nothing here either."

"I'll get a tech team out here," Hunter said. "Hopefully I can get a cell signal outside. If we're really lucky, this boot print will match the one we found near Black's body." He eyed the squad. "Bulldog, you got here first. Any sign of a vehicle having been here recently?"

"Negative. I checked as we approached. After last night's rain, any tracks would've been from today."

Fish offered to wait for the tech team while the rest of them gathered what evidence they could.

When Josh stepped into the bright sunlight, he squinted for a moment while his eyes adjusted. He walked over to his truck and started muttering when he saw the empty cab. "Stubborn, reckless woman." He turned in a circle, trying to figure out where she had gone. His eyes tracked higher, and he saw the opening to another small cave, half-obscured by a bush. Cursing under his breath, he headed in that direction.

———————

Excitement hummed under her skin as the squad disappeared into the cave. She slipped out of the truck and eased the door shut behind her, scanning the area, confirming what her heart already knew. It looked totally different than it had from above or from the opposite shoreline, but this was the place. A grin spread across her face, and she resisted the urge to shout.

After a quick glance over her shoulder, she started up the steep limestone hill, determined to slip into the cave before anyone noticed. Using her hands for balance, she scampered up in her tennis shoes, wishing she'd worn hiking boots for her still-tender ankle. She froze when she accidentally sent some rocks tumbling down the hill. No one emerged from the cave below, so she continued her ascent.

When she reached the little bush that obscured the opening, she turned on her cell phone flashlight as she ducked inside. Yes! This was definitely the cave Mary had declared their private hideout years ago.

Memories flooded her when she spotted the flat rocks they'd used as backrests. She reached behind one, pulled out the tin box of matches, and lit the oil lamp, then held it aloft until she found what she was after.

The small burlap sack was tucked in a niche in the wall. She pulled out the two journals, and as she ran her hands over hers, the fear and confusion she'd poured onto its pages so long ago washed over her. There was no writing or decoration of any kind on the plain cardboard cover, as though she'd avoided drawing attention to herself, even in a hidden journal.

Mary's was different, covered in colorful stickers Delilah had purchased at the farmers market. It reflected her personality, bright and cheerful and brimming with optimism. A huge contrast to the reality Mary was facing right now. Had her sister been here recently?

Delilah flipped to the back of the book, and a folded piece of paper slipped out. Her heart sped up as she read it, scribbled in Mary's looping handwriting.

> *I hope you find this and can find me before my birthday. Please, Delilah. Papa and Aaron are fighting all the time about some kind of alliance. It's somehow connected to my wedding, but nobody will tell me what's happening. I'm scared.*

"I thought I told you to stay in the truck," Josh growled behind her.

Delilah spun around, startled, and almost crashed into him. His arms shot out to steady her, then settled on her shoulders. She clutched Mary's journal to her pounding heart. "Why did you sneak up on me like that? You almost gave me heart failure."

Irritation crackled around him like static electricity. "Someone could have grabbed you."

A chill passed over her at the reminder. "You're right. I wasn't thinking." Then she smiled. "But this is it."

It took him barely a second. "The cave you were looking for?"

"Yes. This was our hideout, and I found Mary's journal. I can't believe it's still here."

Josh narrowed his eyes as he scanned the small cave. "Everyone in your family knows about this place?"

"Probably. I never told anyone we were coming here, but John Henry kept us on a pretty short leash. It wouldn't surprise me if he followed us."

"Did Aaron come here too?"

"At first. He and I found it together. Later, it was just Mary and me."

"Has she been here recently?"

The fear in Mary's note raised gooseflesh on her arms. "Yes." *I'll find you, Mary Lou Who. I promise.*

"Did she say where she is?"

"No." *But maybe I'll find more clues when I study the journal.* As the thought registered, her foolishness slapped her, hard. He was doing his absolute best to help, yet her first instinct was still to keep information from him. Her worry that confiding in him could make things worse for Mary was legitimate. But what if the opposite happened because she *wouldn't* trust him?

That ended now. She reached to hand him Mary's note just as someone shouted his name from below.

"We need to go." He turned toward the entrance.

Frustrated, she tucked both journals inside the burlap sack, blew out the oil lamp, and followed him back to the truck, her mind on Mary's note. What alliance? The possibilities sent another shiver over her skin.

"I'll drive you home, Xena," Josh said when he pulled up beside her truck.

She pulled her thoughts from Mary and raised a brow, smiling. "Xena? Like the warrior princess?" One of her professors had shown clips from the television series in class, and she liked the comparison.

His smile didn't hide the worry in his green eyes. "I get that you're in warrior mode, desperate to protect your sister. I admire it, and frankly, it's sexy as hell. But even warriors need someone to watch their back."

There it was again, the sizzle of attraction that made her want to touch. She gave him a slow once-over, as though assessing his fitness for the job. "You offering, Officer Tanner?"

He gave a mock shake of his head. "I have clearly lost my touch. Have you not heard a word I've said?"

"Oh, I heard." She smiled, and then honesty forced her to add, "But until now, I haven't been ready to listen." She reached for the door, glanced over her shoulder. "I can drive myself, but there are things I need to tell you. Will you follow me home?"

His grin sent a delicious shiver down her spine despite the heat of the day. "Absolutely."

She had mixed feelings as she drove. Explaining why rescuing Mary mattered meant revisiting her past and admitting what a naïve, stupid girl she'd been. Except for Kimberly and her counselor, she'd never told anybody, not even her sweet foster parents. But he wouldn't understand her concerns unless she told him the truth, every ugly bit of it.

He followed her inside and sat down at the dinette. She slid in across from him, then jumped up again. "Can I get you anything to drink? I have sweet tea or water."

"They don't let you live in the south if you don't like sweet tea, do they?"

She appreciated his effort to calm her, but her hands were still a little unsteady as she poured two glasses and set them on the table.

He leaned over and gripped her fingers. "Whatever it is, it's going to be okay. Just talk to me, all right?"

She nodded, sipped her tea. Then she sat up straight and pushed all her namby-pamby self-consciousness aside. This wasn't about her. "Before I tell you what I found in the cave, you need to know why I have to find Mary."

He sat up straighter at the word *cave* but didn't ask. "You haven't been back in a lot of years. I've wondered why you're so determined to find your sister now."

The words came out in a rush. "It's almost her sixteenth birthday, and in my family, instead of a sweet sixteen party, you get a wedding dress. I can't let that happen to her."

He didn't interrupt, but his knuckles went white around the glass, and tension radiated off him.

"Since I left, I've always come back before Christmas and around Mary's birthday to drop off a gift and card, make sure she knows I haven't forgotten her. My research project is a way to be here this summer. I wanted to reconnect with her and Mama, and I was hoping, since they finally raised the marital age to seventeen last year, that she'd be okay. Instead, I found out they are marrying her off anyway." She met his gaze, fury pounding through her. "She's just a girl. She should be worrying about prom dresses and crushes on boys. Not preparing to marry some man old enough to be her father."

"No question." He took her hands and made soothing circles on the backs with his thumbs. "How do you plan to prevent it?"

The steel underneath his casual question reassured her. So did the fact that he didn't immediately jump in with a plan but was listening to what she had to say.

"Initially, I thought I'd just show up at their campsite and offer to take her off their hands. John Henry always complained about all the mouths he had to feed. I figured it'd be easy." She rolled her eyes. "It obviously hasn't worked out that way."

Josh studied her. "Not only have lawmakers raised the age to seventeen with parental consent, the partner can't be more than two years older."

She snorted. "You do remember that my family never lets a little thing like the law get in their way, right?" She muttered a curse. "She doesn't want to get married now. She wants to go to college and choose her own husband when she's ready, way down the road."

"Which is her right, legally and morally." He paused. "Do you think what happened today is connected to Mary?"

"Unless it's connected to my research project."

"Another possibility we're looking into."

Delilah stood and pulled the journals from her backpack and handed him the note from Mary. "Maybe this has something to do with it."

She watched his expression darken as he read. "What alliance? Do you know?"

"I don't. Yet. But her fear is clear as day."

He walked over, tipped her face up. "We'll find her and stop this. Make no mistake." He paused, then asked, "Do you know who the groom is?"

Nate's face popped into her mind at the word *groom*, and she bit back her revulsion. "I'm trying to find that out."

"May I keep this?" He held up the note.

Delilah nodded and started pacing, trying to find the words to tell him the rest.

He leaned against the counter, arms crossed over his chest, jaw clenched. "Did you get a wedding dress for your sixteenth birthday, too?"

Her counselor had called it survivor's guilt. It washed over her, and she swallowed hard, bit her lip. Before she realized he'd moved, he reached out and cupped her cheeks and raised her chin, but she couldn't meet his eyes.

"Is that why you disappeared?"

"I couldn't stay. I was a coward and left Mama and Mary to deal with the fallout."

"Look at me."

She expected judgment, at the very least disappointment, but what she saw was...admiration.

"You're not a coward. You were sixteen years old. It took incredible guts to leave everything behind and start over. I'm proud of you, and I hope you'll tell me the whole story someday." He tucked her hair behind her ears, then stilled. "She's not pregnant, right?" The new law did allow some exceptions.

She shivered. "No, not as far as I know." *Please, God.*

"Good. Then Xena, my beloved warrior, you and I are going to find Mary and prevent her from being forced into an illegal marriage. You are not alone."

Relief slid through her as she absorbed that, but she still had to ask, "What about the FWC investigations?"

He sent her a cocky grin as wide and confident as his nickname implied. "If we all work together, we'll find your sister, stop the wedding, figure out what idiot painted a target on your back, *and* find out what your family is up to."

So many emotions rushed through her, Delilah couldn't sort them out fast enough to put them into words. She reached up and cupped his cheeks, then placed a kiss on his lips, hoping to convey a small piece of what was in her heart. But instead of stepping back, he gripped her hips and kissed her again, pulling her against him in one quick move. She sighed as his arms tightened around her. His tongue teased her lips, and she opened her mouth, savoring the glide of their tongues and the taste that was uniquely Josh. With her arms around his neck, she tunneled her fingers in the hair at his nape, delighted to feel his heart pounding as hard as hers. What would it be like if—

"Stop thinking," he murmured.

She smiled against his lips and did as he instructed. The world faded away as the kiss deepened, and there was nothing but the two of them, need and desire rushing through her. He cupped her backside and groaned deep in his throat. Unable to resist, she ran her hands under the hem of his T-shirt, desperate suddenly to feel all those hard muscles under her palms. He felt as good as she'd imagined, and she made a low sound of approval in her throat as he nuzzled her neck, placing quick kisses behind her ear, then biting gently and soothing the spot with his tongue. His hands slid under her T-shirt, and anticipation built as his palms slowly, deliberately inched their way higher and higher—

His cell phone rang. It took a few seconds to identify the sound, but then he eased away, apology in his eyes. "Tanner. Sure. I'll be right there." Sighing, he holstered the phone. "Report of a nuisance gator in a swimming pool. I need to go."

They studied each other for a long moment. She didn't want him to leave. His look said he felt the same. But duty called.

"You've had one heckuva day, Xena. Get some rest. And call me if anything weird happens, night or day, okay? We'll figure this out."

He leaned over and placed a gentle kiss on her forehead before he walked out the door.

Delilah sank down on the futon after he left, struck by a sense of wonder. This man was far more dangerous than she'd ever imagined. And it wasn't because of his uniform.

He made her feel things she'd never felt before, and she had no idea what to do about that.

CHAPTER 15

"You are not alone."

Josh's words played in a continuous loop in her head. Sure, she'd worked on assignments with other students, and her foster parents had made her part of their family, but she'd still felt a beat apart. When she left eight years ago, she'd sworn no one but her would determine her destiny. If she was lonely sometimes, it seemed a small price to pay for her independence. Even during the two years she'd spent with Andy, he'd been so unassuming and nonthreatening, he'd never disagreed with any of her plans. Now here was Josh, who'd barreled into her life with his kindness and underlying stubbornness and decided they were a team.

It amazed her. She grabbed her gear, figuring an hour or two watching her favorite monkey troop would help her think things through logically and sort out everything that had happened today.

She was also worried about little Oscar. She still couldn't believe she'd actually fed a feral monkey, but what choice did she have? She couldn't just let him starve.

As she followed the sounds of the troop chattering in the treetops, she berated herself. If she heard someone else say that, she'd condemn their actions without a moment's hesitation, calling them self-serving and irresponsible. Funny how everything changed when it was her and sweet little Oscar's life was at stake.

Worry quickened her steps as she found a quiet spot to observe them. There wasn't much daylight left, so she grabbed her camera and quickly scanned the troop, trying to identify the various monkeys she'd been studying. She snapped photos, looking for Oscar, and her breath came out in a *whoosh* when she spotted him above her. He looked at her intently for a long moment as though he recognized her. Then he hopped on his auntie's back, and they clambered higher into the tree.

Relief flooded her. He'd lost that gaunt look, but she enlarged the photo on her camera to be sure. Yes, thankfully, he'd been eating. But he still wasn't with his mother. This female wasn't her. Where was she?

Viewfinder in place, she scanned the troop again, snapping more pictures as she went, her niggling worry increasing as her photos confirmed what she'd seen. Or not seen. Unless she was losing her mind, always a possibility, there were three more mothers missing. Where had they gone?

She stood and walked deeper into the forest, circling around to the opposite side of the troop in case she'd missed them. She took more photos, searching for familiar faces, but they weren't there. Worry dug deeper. None of the monkeys looked sick, so she couldn't assume illness. And why was it just the new mothers who were missing?

Was someone killing them off?

Just as that hideous thought sank in, the unmistakable feeling she was being watched crept over her.

Using her camera as cover, she studied the area around her but didn't see anyone.

Still, given what had happened earlier, caution seemed wise. There wasn't enough light to get any more shots, and since she'd confirmed Oscar was okay, she returned to her truck by a roundabout route, every sense on alert. She stopped frequently to listen but heard no one behind her.

That didn't mean she wasn't being followed.

———

Later, Delilah checked the perimeter of her campsite again, making sure there was no evidence someone had been there, just as she'd been doing every night.

"You are not alone."

She still wasn't sure what to do with that or the explosive attraction growing between them. If his phone hadn't interrupted them, she had no doubt they would have ended up on her futon.

Which would have been a huge mistake. After Andy headed for Peru, she'd dated several nice enough men and slept with two of them, but those encounters left her feeling more alone than before. She wasn't a casual sex kind of person. Physical intimacy without a deeper connection and affection made her feel hollow. It wasn't worth it.

Her growing feelings for Josh would have made it amazing. In the moment, anyway. Afterward, though, everything would be even more of a tangled mess. She couldn't sleep with him without getting her heart involved. And she couldn't get her heart involved because she wasn't staying in Ocala. Not ever. Not with John Henry and Aaron still around and her past liable to pop up at every corner.

It was good they'd been interrupted. It kept things simple. Casual. Her focus had to stay on Mary. Period.

But that didn't stop all sorts of tempting scenarios involving her and Josh from slipping through her mind as she drifted off to sleep.

But then, in that weird way of dreams, her old nightmare kicked in, and Nate loomed over her. She thrashed and fought until her terrified scream woke her and she sat bolt upright in bed.

Heart pounding, covered in sweat, she headed for the tiny bathroom and splashed her face with water, annoyed that he could still rob her of sleep, so many years later.

She started a pot of coffee and peeked out the window, the cold knot in her stomach loosening as she spotted Josh's official F-150 outside. He turned on his dome light and sent her a warm smile and salute with his coffee cup. Delilah raised hers and smiled back.

Should she bring him more coffee? No. Better not. Instead, she remade the futon and reached for her camera. She clicked through the photos she'd taken earlier but found no clues as to where the missing mothers had gone. Was it possible FWC had hired someone to cull the population? Josh had said FWC hadn't made any decisions—yet—on the future of the rhesus macaques. And even if they had, she couldn't imagine a trapper targeting nursing mothers. Anger shot through her at the very idea, but she dialed it back. She had no proof.

After another fortifying sip of coffee, she set her camera aside and reached for the journals. She wasn't quite ready to read her own, so she pulled Mary's out instead.

She found the entry dated a few days after her family disappeared. Guilt clogged her throat as she absorbed Mary's confusion and sense of abandonment that her big sister hadn't tried to find her. "Oh, Mary Lou, it wasn't about you. I was just trying to survive. But I should have taken you with me. I'm so sorry."

She flipped to an entry a year later. Mary's sadness had turned to anger now, at Delilah's disappearance, Mama's never-ending kowtowing to Papa's demands, Aaron's increasing harshness. Mary had lived it all, just like Delilah. But what shredded her heart was that Mary's bright light seemed to have been snuffed out. There was no joy in her entries, no mention of friends, no hint of the fun-loving, smiling, always humming little sister she'd known. Anger at her family and guilt for abandoning Mary hit like a cat-o'-nine-tails, tearing strips off the scars she'd tried so hard to heal.

But Delilah kept reading, accepting the condemnation on the pages, knowing she deserved every word.

Somewhere along the way, she fell asleep.

———

He turned and walked out of the meeting before the frustration boiling inside him spilled over. He didn't have time for their wishy-washy, wait-and-see nonsense. Didn't any of them understand that things had to change? The country needed him. More importantly, they needed him to be their leader. Someone strong. Decisive. Ready to take action. The time for casual alliances and loose associations was long past. It wasn't enough anymore to simply arm those of like mind. They had to do more. The time was right to put their own militia into place, one that was equipped and ready to stand and fight against the government oppressors.

But the established old guard didn't want to see it. Didn't want to listen. They spoke of caution, of more planning, of waiting for the right moment.

The right moment had already been set. He'd set it. In just over a week, everything would be in place, and he'd step up as their leader and take them to the next level. He was the only one strong enough and brave enough to guide them into liberty.

He thought of Black's death and shook his head. The last thing they needed right now was FWC and their idiotic band of fish cops snooping around. That body should never have been found. Hell, the idiot shouldn't have been out there to begin with, poking his nose where it didn't belong.

He sighed. As always, it was up to him to clean up other people's messes. None of them had any idea what he did for them, the spineless cowards. Only he knew the risks he took and lengths he went to, all in order to keep their world secure. He never got the recognition he deserved. But just wait. By next week, all that would change.

There were just a few loose ends to tie up between now and then. He still couldn't believe Delilah had the nerve to come back to town, flaunting her worldly looks and whoring ways. Did she think nobody saw through her flimsy disguise? He'd known her the moment he'd laid eyes on her. How could he not? She was a part of him.

She, too, would have to be dealt with. Nobody and nothing was going to get in his way. Not this time. Nobody. Especially not a so-called monkey researcher.

He lifted his rifle and sighted through the scope. He held the weapon steady, pulled in a breath, then slowly eased off the trigger.

The rabbit exploded in a satisfying burst of blood and fur. He nodded as he set down the weapon. That was what happened to those who tried to get in his way.

Delilah would live to regret the day she came back to town.

He turned and disappeared into the forest. The countdown was on.

———————————

Delilah woke sometime later, coughing. She opened her eyes, but everything seemed blurry. She rubbed them, trying to clear the haze, but it didn't make a difference. Groggy and trying to get her bearings, she heard a crackling noise. What in the world?

She coughed again, and that was when the acrid smell registered. Her head cleared in an instant, and she sat up. Her camper was filled with smoke. A quick peek out the window and she saw flames. Dear God, the area outside her camper was on fire!

Her feet hit the scorching hot floor, and she instantly hopped back onto the futon before she burned the soles of her feet. She slid her feet into flip-flops. She had to get out of here.

She stumbled to the door and reached for the latch, but her brain kicked in just before she grabbed the hot metal. "Right, towel, something. Think, girl."

Crouched low as she'd been taught somewhere along the way, she grabbed a pot holder from the kitchen counter and used it to cover the latch. Though she'd pulled the collar of her T-shirt over her nose and mouth to keep the smoke out of her lungs, she couldn't stop coughing. She pushed against the latch, but it wouldn't budge. She used her shoulder, wincing as the heat from the metal door singed her skin, but she ignored it.

Again and again and again, she slammed her shoulder against the door, but it wouldn't budge.

Frantic, desperate, she turned back into the smoke-filled room and searched for another escape route. The window beside the door showed only flames, and she knew the tiny window in the bathroom wasn't big enough for her to climb through. That left only the window above the futon. She rushed to it and peered out, horrified by the wall of flames beyond.

She knew there were only seconds to make a decision. She spun around, ducked down, and squinted through the smoke, determined to find the journals. They might be the only clues to finding her sister. She spotted her phone, scooped that up, too, and stumbled back onto the futon.

She was fighting with the screen when there was a loud crack. The ceiling above her split open as a flaming branch crashed through the roof and landed inside the camper. By some miracle, it hadn't crushed her. But it had bent the camper enough that the screen popped out. She clawed her way around branches and smoke and debris in a desperate fight to escape.

Once she wiggled her way through the rectangular opening, she landed on the ground with a thump. She could feel the burning embers through her clothes as she struggled to her feet. She had to get away, but if she ran fast, they would burst into flame. She took three stumbling steps away from the camper before she dropped onto a sandy patch not far from her truck and rolled back and forth.

She lay there a moment, trying to catch her breath, coughing. Flames danced into the sky from the trees closest to her camper. *Oh God, the trees.* The whole forest could catch fire. She looked down and saw the burlap bag with the journals still clutched in her fist. Thank God.

She sat up and coughed some more, then pulled her shirt back over her nose and mouth. Where was her phone? Had she lost it somewhere? Relief flooded her when she spotted it on the ground not far away.

Her legs weren't too steady as she hobbled over to it. The camper was now completely engulfed, and her heart slammed into overdrive. The propane tank would blow any second. There was no time to drive away—she didn't have her truck keys anyway—so she clutched the journals and phone to her chest and ran as fast as determination and her shaky legs could carry her.

She'd barely cleared the area when the camper exploded. The blast knocked her off her feet, and she landed facedown on the sandy, pine-needle-covered forest floor. As she tried to get her bearings and draw breath, she looked over her shoulder. The inferno had gotten even bigger. She had to call for help. The fire department.

Getting up on all fours took much too long. She fumbled for her phone and cursed when she saw the "no signal" message. Seconds passed while her fuzzy brain tried to figure out what to do next. Josh. She could text him. She had his number programmed.

Wait. He was here.

She spun around to where his truck had been, but it was gone. For a moment, she froze in absolute terror. Had it exploded, too?

She looked closer, and the breath whooshed out of her lungs. No. The place he'd parked was empty. No debris. He'd left.

The adrenaline coursing through her veins made it impossible to type, so she dictated instead: Camper exploded. Forest on fire. Send help. Fast.

Her whole body had started shaking from shock, and she watched in horror as the flames jumped from tree to tree and the pine needles below caught fire. The only saving grace at this point was that it had rained quite a bit recently, so the ground wasn't completely dry.

Even so, the heat from the flames threatened to scorch her skin. Delilah moved back into the trees, desperate to stay clear of the flames but not so far she'd run the risk of getting lost. The thought of being trapped behind the fire scared her more than she wanted to admit. But she couldn't abandon her little home, either, so she sat on a log and watched it burn.

Time dragged by as she coughed and kept an eye on the dancing flames, but finally, finally, the sound of sirens pierced the forest. "Oh, thank you, God," she whispered.

Headlights appeared and blinded her. She raised one hand to block the light as someone called her name. "Delilah! Where are you? Delilah!"

She tried to answer, but all that came out was a croak. She coughed some more and suddenly found herself wrapped in Josh's strong arms. "Are you okay?"

"Yes, I'm okay." She burrowed against his chest and tucked her face in the crook of his neck, holding tight to combat the shakes that wouldn't stop.

He eased her back slightly and cupped her cheeks in his hands, studying her. "EMTs are on their way. We'll get you taken care of. No one else in the camper, right?"

"Just me." He pulled her close again, and it took a minute to gather her scattered thoughts. She leaned back and clenched his shirt in her fist, her throat like raw sandpaper. "I couldn't get out. The door wouldn't open. I thought I was going to die in there."

Josh's eyes widened before they narrowed to angry slits. "Are you saying someone locked you in?"

Delilah gripped him tighter as another shiver raced over her. "I don't know. I just know I couldn't get out."

He studied her for a moment as the reality of what might have happened snapped in the air between them. She wasn't sure who moved first, but suddenly, she had her arms around his neck, his were around her waist, and their mouths were fused in a desperate kiss she felt all the way to her toes. As his tongue plundered her mouth, she tasted his relief that she was alive but also the fury he was keeping tightly leashed. She soothed him with kisses, running her hands through the hair at his nape, their hearts pounding in unison. She was alive, and he was holding her, and right now, that was all that mattered.

The moment the fire trucks arrived, the firefighters dove into action, desperate to keep the fire from spreading.

"I'm so glad you're okay," Josh said, his hands trembling slightly as they rubbed her back.

"I'm fine," she said.

He looked over her shoulder at the flames raging behind them, and his expression hardened into one she'd never seen before. "I need to check on some things. EMTs are heading over to check you out. Will you be okay here for a bit?"

She nodded, a cough preventing her from saying more.

He strode away without a word.

CHAPTER 16

"I DON'T NEED TO GO TO THE HOSPITAL. PLEASE. I'M FINE."

The EMT ignored her and fitted an oxygen mask over her face. Josh wasn't sure if it was because she needed it or it was an efficient way to stop her protests. Probably both.

"What the hell happened here, Hollywood?" Hunter said from behind him.

Josh turned. Hunter had obviously just crawled out of bed, too, but he looked a lot more pulled together than Josh, who'd barely thrown on a T-shirt, shorts, and flip-flops before he raced out the door. Hunter had taken time to don his uniform and wore the air of command like a second skin. He motioned Josh off to the side so they wouldn't be overheard.

Pete hurried over, wearing the same unmade-bed look as Josh. "Is Delilah all right?"

They glanced over to where the EMTs were checking her vitals.

Josh voiced what they were all thinking. "After the zip line, this was no accident. Plus, I'd been outside her camper earlier and got pulled away on a bogus call no more than an hour ago."

Hunter muttered a curse, and Pete scrubbed the back of his neck.

"Let me talk to the fire chief," Hunter said. Thankfully, the flames had been contained. The recent rain had definitely prevented a huge forest fire. The fact that Delilah's camper stood in a fairly large clearing had also helped.

Josh's mind raced in multiple directions, but he kept circling back to the one question he didn't have an answer to. Why Delilah? Was it because of Robert Black's murder? Her research? Or did it have to do with her sister and, by extension, her family? Because even though someone had taken shots at her before, they'd deliberately missed. Locking her inside a burning camper took things to a whole new level.

"You okay, Brother?" Pete asked.

"Why wouldn't I be? I'm not the one who barely escaped a fire."

Pete just looked at him. "You can keep bluffing, but I'm not buying a word of your crap." He planted his hands on his fists. "I've seen the way you look at her." When Josh started to protest, he held up a hand. "I know. You don't want to talk about it. Just be careful. From what I can see, that pretty lady is a lightning rod for trouble."

Josh's hackles went up, but he didn't respond. He had more important things to do, like figure out how to keep Delilah safe while he hunted down the scumbag who was after her.

Hunter returned, expression grim. "There's evidence of a generator malfunction that caused the fire."

"From inside or outside the camper?" Josh asked.

"That was my question, too. From the outside."

"So someone could have tampered with it." Josh narrowed his eyes. "Any sign that the door was blocked in some way to keep her from getting out?"

"She couldn't get out?" Pete's eyebrows shot toward his hairline.

Josh glanced from one to the other. "That's what she said. When the door wouldn't open, she climbed out the window. And just in time, too."

Josh scanned the area and saw Sanchez and Fish pull up in their separate vehicles. Both hurried over.

"Is Delilah okay?" Fish asked.

"EMTs are checking her over now."

Sanchez scanned what was left of her camper and let out a slow whistle. "Damn, she's lucky to be alive."

As Josh scanned their faces, he couldn't shake the certainty that if he didn't do something desperate, and fast, Delilah wouldn't survive. And that, he didn't think he could survive.

Someone had painted a big target on her back, and until they figured out who, she had to stay hidden. "I say we put the word out that she died in the fire. That will buy us some time to figure out what the hell is going on."

Surprised looks flashed across their faces, but Hunter's turned speculative. "Tell me what you're thinking, Hollywood. How would it help? You think this is tied to Black's murder? Or her family?"

He'd told Hunter and the squad about the guns and money, and Byte was digging into the Atwood family's background. "I don't know, but we sure as hell need to find out. Until now, all the shots have felt like warnings, someone's attempt to keep her away."

"Agreed. But away from what? Her research?" Pete asked.

Josh filled them in on Mary's situation but didn't mention Delilah's past. That wasn't his story to tell. "She's trying to find her sister and stop the wedding. My guess is someone in her family— either her father or her brother—have been trying to scare her off."

"Whoever it is, they're an excellent shot," Fish said.

"Tonight was different, though," Hunter said. "This was an out-right attempt on her life."

Sanchez chimed in. "Byte also found that evidence on Black's computer about ties to some kind of militia here in the forest. We know her family has always been tied to them as well. Is she somehow the link between the two? The militia and Black's murder?"

"She found her sister's journals in the caves today. Mary mentioned something about an alliance but gave no details."

There was a round of collective muttering and cursing before Hunter drilled Josh with a look. "Since you've got this all figured out, Hollywood, what's your plan?"

Josh scrambled for a reply. He had been so focused on protecting Delilah, he hadn't thought through logistical details. But then it came to him. "We borrow my folks' camper, since they're not going anywhere just yet, and I park it in the forest and go undercover as a guy looking to join a local militia. I'll wear a disguise, see where that leads."

"And where exactly will Miss Paige be during this time?"

Josh's chin came up, and he met Hunter's gaze. "She'll be with me."

The chorus of protests was instantaneous, with Hunter's the loudest. "Have you lost your mind? We can't send a civilian undercover. I won't. That's reckless."

"From what I can tell, only Delilah's family knows she's back in town. She's using a different name, and no one has seen her for eight years. And even when she was here before, the family moved around and kept to themselves. She was homeschooled. For her to wear a wig and a pair of glasses would not be a big deal. But it would allow me to keep her safe." When Hunter opened his mouth to say something, Josh cut him off. "I can do this on the payroll or off. But I'm doing it."

"FWC doesn't do protection details, Hollywood," Hunter reminded him. "I'll see if she can stay with Charlee."

"She stays with me," Josh said again.

The two men faced off. Even though Hunter was going to be his brother-in-law, he was also his boss. And Josh had just directly countermanded Hunter's decision. "You are treading on thin ice, Hollywood."

"Yes, sir. I have time off saved up. I'll take a leave of absence, vacation, sick time, whatever you want to call it."

Hunter studied him, eyes narrowed. "Are you sure about this?"

Josh nodded. He couldn't explain it to himself, let alone anyone else. He just knew he had to do it.

The silence stretched. Finally, Hunter said, "I can't tell you what to do on your vacation, Officer Tanner. But I do expect an update twice a day. If I don't get it, I'll call in the cavalry." He waited a beat. "We clear?"

"Yes, sir." Josh released the breath he hadn't realized he'd been holding. He considered the fact that Hunter hadn't fired him out-right a plus. "Thank you."

"I hope this doesn't come back and bite you in the ass. But either way, we've got your back." Hunter eyed his squad. "The quicker we get this plan into action, the better the chances of keeping a lid on the truth. Hollywood, get Delilah and the EMTs on board. I'll talk to the fire captain. Pete, keep things at the sheriff's office need-to-know, and, Sanchez and Fish, you guys have a word with every single person here. If the press shows up, tell them I'll make a statement later this morning. Make sure everyone knows not to talk to a reporter."

Josh stepped up beside Hunter. "Thank you."

"Don't make me regret it. Let's figure out who wants her dead."

CHAPTER 17

JOSH HURRIED OVER TO THE EMTs, WHO WERE STILL TRYING to keep Delilah from climbing off the stretcher. "Give us a second here, guys."

They exchanged a look and stepped away.

He placed a hand on her arm, his voice low. "Stop fighting and listen for a minute. Someone almost killed you tonight, and you're too smart not to realize it. We're going to pretend you died. That will buy the squad time to figure out who's after you."

"I'll be fine. I've got this. I don't need FWC getting any more involved."

Josh laughed. "Like it or not, FWC is already involved. When I said I'd help you, I meant it. You get the whole squad, too, no extra charge." He grinned but then caught the look in her eyes. Now that the shock had worn off, she was furious. So was he, but he wasn't letting her storm off to figure out who set the fire. Not without him.

When she opened her mouth to argue again, he leaned over and whispered, "Close your eyes and play along. I'll explain more later." He leaned back and shouted, "Delilah! Delilah! Wake up!" He patted her face as the EMTs rushed over.

"What happened? She was fine a few minutes ago."

"She stopped breathing." Then he leaned closer so only they could hear. "For her safety, we need to pretend she didn't make it. Will you help?"

The EMTs exchanged a look and then nodded. "10-4."

The older one raised his voice. "Start CPR. Let's get her in the bus and over to Ocala Regional."

When the EMT climbed onto the gurney and pretended to

start CPR, Josh tossed his keys to Pete and climbed into the back of the ambulance with them. The other EMT started the bus and took off, lights flashing and sirens blaring.

Delilah blinked her eyes open and squinted against the sunlight streaming through old-fashioned curtains. She dimly remembered Josh carrying her into a house last night, right before the adrenaline crash knocked her flat. Her glance took in the quilt on the bed, the wicker chair, antique furniture.

The sound of voices from another room, mostly male, brought her to her feet. Every muscle ached, and as soon as she stood up, she started coughing again, her throat like sandpaper. She glanced down at the oversize T-shirt she was wearing, and a little zing slid over her skin. Josh must have put it on her. She buried her nose in the sleeve. It smelled like him, clean and woodsy.

Another T-shirt and basketball shorts were neatly stacked on the chair along with a note in a masculine scrawl. "Help yourself to these until we get you something that fits. Bathroom is down the hall."

Delilah smiled despite the circumstances, grabbed the clothing, and padded to the bathroom where she stood under the spray until the water turned cool and she felt a bit less stiff and creaky. When she reached the kitchen, she found Fish at the counter, pouring coffee.

"Good morning. Did you get some sleep?"

Delilah gratefully accepted the cup Fish offered, added milk and sugar. "I did, thanks. And thanks for the coffee."

Josh stepped into the kitchen, and his eyes immediately sought hers, grinning as he looked her over. "Glad you found the clothes, even though they are a tad big."

She looked down. The T-shirt fell almost to her knees, and if not for the drawstring inside the basketball shorts, she would've had to hold them up with one hand. "Barely noticeable," she drawled and enjoyed his laugh.

"The squad was here this morning for a strategy meeting. I didn't have the heart to wake you."

She stiffened. "You didn't think I'd want to be there, tired or not?"

His smile faded, and he scrubbed a hand over the back of his neck. Fish took her coffee and beat a hasty retreat. "Yeah, when you put it like that, I should have woken you. I figured you needed sleep."

The whole idea of someone doing things "for her own good" raised her hackles, but he was so genuine, she couldn't be too angry. Still, ground rules needed to be set. "Don't make decisions for me. Last night, you and the team didn't give me a choice, just put a plan in motion and said you'd explain later."

"It's a good plan."

"I'm not arguing that. But I'm part of the discussion. I won't be ordered around."

He huffed out a laugh. "I wouldn't be fool enough to try."

Her temper eased somewhat.

"I get that you're used to being alone." He stepped closer, took her hands in his. "But you aren't anymore. I'll be here. The whole squad will be, too. We're trying to help."

"Then treat me as an equal, and remember that I make my own decisions."

"Yes, ma'am." He sent her a grin and a wink, then reached behind him and thrust a newspaper at her. "Check out today's editorial, Madam Researcher. Looks like Commissioner Benson has quite a bit to say about your study of the monkeys."

"Do tell. Based on some of his earlier comments, I can't imagine any sort of wholehearted support coming from his camp." Delilah started reading the commissioner's tirade and then looked up. "I just remembered my laptop. I didn't think to take it with me last night."

"You mean that wasn't your first thought during a fire? Slacker." He nodded to a laptop on the counter. "Feel free to use mine. Password is next to it."

"Thank you. The café has free Wi-Fi, so I back everything up to the cloud. I'll have to replace my laptop, camera, and all my gear, but I only lost the last batch of monkey photos." She'd have to raid her meager savings, but it should cover all of it. She thought of Oscar. "Speaking of monkeys, has FWC hired anyone to cull them out?"

Surprise crossed his features. "No, why? No decisions have been made. I told you that."

"Call me crazy, but I think some of the mothers in one of the troops I've been studying are missing."

His eyebrows shot up. "What do you mean, missing?"

"As in, not there, with aunties taking care of their young."

"Did you just overlook them, maybe? Or they were off on a girl's day out?" He smiled, but his eyes were serious.

"I don't know. But it has me worried."

"Were the infants healthy? Eating enough?"

She thought of Oscar and ducked her head, embarrassed. "One of them had me worried, but he seems to be okay now."

"Then I wouldn't worry too much. You know they sometimes let the aunties take over for a while."

He was right. She was making mountains out of molehills, as Mama would say. Still. "I got the feeling I was being watched the last few times I was out."

He straightened from where he'd been leaning on the counter. "Did you see anyone?"

"No. It might have been an animal, too."

His eyes narrowed. "Don't go out alone until we figure out what's going on."

She raised a brow. Hadn't they just had this conversation? "Really? And are you going into the forest with me?"

He grinned, totally surprising her. "Absolutely. Since I'm

officially on 'vacation'"—he made air quotes—"maybe you can convince me the monkeys should stay."

"And you can keep an eye on me."

"Two birds, one stone."

She couldn't stay annoyed with him, especially when he turned on the charm. "Is this your place? Where are we exactly?"

"This little cottage sits on the edge of the Outpost property. What, you don't like my granny-inspired décor?"

"I sort of expected to see Aunt Bea from *The Andy Griffith Show* bustling about the kitchen."

"Just me, but I make a mean omelet. You game?"

"You cook? Wow. Sure." While he prepared breakfast, she sipped coffee and scanned the article, not really surprised at the ugliness spewing from Commissioner Benson's editorial. Though to be fair, it wasn't so much venom as opposition. She could handle that. "I don't think Benson had anything to do with the fire."

Josh looked up, frying pan suspended over their plates. "I agree. He's against the monkeys, but I don't see him trying to kill you over it."

Delilah shivered at the reminder and focused on the excellent food instead. "Thanks for breakfast, but now I want to know what you and the squad talked about this morning, and don't leave anything out."

"I guess that means the social portion of the day is over," he quipped, then sobered. "News of a suspected death from smoke inhalation will be posted on the newspaper website later today and will be headline news in tomorrow's edition. We'll carefully leak your name so even though it isn't officially reported, people will believe you're dead. That should buy us some time to figure out who's after you." He leaned forward, arms on the table, and pierced her with a look. "I did an online search, and there is no record of Delilah Paige Atwood ever getting married. I assumed you'd gone through with the wedding. Was I wrong?"

Delilah gripped her coffee cup, taken by surprise. "No, I didn't go through with it." She paused. "After my family moved again, without me, I left."

"Can't say I blame you. Who were you supposed to marry?"

His matter-of-fact response soothed more of the jagged edges of her heart, acknowledging that her actions had been perfectly logical.

"I need a name, Delilah."

Her head snapped up. His expression indicated he was prepared to sit there all day.

The clock on the wall ticked loudly. She did not want him to know the mention of Nate's name still made her want to throw up, but that was her problem. She swallowed hard. "His name was Nate, but I think he's left the area. Nothing came up in my online searches or local gossip."

Josh went outside and came back with his FWC laptop. He clicked several keys and said, "Last name?"

"Hamm."

"Middle name?"

"No idea."

He tapped a few more keys. "I see a birth certificate for a Nathan Ezekiel Hamm, born in North Carolina. No death certificate. Nate was a survivalist type, like your family?"

Delilah nodded and forced a neutral expression.

"We'll track down his last known address. Do you know who Mary's supposed to marry?"

"Not yet, but Kimberly is trying to find out. Did my truck survive the fire?"

"It did, but you obviously can't go cruising around town in it. Give me a few minutes to clean up, and we'll start putting the pieces in place. That's the backstory we came up with." He nodded toward a sheaf of papers on the counter.

"What's the plan? And if you say I'm supposed to hide out here, we're going to have a serious problem. This is my sister. I'm not sitting on the sidelines."

He let out a long sigh. "Oh man. Now we'll have to come up with a new plan."

As she tossed her crumpled napkin at him, she noticed the twinkle in his eyes.

"My parents have offered the use of their camper, since Mom's not well enough to travel yet, and we're going to set it up in the forest. You and I will pose as a married couple looking to get involved with a local militia. We'll try to find Mary and also try to figure out who's after you. And hopefully, we'll find out who killed Robert Black and whether the guns and money you saw are part of this, too."

"You think a local militia is involved?" Was that the alliance Mary mentioned?

"We're not sure, but it looks like Black had ties to a local group. We'll tug on those connections and see what pulls loose." He pulled her to her feet and wrapped his arms around her waist. "We'll figure it out." He tucked a strand of hair behind her ear.

Delilah leaned into his touch. She still felt disoriented and slightly groggy from last night, with the worst sore throat she'd had in her life, so it took a minute before the rest of his words sank in. They'd be living together, in a small camper.

Could she keep him at arm's length to protect her heart?

Maybe the bigger question was whether she wanted to.

While Delilah changed into some clothes Fish and Charlee had brought over, Josh fought to corral his wayward thoughts, but all he could think about was how much he liked the feel of her in his arms. And the fact that they'd be living together.

Pete and Hunter and even Charlee had warned him to keep his distance, but it was too late. Though he'd been prepared, even eager to spend his life with Elaine, he'd never felt this primal, bone-deep need to protect like he did with Delilah. And it wasn't as though she wanted protecting. He snorted. Dang woman got all huffy about him getting in her way. His determined Xena warrior with the sad eyes had burrowed under all his defenses and stripped him bare. She made him want to take her to bed and love her forever. His body tightened at the thought of finally running his hands over every inch of her soft skin, while his heart shoved thoughts of the L word firmly away. He didn't have time for all this touchy-feely nonsense. Or to think about her hot body. If he wanted to explore what was between them, he had to keep her alive long enough to do it.

CHAPTER 18

DELILAH STUDIED HER REFLECTION IN THE BEDROOM MIRROR. The clothing that Fish had brought was disorienting. The shapeless Laura Ashley–style dress looked just like the ones Mama used to make for her and Mary. The soft cotton slid over the raw places on her skin and felt as confining as it had when she was a child. She'd never belonged in that world. She was going back, but Josh would be right beside her this time.

She smoothed the front of the dress and straightened her shoulders. She used a piece of pantyhose to secure her hair, then pulled a blond wig over it. After she added the clear horn-rimmed spectacles, even she didn't recognize herself.

When she walked into the kitchen, Josh's jaw dropped and made her laugh. "Kind of a cross between Annie Oakley and the Waltons, right?"

He blinked several times, and the dimple popped out on his cheek when he grinned. "Wow. I can't believe how different you look. Nobody is going to recognize you."

"That's the idea." Nobody had recognized her until now, either. But that wasn't her biggest concern. When he turned toward the door, she gripped his arm, tight. "I know you said you'd try to keep Mary out of any official fallout, but I need something more. I want your word, right now, that no matter what happens to me or how this all ends, you will stop the wedding and make sure Mary is safe."

He cocked his head. "I told you I'd do whatever I can—"

"Promise me you'll save Mary. No hedging, no 'I'll try.' I want your word." She knew if he gave it, he'd never renege on it. She had to know Mary would be safe, no matter what.

He finally nodded once. "You have it. But I plan to help you stay alive so you can protect her yourself."

Delilah released the breath she'd been holding. "Thank you." She stepped back and cleared her throat. "Where to first?"

"There's basketball practice at the community center, and I don't want to let the boys down. I hope you don't mind hanging around for a little while. After that, we'll grab the camper and get it set up."

A little shiver of anticipation slid through her belly, but she focused on the first part of his statement. "Great. That way I can touch base with Kimberly, see if she has any news." An unfamiliar pickup truck sat in the driveway. "Whose is this?" Delilah asked as they walked out of the cottage.

"My dad's. It's a diesel, dually, one he bought to pull the camper. He's letting us borrow both." He patted the back fender as they walked by. "She's a beaut, and she'll help with my disguise, too."

"What is it with men and their trucks?" Delilah teased. He handed her into the cab, and she let out a sigh as her sore body settled into the buttery yellow leather seats. "Never mind. This is an amazing truck. I may just live in here."

"The camper's pretty nice, too. Just saying." He winked at her before he pulled dark sunglasses over his eyes and backed out of the driveway.

Once they reached the community center, she checked that her wig was securely in place before she entered the clinic next door.

"May I help you?" The young girl behind the receptionist desk didn't look more than twelve, but she had to be in high school at least.

"Hi. I'm here to see Kimberly Gaines." Delilah flashed the girl a smile. "I'm a friend of hers." She headed down the hall.

"Wait. You can't just go back there," the girl said, rushing after her.

Delilah ignored her and stepped into Kimberly's office. Her

friend was at her desk, the newspaper's website open on her computer screen. The headline screamed MONKEY RESEARCHER PRESUMED DEAD IN FIERY BLAZE.

"Kimberly. It's me. I'm okay." She said the words quietly, only now realizing they'd come as a shock. She should have thought this through.

Kimberly swung her chair around, tears streaming down her cheeks. She swiped her cheeks, then stood. "I'm sorry. What did you say?"

Delilah closed the door behind her just as the receptionist reached them. "It's me. I'm okay."

Kimberly just looked at her.

Delilah pulled off the glasses and took a step closer. "It's Delilah. I'm okay."

Kimberly blinked rapidly, then cupped Delilah's cheeks and studied her for a long moment. "Oh sweet Jesus, I thought you were dead." More tears spilled out of her eyes as she grabbed Delilah and hugged her tight.

Delilah felt her throat close as they embraced. *Why hadn't she called?* She pulled back and wiped the tears from Kimberly's cheeks. "I'm so sorry."

A knock sounded on the door, then the receptionist's voice. "Ms. Gaines? Are you okay? Do I need to get help?"

Kimberly went to the door and opened it a crack. "Thank you, Cindy. I'm fine."

"You don't look fine. You're crying."

"True, but these are happy tears. I didn't think I was going to see my friend again for a very long time. This is a wonderful surprise."

Cindy's young voice sounded hesitant. "Okay. If you're sure…"

"I am. Thank you. If anyone's looking for me, I'll be there in a few minutes." She shut the door firmly and turned back to Delilah. "Tell me exactly what happened."

They sat on the worn love seat while Delilah recounted the fire and Josh's plan. Kimberly studied the wig. "It's a good plan. You need to figure out what's going on. And most importantly, you need to stay safe."

Delilah rolled her eyes. "Now you sound like Josh. What I need is to find Mary."

Kimberly gripped her hand and gave it a shake. "I know you're trying to make light of it, but someone tried to kill you. And I—" Her breath hitched. "Today was bad enough. Do whatever you have to do to stay safe."

Thoroughly chastened, Delilah simply nodded. Kimberly's concern, coupled with Josh's, started a warmth deep inside.

Kimberly leaned closer. "I overheard a couple people talking yesterday. They didn't think I could hear them, but they were whispering about a meeting."

"What kind of meeting? Did they say where?"

"I heard the word 'militia' a few times, and that of course made my radar twitch. I also heard something about Stevens Point."

"Did you catch when this meeting was supposed to be?"

"No, unfortunately. They realized I was listening and clammed up."

Delilah jumped to her feet. "I need to let Josh know about this."

"No luck finding Mary yet?"

Delilah shook her head. "I found her journals, and she says she's scared, but I can't find their campsite. We have less than a week. Anything on your end?"

Kimberly smiled. "Your mother has an appointment with me the day after tomorrow." She checked the calendar. "About three o'clock."

Delilah's eyebrows rose. "On a Sunday?"

"She said she'd go for an afternoon walk and swing by. I said I'd be here, catching up on paperwork."

"Then they can't be too far away." Delilah reached over and hugged her. "Thank you. I'll be here." Delilah put her glasses back on and said, "Keep your ear to the ground, okay? If you hear any-thing about me or Josh or any of the rest of it, especially Mary, you'll let me know, right?"

"Of course. Do you still have a cell phone?"

"Yes, for whatever reason, I remembered to take it with me last night."

Kimberly smiled. "That's my girl." Then she pulled her close for another bone-crushing hug.

As Delilah left the building, she was filled with more optimism and confidence than she had had since this all began. She truly wasn't alone. They'd find Mary. And she would make sure she—and Josh—stayed safe in the process.

―――――――――

"Hey, copper, how you doing?" Donny Thomas said, bouncing a basketball.

Josh walked onto the court, easily maneuvering the basketball away from the twelve-year-old. He shot it toward the basket and grinned when it swished through the net.

"That would be Mr. Copper," he corrected. "How are you, Mr. Thomas?" he asked as he ruffled the boy's hair. "Or you could just call me Michael Jordan." His grin was cheeky and earned him an eye roll. The boys needed to know the boundaries, to learn respect, but they also needed encouragement and fun. Josh tried to give them a little of all of it.

"Yeah, you wish, old man," Donny said as he grabbed the ball and shot for the basket. It bounced off the rim, and Donny went after it.

The door at the far end of the building opened as a herd of boys came in, laughing, talking, dribbling basketballs, with Hunter and Sanchez behind them. They were wearing T-shirts and basketball shorts, and with one quick blast of the whistle around his neck, Josh got everyone gathered around and started on drills.

As the boys ran up and down the court, Hunter and Sanchez stepped closer. "Where's Delilah?" Hunter asked.

"Next door at the clinic. Kimberly Gaines has been a friend of hers for years. She wanted to let her know she wasn't dead."

Both men frowned. "Not a good idea, man," Sanchez said.

"Agreed," Hunter said. "The fewer people who know the truth, the better."

"The woman's been like a mother to her. And she may be able to help track down Delilah's sister."

As the boys came galloping toward them, their focus turned to drills and good-natured teasing. By the time practice ended, there were a lot of sweaty boys and equally sweaty men running up and down the court.

When the boys came out of the locker room, most of them smelling like they hadn't actually showered, Josh saw Billy, one of the newer boys, sitting on the floor, lacing up a pair of expensive hiking boots. He stood and started walking away, the too-large boots thumping on the all-purpose floor.

Josh caught up to him. "Hey, Billy, nice job out there today."

The boy glanced up and smiled shyly. "Thanks, Mr. Josh. I'm getting better."

"You're making great progress, kiddo. Glad to have you on the team." He paused, searching for the right words. He didn't want to injure the boy's pride. "New boots?"

Billy just shrugged and wouldn't meet his eyes as he walked outside. They had had another rain shower, and Billy squished through the mud toward a rusty bicycle that leaned up against the fence. Josh glanced at the boot prints, and something niggled at the back of his mind. He realized what it was, but by the time he looked up, Billy had climbed on the bicycle and was pedaling away.

Josh pulled out his cell phone and took several pictures. Then he went back into the building and showed them to Hunter and Sanchez. The three men exchanged glances.

"Send them to Byte and have him compare those to the boot prints we found at Black's death scene." As the squad's resident tech and computer genius, Byte could find even the smallest similarities and clues. But in this case, Josh would bet a month's salary that the two prints matched.

"So how would a poor kid from the forest end up wearing a pair of expensive boots, obviously too big, that made an appearance at a murder scene?" Sanchez asked.

"Let's find out," Hunter said. "You and Delilah heading into the forest with the camper?"

"Yep. That's next on the agenda."

Hunter sent him a hard look, then said, "Be careful. And check in."

Sanchez touched a finger to the brim of his hat as they all headed for their vehicles. Josh felt a sudden need to check on Delilah, make sure she was okay.

When she burst out the door and a smile bloomed on her face as she spotted him, his heart rate settled back down as he returned her smile.

There were definitely some good things about this situation.

CHAPTER 19

JOSH ITCHED TO GET THE CAMPER SET UP, BUT FIRST THEY HAD to stop by the bank and then swing by Best Buy for a new laptop, a camera, and accessories, followed by another stop for clothes and toiletries. Thankfully, Delilah didn't shop like his sister Natalie, who would have turned this into an all-day marathon. Delilah was quick, efficient, and focused, qualities he especially admired when it came to shopping.

Afternoon shadows were lengthening as they drove into the forest with the truck and trailer, their pace slowed by the dirt roads. He glanced over at Delilah. Arms crossed over her chest, she stared out the window, shaking her head every so often.

"Are you okay?"

She sent him a small smile. "Kimberly was pretty upset when I got there. She had just seen the article online and thought I was dead. I guess I'm so used to being on my own, it never occurred to me that anyone would really miss me if I was suddenly gone."

The words were said without drama or self-pity, and he found them incredibly sad. His family was loud and boisterous, often bullheaded, and he and his brother thrashed each other fairly regularly, so he couldn't imagine that kind of aloneness. "Then I'm glad we stopped by when we did. She won't say anything to anyone, right?"

Delilah rolled her eyes.

"Okay, I deserve that. Kimberly is awesome. She give you any other information?"

She told him about Mama's appointment. "I'm going to show up at the clinic when she's there. Hopefully I can convince her to let me take Mary with me."

"Do you think she will?"

"I don't know. I've never doubted she loves her children, but I also know she's afraid to cross John Henry." The way she clenched her jaw told him there was more she wasn't saying. "At the very least, I hope she'll tell me how I can find Mary."

He reached across the cab and took her hand, gave it a squeeze. "We'll find her."

Pete had been chatting up his local contacts, hanging around the café, seeing what the local gossip turned up. Fish and Sanchez had been tapping their local informants in the forest as well, trying to scare up any information about this supposed militia group organizing. There were rumors here and there, which usually didn't amount to much. But this time, the rumblings were louder and deeper and the squad—and sheriff's office—put more credence in them.

Based on that gossip, Josh had chosen a spot several miles from where Delilah's camper had been to ensure no one would suspect it was her. It also put them closer to the last known location of her family. Which could be risky.

They passed a small clearing with two campers. Delilah instantly came alert, but then shook her head no. "That's not my family."

"If they see you in disguise, do you think they'll recognize you?"

She thought about it. "Mama would know. So would Mary. I don't know about my father or Aaron. They tend to see through women. Or only see their shape." She indicated the shapeless dress she wore. "And it's not like this tantalizing getup will draw attention."

"I don't know, I hear high-collared cotton dresses can be a real turn-on." He waggled his brows and made her laugh.

"Well then, I'd best be on my guard, or I'll have to beat them off with a stick."

Josh laughed, but his mind again went to what was under the shapeless dress. He knew every other man would be thinking the same thing. She had no idea how attractive she was, how the saucy tilt of her head and her sharp mind turned him on as much as the way the fabric slid over her curves.

He backed the camper to one side of the clearing and was surprised when Delilah hopped out as soon as he stopped. "That should work." She turned in a circle and scanned the area, eyes on the sky. "It will keep the afternoon sun from beating down on the living area."

Without a word, she grabbed the chocks and put them in position under the camper's tires. He leveled everything, and as soon as he got the canopy open, she reached inside and pulled out the floor mat and several folding chairs. Within minutes, she had a cozy living area set up. She headed off into the forest.

"Where you going?"

"I wasn't sure if you brought enough firewood, so I figured I'd grab some kindling."

He watched her disappear, smiling. Several minutes later, she dumped an armload of small sticks and twigs next to the fire ring while he got the fire started.

Tasks complete, they settled into chairs by the fire. "Have your folks taken the camper anywhere yet? It looks like it's never been used."

A shadow passed over Josh's heart. "Not yet. They bought it a little over a year ago, just before Mom's stroke. She isn't strong enough yet for them to go exploring."

"I'm really sorry. I hope they can go soon."

He smiled. "Us, too. Mom is as stubborn as the kids she raised, so if there is a way, she'll find it."

"You have a nice family."

There was such longing in the words, he reached over and took her hand. She looked at their clasped hands, then back at his face, a question in her eyes.

He winked, content to enjoy the quiet of the forest with a woman who apparently appreciated it the same way he did.

They watched the fire for a few minutes before she turned to look at him. "You getting hungry yet? Whoever stocked the kitchen did a really nice job. We won't starve."

"I don't expect you to do the cooking."

"What do you expect from me?"

Their eyes met, held. They were clearly talking about more than dinner. "I'll never expect a single thing more than you're willing to give." He paused. "Even though the timing sucks, you know I'm attracted to you, and I think you're attracted to me, too."

Her eyes widened slightly, and heat ignited in her blue gaze. By the light of the setting sun, she gave him as thorough a perusal as he'd given her. The wanting in her eyes burned as though she'd run her hands over every inch of him. "Good to know, Hollywood," she murmured, the words low, husky. All his nerve endings sprang to attention. He was about to reach for her when she stood. "I'll see what I can rustle up for supper."

Talk about a dose of reality. He stood and paced the clearing, telling his libido to settle down. This was essentially a stakeout, and getting tangled up with her right now was a terrible idea.

His focus had to stay on the mission. As long as he ignored her sharp mind, huge heart, and the growing need to ignite the fire smoldering between them, they'd be fine.

CHAPTER 20

DELILAH STEPPED INTO THE CAMPER, CLOSED THE DOOR behind her, and leaned back against it. Her skin tingled as though his sharp green gaze were still tracking her every move, waiting, wanting. She reached for the doorknob, ready to march back out there, haul him out of his chair, and pull him against her for a deep, wet kiss. For starters.

Still not staying, her self-preservation reminded her. After Andy had disappeared from her life into the wilds of Peru, of course she'd missed him. But comparing that relationship and whatever this…thing was between her and Josh was like the difference between a light summer breeze and a Cat 5 hurricane. With his easy laugh, twinkling eyes, and protective streak, Josh touched her, deep down, and awakened feelings and desires she'd never known she had. He made her loneliness stand out in stark relief and pulled her into the warm circle of his friends. Sleeping with him would pull her so far into his life and world, she wasn't sure she'd survive when she left.

Time for some distraction. She unearthed a large can of beef stew and package of instant rice, which should be enough for the two of them. She put both in the microwave and pulled out Mary's journal while she waited.

She flipped to the last entry and read backward, hoping Mary had added some clue about where the family was staying, where they were headed next. But she didn't find anything except Mary's obvious dread and fear of her upcoming wedding.

When the microwave timer dinged, Delilah stirred the stew and added a few more minutes. She returned to a section where Mary mentioned a man named Eli, a friend of their father's, who seemed to be hanging around more than normal and made Mary uncomfortable.

Mary had also mentioned the Ocklawaha river again and then talked about regular activity at their favorite spot on the river on Friday nights. Delilah straightened. She and Mary used to sneak out and sit high up in a tree overlooking the river. It was peaceful and quiet, and often, the monkeys hung around nearby, and they could watch them play.

It was also where her father and Aaron met with other men. They'd never realized their voices carried over the water, so by sitting really still, she and Mary could overhear what was happening or when they were moving again.

As soon as the stew was hot and the rice cooked, Delilah stuck her head out the camper door. "Food's ready. Not fancy but hot."

Josh had been sitting in a folding chair, iced tea in one hand and his phone in the other, legs stretched out in front of him. He grinned up at her, that dimple popping out in his cheek. "You cooked? That fast?" He pushed out of the chair and stretched, graceful as a cat. The move pulled his T-shirt up, revealing a smooth expanse of taut abdomen. Delilah's mouth went dry, and she quickly looked away when he caught her staring.

"I wouldn't call it cooking so much as opening cans and heating," she said, determined to keep things light.

"I don't care what you call it. I appreciate it." He stepped into the camper behind her, brushing his palms lightly over her shoulders as he passed.

They settled at the table, and out of lifelong habit, she bowed her head and murmured a short prayer of thanks, not really surprised when she looked up and realized he had done the same. She had some serious issues with her parents' view of God, but she didn't doubt there was a higher power, someone who'd put everything in motion and cared about those he created. She always said thanks.

Then she dug in and gulped her food down in record time. After she swallowed her last bite, she looked up to see him hiding a smile, his fork poised over his half-eaten portion. "Are we late getting somewhere? Or are you worried I'll eat your share, too?"

Her cheeks heated. "Growing up, if you didn't eat your first scoop quick, you might not get any more or someone would take whatever you had left." She shrugged. "I'm still trying to break the habit."

"Would you like some of mine?" He nudged his plate toward her.

"No thanks. I'm good."

He bent his head and kept eating, his movements smooth and easy, oblivious to the fact that she was watching him like a hawk, impatience humming under her skin.

As soon as he took his last bite, Delilah said, "I think we should head to the Ocklawaha river tonight." He sent her a questioning look. "I've been reading Mary's journal. She mentioned a place she and I used to go. We'd climb up into a tree over the river and watch the monkeys, but mostly, we'd listen in on conversations."

Josh grinned. "And is there reason to believe there may be conversations to eavesdrop on?"

Delilah smiled back. "Mary mentioned Friday nights." She frowned. "Or maybe she's just a teenager recounting what she's seen, and I am imagining clues where there aren't any."

"May I see the journal?"

She leaned over his shoulder while she turned the pages to show him which entry she meant. When she put her hands on his shoulders, he stilled under her palms. She breathed in the scent of man, with a hint of some woodsy aftershave, and rubbed the back of his neck, kneading the tight muscles.

He purred like a contented cat. "I'll give you two hours to stop that."

Delilah was about to throw self-preservation out the window when he cleared his throat and nodded to the journal. "It seems a bit vague, but it's definitely worth looking into. Especially since it's Friday night."

She stepped back. "I also want to stop by to check on the monkeys, just to make sure the mothers came back from their walkabout."

"You're really worried about them?"

"I can't explain it, but something seems off." She shrugged. "I'll feel better if I stop by."

"Fine by me, Madam Researcher." He called to tell Hunter their plans, then slid out of the bench seat. She'd started the dishes, but he stepped over and nudged her aside with his hip. "You cooked; I clean."

Delilah's eyes widened. "It's okay. It won't take long."

"My mama would smack me upside the head if I didn't take my turn. She taught all her children that. If you hadn't cooked, and she made sure we all know how to do that, too, then you cleaned up. Equal division of labor and all that."

"Who are you? You must be some species of man I've never met before."

"Yes, ma'am," he drawled, pure Hollywood. "There's a whole lot of me you ain't seen yet."

"Promises, promises." She'd meant to sound flirty, but her voice came out a sultry growl, and heat flared in his eyes. He took a step toward her, ran his hand down her cheek. A shiver passed over her skin at the look in his eyes. "Just say the word, Xena," he murmured.

Time stretched as they studied each other. Outside, a hawk screeched, followed by the whoosh of wings and a thump as he snatched some small creature. Delilah shivered, the moment shattered. "Poor thing. I understand the food chain and all that, but I hate seeing—or hearing—it happen." She stepped around him. "I'll just brush my teeth before we go."

They locked the camper and headed for his truck. "I didn't

think to ask," he said. "You guys hiked there, correct? Or did you go by canoe or kayak?"

"Mary and I walked. But we can drive partway. I'll show you." She held up her backpack. "I threw in bug repellent, a flashlight, and some water and snacks, so we should be good."

"I like the way you think. I packed the same, plus binoculars and night-vision goggles."

"Show-off."

───────────

Josh didn't think they would learn anything useful, but he wasn't opposed to spending a couple of hours alone with Delilah.

She gave directions, peering through the windshield and gesturing out the open windows. Finally, she pointed. "We can walk in from here." She slung her new camera around her neck and headed off at a fast clip.

He hurried to catch up, admiring the swing of her shapely rear as she marched ahead of him.

As usual, they heard the monkeys before they saw them. Once they pinpointed the chatter, it wasn't hard to find the swaying branches where youngsters frolicked and played.

They found a comfy spot on a fallen tree, and while Delilah watched the monkeys, Josh watched Delilah. He could see her mile-wide smile behind the camera lens as she panned the troop, snapping photos. "There you are, Oscar. It's so good to see you. You're looking good, little man. Looking good," she crooned.

He leaned closer and whispered, "You named a baby monkey Oscar?"

She shot him a look, grinning. "Yes. He's totally adorable." She showed him one of the photos she'd just taken. "I'm so glad he's okay. I've been worried about him."

Camera to her eye, her smile faded as she continued panning. "But something still isn't right." She twisted around, scanned several other trees. "I can't find them. They're still not here." Her voice rose with anxiety.

"Who? The mothers?"

"Yes. First Oscar's mother disappeared, then the three others I was telling you about." She looked over at Oscar again. "One of the aunties is taking care of him, and I was worried he wasn't getting enough nutrition since she's not lactating, but he seems to be doing fine." She giggled. "Oh, he's playing with something." She zoomed in. "What is that?"

She lowered the camera, showed him a photo.

"It looks like a gum wrapper."

A flock of birds suddenly took flight and startled the monkeys. Within seconds, the troop disappeared.

Delilah leaped to her feet. "I'm going to find it." She tossed the words over her shoulder. "I knew someone's been following me."

"A gum wrapper on the forest floor doesn't necessarily constitute proof."

She threw him a look.

"But it could," he added.

When she bent down, he wrapped an arm around her waist from behind to stop her. "Don't touch. Let me get it." He pulled out the gloves he always carried before he carefully picked up the metallic wrapper and tucked it into a bag. "Definitely looks like a gum wrapper. Maybe we'll get lucky and Byte will find prints on it."

Her body fairly vibrated as she stomped ahead of him, both of them scanning the ground, looking for more evidence, but they didn't find anything.

They didn't find any clues to the missing mama monkeys, either.

He waited until they were heading back to the truck before he said, "Tell me about every time you thought you were being followed, and don't leave anything out."

She did, as clearly and methodically as if she were presenting a research paper. But he sensed the anger simmering inside her, and it matched his own. He'd definitely have Byte look into this further.

Her directions led them to an area close to the Ocklawaha River, and they walked in, following what looked like a game trail that ended at the water's edge. It was almost full dark, but he didn't turn on a flashlight for fear of calling attention to their presence. Delilah must've been thinking the same. At least there wasn't a full moon tonight.

She stopped at the river's edge and pointed to a huge bald cypress tree behind her, grinning. "Race you to the top." Before he realized what she was doing, she started shimmying up the trunk like one of the monkeys she loved. He stepped closer and laughed when he spotted the strips of wood nailed to the tree, creating a ladder. She disappeared into the canopy, her skill telling him again that this was something she had done many times before. Her quiet voice filtered down, "You coming, Hollywood?"

He loved the sound of his nickname on her lips. He slung his backpack over one shoulder and quickly followed her up into the notch of the tree. She sat on a large limb, her back against the trunk, and nodded toward a nearby branch. He settled in next to her and looked around, realizing they had a perfect vantage point to watch any comings and goings on the water. The river narrowed here and acted as a funnel. He glanced her way. "Nice observation deck. Good choice."

In answer, she smacked a mosquito. "Annoying bugs." She rooted around in her bag and produced one of the vials of essential oils his sister sold at the Outpost. He heard buzzing around his own head and reached into his backpack for a can of Deep Woods OFF!

"That stuff is terrible for your skin and for the environment."

"No argument," he answered, spraying himself liberally while she exaggerated major coughing beside him.

She waved a hand in front of her face. "Geez, Hollywood, give a girl a break."

"Sorry about that, but this stuff works. That oil doesn't do a thing for me." He shot her a grin as he tucked the can back into his backpack. Hunter was going to wait on the other side of the river until Josh let him know their location, but the ever-popular "no service" message popped up when he tried to call. He sent a text with as much location info as he could and hoped it went through. You never knew out here.

As the shadows lengthened and dusk turned to full night, they fell into easy conversation. He asked her about growing up, what it was like to live in a camper and move around all the time, how she liked being homeschooled.

"As a kid, you don't realize your upbringing is different from anyone else's. That was my normal, and I didn't realize other families did things differently. Don't forget, we didn't socialize much, and the people our family spent time with all thought and did things the same way my parents did."

"Your father seems like a very strict, very stern man. Was he always like that? Or did he loosen up and play with you when you were a kid?"

Josh watched a flurry of emotion pass over Delilah's face before she answered. "He was definitely strict and usually stern, sometimes much more than that. It got worse after his brother was killed by FWC when I was little. But he changed whenever someone started playing music." A small smile tipped up one corner of her mouth. "He had a great voice, and he'd start tapping his toe, and next thing you know, he'd start singing. He'd grab Mama by the elbow and swing her around and get everyone else up dancing and do-si-doing, too." She paused. "I'd forgotten about those memories, buried them under all the ugliness."

He waited for her to say more, but she didn't.

"How did you like school? Were you a bookworm?"

She laughed. "How did you guess? I've always been a big reader, and I enjoyed homeschool, enjoyed learning new things."

"What made you become a monkey researcher? Besides growing up out here?"

She didn't answer for a long time, and he wondered if he'd crossed some boundary he shouldn't have.

"I was fascinated by the monkeys, especially the way they interact with each other. Mary was too. Some of their behavior seems very human. I liked watching the mamas handle their young. They are tough, and they don't put up with any shenanigans." She smiled. "When I needed to choose a major at FSU, this seemed like the logical choice."

He heard something in her voice. "Is it still the logical choice? Or are you rethinking your future plans?"

"I will always want to work outside with animals, especially monkeys. I'd love to do more teaching, especially with children, sharing my love of the rhesus macaques with them. It's the research part I'm second-guessing. I've discovered I don't really like spending days on end by myself. I guess I'm more of a social animal than I realized." She sent him a rueful smile. "This grant research study is my final project. Then I'll have to figure out what's next."

"Would you ever come back here? To live?" The question popped out, and he froze, waiting, feeling like his future hinged on her answer.

She met his gaze for long moments, and he saw longing, attraction, and regret swirling in the blue of her eyes. "No. I can't stay here. Not ever."

Despite the finality in her tone, he turned on the charm. "You know the old saying, Xena. 'Never say never,'" he teased.

She shook her head and opened her mouth to argue, but then they spotted lights approaching on the river.

He pulled out his night-vision goggles and handed her the binoculars. "Not sure how much you'll be able to see, but it can't hurt."

The sound of an outboard motor pierced the quiet. Instead of the usual running lights, it looked like someone was sitting at the bow of a small johnboat, shining a flashlight into the water ahead of them. Josh could make out a second man at the stern, hand on the tiller, guiding them through the water.

As they watched, a light flashed on and off from the opposite bank, almost directly across from their location. Josh went on alert, and he felt Delilah stiffen beside him. They waited as the boat slowly made its way toward them and then pulled into a small natural alcove where the light had been.

Josh wished there were a way to get close enough to hear what was being said. He glanced up into the tree canopy. Though the trees met halfway across the river, he could never cross from one to the other without anybody hearing or seeing him.

The two men climbed out of the boat, tied the bowline to a tree, then disappeared several paces into the forest. The light came on, and Josh could make out two additional men. There were stacks of boxes on the ground, and he leaned forward, straining to see, when one of the men used a crowbar to pry open the lid on the first box. Unfortunately, from this angle, he couldn't tell what was inside, but the crates looked the right length to hold guns. Of course, they could be filled with something completely innocuous, like canned goods, but you didn't schedule a clandestine meeting to hand off SpaghettiOs.

He reached for his phone, knowing he wouldn't be able to zoom in far enough, when he heard the soft click of a shutter beside him. Delilah was busily snapping pictures of what was happening. He hoped she could capture their faces, but he knew it was a long shot. They were all wearing ball caps pulled low.

They heard the quiet murmur of conversation, and then the men picked up the boxes, two people per box, and loaded them into the boat. Josh shifted, trying to get a better look, and knocked his backpack out of the tree. He lunged for it and almost lost his balance. Delilah grabbed the back of his shirt and held tight while he caught his balance.

They both froze, horrified, as the heavy pack landed with a thump. He winced as his metal water bottle clanked against a rock below. The sound carried across the water, and the men's heads snapped up. Josh clasped Delilah's hand as one of the men turned on a powerful spotlight and scanned the area. When the light hit the ground beneath their tree and started moving higher, Josh whispered, "Close your eyes." The reflection could give away their location.

They sat, hands clasped and hearts pounding as the man shone the light around for what seemed like hours. He finally turned it off, and they let out a sigh of relief. The men quickly loaded the rest of the boxes, and less than ten minutes after they'd arrived, the boat pulled away and headed back the way it had come, sitting much lower in the water.

Josh and Delilah stayed where they were until the sound of the motor faded in the distance. When she would have started down, he put a hand on her arm and whispered, "Give it a few more minutes. In case the guys on shore haven't left yet."

She nodded and tucked her camera away while they waited. Sure enough, several minutes later, Josh saw the light flash on and off once more, and a few minutes after that, they heard the sound of a truck starting off in the distance.

To be safe, he waited another ten minutes before he said, "We should be okay to leave now."

If they were lucky, Hunter would have intercepted the truck near the paved road. Delilah nimbly climbed back down the tree and waited for him at the base. As they headed toward the truck, he admired her sure steps in the dark. She was a mass of contradictions but definitely a woman who could take care of herself and knew her way around a forest. The thought made him grin.

———————

Delilah hurried toward Josh's truck, eager to see if she had caught anyone's face. She wavered between hoping it was Aaron's and hoping it wasn't. The whole crazy merry-go-round made her feel seasick, but she was determined to get answers. No matter what they were.

Josh held the door for her, and she climbed inside. Once he slid in, he pulled up a map on his phone. "Nothing from Hunter, so I don't know if he got my text, but I'll try again. Hopefully, he can find that spot across the river. If we're lucky, we'll get a match to the tire treads or find some other evidence at the site of the meeting."

As he drove toward their campsite, Delilah scrolled through the photos, hope sinking as they confirmed what she already knew. Everyone had kept their heads down, making it impossible to see past the bills of their caps. She sank back with a sigh.

"Nothing?" Josh asked.

"No. They were very careful."

"I'll still send the pictures to Byte, our tech wizard, see if he can get something."

When they pulled up to the camper, Josh put a hand on her arm to stop her from sliding out immediately. "Let me check it out first, okay?"

She watched him step inside, gun drawn, completely calm, and her heart rate settled. His confidence bolstered her own. They were going to figure this out.

Once he gave the all clear, they sat side by side on the sofa as she showed him the photos. They hunched over the small screen, desperate for some clue, some small movement that would help them identify the four men, but found nothing. Delilah handed him the SD card, and he sent the images to Byte, then emailed Hunter whatever info they had.

"I asked Hunter to check if anyone has a permit for trapping rhesus macaques out here, just in case. We'll also see if the gum wrapper turns up anything."

"Thanks. I appreciate it. I know the monkeys aren't your favorite thing."

"I never said that. I don't know what the answer is, but the increasing cases of aggression mean there has to be some kind of management plan."

Delilah didn't like it, but a part of her understood. She slumped back against the sofa. "What do you think was in those boxes?" They looked similar to the ones she's seen in Aaron's pickup.

He looked up from the computer. "Based on the weight and size, my money's on guns."

"Who were those men? Since Mary wrote about the place in her journal or at least about some sort of meeting, this has happened before. But is it connected to this militia meeting Kimberly mentioned?"

Josh sent her an admiring glance. "That's what we have to find out."

Delilah leaned her head back and closed her eyes, trying to put the pieces together, but the picture wouldn't come clear. None of it seemed to fit together, and none of it made sense. Maybe it wasn't supposed to. Maybe none of this had anything to do with her family or with Mary. And maybe there really was a Santa Claus.

Her eyes popped open when Josh took her hands and pulled her to her feet and into his arms. He steadied her and then tucked her hair behind her ears, making her glad she'd pulled off the wig as soon as they'd gotten back. He cupped her cheeks and smiled gently. "We're getting closer. And we're going to find your sister. Don't get discouraged. And don't give up."

His eyes flicked to her lips, and Delilah licked them self-consciously, drawing his eyes again. He leaned in slowly, and so did she, his breath warm on her face. He stroked his thumb over her cheek, and awareness rippled through her. She reached up and wrapped her arms around his neck, desperate suddenly to feel his lips on hers.

"If you don't want me to kiss you, now's the time to say so." His voice was low, but his eyes blazed green fire.

Delilah's stomach swooped at the look in his eyes, and she

smiled as she pulled him close, sighing as they fit together, curves and angles meeting at just the right places. She sent him a saucy smile. "What took you so long, Hollywood?"

He was smiling as his lips closed over hers, warm and feather-light as he ran his hands over her back and down the curve of her backside. She tunneled her hands into the hair at his nape, enjoying the feel of the soft strands.

He pulled back slightly, and they studied each other before he leaned in slowly and kissed her again, soft and tempting, nibbling at her lips as though he had nothing more important to do for the next millennia.

After a while, impatience got the best of her, and she ran her tongue along the seam of his lips. He opened his mouth, and the passion he'd kept banked till now burst into flame. The kiss went deeper, hotter, the glide of teeth and tongues sending a shock of pleasure to her very core. Her hands reached up to tangle in his hair again as she plastered herself against his rock-hard chest, wanting to get closer, ever closer.

His hands tightened on her waist, and he bit down lightly on her lower lip. She moaned and ran her hands under his shirt while his lips blazed a trail from her neck to the vee of her blouse. His eyes blazed fire as he unbuttoned first one button, then another, until they were all undone and he pushed it from her shoulders.

"You are so beautiful." He trailed kisses over her collarbone, then across her chest and between the cups of her white cotton bra. He looked up, grinned. "Very practical. But in the way."

His hands left a trail of fire everywhere he touched, and she arched her back, wanting more.

The world tilted suddenly as he scooped her into his arms, heading for the bedroom.

"I'm not staying." The thought screamed through her head, a loud screech reminding her to stop and think. To decide. Instead of getting swept away by passion.

He froze, and his eyes shot to hers.

Her face heated like it was on fire. *Had she really said that out loud?*

Apparently, she had.

He slowly lowered her to her feet. "Then it's better we don't start something that isn't going anywhere."

She wanted to argue, say they'd just enjoy the moment and not worry about tomorrow, but the words wouldn't come. It wasn't that simple, and they both knew it.

He leaned in for one quick kiss, then smiled at her. "Off to bed with you, woman. I'll take the bunks."

She opened her mouth to say more, to try to explain, but he stopped her with a finger on her lips. "Go to bed, Delilah. Or we'll both regret it in the morning."

Heat and want still blazed in his eyes as he stepped out of the camper and closed the door behind him.

She tugged her shirt on, heart still pounding. She had her hand on the knob to burst through the door and tell him she'd changed her mind, but she pulled it back. It was better this way. If she wasn't careful, she'd fall in love with the green-eyed lawman.

She ignored the little voice in her heart that told her she already had.

CHAPTER 21

DELILAH WOKE JUST PAST DAWN THE NEXT MORNING, DISORI-
ented. She raised up on her elbows and looked around. Tiny windows, built-in cabinet, small television mounted to the wall. The
Tanners' camper. Got it.

She'd slept better last night than she had in a very long time,
which surprised her. After that epic faux pas, she'd expected to stay
awake, obsessing and replaying the embarrassing scene. Maybe
the exhaustion of the past week had caught up to her, or maybe it
was knowing Josh was nearby.

As she slid out of bed, she decided she'd pretend nothing had
happened. After a quick stop in the bathroom to get dressed, she
tiptoed into the kitchen and quietly searched the cabinets, looking
for coffee.

"I'm up. No need to be quiet."

Delilah spun to find him lying on the couch, the blanket low on
his hips, bare chest and washboard abs on display. He had one arm
tucked behind his head, and between that and the low rumble of
his voice, her mouth went dry. *Be still my heart.* "I, ah, thought you
were sleeping in the bunks."

The camper had one bedroom plus a built-in set of bunks at
the other end. "I had planned to. But I fell asleep before I made it
that far." He tossed the blanket aside and stood, and Delilah swallowed hard at the sight of him wearing nothing but a pair of blue
plaid boxers. Boxers that were tented in front, she noticed.

"You sleep okay?" he asked.

It took a moment for his question to register, and when her gaze
slid up to his face, his twinkling eyes said he'd caught her staring.

"Ah, yes. Thanks. You?"

"As well as could be expected. Considering."

She stiffened. "Considering what?" Her hands fisted on her hips.

"Considering my feet hang off the end of the sofa and the cushions are lumpy." He cocked one eyebrow. "What did you think I meant?"

Oh, she so wasn't going there. As he walked by, he chuckled as he cupped her shoulders and kissed the top of her head.

She had toast going, coffee ready, and was whipping a few eggs by the time he reemerged, fully clothed, the spicy scent of whatever soap or aftershave he used drifting in his wake. He reached around her for a mug, purposefully crowding her, and poured coffee.

She looked over her shoulder, and their eyes met, his lit with a teasing glint. "Cut it out," she warned, carefully pouring the egg mixture into the frying pan. The man was making her crazy. She let out a sigh of relief when his cell phone rang.

"Tanner." He glanced at the clock. "We can be there in about thirty minutes. 10-4. See you then." He set the phone on the counter. "That was Hunter. He's got some new information."

Delilah scrambled the eggs while he sent a few emails. Then, while he did dishes, she put on her wig, reminding her reflection to quit thinking about Josh's gorgeous body and focus on finding her sister.

━━━━━━━━━━

As Josh drove toward Tanner's Outpost, he searched for a way to dispel the lingering awkwardness. He'd tried teasing Delilah, but that hadn't worked, especially since his first thought was to yank her into his arms for a repeat of last night. Just thinking about it had kept him up far too late—and had woken him up hard as a rock this morning.

But that was his problem and one he needed to deal with. Fast.

Though he was technically "on vacation," he was still an FWC officer. And she was still tied to a current case.

"I'm not staying."

She hadn't meant to say that aloud, given her shocked expression, but the reminder had knocked him upside the head. He didn't do casual sex or halfway relationships, and he was pretty sure she didn't either. If he was in, he was all in. Which meant he shouldn't start something with a woman who'd be leaving in a week or two. That was just stupid. He wasn't looking for more heartache, thanks very much. He still had the scars Elaine left behind.

When they reached Charlee's cottage, Delilah pulled a ball cap over the blond wig she'd braided on the drive and added glasses, ready to hop out of the truck.

"Look, Delilah. About last night—"

She aimed an impersonal smile over her shoulder. "We should get in there."

Guess she didn't want to talk about it.

He kissed Charlee's cheek, and they joined the squad in her small living room. Pete, in his green sheriff's deputy uniform, stood off to one side in a heated discussion with Fish, who was dressed in FWC khaki. He towered over her, but that didn't stop her from propping her hands on her hips and giving attitude right back. Josh's eyes met Hunter's, and the other man rolled his eyes. Pete and Fish were like oil and water, forever arguing about something.

"Did Byte get anything from Delilah's pics?" Josh asked.

Hunter shook his head as he scrolled through the photos. "These guys were really careful. He's hoping to enhance the images enough for facial rec, but…" He shrugged. "I did find the meeting place, though. Good directions, Hollywood, and Pete had the sheriff's techs take tire impressions and search for any other evidence. They're also combing databases for folks with militia leanings, any mention of an alliance, and comparing notes with Byte."

Sanchez leaned against the wall. "Want me to check for trail cameras in the area? They wouldn't have met there if one was nearby, but maybe they passed one on the way in or out. Might give us a license plate or the make and model of a truck or two."

"Good plan. Thanks, Sanchez." He turned to the others. "Byte also compared Billy's boot print to the one near Black's body, and they're a match."

Fish spoke from where she'd plopped on the couch. "Do we know yet where he got the boots?"

"I spoke with Billy's mother just before you arrived," Hunter said. "She claims she got them from her sister, who cleans house for none other than our favorite county commissioner, Dwight Benson."

Pete sat in the armchair across from Fish. "I'll head downtown and have a chat with him as soon as we're done here."

"Thanks, Pete," Hunter said. "Keep me posted."

"Of course." He shot a grin around the room. "Let's hope he confesses nice and easy-like and we can call the Black case cleared."

Everyone laughed, because things only wrapped up that neatly on television. Real-life investigations were usually a lot more tedious, less cut-and-dried, and not nearly as exciting.

"I have one more interesting piece of information." Hunter tapped more keys on his laptop. "Byte put a notification on Black's email to see who was still sending him messages. This just came in, mentions an informal meet-up for possible militia joiners. Tonight." He turned the laptop around so they could read the short message.

"Can Byte trace the IP address?" Sanchez asked.

"Already working on it," Hunter said.

"We can put our cover to the test," Josh said, excitement building. "We'll show up, introduce ourselves, see what we can find out." If a group planned an armed protest, law enforcement would show up in force, armed and ready. But an informal gathering? Perfectly legal—and often a great source of information.

"I'll be nearby, keeping an eye on you both," Hunter said.

Josh was shaking his head before Hunter finished speaking. "If they suspect someone is watching, our cover is toast. You'll have to stay a good distance away."

Hunter crossed his arms over his chest and raised an eyebrow. "You figure this is my first day on the job, Hollywood?"

Josh debated how to respond. The fact that Hunter had gotten the promotion Josh thought was his still grated like a burr under his saddle. But that was his issue and not part of this. "My priority is to keep Delilah safe."

"Then you work on that and let me work my end." He waited a beat, then picked up an FWC mug and held it aloft. "Before we head out, it's time for the monkey suit lottery."

The men groaned.

"At least you guys get to take turns," Fish complained. "It's always my turn."

"That's only because I look terrible in a dress," Josh quipped, batting his eyelashes.

Delilah laughed with the rest of them but still looked confused.

"Every year, FWC sends two officers to the Mayor's Ball to do meet-and-greet duty while the rest of the squad provides security," Charlee said. "Fish gets to wear a gorgeous dress, but she has to go with one of these lunkheads."

Hunter held the mug out to Delilah. "Draw a name, and let's see who this year's monkey suit winner is."

She pulled out one of the folded pieces of paper and handed it to Hunter.

"And the winner is…"

Sanchez tapped his palms on the table in a drum roll.

"Josh." The minute Hunter read the name, Pete and Sanchez high-fived, and Josh groaned.

"Right back at you," Fish said, laughing.

Josh's gaze flicked to Delilah and saw her eyeing Fish speculatively. Was that a flash of jealousy he spotted?

"In case you didn't read the memo I forwarded last week," Hunter continued, and there were more groans, "Dwight Benson is scheduled to be the MC for this year's ball, which will give us a chance to keep a close eye on him. That's all for now."

A timer rang in the kitchen.

"If you ask nicely, I'll let you have a treat before you go," Charlee said.

The squad practically stampeded for the kitchen.

"Do I smell cupcakes?" Josh asked, sniffing the air as he entered.

Charlee grinned. "Or cookies. You'd think you'd know the difference by now."

He poured coffee, saluted her with his cup. "I don't care what it is, Sis. If you're baking, I want some. Pretty please."

A chorus of "hear, hear" came from around the room.

While Charlee pulled a tray of cookies from the oven, Hunter set a plastic bag on the table in front of Delilah. If Josh hadn't been watching, he would've missed the way her eyes widened and she sucked in a quick breath before all emotion disappeared from her face.

"We found this in the woods just beyond your camper. Do you know who it belongs to?" Hunter asked.

All the color leached out of her face. "It's a common enough logo, especially around here." The silence lengthened, and then she said, "My brother was wearing one like that the last time I saw him. But it doesn't prove he burned down my camper," she added.

"You're right. It doesn't. But we do have some questions for him. Had he come to visit you?"

Her chin came up. "No. I've been trying to track him down."

She looked outwardly calm, but Josh had seen the flash of worry, so he said, "I'll see if I can find him. See what he has to say for himself."

Hunter raised a brow. "Since you're on 'vacation'"—he made air quotes—"Hollywood, we'll go together."

"I'm coming with you," Delilah said.

Both Josh and Hunter said no at the same time.

"He's my brother."

"And he may very well have tried to kill you." When she opened her mouth to argue, Josh continued, "Right now, your biggest protection is the fact that he thinks you're dead."

Tension crackled in the air as they stared at each other, but Josh wouldn't back down. Not on this. Delilah scanned the room, and he knew everyone wore the same implacable expression. Finally, her eyes came back to him.

"All right. I'm going to the Saturday market downtown, then. Mama and Mrs. Fenton sometimes set up there on the off weeks from the regular farmers market. I'll go in disguise and see if I can find out where Mary is or what's going on."

"I have a change of clothes in the car," Fish said. "We'll stroll around as two friends out shopping on a Saturday morning."

"I love the Saturday market," Charlee said as she transferred cookies to the cooling rack. "I'll go with you."

"Don't you have a kayak tour in a little while?" Hunter asked.

Charlee huffed out a breath as she turned off the oven. "Yes, dang it. I forgot about that."

"Sorry, *cher*," Hunter said. He sent a text to update the captain, closed his laptop, and kissed Charlee soundly on the mouth. "Let's do this. Be safe out there, everybody."

Fish pulled up to the grassy parking area in Mrs. Tanner's nondescript sedan. It wouldn't do to show up in either an FWC truck or Delilah's vehicle. Both women wore long cotton skirts and long-sleeved blouses. They had traded ball caps for big floppy hats and wore sunglasses to hide their eyes. Delilah had no doubt Mama would recognize her, but she worried how she would react. Maybe she should wait until tomorrow, when Kimberly would keep them safe from prying eyes.

"Easy, girl," Fish whispered. "No one will recognize you."

Delilah didn't argue, just pulled down the brim of her floppy hat and marched off toward the produce section. "There's a vendor just inside who sells recyclable bags. We should grab a few to put produce in."

Fish hurried to keep up, eyeing the change in Delilah's demeanor. "You sure you don't want to join FWC? You're a natural at this undercover stuff."

"I've just learned to blend in over the years." It was a survival skill she'd learned early.

"Then lead on. This is your turf, not mine."

They purchased bags, then wandered up and down the rows, chatting with vendors as they scanned the area, looking for her mother's booth.

Delilah bent down to inspect a basket of beefsteak tomatoes. "I don't see Mama anywhere. But if Mrs. Fenton is here, she may know if Mama came today."

Fish held up a fat tomato and nodded. "This looks about perfect, doesn't it?"

Several minutes later, Delilah spotted Mrs. Fenton returning to her booth. She caught Fish's eye and nodded to the empty space beside it.

"Hey, good morning," Fish said. "I was kinda hoping to get some bread-and-butter pickles from the lady next to you. Atwood, I think her name is. She not here today?"

Mrs. Fenton smiled sadly. "Sorry, you just missed her. She already sold out."

"Oh, she was here today? How long ago did she leave?"

A look of caution slid over the woman's face. "I really couldn't say. Why?"

Fish laughed as Delilah joined her. "Sorry. That came out sounding pretty stalker-ish. I just love those pickles, and I've been raving about them to my friend." She nodded to Delilah. "I was hoping we could either buy several jars or place an order for next week."

Mrs. Fenton's caution melted into a sunny smile. "If you hurry, you might still be able to catch them. They just headed out a few minutes ago." She indicated the vendor parking area off to one side.

"Can you tell me what kind of vehicle they're in?" Fish asked, shading her eyes as she scanned the area.

The older woman shrugged. "Sorry. I was too busy setting up my booth to pay much attention."

Delilah's heart pounded. Did "them" mean Mama and Papa or Aaron? Or did it include Mary, too? She thanked Mrs. Fenton and started running, but Fish put a hand on her arm.

"Let's not draw undue attention to ourselves."

Delilah forced herself to slow down, but it was hard. Every instinct urged her to run full tilt lest she miss them. Once they reached the parking area, they searched for any vehicle that was occupied or loading up. There were quite a few. Some were leaving, while others were offloading more product.

Two rows over, a pickup started. Delilah's eyes widened when she saw her father behind the wheel and two more people in the cab. One of them looked like her mother, which meant the other could very well be Mary. "That's them!"

Delilah rushed between two trucks and smacked her shoulder on a side mirror as she ran, but she didn't slow down. They were almost to the exit! She tried to flag them down, but before her arms were halfway up, Fish ran up behind her and yanked them down. "Don't blow our cover," she hissed in Delilah's ear. Delilah struggled to free herself, but Fish was stronger than she looked. "We need to do this another way, Delilah, and you know it."

She did know it, and her heart sank, defeated. They had been so close. She was almost positive Mary had been sitting between her parents.

"Let's go back and talk to Mrs. Fenton. Maybe your sister left a note."

"She's never done that before, but even if she did, unless Mrs. Fenton knows it's me, she'll never hand it over."

"Can you trust her?"

"I have no reason not to. I've been leaving cards and notes for Mary with her for years."

"Then maybe today is your lucky day."

Delilah didn't feel particularly lucky, but she wasn't giving up. When they reached Mrs. Fenton's booth, they waited politely until the other customers left.

"Did you catch them?" Mrs. Fenton asked.

"Unfortunately, no, they were just pulling away as we got there." Delilah leaned closer, "Mrs. Fenton, did Mary leave a note for me?"

Mrs. Fenton studied her face for a long moment and then her eyes widened. "I've heard blonds have more fun."

Delilah smiled. "I've heard that, too. I'll let you know if it's true." She paused. "Please, Mrs. Fenton. It's important."

The woman looked both ways to be sure no one was watching, then reached under the table and pulled out a small envelope. She passed it to Delilah with a basket of cucumbers and whispered, "She was hoping you'd come."

Her heart pounded with anticipation as she paid, then stashed everything in her bag. "Thank you, Mrs. Fenton."

She patted Delilah's hand. "She's a lovely girl. I hope you two are able to connect."

Delilah and Fish didn't speak as they hurried back to Mrs. Tanner's sedan. Once inside, she pulled out the envelope and relief flooded her at Mary's familiar, looping handwriting. "It doesn't say much. 'Tomorrow after church, our favorite spot. Please come.'"

Fish sent her a quick grin. "It may not be a lot of words, but it tells us everything we need to know."

The hard knot of worry inside Delilah loosened slightly as the words sank in. Mary believed Delilah was looking for her and had just told her where she could be found. This was exactly what she'd been hoping and longing for. If all went according to plan, she'd have Mary safely with her tomorrow.

CHAPTER 22

Josh and Hunter checked the Corner Café first, but Aaron wasn't there. According to Liz, he hadn't been there at all during the past several days. There was no sign of County Commissioner Dwight Benson either, and Liz couldn't say for sure when she'd last seen the man.

"Interesting," Josh said when they were back in Hunter's truck. "Benson's a regular fixture at the café, so this is out of character."

"I agree. Let's go see if Mama T has anything useful to tell us." The tiny older woman had been operating a small convenience store out in the forest for decades and always had her ear to the ground. If you wanted to know what was happening, you asked Mama T.

Hunter drove into the forest but hadn't gone far when Pete called. Hunter put him on speaker. "Did you bring Benson in for questioning?"

"Negative. He wasn't at his office, but Mom knows his secretary, so I called Janet at home. She was frantic that he'd been out of pocket for the last two days, which she says is completely unlike him. I'm heading to his house now to do a well check. If he doesn't turn up, I'll be at his office first thing Monday morning to look around."

"Keep me posted." Hunter thanked him and disconnected.

The two men exchanged looks. "Looks like Mr. Benson has something to hide," Josh said.

"Sounds like." Hunter dialed his cell phone. "Hey, Byte, I need a favor. Do a search to see if County Commissioner Dwight Benson has any other property in the area that he might use as a hidey-hole."

"10-4, boss. I'll get back to you."

Josh flipped through the facts of the case as they drove out to Mama T's place. "We still have no motive for Benson to kill Black. Benson has an election coming up, one he's been pretty determined to win, so killing somebody doesn't seem like a smart political move."

"Unless it wasn't planned, and Black showed up at the wrong place at the wrong time, and Benson didn't feel he had a choice."

"Which still doesn't tell us why."

"And we still don't have any solid proof he did it."

Josh grinned as they parked. "Details, details."

When they stepped onto the rickety porch at Mama T's, the tiny older woman greeted them like long-lost family. She gave hugs, patted cheeks, and generally treated both men as though they were twelve. Josh half expected her to tweak his cheek before it was over. Once they'd exchanged the requisite pleasantries, she propped her hands on her hips, expression stern. "Much as I enjoy seeing you, y'all have the look of men on a mission today. How can I help?"

"We're trying to find Aaron Atwood. He been around here lately?" Hunter asked.

Mama T's eyes clouded, and she shook her head and clucked her tongue. "Don't know what's gotten into that boy lately. He and his father used to come by, regular like, and then Aaron started coming by himself, strutting around like he was all that and too good for the rest of us."

"About how long ago did you notice the change?" Josh asked.

She thought about it for a minute. "Least a year ago now, maybe going on two."

"When was the last time you saw him?" Josh asked.

She squinted. "Must've been a few days ago now. He got another propane tank for his camper, a few supplies, but he wasn't in no mood to talk."

"Any guesses where we might find him today?" Hunter asked.

"John Henry came by earlier for live bait, so the two of them might be fishing together."

Hunter and Josh exchanged a look. "Mama T, have you heard any rumors or rumblings about somebody trying to start a militia in this area? Or anything about guns?" Josh kept his eyes on her face as he asked the question.

Instead of answering, Mama T reached under the counter and pulled out a flyer. It was the same invite to a meet and greet that had shown up in Black's email. "Some man I ain't never seen before came by and asked me to post this for him. I said no, and he wasn't none too happy about it."

"Can you describe him for us?" Hunter asked.

"All's I can tell you is that he was tall and had red hair. And a red beard, too."

"Thanks for your time, Mama T," Josh said. "You let us know if he comes around again or if anyone bothers you, you hear?"

She patted his cheek. "You're a good man, even if you is a copper."

Josh and Hunter laughed, then each one hugged her and kissed her cheek before they climbed into the truck and headed for the nearest boat ramp.

"I've not heard mention of either Atwood owning a boat, so maybe we'll get lucky and they're fishing off the dock."

When they pulled up at the boat ramp, Hunter hitched his chin and grinned. "Looks like we got lucky." He grabbed the ball cap, and they approached the two men leaning over the dock railing, poles in the water.

"Afternoon, gentlemen," Hunter said. "How's the fishing?"

John Henry kept his eyes on the water, pretending he didn't hear them. Aaron, however, glanced their way. "No keepers so far, but that's why they call it fishing, not catching, right?"

After polite chuckles, Hunter said, "I have a couple questions for you, Aaron."

"All right. How can I assist FWC today?"

Interesting, Josh thought, that all of a sudden, the son of a survivalist gets chatty with law enforcement.

Hunter held the ball cap out to Aaron. "Is this yours?"

Aaron leaned forward but didn't touch it. John Henry had obviously cautioned him about giving his fingerprints to the government. "I suppose it could be. Course it could belong to any number of people, what with the feed store giving them out like candy."

"Let me ask it another way. Do you own one of the many hats the feed store gave out, Mr. Atwood?" Hunter pressed.

"I used to. But I don't recall seeing it for a while." He shrugged again.

"Did you hear about the camper that burned down in the forest the other night?" Hunter asked.

Aaron clicked his tongue. "I did. Sad story that. At least with the rain we've had, the fire didn't spread too far."

Was this guy for real? "You also heard someone died as a result of that fire, correct?"

Josh saw John Henry clench his jaw and couldn't tell if the other man was angry or suppressing emotion. "They've identified the victim as Delilah Paige. Also known as your sister, Delilah Atwood."

John Henry's grip on the pole tightened.

Aaron's expression turned sad. "I'd heard that, yes, but I—we—were hoping it wasn't true."

"You knew she was back in town?"

Aaron looked away, nodded. "Just heard that recently." He paused. "Any idea what caused the fire?"

"The fire marshal is still conducting his investigation," Hunter said.

"Did you set it?" Josh demanded. Hunter sent him a quelling look, but he ignored it.

206

Aaron's incredulous smile made Josh itch to punch him. He clenched his fists to keep from doing it.

"I had no idea that was my sister's camper, and even if I had, what possible reason would I have for setting fire to it?" Aaron shook his head. "That doesn't even make sense. I don't know what kind of fishing expedition you gentlemen are on, but you're in the wrong pond."

"We found the ball cap near the camper."

"And that means I set the fire?" He laughed. "If that's all you have to go on, this conversation is over."

Josh stepped in and grabbed Aaron by the shirtfront. He pulled him up onto his toes and hissed, "If I find out you were behind this, there will not be a hole deep enough for you to hide in."

"This is police harassment," Aaron said to Hunter, calm as you please.

Hunter moved next to Josh. "Let him go."

Josh's grip tightened, fingers itching to slap the smug expression off Aaron's face. With one final glare, he slowly set the other man back on his feet.

Aaron rolled his shoulders, then picked up his pole and reeled in his line, completely ignoring them, just as John Henry had been doing since they arrived.

Once back in the truck, Hunter speared him with a look. "Keep your feelings out of this, Hollywood, or you're going to screw it up."

"You think Aaron set the fire?"

"I don't know. He's pretty sure of himself. I can see him getting someone else to do his dirty work for him, though." His cell phone rang, and he put it on speaker. "What do you have, Pete?"

"I'm at Benson's house, and there's no sign of him. According to the housekeeper, she found the boots in the trash and gave them to her sister for her nephew, thinking they were about the right size. Benson hasn't been here in the past two days, and there's no evidence he packed a bag before he left. Housekeeper comes twice a week and says she has no way of knowing when he might have left town."

"Thanks, Pete. Anything else lying around that caught your interest or attention?"

"Negative, but I'll look around some more, just to make sure. No sign of his body, but I'll check the perimeter of the property before I leave."

"We just had a chat with Aaron Atwood. John Henry was there, too, but he had nothing to say."

"Aaron come clean about the ball cap?"

"Danced around it and was pretty damn smug. Made sure we didn't get his prints either."

"That doesn't surprise me, not with the Atwoods."

"We'll keep working all the angles. We stopped by Mama T's, and she had the same flyer about a militia meet and greet that was emailed to Black."

"Hollywood, you and Delilah be careful tonight."

"10-4, Bulldog," Josh said.

Nothing would happen to Delilah. Not on his watch.

─────────────

Delilah glanced in the mirror with equal parts dread and determination. She knew no one would recognize her dressed like this, but deliberately breaching the lion's den of her former life was going to be risky.

She stepped into the living room, chin up, and Josh gave her a thorough once-over. "Perfect." He stepped away from the counter and tipped her chin up. "Besides, everyone thinks you're dead, so no one will be looking for you." He ran his thumb along her jawline, and his calm steadiness settled her. He reached in his pocket and pulled out two plain gold bands. "Before I forget, we're supposed to wear these." Without ceremony, he slid the smaller one on her ring finger and the other on his own.

He looked up, and she swallowed hard as they studied each other. What if they weren't pretending? Apparently, the significance of the gesture wasn't lost on him, either, for his green eyes lost their teasing glint, and Delilah caught a flash of what might have been longing before it disappeared.

He lowered his head, and she thought he was going to kiss her. As his warm breath touched her face, Delilah tilted her face toward his.

At the last second, he pulled back. Green eyes burning with some unnamed emotion, he slowly brushed his lips over her knuckles, sending a little thrill through her.

He stepped back and winked. "Let me change, and we'll go conquer the world, Xena."

The fact that he saw her as a warrior gave her confidence a boost, as did knowing he'd have her back tonight. Still, she wasn't taking any chances. She went into the bedroom and tucked her knife in the pocket of her long skirt. She stashed her gun in her backpack, too, just in case.

Stay strong, Mary. We're coming to find you.

CHAPTER 23

DELILAH'S EYES WIDENED WHEN JOSH EMERGED FROM THE bathroom. Instead of his usual FWC baseball cap, he wore a battered cowboy hat and sported a brown, close-cropped beard. He'd added a pair of thick glasses that completely changed his face. Her eyes traveled down his body, and she realized he was wearing some sort of padding under his loose-fitting shirt. Instead of the clearly delineated muscles she'd spent far too much time drooling over, now he looked middle-aged and lumpy.

He grinned at her appraisal and said, "Jim Brown here, and this is the little woman, Donna."

"Little woman, huh?" she teased. But that was the mindset they were walking into. "Why Brown?"

"Because it's so ordinary, people won't remember it. They'll say, 'What was their name? Something like Smith or Jones or something.' It helps our cover."

"What are you wearing under that shirt?"

A wicked gleam appeared in his eyes. "I'll show you mine if you show me yours." With a laugh, he pulled up the edge of the fabric. "It's a modified Kevlar vest. The padding is thick enough to help protect me but not so stiff that it doesn't look like part of my body."

Delilah shook her head. "I can't believe how different you look."

"Right back at you, Donna, dear." He winked and held the door open so she could precede him. " Let's do this."

On the way to the meeting site, Josh went over their cover story again. "Jim and Donna Brown, just down from Ohio, have been married a little over a year. We met, ironically enough, at a militia meeting, because your family was part of it. We don't like the direction this country is going and worry about our freedoms being taken away, so we decided to embrace the survivalist lifestyle, live in our camper, learn to protect ourselves, and be ready for anything."

"What was my maiden name?" Delilah asked.

He grinned. "Let's keep it simple, Donna Jones."

She nodded and glanced out the window, her mind replaying the long list of things that could go wrong tonight.

As though he could read her mind, he said, "We're going to be fine. People see what they expect to see. Stick with our script, pretend you're really shy, and follow my lead."

The dread persisted, but when they pulled up to Stevens Point, she shoved it aside. She'd been playing a role most of her life. This wasn't any different. She was an expert at being invisible.

There were far more pickup trucks in the clearing than she had expected. Josh parked at the end of a row so they could make a quick getaway if necessary. He reached into the bed of the truck and grabbed two camp chairs and slung them over his shoulder before he took her hand and they headed toward the campfire. It was almost dark, so faces were hard to distinguish. Which kept them concealed but made it harder to recognize others.

As they approached, a tall, thin, middle-aged man with red hair and beard separated himself from a knot of men. "Evening. You folks new here?"

Josh sent the man a warm smile, wrapped an arm around Delilah's waist, and tucked her against his side. "Yes, sir. Me and the missus just came down from Ohio. Looking forward to getting to know some folks here."

The man extended his hand. "Eli Foster. Welcome. I'm one of the organizers. Let me introduce you around."

Mary mentioned a guy named Eli, Delilah thought.

With a hand on Josh's shoulder, Eli steered him toward a group of men, leaving Delilah standing alone. Before she could figure out whether to follow, an older woman with a graying ponytail approached. "Don't worry. Eli won't take him far. I'm Sue, his sister. What's your name?" After Delilah gave it, Sue said, "Let me introduce you to some of the womenfolk."

Delilah found herself surrounded by fifteen women, all of them wearing the same old-fashioned garb, all looking at her curiously. She smiled shyly.

Sue wrapped an arm around her waist. "This here is Donna. She and her man are new."

The women said hello, most of them warm and friendly, but a few looked at her askance. Since she remembered wondering whether a newcomer was friend or foe at gatherings like this during her childhood, Delilah didn't hold it against them. She widened her smile and said, "Thank you. We're glad to be here. I'm looking forward to getting to know you ladies."

Sue invited her to sit beside her, their circle of chairs separate from the main campfire where the men were holding court. Several women came over, and Delilah scrambled to remember everything Mama had taught her about herbs and gardening and favorite recipes.

The conversation flowed around her, easy and light, and when she felt Josh's eyes on her, Delilah glanced toward the men's circle. He smiled and winked, and Delilah ducked her head, blushing like the newlywed she was supposed to be. Good-natured teasing came from several of the ladies.

"Oh, honey," Sue said. "Enjoy those looks while you can." She looked around the circle. "Once the babies start coming, those looks get fewer and farther between."

The other women chuckled, and the conversation continued, but Delilah found her eyes drawn back to Josh again and again. Every time, she found him looking right back at her. With every glance, every secret smile, the line between the part she was playing and reality blurred a little bit more.

———

Josh let the men's conversations flow around him as he pretended to sip a beer.

"Does anyone know who this Black guy was? He wasn't part of us, was he?" a rail-thin man asked. Josh tried to see his face, but it was hidden by the ball cap pulled low over his forehead.

"Paper said he wasn't from around here," a heavy-set bald man offered.

"I heard he had one of the flyers about tonight."

Josh went on alert at that, especially when he recognized County Commissioner Rory Fitzpatrick's voice. He kept his body language loose and casual. That piece of information hadn't been in the paper. So how did Fitzpatrick know about it?

"Maybe he was looking to join up," thin guy said.

"Tallahassee is a long way to come for meetings," bald guy argued.

Aaron Atwood suddenly appeared and exchanged greetings with the men. Josh kept his face in the shadows.

"I want a word with you," Fitzpatrick said quietly, and the two men stepped away from the group. Josh slowly walked past on his way to get another beer so he could hear their conversation. "What the hell happened out there, Atwood? Black was found near your family's old campsite. And I can't get hold of Benson."

"What makes you think I had anything to do with it?"

Fitzpatrick clenched his fists. "Don't you go acting all innocent, Atwood. I want to know what happened, and I want to know where Benson is."

Aaron didn't raise his voice. Actually, none of it seemed to affect him in the least. "I don't know, as I wasn't there when Black was killed. You want to know more, find Benson. I'd be interested in his story, too." With that, Aaron walked back over to the group, and Josh casually rejoined them as well. Interesting that Fitzpatrick didn't know where Benson was, either.

A few minutes later, another man joined them, and tension

suddenly crackled in the air. Men eased away from Aaron as the newcomer entered the circle, and the two men faced each other. The other man stuck out his hand. "Glad you could make it tonight, Atwood. Always good to see you. Is John Henry here, too?"

Aaron ignored the outstretched hand and stepped closer, hands on his hips. "What were you thinking, sending out flyers and starting a Facebook page, for cripes' sake? Do you want every fish cop in the state trying to shut us down?"

"We aren't doing anything wrong, just gathering with like-minded individuals. Nothing wrong with people knowing we're a welcoming group."

"We fly under the radar. We don't put up neon signs announcing our presence."

"This is the way of the future. Time to use social media to our advantage. I say we make our presence known." He scanned the men around him, nodding to those who murmured agreement.

Aaron simply stood, arms folded, vibrating with fury.

John Henry appeared next to his son, put a hand on his arm in some sort of signal, and extended a hand to the other man. "Good to see you tonight."

The other man returned the handshake before he turned to the group. "Gentlemen, please excuse us a moment. John Henry and I need to discuss his daughter's wedding."

Josh followed them as far as he could without being completely obvious, but he still couldn't hear what they were saying. *Damn.*

Delilah kept waiting for an official meeting to start, but none did. As the night got darker, Sue led her over to a dessert table, and she spotted Aaron pulling beer from a cooler. Nerves hummed under her skin, but she relaxed a bit when she realized Josh was watching him closely. She didn't see Mama or Mary, but she turned her chair so she could keep an eye on both circles.

When the first notes of a fiddle echoed through the night, it was met with hoots and hollers and loud applause. "Grab your chair," Sue instructed as the women joined the men's circle. The fiddle was joined by a banjo, a harmonica, and even a washtub.

Voices joined in, and soon the traditional songs of her childhood drifted through the forest. Delilah's throat closed up as memories assailed her, of her father laughing and smiling at Mama as he swung her around the dance floor. Delilah found herself missing that man in ways she never had before.

She swallowed hard and set her chair just beyond the makeshift dance floor, eyes averted. She tapped her toe in time to the music, clapping as the dancers swung and spun, the ladies' dresses belling out. After a rousing rendition of "Don't Sit Under the Apple Tree," the band swung into "Tennessee Waltz."

"May I have this dance, Mrs. Brown?" Josh asked, bending down beside her.

Delilah saw the invitation in his green eyes as he held out a hand. She slowly put hers into it, finding it harder and harder to keep her emotional distance. Once they reached the dance floor, he turned her toward him and pulled her close, one hand at the small of her back, the other folding her hand in his much larger one. He started moving in time to the music, and with every step, he shifted her closer.

Delilah looked over his shoulder and almost tripped over her own feet. As though her memories had conjured him, she spotted her father at the edge of the crowd, clapping in time to the music. Past and present collided, and she stumbled again, desperate suddenly to stay out of his line of sight.

"Relax, Delilah," he whispered in her ear. "This won't work if you look like you're trying to escape."

If it wasn't all so convoluted, she'd have laughed. She did want to escape. The situation, not him. But she had a part to play tonight, so she took a deep breath and relaxed in his embrace, her head on his shoulder. His arm tightened around her, and she let everything go except the feel of him holding her, the music flowing around them, the smell of the campfire and the crackling flames.

Suddenly, the crowd parted like the Red Sea, and a deep voice said, "Evening, everyone."

Delilah's head almost snapped up, but Josh kept a firm hand on her neck. Despite the warmth radiating from him, her blood turned to ice.

She knew that voice.

"Just keep dancing, Delilah," Josh whispered. "We've got this."

Her heart pounded until she was sure everyone around them could hear it. She realized her breath was coming in short pants and forced herself to slow it down. She couldn't blow it now.

She kept her eyes averted as the man tapped Josh on the shoulder. "You folks new here?"

He stopped moving but tucked Delilah against him, keeping her face in the shadows. "I'm Jim Brown, this here is the missus." He held out his hand to the other man. Delilah held her breath.

"Nathan Hamm, but my friends call me Nate," he said.

"He's the one who organized tonight's little get-together," Eli added from beside him.

Delilah willed herself to stand still and not look up. When the man thrust a hand in her direction, she shook it firmly, head down.

"The wife and I just moved down from Ohio, and we're looking to meet some like-minded folks."

"Then you've come to the right place. We're happy to have you."

The conversation swirled around her, but only one thing registered. Nate was here. *Oh, God.* When she'd heard no mention of his name, she thought he'd left town. What would he do if he found out she was back? Far more terrifying, had he acquired another child bride and subjected her to the kind of "love" he'd tried to force on her? Was it even possible he was Mary's groom?

It was suddenly too much. She mumbled, "Excuse me," and

rushed past the edge of the crowd and threw up in the bushes. She heard laughter behind her and then Nate's voice. "Looks like maybe the missus has a bun in the oven."

"Nothing would make me happier," Josh responded. "But if you folks will excuse us, I think we'll head home."

"Here's my email address," Nate said. "Get in touch, and I'll make sure we keep you up-to-date on what our plans are."

"Appreciate that. Good night, all."

Delilah felt rather than heard Josh step up behind her. He thrust a handkerchief in front of her, and she sent him a grateful glance as she used it to wipe her mouth. "Sorry about that."

He didn't say anything for several seconds, just watched her. "Are you all right?" His voice was quiet, concerned.

Her stomach gave another lurch, and she wrapped her arms around her middle as she stood. "I will be. Can we get out of here?"

"Of course." He tucked her against him as they made their way around the outside of the crowd. Eli Foster intercepted them, holding both their chairs. "Nice to have met you folks. Hope we'll see more of you."

Once they reached the truck, Delilah sank back against the seat and willed the churning in her stomach to stop.

Dear God. Nate is still in town.

Josh watched Delilah's eyes slide closed and temporarily shelved his need to question. He'd learned some interesting things tonight, not the least of which was County Commissioner Rory Kilpatrick's conversation with Aaron. But he was more concerned about her.

When he pulled into their campsite, he laid a gentle hand on her arm, and she startled awake, eyes wide. "We're home. Let me check the camper first."

Once he gave the all clear, she hurried past him, straight toward the bedroom.

He stepped in her path. "Are you okay?"

"I will be. I'll see you in the morning."

He settled his hands on her shoulders, rubbed the tight muscles. "Talk to me, please." He'd noticed she retreated into herself when she was shaken, but she needed to talk, even if she didn't realize it. This hunched, frightened version was not the Delilah he was getting to know. That Nate could do this to her, after all these years, made him see red.

She sighed. "Let me get out of this getup."

He made coffee, then booted up his laptop and grabbed the tub of chocolate chip cookies Charlee had sent along. He'd completed a background check and was on his third cookie by the time Delilah ventured out of the bathroom and sank down across from him at the dinette.

"Coffee?" he asked.

"Sure. Thanks." She wrapped her hands around the mug as though trying to warm them.

"I'm guessing you haven't seen your erstwhile groom in eight years."

"No. There's been no mention of him anywhere since I've been back. I'd hoped he'd left town." She studied her coffee cup. "He didn't have a beard before, but I'd recognize him anywhere."

"Is the scar on his cheek courtesy of Xena?"

Her chin came up. "Yes. I was desperate to get away."

He leaned forward and wrapped his hands around hers. "Good! I hope that bastard thinks of you every time he looks in the mirror."

She froze. "That's what I'm worried about."

"What do you mean?"

"My engagement to him was part of some business deal between him and John Henry. When I disappeared before the wedding, he would have been royally ticked off and would have taken it out on my father. He's the sort to hold a grudge, so if he finds out I'm alive…" She shook her head. "There's no telling what he'll do."

He tilted her chin up, furious at the anxiety shimmering in the blue depths of her eyes. "He will not hurt you again, Delilah. I will make sure of it. Don't let him do this to you. Don't let him make you afraid."

Flames suddenly shot from her eyes, and she jerked her chin away and jabbed a finger at him. "Don't you dare say things like that to me. You're strong and male and can protect yourself. You don't know what it's like to be overpowered and trapped and terrified, afraid for your life. So don't you dare tell me how to react. You have no idea what you're talking about." She huffed out a breath.

Pride shot through him. *Damn, she is incredible when she shows her power.* Eyes flashing, shoulders back, she looked ready to take on the world.

"There's the Xena I know." Then he sobered abruptly, captured her hands again. "But you're right; I don't know. I'm so sorry you went through that, especially as a teen. And I'm furious your family didn't protect you. I'll make sure you never have to deal with him again. I'm also going to make sure he gets what he deserves." When she winced, he realized he'd squeezed her fingers harder than he intended.

She met his gaze, eyes still spitting blue flames. "No. You're not doing anything. It's over, and it was too long ago to do anything legal about anyway. I checked."

"I can check on a civil—"

Her chin came up, and this time, she clamped down on *his* fingers. "Let it go. I've moved on. My focus is on making sure Mary is never in the same situation."

He snorted. "The guy shows up and you puke. How is that moving on?"

"You don't understand." Delilah's voice had an edge he'd never heard before.

"Then explain it to me. Why won't you go after him?"

"Even if legal action were possible, I don't want to relive it all for months on end, especially when it amounts to nothing more than a she said, he said situation. I won't put myself through that. I'm going to do whatever it takes to get Mary safely away from all of this and then move on with my life." Her eyes drilled into his. "That's my choice." She took a sip of her coffee. "Did you learn anything else tonight that might help us find her?"

He accepted the change in topic. "Hamm said he had to talk to John Henry about his daughter's upcoming wedding."

Delilah's jaw clenched. "Did he say anything else? Tell you who she's marrying? It's not Nate, is it?"

"I don't know. I tried to get close enough, but they moved out of earshot. And just so you know, sometime after we find Mary, Hamm is going to get a beating he will never ever forget. It's that or I shoot his balls off." He shrugged. "Either way, nobody treats my Xena like that and gets away with it."

Her eyes widened, and then she huffed out a laugh, shaking her head. "I never know what to expect from you, Hollywood."

He sobered. "Start by expecting respect, and we'll go from there, okay?"

She nodded and set her cup in the sink, swaying slightly from exhaustion. "I'm done. Good night." She paused by the bedroom door. "And thank you."

He waited until the bedroom door closed before he stormed outside. It had taken every ounce of his self-control to keep his fury under wraps, but now he muttered and paced, fists clenched. He'd make sure Nathan Hamm got his.

After he'd calmed slightly, he called Hunter and told him about seeing Commissioner Kilpatrick at tonight's gathering. "Aaron and John Henry Atwood also made an appearance, but Aaron disappeared before I could follow him. And interestingly enough, I heard a few men arguing about the risks of drawing attention to their group via the Mayor's Ball."

"Isn't that interesting," Hunter responded. "Any weapons talk connected to the ball? Or any kind of protest?"

"No. It sounded like they were going to talk up their group, if you can believe that."

"At a ball? That's not the usual MO for groups like this, especially at a political fund-raiser. Good thing you'll be there in your monkey suit to figure out what's going on, Hollywood."

Josh snorted. "Thanks for that. In the meantime, I'm going to dig deep into Nathan Hamm's background. He seems to be the head of this new group. He also has ties to Delilah's family. And he mentioned Mary's wedding, but I couldn't get any details."

"That's more than we had before. Let me know what else you turn up."

"Of course. I'll be in touch."

He rubbed the wedding band with his thumb, remembering the look in Delilah's eyes when he'd slipped hers on her finger, but then he shoved that thought firmly away. Whatever was between them had to wait. His priority right now was keeping her safe. He went back inside and pulled out the sofa-bed, imagining all sorts of ways Nathan Hamm would pay for what he'd done.

CHAPTER 24

DELILAH HAD EXPECTED TO FALL ASLEEP IMMEDIATELY, BUT she kept replaying her conversation with Josh, and she wasn't happy about what it said about her. She couldn't deny that seeing Nate had rattled her. But had he made her afraid, as Josh said? She hated to admit it, but in that moment, yes. Suddenly she was sixteen again, helpless and terrified.

But she wasn't that girl anymore, and she had to keep living like she believed it. Despite Josh's desire to protect her, which touched something deep inside her, she'd also learned that her safety, physical and emotional, was ultimately up to her.

Her worry now was for Mary, a bone-deep determination to keep her from the same hellacious situation.

But were her old fears sabotaging her relationship with Josh? In an effort to play it safe emotionally, was she depriving them both? If they got involved, saying goodbye would be brutal. Oh, who was she kidding? It would be anyway. So why not enjoy every minute they had together?

She tiptoed into the living room, worried he might have fallen asleep already. Seeing him sprawled across the middle of the sofa bed, blanket bunched around his hips, made her want to touch.

As she approached, he sat up, scrubbed a hand over his face, and held out a hand in invitation. "Everything okay?" The husky timbre of his voice slid over her skin like a caress.

"It is now," she whispered as she climbed onto the bed and sat beside him. She cupped his jaw and brushed a kiss over his lips, once, twice, before she pulled back.

In the dim light, she saw the question in his eyes, the barely banked fire. "Tell me what you want," he whispered, pulling her close and kissing her, long and slow and deep.

When they pulled apart, she studied him a moment. What she wanted was him, with a desperation that frightened her, but she couldn't offer forever, wouldn't weave fantasies that could never come true. But she could give him honesty. "You know I'm not staying in Ocala. I can't. But what if we make the most of the time we have?"

Their eyes met, and the silence lengthened as he studied her. "You're sure?"

She ran the back of her hand down his cheek and smiled. "I'm sure."

He leaned closer and tucked her hair behind her ear, his voice a low rumble. "Then let me love you tonight, and we'll let tomorrow take care of itself."

When his lips met hers, they slipped into that magical world where only the two of them existed. His tongue swept into her mouth and shut down her busy brain. All that existed were him and her and this moment.

She cupped his cheeks as she kissed him, determined to show him all the feelings she couldn't put into words. Hands tangled in his hair, she gave him everything in her heart, and he did the same. Her eyes slid closed as he nuzzled her neck, then ran a line of kisses down her arm before he placed a tender kiss in her palm. She took his hand and did the same, the green fire in his eyes scorching everywhere it touched.

Their mouths met again, and their tongues danced, the heat in her belly coiling tighter and tighter. Frustrated that she still couldn't get close enough to him, she swung her leg over and straddled his lap, enjoying his low moan when she settled over him, running her hands over his shoulders and chest, enjoying the feel of the crisp hair covering his pecs.

"I like the way you think, Xena," he murmured and pulled her flush against him.

She sighed and nibbled the side of his neck, enjoying the idea that she could make him moan. His hands slid under her sleep shirt, and this time, she was the one who moaned.

"You feel good," she said, running her tongue along his collarbone, then nipping his ear.

"I was thinking the same thing about you," he said, then gripped the edges of her shirt, yanked it over her head, and tossed it away. "You take my breath away." He studied her, trailing a hand from her neck to her waist and back again, touching and caressing along the way. Heat spiraled through her, and she pulled him closer, shifting restlessly.

"Hold that thought," he muttered, then reached over the side of the bed for his pants. Once he found what he needed, he pulled her down to stretch out over him, and she sighed at the feel of his body under her.

With every touch, every caress, every slide of skin against skin, the heat built as their kisses grew more frantic, more desperate. He gripped her backside while their tongues tangled, fought.

Finally, when she thought she couldn't stand it another minute, he threaded his fingers through hers. "Look at me," he ordered, and she met his eyes. Gazes locked, they climbed to the stars together, higher and higher, until they reached the heavens and shattered in a burst of light.

A long time later, when their heartbeats had returned to normal, he pulled the covers over them and tucked her against his side.

"Sleep, Xena. I've got you."

"And I've got you," she murmured and burrowed closer. She listened to the steady beat of his heart and slid into a deep, dreamless sleep.

———

Several hours later, Josh's eyes snapped open. He woke completely alert, as always, but it took a second to identify where he was and the warm body snuggled in close to him, her arm across his belly, her hair tickling his cheek. He grinned. He could get used to this.

Or not.

He frowned as he watched her sleep, the furrow between her brows gone, all her sharp edges erased for the moment.

I'm not staying...

She'd warned him, had been up front about their relationship or whatever the hell she wanted to call it, and he'd agreed to her terms.

His gut clenched. He'd been a fool. Somehow, when he wasn't paying attention, she'd snuck past all his defenses.

She stiffened suddenly and started shifting restlessly, caught in the midst of a nightmare. He tightened his hold on her and murmured soothing words in her ear until she calmed again and settled back into sleep.

He watched her as the minutes ticked by, running his hand up and down her arm as he absorbed the fact that her happiness, her safety, meant everything to him. Ready or not and despite all her secrets, she'd burrowed into his heart, way down deep, to a place no one had ever touched before.

As he tucked the covers over them both, he decided he had neither the strength nor the desire to push her out. Ever.

And he was okay with that.

Now all he had to do was keep her alive while they rescued her sister.

And then figure out how to let her go.

―――――――

The sun was barely up when she woke, and it took a moment to figure out where she was. Josh was gone, but she heard his voice outside, probably on the phone. She stretched, then sighed, remembering the way he'd made love to her during the night, the way he'd held her close. But it went deeper than that. Nobody had ever seen her the way he did, had ever touched her with such tenderness and want. When worries about how she would ever manage to say goodbye tried to intrude, she locked them away to think about some other time.

Today was Sunday. If all went well, Mary would be safely in her arms in just a few hours. She sent up a quick prayer. *Please God, let her show up.*

She grabbed a shower, packed her research gear, and headed to the kitchen. "I'll go crazy sitting here all morning, so how about we check on my favorite monkey troop after breakfast?"

"Good morning to you, too," he drawled, leaning against the counter sipping coffee. He was already fully dressed, and Delilah hid her disappointment. Though the way that T-shirt molded to his chest offered ample compensation.

She walked over, gave him a long, lingering kiss. "Sorry. Good morning. I'm a little wound up."

"Do you still want coffee, then?"

"Oh, I'm never that wound." She smiled and reached past him for a mug, brushing a hand along his jaw as she did.

After breakfast, they drove to the same location as before, but it took longer to find the troop, since they'd moved much farther into the forest. As before, Josh kept his eyes on their surroundings while Delilah pulled out her camera and started cataloguing the monkeys' faces.

"Did you name them all?" he asked after he overheard her talking to them.

She flushed. "Not all. Several of the alpha males, certainly, some of the females. But mostly the little ones."

"I'm onto you, Miss Atwood. It's not really about research. You're just a sucker for an adorable monkey face."

She lowered her camera. "Busted. Aren't they sweet?" She showed him several pictures of Oscar, then sobered. "But I still can't find the mothers. It's like they've vanished."

"You're absolutely sure?"

She drew a shaky breath. "As sure as I can be. Not only are those four gone, but two more are missing."

"Mothers?"

"Yes. It looks like two of the other mothers adopted the infants." She scrolled through her photos. "See, they've each got two now, where they only had one before."

Josh scrubbed his chin. "Hunter checked. Nobody has a permit to trap them out here. Let's see if there is any more evidence of humans in the area before we go."

There wasn't, but that didn't make Delilah feel any better.

"We'll get our biologist to check it out, see if he can give us any answers," Josh said as they returned to the truck.

When they reached the main road, they had barely enough time to get to the church before services let out. Josh reached over the truck's console and gripped her hand. "Breathe. It'll be okay."

Worry hummed under her skin. "What if she can't get away? What if John Henry—"

He gave her hand an extra squeeze. "Let's just get there first."

They parked in the dense forest and quietly wound their way to the secluded clearing she and Mary used to disappear to.

Josh propped one leg on the log where Delilah sat, leaned on his forearm as he looked around. "Why this spot?"

She smiled. "As soon as the preacher said amen, the men would congregate outside on one side of the church and the women on the other, and rather than stand around in the heat, starving, Mary and I would sneak into the woods until we heard Mama calling. It was cooler here and quieter, and as a bonus, it kept me from getting recruited to help with canning and birthing." She shuddered. "And from getting shanghaied into babysitting or meal prep duty for moms who had just given birth."

"I take it those weren't your favorite assignments?"

Delilah shook her head, remembering. "I'd much rather fish or be part of target practice. But I only got to do those things when we were alone. Otherwise, things were strictly divided along male-female roles."

"Have you really helped deliver a baby?"

Just as she opened her mouth to respond, she heard a *whooshing* noise. Without thought, she dropped down beside the log. Josh landed on top of her, covering her with his body.

They stayed that way for several seconds before Delilah raised her head. She locked eyes with him, and they both looked up and spotted it at the same time.

There was a knife embedded in the tree just beyond where they had been sitting. Had they not ducked, it would have hit one of them.

"Stay down." Josh crouched by the log, weapon drawn, prepared to head into the forest.

"Mary! Let's go. What are you doing out here?"

At the sound of John Henry's angry growl, Delilah froze. Had he followed her? She waited, heart pounding.

"I'm sorry, Papa. I was just taking a walk."

Delilah's heart clenched at the way her sister's voice shook.

"You know better than to disappear without permission."

This was her chance. Delilah opened her backpack and closed her hand around her gun. She'd force him to let Mary go. Right now. She lurched to her feet, gun down at her side, ready to burst out of the trees and get her sister.

From somewhere nearby, she heard pounding feet and children's laughter as they ran by.

She hadn't taken more than a single step when Josh wrapped his arms around her from behind and pulled her back against his chest. She elbowed him in the ribs and tried to break free, but he simply tightened his hold. "Let me go," she hissed. "What are you doing?"

His voice was quiet in her ear. "Too many people. Children. And whoever threw that knife is probably still out here."

She hadn't considered any of that, all her focus on Mary. Had John Henry thrown the knife, knowing Mary was coming to meet her? That didn't make sense. So it had to be someone else. If Delilah showed herself, would whoever it was hurt her sister? Or the children?

More childish giggles rang out, and she froze. *Oh God. She couldn't get her sister without risking innocent lives.* With every passing second, Mary and John Henry's voices faded, and her window of opportunity disappeared.

Delilah stepped out of Josh's arms, saw the way he eyed her gun, and anger flared, hot and bright. Right. FWC officer. He couldn't stand by and watch her threaten her father at gunpoint. Dammit. Another reason she shouldn't have gotten involved with him. She squeezed her eyes shut, beyond frustrated with him, herself, the whole freaking situation.

She tucked her weapon in her backpack, cataloguing options, searching for another way to rescue her sister.

Josh pulled gloves and a plastic bag from one of the pockets of his cargo pants. After a quick look around, he stepped over to the tree and quickly bagged the knife. "Let's find a better hiding place. Whoever threw this will be coming back to see what he hit. I want to be ready."

Delilah marched after him, and they crouched in the bushes for almost an hour, but no one showed up. Frustrated anger still churned under her skin when Josh stood and pulled her up beside him, apology thick in his expression. "I'm sorry."

Without a word, she headed for his truck. Logic told her he'd done the right thing, but she still wasn't feeling very logical. She only knew Mary had been close enough to touch and she'd lost her chance.

———

Neither said a word as they waited outside the community center. Delilah used the time to wrestle her frustration under control and think about her upcoming meeting with Mama. Would she be able to convince her?

When her mother appeared, Delilah's heart clenched. She looked so much older than her years. Her life was not an easy one, and her body bore the evidence.

"What are you hoping to accomplish?" Josh asked quietly as she opened her door.

She glanced over her shoulder, ignored the caring in his expression. "Ideally, Mama will agree to help me get Mary away from the campsite. But I'm not holding my breath on that one," she added when Josh started to protest. "If not that, I want to know who they're marrying her off to."

"You'll try to convince the groom to back out of the deal?"

Delilah kept her expression bland. "Something like that. Though I don't figure this scumbag will want to give up his child bride willingly," she muttered.

"You know you can't just pull a gun—"

Delilah held up a hand. "Do not tell me what I can and cannot do. I am going to keep my sister from getting married at sixteen. End of story."

"It's not the end of the story and you know it. I said I'd help. But you have to follow—"

Delilah missed whatever else he said, because she slid out of the truck and slammed the door. Let Mr. By-the-Book do things his way. She'd make her own plans.

At the door to the clinic, she paused and took a deep breath before she walked inside. Then another. Honesty forced her to admit that her anger at Josh was misplaced. She was beyond furious with her father and the whole situation. Josh was just a convenient target. And that wasn't fair to him. At all.

She forced a smile at the older woman who manned the receptionist desk. "Good afternoon. I'm here to see Kimberly Gaines."

"I'm sorry, but Ms. Gaines is currently with another patient," the woman said.

"Yes, I know. I'm supposed to be part of that meeting. Thank you." She strode down the hall and straight into Kimberly's office, closing the door behind her before the woman could cause a ruckus.

"Hello, Ms…ah…Kimberly."

Hello, Mama." She leaned down to her mother's chair and gave her a quick hug.

After a stunned moment of disbelief, Mama hopped up and wrapped Delilah in a fierce hug. "Oh, baby girl. I thought you were dead." Tears poured down her cheeks as she pulled back and cupped Delilah's face with her warm hands. "You're okay. Oh, thank you, Jesus, you're okay."

Delilah met Kimberly's chiding expression. She'd totally forgotten that her mother thought she had died, too. She'd always felt socially inept, like she regularly missed social cues, but never more so than now. "I'm sorry you thought I was dead, Mama."

"But why are you letting people think that?"

Again, she and Kimberly exchanged looks. Could she trust Mama? How much would she feel compelled to tell John Henry? "It's better this way."

"Better for whom? What's going on, Delilah?"

"Why don't we sit down and talk this through?" Kimberly ushered them to the sagging love seat while she took the chair opposite.

Delilah opened her mouth, but all her carefully rehearsed words didn't seem appropriate. Or maybe they were, since the bottom line was the same. "I need to talk to you about Mary." Delilah leaned forward and grabbed both of Mama's work-worn hands in her own. "She's only sixteen, Mama. It's too young to get married. She wants to go to school and be independent and choose her own husband someday when she's ready. Can you understand that?" she asked gently.

Mama waved that away. "She doesn't know her own mind. She needs a strong man to guide her, to help her mature and give her the chance to be a mother."

Delilah's stomach turned at hearing the exact same words Mama had said to her so many years ago. Words John Henry had clearly drilled into her. "Wouldn't it be better for her to make her own choices? When she's older and does know her own mind? Don't you want that for her?"

Mama reared back as though Delilah had slapped her. "You don't think I want what's best for my daughters? I've spent my whole life trying to do right by my family."

"I've never doubted your love for us, Mama. Not once. But right now, if you love Mary, you need to convince Papa to call this off."

All the color drained from Mama's face. She gripped her hands together and looked away, and Delilah's hope sank.

"Your father makes the decisions he thinks are best. It is my job to support them."

"Even if he's wrong? Even if this is a terrible idea?" Mentioning it was also illegal wouldn't help.

"Eli is a good man. He'll take good care of Mary."

"Eli Foster?" she asked. Nausea threatened as Delilah pictured the tall, middle-aged man they'd met at the campfire putting his hands on her sister.

"He's a good man, Delilah," her mother repeated. "His son needs a mother. And Mary needs a firm hand." Then her chin came up, and accusation filled her eyes. "When you turned your back on Nate, you brought shame to our family. This is your father's chance to make it right. John Henry needs to reclaim his place in our world. Mary is the key to that."

Delilah gripped Mama's hands, hard. "Don't allow this, Mama. It's not right. Please, let Mary come live with me."

Mama stood and grabbed the straps of her purse, chin up. "I will not go against my husband's wishes. And I will not interfere between a husband and his wife. I'm very glad you're okay." She turned toward the door.

"Wait. When is the wedding?"

Mama paused, hand on the doorknob. She didn't turn, just whispered, "On her birthday," and then left.

Delilah tried to follow, but Kimberly stopped her with a hand on her arm. "Let her go. She won't listen, not now."

Delilah spun and slammed a hand against the wall. That was the second time today Mary had slipped through her fingers.

Kimberly wrapped her arms around her, and Delilah stiffened. She didn't need comfort. She needed a plan. "We'll figure it out. We'll figure it out," Kimberly murmured.

When Kimberly finally released her, Delilah said, "Thank you for trying to help. I need to go."

She hurried out of the building and didn't stop until she climbed into the cab of Josh's truck. He sent her a sympathetic glance, put the truck in gear, and headed out of the parking lot.

Her mother's predictable response shouldn't hurt as much as it did. She rubbed a hand over the ache in her heart and focused on finding another way to get her sister. She wouldn't stop until she did.

They only had four more days.

———

Josh watched her ruthlessly bring her emotions under control. He hadn't expected the meeting to go well and figured she hadn't either. But his heart still hurt at the anguish etched in her face.

"What are we doing here?" she asked as he pulled up at his place. Judging by the vehicles, the rest of the squad had already arrived.

"Quick strategy meeting to go over details for the Mayor's Ball tomorrow night. County Commissioner Benson is slated to be the master of ceremonies, but no one has seen him in two days."

Delilah nodded and climbed out of the truck, her mind obviously elsewhere.

"Look, about before—" he began, but she didn't let him finish.

"I understand that you were trying to protect me—and Mary. I do." She huffed out a breath, sighed. "Let's just move on, okay?"

He narrowed his eyes, and his radar twitched at how easily she let him off the hook.

Once inside, Josh recapped what happened outside the church, and Sanchez offered to check the knife for prints and see if it matched the one used in Black's murder.

"I'm sorry you couldn't get your sister to come with you," Fish said.

Delilah looked surprised, then nodded her thanks.

Hunter spoke up. "We think it's time to shake a few trees, see what falls out. Commissioner Benson's secretary said he's checked in by phone, so he's alive, but he's not returning our phone calls. We're hoping to question him at the ball. In the meantime, we're still picking up rumors about gun shipments and trying to figure out if either of those things are connected to Black's death." He nodded to Josh. "Hollywood discovered that Nathan Hamm is a big contributor to Commissioner Benson's reelection campaign. So is Eli Foster, although he's not given nearly as much."

Delilah's eyebrows shot to her hairline. "You're saying these two antigovernment types are now going to balls and contributing to election campaigns? That makes no sense."

"Agreed. It's out of character, which means there has to be some agenda we don't know about." Hunter leaned forward. "We believe you're the thread that connects it all. If you're willing, we're going to send you to the ball as Josh's date. We're hoping the shock of seeing you alive will loosen a few tongues." He quirked a smile. "A generous dose of free alcohol never hurts, either."

She looked around the room, then back at Hunter, and a

calculating expression darted over her features. "What about the rest of the team?"

"Everyone else will be working security. And we'll be keeping a close eye on you. Don't worry. You'll be perfectly safe."

"All right. I'm in."

Her calm acceptance confirmed his suspicions. Josh tried to catch her eye, but she avoided his gaze. She was hatching a plan in that beautiful head of hers. He just had to figure out what it was before she put herself in danger.

CHAPTER 25

DELILAH KNEW SHE'D GO STARK RAVING MAD—OR COMPLETELY give herself away—if she hung around all day, so while Josh was in a squad meeting, she quickly slipped into the forest. It didn't make sense that the mama monkeys would leave their infants without good reason. She hadn't found any bodies, thank God, and no evidence that anyone was trapping them. So where were they?

She parked and then hiked to where she and Josh had seen the troop before, but they weren't anywhere around. Which wasn't unusual, as they regularly roamed over a pretty large area. She hiked a good half mile in every direction before she gave up. More worried than before, she headed back to her truck.

By six o'clock that evening, she'd forced everything aside except tonight's mission. Her plan would only work if the timing was just right.

Earlier, she and Josh had met the squad at Charlee's cottage as they reviewed last-minute details and tested earbuds and equipment.

But now, as Josh sauntered into the room wearing a perfectly tailored black tuxedo and crisp white shirt, she sucked in an audible breath. He looked that good. *Be still, my pounding heart.*

The rest of the squad looked pretty amazing, too, and Delilah felt a little overwhelmed by all the blatant maleness on display. She saw the way Charlee looked at Hunter and figured the look on her face was an exact match. Like she could eat Josh with a spoon.

He had been sending her speculative glances all afternoon, as though he was trying to read her mind. She sent him a flirty little smile, the way she'd seen Charlee do to Hunter, and watched as his eyes widened and the dimple popped out on his cheek. That should distract him.

"I'll see you at the ball, Cinderella," he said and placed a quick kiss on her cheek. "Let me know when you're in the parking lot," he added before he walked out the door. The squad was heading over early to be sure everything was set, and she'd meet him there later.

To keep her nerves at bay, she curled up on the sofa with her laptop and typed up some research notes while she waited for Fish, who'd run out earlier to exchange her ball gown for one in Delilah's size.

She finally closed her laptop, unable to concentrate, and replayed yesterday's conversation with her mother. Again. She'd known Mama's loyalty to her husband was unshakable, but she had hoped that worry for Mary's future would push her to take action. It hadn't been enough when Delilah was sixteen, so it shouldn't have been such a painful shock now. But the hurt cut deep.

Despite what Josh claimed, rescuing Mary was ultimately up to her. She reached into her tote bag and opened the fancy clutch she'd borrowed from Kimberly, reassured by the feel of her Glock inside. She tucked her keys in, too, glad they'd hidden her truck behind Charlee's cottage after her camper burned.

Fish burst in with the ball gown and a toiletry bag, and Delilah jumped. "Sorry it took so long. Traffic on Silver Springs Boulevard was a nightmare." Fish headed down the hall.

Yummy smells said Charlee was in the kitchen, baking. Delilah's heart rate sped up. It was time. She followed Fish into the bedroom and gasped when the other woman unzipped the garment bag. "Oh, wow. That's gorgeous." Navy-blue lace covered the slim column of fabric, and she reached a hand out to touch.

One corner of Fish's mouth quirked up. "All I can say is better you than me." She handed the toiletry bag over. "The woman at the cosmetics counter said this is everything you need for a nighttime formal." Fish rolled her eyes.

Delilah took the bag and poked at the eyeliner and dark shadow, deep lipstick and bronzing powder. Worlds away from the barely there makeup she usually wore. "Thanks for getting all this. I wouldn't have known where to start." She sat down at Charlee's small dressing table and spent the next twenty minutes layering on more makeup than she'd ever worn in her life. She studied the results, pleased. Her eyes look bluer than she'd ever seen them, her cheekbones more defined. She wondered what Josh would say.

Fish had been leaning against the wall, watching her as they chatted while she primped. When Delilah added the last spritz of hair spray, she turned serious, eyes narrowed. "What are you planning to do once you get there?"

Delilah stilled, and their eyes met in the mirror. "What I've been trying to do all along. Stop my sister's wedding."

"How specifically do you plan to do that?"

Delilah hitched up her chin. "I'm going to corner Eli Foster. Get him to see the benefits of calling off the wedding."

"And if he won't?"

"I'll offer him money."

"If that doesn't work, then what?" Fish demanded, eyebrows raised.

Delilah looked away, then back at the determined cop. "Whatever it takes to keep her from 'marrying' the scumbag in an illegal ceremony! She's only sixteen!" Her voice came out louder than she intended.

Sure enough, they heard footsteps in the hallway, and then Charlee barged into the room. "What's going on? Why aren't you both dressed yet?"

After a long beat, Fish said, "We just had a few details to talk through." She went to the closet and pulled out her black pantsuit.

Charlee looked from one to the other, but neither offered more information. "Fine. Let's get this show on the road, or you'll both be late."

Once Charlee zipped her into the navy-blue ball gown, Delilah turned toward the mirror. The lacey fabric hugged every curve and made her feel both sexy and exceedingly self-conscious. She'd never worn anything even remotely like this. Every inch of the gown was designed to garner male attention, and she worried if she breathed too deeply, she'd pop right out of the low-cut bodice. She tugged and pulled, biting her lip, but Charlee brushed her hands away.

"Stop. You look amazing. Josh is going to swallow his tongue when he sees you."

Her grin started another flock of butterflies swooping in Delilah's stomach, so she focused on walking in high-heeled sandals. After three turns around Charlee's tiny living room, she thought maybe she could walk without falling flat on her face. *Focus on your mission. Ignore it if anyone stares. It's just another role to play.* The lecture didn't help.

Fish walked out of the bedroom in her sedate black pantsuit, tucking her weapon into her shoulder holster. "Are you ready?"

She took a deep breath. "Ready."

Charlee put her hands on Delilah's shoulders. "You're going to be fine. Fish, Josh, and the rest of the squad will make sure of it." She glanced at Fish. "You have an extra earbud for her?"

"Absolutely. You going to be okay here by yourself?" Fish asked.

Charlee grimaced. "It still feels really weird not to be part of the squad, but I'm getting used to it. Besides, I have a hot date with my parents and a deck of cards tonight."

Delilah climbed in her truck, then followed Fish to the hotel in Ocala where the ball was being held. Charlee hadn't realized that mention of the squad wasn't reassuring. Delilah was more concerned about avoiding them.

When she reached the ballroom doors, she took a cautious breath as she tugged on the bodice, then squared her shoulders and headed inside.

The girl who'd always been invisible was about to make a grand entrance.

━━━━━━━━

"Anyone got eyes on Benson yet?" Hunter asked.

A chorus of nos responded.

"Where the hell is he?" Josh growled. "He's the MC, for cripes' sake."

"Relax, Hollywood," Hunter murmured in his ear.

Josh scanned the crowd and forced a polite smile at the older woman headed his way. Hunter was right. He had to chill or he would draw attention to himself. But he couldn't escape the nagging feeling that Delilah was up to something. Until he knew what that something was, he couldn't focus, and that could put all of them in danger.

"Well now, young man, don't you look lovely tonight."

Josh flipped through his mental files, trying to remember if he knew this woman or not, but came up blank. The scent of Chanel No. 5 applied with a liberal hand wafted up as she leaned closer and patted his arm, her age-spotted hand adorned with expensive rings. "Seeing a young, handsome buck like you reminds me of my Melvin. We lost him last year, God rest his soul, and I miss him, especially on nights like this."

Josh smiled kindly. "I'm sure you were the belle of the ball, and Melvin was lucky to have you." His smile faded. "I'm very sorry for your loss."

"Thank you, young man." She patted his hand again, then looked over his shoulder and grinned. "I'm sure you have better things to do than be seen with an old woman like me. The lovely young lady who just came in can't take her eyes off you, so I'll leave you to it."

Josh turned, and all the breath backed up in his throat as he stared, then swallowed hard. Delilah looked like every man's fantasy, standing in the doorway in a shimmery blue dress that outlined every curve and gave a tantalizing glimpse of cleavage. His mouth went dry. Their gazes locked as he walked toward her, taking her in from head to toe. She scanned him in return, and her smile said she liked what she saw. When he reached her, he took both her hands in his and kissed her knuckles. He realized she must be wearing heels, because they were almost eye level, and he decided he liked looking her straight in the eye. She was wearing more makeup than usual, and whatever she'd done to her eyes made them bluer than he'd ever seen them.

She glanced around as though suddenly aware of the avid gazes aimed their way. A flicker of uncertainty crossed her face before she hitched her chin up and widened her smile.

He cupped her cheek and stroked his thumb over the smooth skin. Did she have any idea how proud he was of her? "You look absolutely stunning, Xena." She cocked a brow, and he leaned forward to kiss her cheek. "Every woman wants to be you, and every man wishes you were his." He whispered the words against her ear and felt her shiver.

The band started up a waltz, but before Josh could draw her into his arms, she sent him a blinding smile that burned his nerve endings, and slid from his grasp, trailing her finger down his cheek. "There's someone I need to see. Don't follow me," she whispered before she glided away.

Damn. He'd been right. His eyes followed her, mesmerized by the sway of her hips, glaring at any man who'd also noticed. He stayed back far enough to give her the space she demanded but close enough to intervene if she ran into trouble.

———

Delilah felt Josh's eyes on her as she crossed the room. A quick scan showed Fish near the punch bowl, Hunter not far from the orchestra, and Sanchez chatting with some folks near the buffet table. She had not seen Aaron or John Henry, which didn't really surprise her. She couldn't imagine her father in a place like this, dressed in a tuxedo. Not for any reason.

With a silent apology to Josh, she removed the earbud and put it in her purse. She didn't want him to overhear what she was about to do.

Across the room, she spotted Nate Hamm, also wearing a black tuxedo, holding court with the mayor. The way women's eyes followed him made bile rise in her throat, but she pushed it down and focused on Eli Foster, who hovered beside him.

When Eli headed toward the bar, she intercepted him and maneuvered him against the wall, out of the main traffic flow. "Hello, Eli," she said, her voice pitched low.

He looked at her with confusion. "Hello, pretty lady. Have we met? I'm sure I would have remembered."

Delilah stepped closer, watched his eyes dip to her cleavage, and ignored the way her skin crawled. "I hear you're planning to get married soon."

His eyes widened, and then he grinned. "Why, yes, as a matter of fact, I am. But that doesn't mean we can't have a little fun, does it?" He ran a finger down her arm.

Delilah placed both hands on his chest. "Actually, Eli, it does. You're going to call off the wedding, and if you really want to get married, you'll find yourself a grown woman, not a child."

"Now just a minute here. Who are you to tell me what to do?"

"I'm Mary's sister, Delilah Atwood, monkey researcher for FSU. And unless you want a two-page spread on the front page of the local paper about the dirty old man who is 'marrying' a teenage girl in an illegal scam of a ceremony, you're going to quietly call it off, understand?"

Eli stiffened as his face went pale. "Even if I wanted to, which I don't, I can't do that. It's all arranged. Nate said—"

"Ah yes, Nate. What's he have to do with all this?" She took another step toward him, giving him a clear view down the front of her dress.

His eyes almost bugged out of his head. "He-he set it up. The marriage is an alliance, a strategic partnership between us and your family. I can't just back out."

Delilah wrapped her arms around his neck, whispered in his ear. "You can and you will. You'll arrange to meet with Mary, and then you'll bring her to me. In return for your change of heart, I'll give you five thousand dollars to ease your conscience. Do you understand?" She pulled back and ran one finger down his cheek, like a caress.

His eyes narrowed. "And if I refuse?"

Delilah's grip tightened in his hair, and she smiled as another couple passed by. She turned back to Eli. "Then I'll kill you in your sleep." She kept her gaze steady on his, unblinking. His throat worked, and Delilah let the words hang in the air. She could never actually follow through, but he didn't know that. "Do we have a deal?"

"Well, well, well, look who's here," the voice from her nightmares drawled from behind her. "I heard you were dead."

Delilah wanted to snarl at the untimely interruption, but she turned and gave Nate a casual once-over. "Hello, Nate." Behind her, Eli muttered something and hurried off, the lily-livered coward. She'd hunt him down later.

In her heels, they were almost eye level, and Delilah pulled her shoulders back and looked at him with disdain. He wasn't quite as intimidating as he used to be. All that hard muscle had turned to fat, and his tux strained at the waist. If she had to guess, she'd say his drinking had gotten worse. She made sure her voice was cool and indifferent. "It looks like the reports of my death were greatly exaggerated, as Mark Twain said."

"You have a lot of nerve showing up here."

"And you have a lot of nerve trying to marry my sister off to one of your minions."

When he stepped into her personal space, Delilah didn't back up a single inch. His hand snaked out and gripped her upper arm, hard, as he muttered, "Let's have this conversation in private."

He all but dragged her toward a side door, and Delilah hissed, "Take your hand off me right now, or I'll scream the place down."

Surprisingly, he did as she asked but kept his other hand at the small of her back, making her skin crawl. She could feel Josh's eyes on her, and the knowledge that he was nearby gave her the courage to keep walking.

They exited the ballroom onto a tiled patio area where several other couples had gone to escape the noisy crowd. There were comfortable chairs and low lighting, and if it was anyone but Nate, it would've been a romantic spot.

The moment they were out of earshot of those around them, Delilah spun around and poked him in the chest. "Eli is not going to marry my sister."

He had the gall to laugh as he crossed his arms over his chest. "But he is, with your parents' blessing, I might add. I'm thinking she'll be a mite more trainable than you turned out to be."

Delilah thought she would explode from the fury coursing through her veins, but she kept her demeanor calm. She knew a shouting match wouldn't gain her anything. She mimicked his stance, then raised her chin. "What kind of deal did you make with my father for Mary?"

"What's it to you?"

She shrugged as though it didn't matter. "If you cancel the wedding, I'll make you a better deal."

He leaned closer and suddenly grabbed her upper arms and hauled her against his chest. "You haven't fulfilled your last deal, but I plan to rectify that. You'll marry me, Delilah," he ground out.

She fought like a wildcat to free herself from his grasp. *Marry him? Was he insane?*

"Hey! What are you doing?" Josh suddenly appeared beside

them and hauled her out of Nate's grasp. He grabbed the other man by the shirtfront and shoved him backward. "Take your hands off my fiancée," he growled. "What the hell is the matter with you?" He kept an eye on Nate as he asked, "Did he hurt you, honey? Do I need to call the police?"

At the word *police*, Nathan held up both hands. "No hard feelings, man. In the dim lighting, I thought she was someone else," he said, then backed away and disappeared into the crowd.

"Damn coward," Josh muttered. His eyes glittered with fury as he turned toward Delilah, but his touch was gentle as he brushed a strand of hair off her cheek. "Did he hurt you? Are you okay?"

Nate's threat of marriage had made the hair on the back of her neck stand up. He'd scared her with his tight grip, but she'd held her ground. She drew in a deep breath and straightened her shoulders. She hadn't cowered or caved. She'd faced down the monster on her terms, and it felt good, damn good. A slow smile bloomed. "I'm fine, actually. Finally."

He picked up her hand, and the way he looked at her as he kissed her knuckles said he not only understood but he was proud of her.

A waiter suddenly appeared, and Delilah decided this was cause for celebration. Despite the situation with Mary, she was finally free of the past, and Josh's look of pride had been replaced with a blistering heat she felt all the way to her toes. "Champagne, miss?"

"Yes, thank you," she said as she took the flute and raised it to Josh in salute. She took a sip, savored the crisp taste, then swallowed some more. "You don't want any?"

"I'll grab some ginger ale from the bar," he said.

Right. FWC officer on duty. Even that reminder of their purpose tonight couldn't dim her mood. "Okay. Meet me at the buffet table. I'm starving." Then she'd go finish her little chat with Eli.

He studied her for a long moment. "Put the earbud back in, and stay where I can see you."

Delilah took it out of her purse and tucked it into place, relieved he hadn't lectured. His bossy tone chafed, but she couldn't ignore the seriousness of the situation. Until now, she'd been convinced Aaron or John Henry had been behind the warnings and attempts on her life, but now she wasn't sure. What if it was Nate? She took a plate and wandered past the hors d'oeuvres, replaying their conversation. If he still wanted to marry her—which was completely insane—he'd have no reason to kill her, would he? That didn't even make sense. Who, then?

She nibbled on a bacon-wrapped date and sipped more champagne as she tried to puzzle it out. Suddenly, a wave of dizziness hit her. She set her glass down with a shaky hand and braced herself against the table. What in the world?

Although she hadn't had champagne in a while, she'd never reacted like this. Maybe it was nerves and the fact that she hadn't eaten much today. Her stomach gave a sudden lurch, and she turned and searched for the nearest restroom.

She spotted the sign across the room and headed that way, taking slow, deliberate steps, since the room had an unfortunate tendency to spin. She handed her glass and plate to another passing waiter as she made her way to the hallway. Once there, she had to pause and brace her hand against the wall, since the spinning was getting worse. She kept walking and heard someone whisper about obnoxious drunks, but she couldn't seem to form the words to protest.

On her third attempt to push open the restroom door, someone opened it from the inside, and she almost fell at their feet. She murmured something as she tottered into the room and braced her hands against the counter. When she looked in the mirror, there seemed to be four of her, which couldn't be right. It took a few tries to turn on the water, and she ran her wrists under it, hoping that would help. It didn't. The dizziness got worse.

She heard a toilet flush, and a woman came out, eyed her askance, and left without even washing her hands.

She heard Josh growl, "Where are you, Delilah? I told you to stay where I can see you."

Where was his voice coming from? She looked over her shoulder and almost lost her balance. He would know what to do. "Not. Feeling. Good."

"Delilah? I can barely hear you. Where are you?"

"Here," she whispered. "Bathroom."

"Delilah! Tell me where you are!" She heard Josh's voice and the worry in it, but it sounded like it was coming from very far away.

Suddenly, she heard another voice, closer, softer. It sounded like a man's voice, but she couldn't be sure because her eyelids kept wanting to slide closed.

"I'll take care of you. Just come with me."

A hand slipped around her shoulder and turned her gently toward the door. Delilah couldn't focus on the face, but she thought the voice was vaguely familiar, even though she couldn't place it. Her knees threatened to buckle, and suddenly, an arm came around her waist to support her. She laid her head against the warm shoulder and let herself be led from the room.

They must've stepped outside, because she felt the familiar wall of humidity wash over her. She tried to get her bearings, to figure out where she was, but then another wave of dizziness hit, and she sank toward the ground.

CHAPTER 26

"Delilah!" Josh hissed into his microphone, scanning the room. "Where are you, dammit?" He pushed and shoved his way across the ballroom, frantic to spot her through the crush. "Who has eyes on her?"

"Negative," Fish said.

"Looking," Hunter chimed in just as Sanchez said, "Last I saw her was at the buffet table."

"I thought you were over there, Sanchez. How'd she get by you?"

"I thought I saw Benson, so I followed, but it wasn't him. When I turned back, she was gone."

"Anyone seen him?" Hunter asked.

More nos.

"Spread out," Hunter commanded. "Fish, check the women's restroom."

"Already on it, boss," she said.

Josh felt the pressure tighten in his chest. She should never have been there.

He elbowed his way through the crowd, trying to spot her, but it was like she had vanished into thin air. When he reached the hallway leading to the restrooms, the crowd thinned, and he picked up his pace. "Fish, did you find her?"

"She's not in here. Wait. I think I found her purse."

Josh didn't slow down. If her purse was in the restroom, someone had taken her. They wouldn't have gone back through the ballroom, so they must have headed this way. Several closed doors lined this corridor, and he banged on each one and rattled the knob to make sure they were locked. When we got to the last one, it opened, and he found a storage closet packed with supplies. Along the back wall, a partially opened door led outside.

He held his weapon down as he eased out the door and into a narrow alley. Next to several overflowing dumpsters, a couple walked away from him, the man's arm around the woman's waist as she stumbled. *Delilah!*

He raised his weapon. "Stop! FWC!"

The man glanced over his shoulder, shoved Delilah into the nearby bushes, and took off running. Josh raced over to her, shouting into his earbud, "We've got a runner. I'm outside, last door past the bathrooms. See if you can intercept him."

"Headed that way," Sanchez said just as Hunter said the same thing.

Josh heard their staccato conversation in his earbud, but all his focus was on Delilah. He gently rolled her over and tapped her shoulders. "Delilah? Can you hear me?" When she didn't respond, he leaned closer, relieved to feel the breath coming out of her mouth and her heart racing under his hand.

He tapped her cheeks. "Delilah, honey, wake up." He shook her slightly, his panic ratcheting up when she didn't respond. "Somebody call 911!"

"Already en route," Hunter said as he dropped down beside him. "How is she?"

"I can't wake her. Come on, Delilah. Open those pretty blue eyes for me."

Josh kept talking while he ran his hands over her arms and legs and checked her torso, looking for any signs of injury. Except for a few scrapes from the bushes, she seemed fine. Which told him she'd been drugged.

Unsure what else to do, Josh gathered her close and whispered in her ear, "We need to find Mary. You need to wake up so we can find your sister."

That got through. "Mary. Find Mary," she muttered.

"I'll find her. And so will you. But right now, you need to wake up, okay?"

He watched her face as she fought her way back to consciousness. Her whole body tensed, her eyelids flickered, and finally, finally, her eyes opened. He'd never seen anything so beautiful in his entire life. "Welcome back, Xena."

She sent him a sleepy smile as her lids slid closed again.

"Oh no you don't. Stay with me, girl."

Sirens approached, and shortly afterward, two paramedics nudged Josh out of the way as they crouched beside her. He gave them what information he could as they checked her vitals and readied her for transport. He kept hold of her hand, and when Hunter indicated they should step away, she tightened her grip and wouldn't let go. He leaned closer and whispered, "I'll be right back. Stay tough."

Sanchez and Fish stood guard over the young man he'd seen with Delilah. An Ocala Police Department officer stood beside them, waiting to take him into custody.

Josh stormed toward them, but Hunter grabbed his arm. "Easy. We want information. Don't put his hackles up."

Josh nodded and rolled his shoulders to loosen some of the tension. Hunter was right, dammit, but that didn't mean he liked it. He wanted to beat the guy to a pulp and ask questions later, but Delilah expected and deserved better than that. Something was still off about the whole situation, and this guy was their best shot at figuring out what.

He stood to one side while Hunter pulled out his Louisiana Cajun charm.

"So, Jimmy," Hunter said casually. "How did you and Miss Atwood come to be walking around out here by yourselves?" Hunter indicated the smelly alley. "This isn't exactly a great place to get romantic."

"Nah, we weren't going to stay. We was just walking to my car."

"Hmm. What were you going to do when you got to your car? Were you and Miss Atwood going for a drive somewhere?"

Jimmy looked around, unsure. He shrugged. "We were, you know, just hanging out."

Hunter stepped closer. "You and Miss Atwood know each other? How long have you two been an item?" Hunter asked the questions as though they were just two guys sitting in a bar, getting to know each other.

Jimmy's eyes darted around again, and he muttered, "Awhile, I guess."

"I'm wondering what Ms. Atwood will say when she wakes up." He raised an eyebrow. "You're not giving me much here, Jimmy, and if she wakes up and her story is different, then I'm going to have a problem. Which means you're going to have a problem. It's never a good idea to lie to me." Hunter took a step closer. Not enough to intimidate him but as though he were ready to exchange confidences. "Here's what I think. I think money is a little tight, am I right? And somebody came along and offered you enough to pay the bills for maybe a month or two. All you had to do was get Miss Atwood out of the building."

Jimmy's eyes widened in surprise. "I wasn't going to hurt her. I just needed a little extra, you know?"

"I understand. A guy has to pay the bills. Was somebody coming to pick her up? Or were you supposed to take her somewhere?"

"I wasn't going to hurt her, I swear. That wasn't part of the deal."

Hunter nodded. "I believe you, but you still haven't told me the whole story. Why don't you start at the beginning, so you don't end up charged with attempted murder."

Jimmy's eyes widened in horror, and he started shaking, waving his arms frantically. "No! No! No! I wasn't going to hurt her! I was just supposed to take her somewhere."

"Okay, where were you supposed to take her?" Hunter's voice

never changed pitch, his tone calm and conversational. "Who were you supposed to meet?"

"I was just supposed to drop her off behind that old gas station off 314, that's all."

"Who asked you to do this?" Hunter continued. "I need a name, Jimmy."

Jimmy was shaking his head before Hunter finished speaking. "Dude, I don't know his name. I just got a phone call. Said he heard I needed a little extra cash. I take her from the party and drop her off, he'd pay me a thousand bucks."

Hunter whistled. "That's a lot of cash, Jimmy. I bet that will pay a few bills. How is he going to get you the money?"

"Said if I did what he asked, I'd come back in two days, and the money would be in an envelope behind the rack of tires."

Hunter never took his eyes off Jimmy, but Josh turned and hurried back to the EMTs, who were preparing Delilah for transport.

At that moment, Pete came running up to the ambulance. He turned to Josh. "What happened?"

"Somebody drugged Delilah." Knowing he'd let it happen, that someone had gotten to her on his watch, churned in Josh's gut and made him nauseous. And furious. Not just with Jimmy but with himself. He should never have let this happen.

Pete stopped, rubbed a hand over his face as he scanned the area. He spotted Fish standing beside the Ocala Police Department officer, and his breath came out in a rush. He turned back to Josh. "Is Delilah okay?"

"She will be." Josh studied his brother. "You okay, Pete? You look a little green around the gills." He couldn't remember ever seeing his brother like this.

Pete nodded and headed toward Fish without a word. Josh shook his head and bit back a chuckle when the two immediately faced off. The fireworks should be interesting to watch.

After the ambulance doors closed and they pulled away, Josh

joined Hunter and the rest of his squad while OPD took Jimmy away in handcuffs.

Josh only half listened as Hunter and Sanchez devised a plan to intercept whoever was supposed to show up at the gas station. His mind was on Delilah. She could have died tonight because he'd seriously underestimated her determination. A mistake he would not make again.

He tuned back in when Fish said, "It feels like we're chasing a ghost. Who wants her dead?"

"Right," Hunter said. "Let's think about this a different way. What does Delilah know that someone might kill for? Who would benefit from her death? If we can figure that out, we'll have a better idea of who's after her."

"I still think it's her brother, Aaron." Josh felt it, deep in his gut. "If he's connected to the militia, and we think he is, and if he is connected to the guns that we've heard are coming through here, then it makes sense he'd want to keep her away."

"But we don't have any hard evidence that he's connected." Hunter held up a hand when Josh started to protest. "Not that I'm doubting your gut, Hollywood. But we need proof."

Pete joined the group, standing beside Fish, sparks still shooting between them.

As Josh drove to the hospital, his mind played and replayed scenarios and possibilities. Hunter was right. They needed proof.

———————————

Delilah felt like her head was filled with cotton. Thinking was work. She felt groggy and disoriented, and with Josh watching her like a hawk, she was decidedly uncomfortable. "Stop looking at me like I'm a grenade about to explode," she said, shooting him a frustrated glance across the cab of the truck.

"Somebody drugged you and then tried to kidnap you. So yes, I'm a little concerned. Deal with it."

She wasn't sure what to do with that. Or with the idea of people worrying about her.

At the hospital, they'd found Rohypnol in her system and kept her under observation for several hours despite her protests. It was nearly dawn when they got back to the camper.

Her emotions were a whirling mix inside her fuzzy head. Josh made the kitchen feel too small, so she got flustered and edgy. They did an awkward little dance as she reached for a glass of water just as he did. Their eyes met, and his worry made her hand tremble as she watched him over the rim.

Suddenly, he stepped over, set her glass down, and yanked her into his arms. "Damn, woman, you scared the crap out of me tonight."

After a second of surprise, she knew this was what she'd subconsciously been waiting for. The tension in her shoulders relaxed as she breathed in his scent, then reached under his tuxedo jacket to wrap her arms tight around him. As she held him, every insane minute and conversation of the evening slipped into the background as she focused on his heart beating under her ear. He was here. She was safe. "I'm sorry."

He eased her back, ran the back of his hand down her cheeks. "I understand your concern for your sister. I also get that you didn't want anyone to know what you said to Eli. Or Nate." He raised a brow, and she shrugged, unwilling to put him in a tougher spot than he already was. "But I'm on your side. I need to keep you safe. Don't shut me out, Delilah."

Time stretched as the emotion behind his words unfurled the tight knot in her belly. His hair was rumpled like he'd been running his hands through it, and his tie stuck out of his pocket. She pulled him close, cupped his cheeks in her hands, and kissed him. His indrawn breath made her bolder. She traced the seam of his lips with her tongue, and he opened his mouth and growled low in his throat as she slipped hers inside and explored.

He gripped her waist, then ran his hands up and down her back, pulling her ever closer as though he wanted to climb inside her skin. She wrapped her arms around his neck and found she liked being eye level with him in the heels. The desire burning in his green eyes ignited her own, and with a wicked grin, she dove into the want shimmering between them, determined to take everything he had to give tonight. And to give all she had to him. "Come here, Hollywood. You must be burning up in all these clothes."

He threw his head back and laughed as she pushed the jacket off his shoulders. "Definitely burning up." When she would have hung it over the back of a chair, he grabbed it and slung it in the direction of the sofa.

She started undoing the buttons of his shirt slowly, enjoying the play of muscles under his skin. Once she had it undone, she spread it open like a birthday present and ran her hands over the hard ridges, running her palms over the light furring of hair, humming her approval.

He reached for her, pulling her flush against him again, and she sank into the kiss. Where she expected hurry and depth, he kept it slow and light, nipping at her lips, then planting light, feathery kisses along the line of her jaw. She did the same to him, hands tangled in the hair at his nape while his roamed her back. Her knees threatened to buckle in the wobbly sandals when he nipped her earlobe.

Frustrated with his slow pace, she pulled his mouth back to hers and slid her tongue inside. There was a moan of pleasure as their tongues played, sliding together, but she couldn't tell if it came from her or him, and she didn't care.

"I love the way you taste," he murmured, his hands slipping over her hips to cup her backside and pull her closer still.

"Shirt. Off." She issued the command between kisses, tugging at the fabric.

He chuckled low in her ear. "Yes, ma'am." The shirt landed on the floor.

She burrowed against his bare chest, but it wasn't enough. She wanted to feel his skin next to hers.

His hands went to the long zipper at the back of her dress as though he was thinking the same thing. "Now you're the one wearing too many clothes."

Inch by agonizing inch, he tugged the zipper down, kissing every bit of flesh he exposed on the way. The slope of her neck, the curve of her shoulder. Finally, he slipped the dress off her shoulders, and it slid down and pooled at her feet. He sucked in a breath at the sight of her in nothing but lacy black panties and the towering heels. "You're killing me, Xena."

Slowly, reverently, his hands caressed her, and she sighed with pleasure. Their mouths met again, and the kiss went from leisurely to desperate between one heartbeat and the next. He scooped her into his arms and carried her to the bedroom where he gently laid her on the bed.

The room spun, partly from leftover drugs but mostly from the sight of Josh wearing nothing but a pair of black boxers. He slid the sandals from her feet, then ran his warm palms over her calves, grinning wickedly.

She crooked a finger at him. "Come here, Hollywood, and show me what you've got," she purred, amazed that her voice could sound so sexy.

His eyes glittered like emeralds. "With pleasure." The rumble of his voice sent more shivers over her skin, and she sighed when he stretched out on top of her.

Their hands stroked and touched, learning each other, smiling and laughing and kissing until Delilah felt like she'd been drugged all over again.

When they finally came together, the sense of rightness, of completion, formed a lump in her throat. The pace increased, and the flames burned hotter, and she let go of every thought, every feeling except the exquisite sense of knowing she was free to fly, because Josh was with her.

CHAPTER 27

WHEN DELILAH WOKE LATER THAT MORNING, SHE STRETCHED and rolled over, burrowing her face into the pillow, breathing in Josh's aftershave. She hadn't thought anything could be better than the first time they made love, but last night had been even more amazing. He made love like he did everything else, with intense focus and concentration, as though there was nothing on his mind except her and this one magical moment in time. But he'd also made her laugh, which she'd never associated with lovemaking.

Being with him could quickly become an addiction, one she wasn't at all sure she could recover from when she left. Which meant she had to keep her heart off the slippery slope toward love she was careening down.

Too late, a little voice whispered, but she ignored it.

She'd just have to keep her focus where it belonged, on Mary.

When she walked into the kitchen, he was already there, wearing a T-shirt and shorts, on the phone with Hunter by the sound of it. He smiled and lifted his coffee cup toward the pot behind him, nodding in response to something Hunter said. Delilah gulped down a big glass of water, hoping to clear the last of the drugs out of her system, and then poured coffee.

"How are you feeling?" he asked after he hung up. "You were dead to the world when I got up."

"Much better." Delilah smiled. "But you could have woken me." The words popped out before she thought them through.

He stepped closer and pulled her tight against him for a long, lingering kiss she felt to the tips of her toes.

She was ready to suggest they go back to bed when reality smacked her and she eased away. At his frown, she sent him an apologetic look and nodded toward his phone. "Did Hunter have any new information?"

He scrubbed the back of his neck, apparently having as much trouble switching gears as she was. He paced away, then back. "Not nearly as much as we would like. Our friend Jimmy is sticking to his story that he doesn't know who hired him. He's also not budging from the idea that he did not drug you. His job was merely to find you and escort you out of the building, then bring you to the drop-off location. Unfortunately, even though Sanchez spent the night staking out that old gas station, nobody showed. Which tells me that whoever set this up realized Jimmy had been caught."

"So we have no way of knowing who was behind it." She sighed, frustrated.

"For now. But we're getting closer. Security footage caught a glimpse of both Benson and Eli Foster in the hallway near the restrooms during the right time frame. Apparently, Benson was skulking around before his official duties and then disappeared again afterward. Sanchez is going to question him this morning. But we also have Foster watching you throughout the evening."

Delilah shuddered. "He seems to be Nate's second in command, but I don't think he's running the show." She looked up from her coffee mug. "I tried to get him to call off his wedding to Mary, but he said it was an 'important alliance,' and he couldn't disappoint Nate. He could have drugged my drink, but I don't think he came up with the plan on his own."

"That was my take on him, too. If this wedding is some sort of strategic move, the alliance Mary alluded to, then the reasons someone wants you to stop interfering have just become clearer."

He folded his arms over his chest, and Delilah forced her eyes back up to his face. She couldn't think about how amazing it felt to be held by him.

"Just what in the name of all that's holy were you thinking to confront Nate in the middle of the ball?" he suddenly demanded, his expression rock hard.

Delilah's back went up at this tone. "I was thinking that because it was the middle of a crowded ball, he wouldn't risk doing anything stupid where people could see him. Nate might be a bully, but he's a smart bully. He generally chooses his targets and locations pretty carefully."

"What did you say to him?"

"I told him he wasn't going to marry my sister off to Eli and that I would make it worth his while if he called it off."

Josh narrowed his eyes. "And how did he respond to that exactly?"

A chill ran down Delilah's back as Nate's words echoed in her head. She reminded herself he didn't have any power over her. She wasn't a victim. She was Xena, warrior princess. She raised her chin and looked him in the eye. "He said that not only was Mary going to marry Eli but that I hadn't fulfilled my obligation and he still planned to marry me." She hated the way her voice stumbled, just a little, on the last few words.

"Oh hell no." He took both her hands in his. Fury snapped in his eyes as his thumbs gently brushed over her knuckles. "You're not alone anymore, Delilah. And there is no way he's going to get his hands on you ever again. You have my word on that."

Delilah squeezed his hands and said, "I know and I believe you. You're a good man, Josh Tanner." She leaned forward and brushed her lips over his, then stepped away before she threw herself into his arms. They had work to do. "Now that we know the motivation behind this sham of a marriage, it's more important than ever that I find Mary and get her out of that mess."

Josh jammed a hand through his hair in frustration, his rumpled look making him even more attractive. "I checked with every informant I know and had them check with everyone they know, and nobody can tell me where to find the Atwoods' campsite.

Wherever they set up camp, they've been careful to make sure no one knows where it is." He huffed out a breath. "Neither Aaron nor John Henry has been to the café or been seen at the fishing pier, either."

"I have an idea." Delilah went into the bedroom, grabbed the map of the forest Kimberly had printed for her, and spread it out on the dinette table. She used a yellow highlighter to mark all the locations she and Mary used to go. She included the tree by the river, the old quarry turned zip-line park, and then she added dots for all the places she'd gone to watch the monkeys as part of her research. She had chosen most of those locations from memory, based on where she and Mary used to watch them years ago.

Josh leaned over her shoulder as she worked. He tapped a spot. "This is the last place they set up camp." His finger slid over a little bit, and he said, "And this is where you met with Mary the other night."

Delilah grinned at him. "Now we're getting somewhere." She chewed on the end cap while she studied the terrain. "I'm thinking the hunter was found right around here?" She pointed with the marker.

"That looks right. Can you remember any other locations your family camped at over the years?"

Delilah studied the dirt roads that crisscrossed the forest, then shook her head in defeat. "Even with all John Henry's training about situational awareness, when you're a kid, roads and streets don't mean a whole lot. Or they didn't to me anyway. I remember landmarks, but those, unfortunately, are not printed on a map." Delilah drummed her fingers on the table, her frustration growing. "We still don't know where she is or where the wedding is supposed to be. All we know is that it's on Thursday. We're running out of time."

Josh eyed her speculatively. "What are you thinking?"

"I'm going to cover every inch of forest within the circle of these locations and pray I get lucky and find John Henry's campsite."

"And when you do?"

She hitched up her chin. "I'll figure it out when I find him." She headed toward the bedroom to grab her backpack and her gun.

All he said was, "I'll meet you at the truck."

———————

Josh drove and Delilah spread the map across her lap, unable to ignore the little bubble of hope inside her. He stopped at several locations, including Mama T's small convenience store, but nobody had any information on the Atwoods' whereabouts.

Defeat swamped her when they'd gotten nowhere by early afternoon.

"Why don't we swing by the Corner Café? I could use some caffeine and a cupcake—and maybe Liz and Charlie have some local intel that might help."

Delilah sighed. "We might as well, because this sure isn't accomplishing anything."

"On the contrary," he countered. "We now know all the places your family isn't. I know it doesn't sound like much, but it's more than we knew this morning." He held the door of the café open, and all conversation ceased when they walked through the door. After last night, they hadn't bothered with disguises. What would be the point?

Liz hurried around the counter and grabbed Delilah like she was a long-lost relative. "Oh goodness, Delilah. I am so very relieved to hear you're not dead."

Delilah laughed as the other woman wrapped her in a tight hug. "Yeah, me, too. Thanks."

When Liz let go, she turned and speared Josh with a look. "What is it with you scaring people to death, Hollywood? You are putting some serious strain on my heart lately."

"Completely unintentional, Liz. You know that. But thanks for the concern."

Delilah leaned closer to Liz so they weren't overheard. "I need to find my family's campsite. Do you have any idea where it might be?"

Liz shook her head. "I wish I could help. I truly do. But I have no idea. For a while, your brother would swing by here pretty regularly, but he hasn't been in, in a few days." She looked from one to the other. "But if I see him, I'll be sure to let you know."

"Thank you, Liz," Delilah said.

They took their coffee and cupcakes to a table at the back. Delilah was surprised at the number of people who seemed to know who she was and expressed their relief that she wasn't actually dead. It was a very odd feeling for a woman who had spent most of her life being invisible, either by training or necessity. But she found she liked it.

They got back in the truck and kept searching. The shadows were lengthening when she finally gave up. They had bounced and jostled over miles of dirt roads and barely there paths but had found no trace of her family. None of the folks they asked would admit to seeing them or knowing where they were, either. Leaning her head back against the seat, she looked over at Josh. "We're not going to find them today."

Josh reached over and squeezed her hand. "We'll widen the search in the morning. We will find her, and we won't give up until we do." He quirked a brow and grinned. "But in the meantime, what do you say we grab a pizza and a couple of beers to take back with us?"

Delilah grinned back. "I like the way you think, Hollywood."

"I hope you like more than that, Xena." He picked up her hand and kissed her palm, the scorching look he aimed her way sending a slow shiver of anticipation down her spine.

CHAPTER 28

DELILAH FELT JOSH'S EYES ON HER AS THEY DROVE TOWARD the camper, a fresh-from-the-oven pizza balanced on her lap. The smell of melted cheese made her mouth water, but it was the hungry looks he aimed her way that started a fire deep in her belly.

"That smells amazing. I'm going to enjoy getting my hands on some of that deliciousness." His smile had Delilah shifting in her seat.

She tried to think of some witty little remark, something to keep things light, casual, but came up empty. How was she going to keep her distance if he kept looking at her like that?

"It's a beautiful night," Josh said. "Why don't I start a fire, and we can sit outside before the bugs get too bad?"

As darkness fell, it felt like they were the only two people on earth. Above them, stars appeared in the night sky, and the fire kept the worst of the bugs at bay. Her tummy was full, and the beer gave her a nice feeling. She let herself slide into the moment, decided to simply enjoy the night and the handsome man beside her and the way peace settled around her whenever he was near. Tomorrow would take care of itself.

After a while, Josh gathered up the trash and took it inside. The first strains of the "Tennessee Waltz" floated from the outdoor speakers. He came down the steps and held out a hand. "I don't believe we ever finished our dance, mademoiselle. Care to join me?"

Delilah smiled as he pulled her up and into the circle of his embrace. One arm came around her waist, while the other clasped her hand as they slowly turned in time to the music.

Around them, the night deepened, and one song led to another as they danced and held each other. Gradually, the fire they'd temporarily banked burst back into flame.

She leaned back and tilted her head up so she could see his face. She ran her fingers over the soft skin of his cheekbones and the bristle of his five-o'clock shadow. He didn't react, didn't move, simply watched her out of eyes that had gone dark with passion.

She pulled his mouth to hers, and the explosion when they touched was like throwing a match on kindling. Heat roared between them as their mouths tasted and explored and the kiss deepened, pulling them closer still. His lips were firm and sure, and every flick of his tongue melted more of the starch in her knees. She gripped his upper arms for balance as he nuzzled her neck, then nibbled along her jaw and nipped her earlobe. She shivered and did the same to him, delighting in his low moan.

He leaned in for another kiss just as a mosquito buzzed past her ear. "I think we should take this party inside before the bugs eat us alive."

"Right there with you," she said, swatting another one. "Vicious beasts." He chuckled, and she marveled again that passion and laughter could coexist, but it felt...right.

After he doused the fire, he took her hand and led her up the steps and into the bedroom.

Once they were curled up together, he brushed the hair out of her face and ran his hands slowly, reverently, over every inch of her. "Have I told you how incredibly beautiful you are?"

Until she'd seen herself through his eyes, Delilah had never felt beautiful. "You make me feel that way."

Eyes locked on each other and hearts thundering in unison, they flew through the night together.

CHAPTER 29

DELILAH WOKE TO AN INSISTENT BUZZING AND HEAVY WEIGHT across her chest. It took a few seconds for her brain to register that the weight was Josh's arm and the buzzing was her cell phone. She scrambled out from under him and stumbled into the kitchen, trying to remember where she'd left it.

By the time she located it, it had stopped buzzing. She shoved her hair out of her eyes and tried to figure out who had called.

"What's going on?" Josh asked as he came into the room wearing nothing but boxers. He scrubbed a hand through his hair, making it stand up even more, and then rubbed his bare chest. He ran his gaze over her, quirked an eyebrow, and asked, "Why aren't we still in bed?"

Delilah glanced down at the T-shirt that barely reached the middle of her thighs and shoved aside the heat that memories of last night stirred. She held up one finger while she stabbed buttons to retrieve her voicemail.

Kimberly's voice came over the line, sounding unusually urgent. "Good morning, Delilah. Sorry to call so early, but I wanted to make sure I got hold of you right away. When I got to the clinic this morning, there was an envelope addressed to me taped to the door. Inside was a note for you from Mary. I didn't open it, but I figured you would want to come get it right away."

Josh moved closer, his teasing gone. "Delilah, what's going on?"

"It's Kimberly. She found a note for me from Mary. I need to get to the clinic right away." She started for the bedroom, urgency nipping at her heels.

"Did the call just come in, or was this one of those reminders that you hadn't checked your voicemail?"

She paused midstride. "I thought it just came in, but—"

She handed him the phone, and he tapped the screen, then checked the dive watch strapped to his wrist. "It's after nine now. The time stamp says the call came in at 7:30."

"I need to go." She ran into the bedroom, grabbed jeans and a T-shirt. *What if I'm too late? What if I missed Mary?* She couldn't think like that or she'd go mad, so she focused on getting dressed. Then she grabbed her backpack, checked she had everything, and ran back into the kitchen.

Josh was already there in his FWC uniform, expression grim as he checked his weapon before he holstered it.

"What's happened? I thought you were on vacation."

"Just got a call from Charlee about a capsized kayak. They can't find the kid who went in the water, so it's all hands on deck. I'll meet the squad at the Outpost." He pressed a quick kiss to her forehead. "Let me know what the note says, and I'll catch up with you as soon as I can."

"Be careful." She pulled him in for a quick hug, then touched his cheek. "I hope you find the child safe and sound."

"That's always the hope."

He hurried out to his father's truck, and Delilah locked up and headed for her own, whispering a prayer for the missing child. And for Mary.

Kimberly was waiting for her at the clinic, a worried frown furrowing her brow. "What took you so long to get here?" She glanced at the clock.

Delilah ignored the flush heating her cheeks. "I was asleep and didn't hear my phone. Sorry. May I see the note?"

The plain white envelope had Kimberly's name on the front. Delilah's pulse sounded in her ears as she pulled out the smaller envelope inside it. *Please don't let me be too late.* Below her name, the initial M was written in what looked like Mary's looping script. She unfolded the sheet of paper and sucked in a breath.

Find me, please. 1:00 p.m. River tree. Come alone.

She showed Kimberly the note, and the other woman grinned. "This is the break you've been waiting for." She gripped Delilah's hand. "Just a few more hours, and you'll have Mary with you."

Delilah pulled in a deep breath as hope bubbled up from the depths of her heart. She closed her eyes. *Thank you, God.*

When she opened them, Kimberly was giving her the kind of once-over that made her want to squirm, but she held her ground.

"Where's Handsome?"

"Out on another call. Charlee says a child fell out of a kayak near the Outpost." Her heart hurt just thinking about it.

Kimberly gasped and made the sign of the cross, murmured a quick prayer. Then her gaze sharpened. "How's it going, living with him?"

"I'm not living with him. We're sharing space as part of an operation."

"Uh-huh." She crossed her arms and nodded toward the local paper where a picture of them was featured in a collage with several others. "That was quite the dress you had on. And he didn't look too shabby in that tux, either."

Delilah decided a change of subject was in order. "Someone drugged me"—at Kimberly's gasp, she held up a hand—"but I'm fine."

Delilah was spared having to rehash the whole thing when there was a knock on the door.

"Patient in room three for you, Ms. Gaines."

Kimberly stopped muttering long enough to say "Be right there" before she gave Delilah a stern look. "You keep Hollywood close, you hear? Now is not the time to wave your independence like a flag, not when crazy people are trying to kill you. He's a good man. He'll keep you safe."

Delilah followed her out and headed for her truck. It was true.

Josh was a good man, and he would keep her physically safe. It was her foolish heart that was in danger. She shoved the key in the ignition and tucked all thoughts of him into a tidy little box in the corner of her heart to deal with later. She had other priorities today.

A wide grin split her face.

In less than four hours, Mary would be safe.

CHAPTER 30

HUNTER, SANCHEZ, FISH, AND PETE WERE ALREADY AT THE Outpost when Josh arrived. Hunter and Sanchez had just launched their patrol boats and were trying to get last-known-location information from the frantic parents, a couple in their forties. The wife wore a long cotton dress and twisted the ends of her braid in her hands. Her husband wore jeans and thick boots, face hidden under a ball cap like the one they'd found near Delilah's camper.

Charlee, looking pale, hurried over and briefed him. "They were the first ones here when we opened this morning. Two adults and two teens, boy and a girl. They rented four kayaks."

Josh looked around. "I thought the boy was missing. Where's the girl?"

"Don't know where either one is. Just the parents came back."

His eyes narrowed as he studied the parents. "They say what happened?"

"Just that the teens got ahead of them, and when they came around the bend, they found the empty kayaks."

"Hollywood! Let's go!" Hunter called from his boat.

He hopped aboard, and Fish boarded Sanchez's boat before they took off down the river, single file.

Nobody said much as they headed toward the area the parents had described, scanning every little cove and bend for any sign of the teens' kayaks.

Once they reached the location, a large cypress tree someone had nailed pieces of wood to as a ladder, Hunter and Sanchez slowed to an idle. Just as the parents had said, they found the first kayak but not the second.

Josh pulled his FWC ball cap lower and squinted into the shadows as Hunter pulled alongside it.

Fish cupped her hands around her mouth. "Tommy! Alice! Where are you? We're here to help!"

They waited, but there was no response.

"Sanchez, you guys go downriver, see if you can find that other kayak—and hopefully the kid who was paddling it. Hollywood and I will check this area more thoroughly."

Hunter nosed his patrol boat into the banks next to the empty craft, and Josh tied both to a tree.

"Tommy! Alice! Let us know you're okay!" Josh called.

Still nothing.

He scanned the shore but didn't see footprints or any signs that anyone had been here recently. But then he glanced across the river, and his heart slammed into overdrive. "There!" He pointed. "Get me over there."

Hunter didn't hesitate. As soon as the line was clear and Josh hopped back into the boat, he motored in the direction Josh was pointing.

When they reached the opposite shore, Josh stripped off his utility belt and unbuttoned his shirt.

"What are you doing?"

"I'll dive down, just to make sure."

They'd both spotted what looked like a length of rope extending from a cypress tree and disappearing under the water.

"Let me get the dive team out here."

"You know we don't have time."

Hunter blew out a breath and accepted the phone Josh handed him. He tucked it in the front compartment along with Josh's utility belt. "Be careful."

Josh didn't hesitate, just dove into the tea-colored water, dreading what he would find.

When Delilah left the clinic, she knew she'd go crazy if she didn't find something to occupy her mind until the meeting. Her phone calendar chirped a reminder that she had a progress report due, so she parked the truck and went with her favorite distraction—time with Oscar—and hopefully the missing mamas.

There was no cell service, so she sent Josh a quick text with her whereabouts before she slung her backpack over her shoulder and set off.

Walking through the forest as she'd been taught, quietly, eyes on the ground to look for snakes, she kept her ears cocked but didn't hear her furry friends. She didn't find any sign of them where she'd last seen them, either.

She was hot and sweaty and her essential oil had worn off by the time she turned back. But then she heard it: the faintest chattering, a whisper of sound on the breeze. She paused to see if she could tell which direction it came from, then followed the rustling leaves north, surprised when she emerged in a clearing near Mooney's Pond. The forest opened up around the oblong body of water, and she ducked behind a tree when she heard another sound. A voice, young and distinctly female.

Mary? Her heart pumped with hope, and she was ready to burst from her hiding place when the girl stepped from the shadows. She wore an old-fashioned, long cotton dress with flowers on a bright yellow background, her hair in a thick braid down her back. Mary was taller, more slender.

Disappointment slammed through her, and she eased out of sight. It wasn't Mary. Who, then? She pulled out her camera and used her zoom lens to focus on the teenager's face and snap a few pictures. Unless she missed her guess, this was the same girl she'd seen riding bikes with a boy the day she'd found Mary's doll at her parents' campsite. Did she know where Mary was?

Delilah was shoving her camera into her bag, prepared to

confront her, when the girl aimed binoculars into the trees and started calling, "Come here, mamas. Don't be shy. I brought food. You'll like it."

A stern lecture about feeding wildlife crowded Delilah's tongue, but she stayed put when several monkeys swung down from the trees. Were these the missing mamas?

As the monkeys approached the girl, Delilah scanned their faces with her zoom lens, and a hot jolt of relief shot through her. Yes! Oh, thank goodness, they were back. But where had they been?

The girl tossed a handful of what looked like nuts to one of the mamas, but before she could come get it, the alpha male let out a screech as he leaped down from a nearby branch and scooped up the food, scolding the whole time. The mothers scampered back into the trees, chattering in protest.

Once the mamas had fallen back in line, the alpha male climbed back up the tree and sat on a branch while he chewed the nuts, eyes darting from one mama to the next, a stern warning in his gaze.

Delilah waited, eyes on the male, until suddenly, the babies appeared. They emerged from their hiding places behind limbs and leaves and climbed onto their mamas' backs, jumping and playing without a care in the world. *Where are you, Oscar?* She couldn't find him.

Once the male finished eating and quit scowling, the troop resumed their usual activities. While the adults groomed one another and ate, the babies leaped from tree to tree, cavorting like children.

When Oscar's sweet face finally appeared in her viewfinder, unexpected tears threatened. *There you are, sweet guy.* The mamas were all there, too, and she let out a relieved sigh. They were all right.

She must have made some sound, because the girl's head suddenly whipped in her direction. For one moment, their eyes met, held. The girl's widened in fear just before she leaped up and disappeared into the forest.

"Wait! Don't go!" Delilah ran after her, determined to catch up, but as before, the girl was quick. Delilah swerved around trees, and despite her best efforts, she came around a huge cypress and stopped, scanning the area. The girl had disappeared.

Frustrated and panting, Delilah searched the area for several more minutes before she gave up and headed back to her truck.

Thank goodness the mamas were all right. But why had the girl looked so scared?

CHAPTER 31

JOSH CLUTCHED THE T-SHIRT HE'D PULLED FROM THE RIVER bottom as they slowly headed toward the Outpost, the empty kayak in tow. The shirt matched the description Tommy's mother had given them, and it made the knot in the pit of his stomach tighter. The dive team was on its way.

Hunter checked in with Sanchez and Fish. They hadn't found any trace of the missing siblings, either.

He glanced at Hunter. "Something seem off about this to you?"

"Everything seems off. Parents claim they didn't have their cell phones with them, which I can understand. But they didn't check along the riverbanks, just headed back to report it?" He shook his head in disbelief.

"And how do both kids disappear? If one fell in, wouldn't the other have tried to help? It's unlikely they'd both drown."

"Stranger things have happened." Hunter narrowed his eyes as they scanned the banks, stopping to poke at half-submerged snags, looking for something, anything that would tell them what happened and, most importantly, where the kids were now.

They rounded another of the many bends in the river, and Josh straightened as something caught his eye. "Hang on. Go back." He pointed, and Hunter put the motor in reverse.

He squinted into the gloom and made out what looked like a scrap of yellow fabric. Hunter brought the boat close enough that Josh hopped onto the bank and pulled it from the branches it was tangled in. "Didn't the mother say Alice was wearing a yellow print dress?" He held up the cloth.

"She did."

Josh scanned the ground. "I've got footprints. Two sets." He followed them away from the river, the muddy ground making it easy to follow their trail. The mud turned to solid ground, and several yards later, the footprints ended at a set of tire tracks. He reached for his phone to snap a picture and realized it was on the boat.

When he returned for it, Hunter was scowling. "Let's go. Charlee just called, said the teens called their mother and told her they were fine."

Josh climbed aboard and regarded him steadily. "Just like that? No questions, no explanation?"

"None they gave Charlee. But they'll have to do better with me if I find out they tied up my squad for no reason."

CHAPTER 32

DELILAH KEPT ONE EYE ON THE DASHBOARD CLOCK, HANDS clenched around the wheel. It had taken longer than expected to get back to her truck, but she couldn't be late. Not when Mary was finally participating in her own rescue. She had to get there in time.

As she neared the meeting spot, a weird sense of déjà vu floated over her as her father's safety instructions from childhood and Josh's more recent admonitions echoed in her head. She parked several hundred yards from the river and made sure the truck was not easily visible. Just in case. She still had no cell service, so she sent Josh another quick text: Found note. Meeting Mary 1 p.m. at river tree. She said to come alone.

She eased the door closed, tucked her phone in her back pocket, and headed for the rendezvous. As she slipped from tree to tree, she identified the forest creatures and tried to discern any noises that indicated a human in the area. All she heard were the sounds she expected.

The river came into view, and anticipation flooded her. Finally, finally, she'd have her sister with her. She couldn't wait.

She picked up the pace, ready to wrap Mary in her arms and whisk her to safety. She took another step and suddenly found herself upside down and flying into the air.

Her upward trajectory stopped with a jolt, and she swung, suspended high above the forest floor. Her heart pounded, and it took a moment to figure out what had happened. She was up in a tree, trapped inside a makeshift game net. She hadn't seen it and had stepped right into it, no doubt triggering a hidden mechanism that scooped her up.

She wrapped her hands around the thick rope that formed the web. "Think, Delilah. There has to be a way out of this." She reached for her cell phone, but it wasn't there. She looked down, way down, and glimpsed it lying on the ground below. It had no doubt fallen out of her pocket when she got scooped up.

Okay, fine. She could handle this. All she had to do was slip out of the net. Once she did, she could shimmy up the rope and climb onto the branch from which it was suspended. She started climbing, using the small openings like rungs on a ladder, confident that once she reached the top, she could figure out how to wiggle out and escape.

But her optimism turned to terror when a male voice spoke from below. "Hello, Delilah. I've been waiting for you."

Hunter drilled Mr. Simms with a hard look. "You're telling me Tommy and Alice called a friend to come get them, set their kayaks adrift, and took off without a word to you?"

The man nodded soberly, though a muscle ticked in his jaw. Beside him, his wife continued to wring her hands as she'd been doing since they'd returned to the Outpost.

"Does this sort of thing happen often?" Hunter asked.

The wife said, "Sometimes," at the same time as her husband said, "No."

Hunter didn't miss the quelling look Simms shot his wife or the way she ducked her head. Hunter turned to her. "What did you mean by that, ma'am? What else has been happening lately that's odd?"

She glanced at her husband, then back at Hunter and shrugged. "Just being more unpredictable is all. I guess it comes with them both being teenagers. They're just over a year apart in age."

Josh stood off to the side, Hunter's growing frustration matching his own. "And where are Tommy and Alice now? We need to speak with them."

"Couldn't say," Simms said with a shrug. "They just said they had something to take care of and we'd see them later. If there's nothing else, I'd like to take my wife home. We're sorry to have troubled you." He took his wife's arm as he led her to their pickup and helped her inside.

"I'll stop by your place later to talk with them," Hunter said, and Mrs. Simms paled slightly.

Simms nodded but aimed a quelling glance their way before he climbed behind the wheel.

Josh was still trying to make sense of this weird situation when his phone buzzed with an incoming text. He'd fastened his utility belt and gun over his damp uniform as they approached the Outpost and had stuck his phone back in the holster. There were no missed calls or messages then. He checked now and froze. There were two, both from Delilah. "Dammit. You shouldn't have gone without me," he muttered.

"What's going on, Hollywood?" Hunter asked.

"Delilah got a note." He checked his watch. "She was supposed to meet Mary at one o'clock, down by the river." It was now 1:20.

"Why didn't she call you?"

"She'd been out by the monkeys where cell service is spotty. She texted, but they just came in." Fear clamped down on his insides. "I need to get there." God forbid she needed him and he wasn't there because of lousy cell reception.

Hunter kept pace as Josh hurried toward his truck. "The paperwork on this fiasco can wait. We'll both go." He texted Sanchez and Fish what was happening, and they hopped in their vehicles and raced toward the river.

Uneasiness slid over Josh's skin as he drove, desperate to remember the exact location he and Delilah had gone to before, but everything looked different in daylight.

Somebody had a motive for keeping the sisters apart, and all the possible reasons had him pressing down hard on the accelerator.

Hang on, Delilah. I'm on my way.

————————————

Delilah gripped the ropes as she stared down at Nate. He'd tried to overpower her once before, but she'd escaped. She would use that knowledge to fuel her strength now. He wouldn't win this time, either. "Put me down. What kind of nonsense is this?"

She'd barely finished saying the words when the net suddenly dropped and she hit the ground. Hard. She lay there a moment, trying to catch her breath. When she looked up and saw him standing over her, that oily grin made her stomach churn. "Your wish is my command," he drawled. Then he straightened and barked, "Stand up."

"And if I won't?"

"I'll have to make you. I'm pretty sure you won't like it."

They stared each other down while Delilah debated her next move. She finally rose to her feet, her eyes never leaving his. "What's this all about?"

"You'll find out when I say it's time. Not before." He sighed. "I guess there will be lots of retraining before you're the wife I want." He grinned, his smile pure evil. "But I'm going to enjoy the process."

"Let me out of here, you creep."

His hand slapped her face with enough force to knock her off her feet. She carefully rubbed a hand over her jaw and moved it slowly, relieved that nothing felt broken. Her cheek burned like fire, though, and she was pretty sure she'd have an impressive bruise. He'd pay for that. She slowly got to her feet once more and stood, glaring at him through the ropes. He reached down and did something to the net and then flung it off her.

Delilah spun around to run but froze when she heard the click of a magazine being loaded into a weapon.

"Don't think I won't shoot you in the back if I have to."

Delilah had no doubt he meant it. She turned back toward him. "Where's Mary?"

He shrugged. "I have no idea. Probably getting ready for the wedding."

The truth dawned and made her shiver. "You wrote the note, not Mary."

He smiled at her like a teacher whose student had finally gotten the right answer. "I knew there was a sharp brain hiding under all those ridiculous notions of independence and other nonsense. But don't worry. I'll soon beat those out of you." His conversational tone confirmed he had well and truly lost his grip on reality.

He kept the gun in his right hand and reached down to scoop her phone from the dirt. "Move," he said, nudging her with the gun. "We still have a ways to go. But if you want to live to see your sister wed, you won't do anything stupid."

Delilah had no intention of doing "anything stupid." She'd be smart and escape. She suddenly heard her beloved monkeys chattering in the distance, and her heart clenched. They'd be the perfect distraction, but she didn't want to risk Nate shooting one of them. She kept her head down, ears trained as she waited for her opportunity.

The troop suddenly appeared above them, and when the alpha male let out a shriek, she pretended to stumble, jerked out of Nate's grasp, and took off running. She didn't get very far before his big body landed on top of her. All the air escaped her lungs as she squirmed under him, gasping and terrified.

"I'd forgotten just how feisty you are, my dearest fiancée."

She wanted to gag but held herself perfectly still until he shifted his weight. Then she elbowed him hard before she flipped over and kicked him with everything she had.

He roared with fury and grabbed her, his arms like a vise, the smell of his sweat making her stomach roil. She struggled and twisted and tried to break free, but he tightened his grip, pinning her against him with one arm while he fished in his pocket with the other. Before she knew what he had planned, he'd yanked her hands behind her back and secured them with a zip tie.

He hauled her to her feet. "Enough games. Move."

Delilah kept her expression bland as she walked, but her mind raced, determined to find another way to escape.

Josh huffed out a relieved breath when he spotted Delilah's green pickup hidden near the river. He raced over to it, but it was empty.

"I'll head toward the tree while you skirt around from the other side," he said when Hunter joined him.

"I've got your back, Hollywood. Don't be a hero."

Josh ran in a crouch, gun in hand, eyes scanning, ever alert for trouble. He stopped short, surprised, when he spotted a cargo net lying in a heap several hundred yards from the tree. His eyes followed the rope up to the tree and back down. A chill slid over his skin. He didn't like what he was thinking.

But he didn't want to jump to conclusions, so he made his way to the meeting tree. There was no sign of either Delilah or Mary and nothing that said either one had been there recently. He signaled Hunter, who jogged over and met him at the cargo net.

"What the hell is that doing here?" Hunter asked. "Looks like it came off a container ship."

"Handy for moving gun crates," Josh muttered, tempted to howl with fury. Unless he missed his guess, Delilah had walked right into a cleverly set trap. And he had absolutely no idea where to start looking for her. He spun in a circle, heart pounding, searching the trees as though they could provide the answer. *Dammit.*

"Head in the game, Hollywood," Hunter said. "We've got footprints. Two sets. Let's see where they lead."

CHAPTER 33

HUNTER AND JOSH FOLLOWED THE FOOTPRINTS UNTIL THEY ended abruptly. The sand and dirt were churned up as though there'd been a struggle, but thankfully, there was no blood.

"Over here," Hunter called. "Only one set of tracks heads away from this spot. They're deeper, too."

Josh turned in a slow circle, studied the area. "He carried her from here."

"Looks that way."

They followed the trail until it ended beside one of the dirt roads that crisscrossed the forest. It was well traveled, with evidence of multiple vehicles coming and going. Josh studied the tire impressions and then slammed his hand against a tree trunk in frustration. Everywhere he turned, they ran into nothing but dead ends. Hunter took pictures just in case, but neither man held out much hope. Even if it did lead to a particular vehicle, none of that would help Delilah in time.

He'd promised to protect her, but he hadn't been there when she'd needed him. He rammed a hand through his hair. Crappy cell service wasn't his fault, but she didn't know that. All she'd know was that she'd reached out and he'd abandoned her.

His mind tossed up all manner of horrible scenarios, and his stomach churned just thinking about what she might be going through.

"We'll find her," Hunter said.

Josh nodded absently, his mind scrambling to figure out what they'd missed. Who had her? He pulled out his cell phone, relieved to see a measly two bars. He'd take it. "Did Byte get back to you about Benson's properties?"

"Not yet," Hunter responded.

"Hey, Byte," Josh said when the other man answered. "Did you find out if Commissioner Benson has a hunting place out in the forest?"

"I didn't find anything, but let me make sure." He heard keys tapping. "No. Nothing shows up."

"What about Eli Foster or Nate Hamm? Or the Atwoods? John Henry or Aaron?"

"I'll check, but it'll take a little while."

"Nate said he still plans to marry me."

Delilah's words hit him like a slap, and his whole body stiffened. What if they'd been coming at this all wrong? What if it had been Nate all along? "Byte, move Nate Hamm to the top of your list and see what you can find out about any property he owns, rents, or uses in this area. Right now. Then get me anything you can find on the others. Properties in the area, places they like to go. Anything."

"On it. I'll get back to you as soon as I can."

"I need it yesterday, Byte. Delilah's missing."

"Missing? Damn, Hollywood. You should have led with that. I'll get you whatever I can, as fast as I can."

He thanked the other man, then turned to Hunter, heart pounding with the need to rush out and find her. Now. But to do that, the squad needed info. He took a breath. "Years ago, Delilah's family tried to marry her off at sixteen, which is why she ran away. She thought the guy had left town. But Nate Hamm is still here, and at the ball, he told her he still planned to marry her."

"Crap." Hunter rubbed a hand over the back of his neck. "Why am I just hearing this now?" He sighed. "Never mind. Just get over to Hamm's place, and I'll—"

"Wait a minute. The map." Josh turned and started running back to their vehicles, Hunter right behind him.

"What map? What are you talking about, Hollywood?"

"Delilah and I made a map of all the places the Atwoods might be. We couldn't find them, but we know they move around a lot. Let's split up and start over, and hopefully, Byte will come up with something to narrow the search."

When they reached the trucks, he spread the map over his hood and divided it into sections. He texted pictures to Fish and Sanchez, assigning each another piece of the pie.

"Call me as soon as you find anything," Josh called as he climbed in his truck.

"Same goes, Hollywood. And don't do anything stupid."

He put the truck in gear and took off.

"Stay tough, Delilah. I'm coming."

CHAPTER 34

DELILAH CAME AWAKE SLOWLY, COMPLETELY DISORIENTED FOR a moment. Where was she? Her cheek ached and she almost moaned, but some sixth sense kept her quiet. Without raising her chin from her chest, her eyes darted around the room, lit only by a single kerosene lamp.

She was sitting in a hard wooden chair, her arms tied behind her back, her ankles secured to the chair legs.

Her mouth felt like it was filled with cotton, and she'd give anything for a sip of water. The dimly lit room was stifling. Perhaps that was why she'd dozed off.

A shadow separated itself from the darkness beyond the lamp, and Nate's face appeared. He leaned over her, his fetid breath making her gag. "Welcome home, Delilah. I've been waiting a long time for you to come back where you belong. With me."

"I didn't come back, and I'll never belong here," she spat. "Let me go. This is kidnapping. You know the cops will come looking for me."

He looked surprised. "Why would they? They have no way of knowing that you're with me. And even if they did, what harm is there in a husband and wife having a little reunion?"

"We are not husband and wife, never have been, so there is no reunion. Let me go."

He laughed and then patted her uninjured cheek before he left the room. "We'll see."

Those two words sent chills down her spine, and she held herself stiffly, braced for his return. The silence lengthened as the minutes ticked by. Finally, the outer door opened and closed, and then a key turned in the lock.

He was gone. For now.

Which meant she didn't have a minute to waste. She started trying to work her hands free, but good survivalist that he was, Nate had replaced the zip tie with para cord. She couldn't remember what kind of knot it was, except that the harder she tugged, the tighter it got.

She pulled and tugged until sweat plastered her clothes to her skin and defeat sapped her resolve. Angry tears slipped down her cheeks. But then Josh's smiling face popped into her mind.

Her head snapped up, and she shook it hard to clear it. "You are not a sixteen-year-old weakling anymore. You are Xena, so act like it. You can beat Nate and you will." Memories of her time with Josh sent adrenaline shooting through her. He wouldn't quit until he found her, and he—and Mary—were counting on her not to give up. She wouldn't let them down.

Somehow, she had fallen head over heels in love with the handsome lawman. And though he might not know it yet, she suspected he'd fallen in love with her, too, despite her fears and attempts to push him away.

The knowledge terrified her in the most amazing way. She'd never thought further than rescuing Mary and completing her research study. But what if she did?

For Mary, for herself, and for Josh, she'd fight with every bit of her strength.

She wouldn't let Nate destroy any chance she and Josh had for a future she'd never before allowed herself to want.

As the hours dragged by, Delilah worked to loosen her bindings and plotted her escape.

Josh searched in a grid pattern, determined not to miss a single structure, cave, or hollow tree where Hamm might have taken her. Hunter had checked the man's house, but there was no sign of him—or Delilah.

If he hadn't been driving so slowly, Josh would have missed the small cabin. He pulled behind a clump of scrub palm and moved in on foot.

There was a huge hole in the roof where a tree had fallen through. But was it empty? He climbed through one of the broken windows to be absolutely sure, but his were the only footprints on the dusty floor.

He walked around the structure, surprised to find a small outbuilding that was in much better shape.

Were those tire tracks?

Sure enough, an aging pickup sat in the weeds at the back. He felt the hood. Still warm. Was Delilah in here? Hand on his weapon, he slipped around the building, avoiding the garage door, and tested the knob of the smaller side door. It wasn't locked.

He eased it open, then slipped into the dimly lit room and stepped behind the male sitting in a camp chair, flipping through a magazine, wooden crates surrounding him.

Gun steady, he said, "FWC. Hands where I can see them."

The man leaped up and spun around, hands raised, eyes wide with fear.

What the hell? This was no man. This was a boy, no more than fourteen or fifteen years old.

"You have any weapons on you?"

"No, sir."

"Empty your pockets." The boy did. "Now raise your pant legs." Josh zip-tied the kid's wrists together and then patted him down, just in case. Satisfied, he pushed him down in the chair and holstered his weapon before he studied the room. Crates of wooden boxes were stacked like cordwood. When he inspected one of them, he found semiautomatic weapons. Lots of them.

After he notified Hunter by radio, he demanded, "What's your name, kid?"

The teen looked mutinous, but then muttered, "Tom Simms."

Josh huffed out a laugh and shook his head. "Small world." Then he sobered. "Your folks were pretty worried about you and your sister this morning. Not nice letting them think you drowned."

The boy shrugged. "I had things to do."

"I can see that." They'd sent a kid to guard their stash? That was pretty cocky. "Is your sister all right?" First things first.

He looked down, mumbled, "She had stuff to do, too."

"More guns to guard?"

He shook his head no.

Josh leaned closer, applied a bit of pressure. "Who paid you to pull that stunt this morning?"

Simms visibly paled. "I can't tell you. He made me promise. Said bad things would happen if I told."

"Is that the same person who paid you to sit here?"

The teen nodded.

"I need a name, kid. Now. Or this is not going to go well for you."

Tom swallowed hard, his Adam's apple bobbing. "Will he know I told you?"

"I'll do my best to make sure he doesn't. Who hired you?"

"Aaron Atwood."

Josh straightened. "Do you know where he's taken Delilah Atwood?"

"I don't know anything about that. He just told me to sit here."

Frustration burned in Josh's gut as he waited for Hunter. Keeping these weapons out of the wrong hands was good, but he still had no way to find Delilah.

The moment Hunter arrived, he filled him in, then took off for his truck.

———————

It was dark when Delilah heard the sound of the key in the lock. By then, her stomach rumbled, and she had to pee, bad. She tensed, hoping her flimsy little plan would work. It wasn't much, but it was all she could come up with.

She heard the sound of a match, and then the kerosene lamp flared to life. He came into the room and leaned over her, holding the lamp high so he could see her face.

Delilah made her voice soft, pleading. "Please. I need to use the bathroom."

He studied her a moment longer, then left the room and returned carrying a five-gallon bucket, which he set beside the bed. He reached for one of the bindings around her wrist and made a *tsk*ing sound. "You should know better than to tug on these. You've practically cut off your own circulation. You should take better care of yourself."

Delilah bit back words and waited. He pulled out a knife and kept it trained on her while he untied the cords with the other hand. When she was free, he raised the knife. "If you try to run, I'll have to hurt you. Do you understand?" When she nodded, he rose and leaned against the wall.

She stood up slowly, rubbing her wrists to get the circulation going again. He'd positioned himself right by the door, so there was no hope of escape in that direction. She lifted her chin. "I need some privacy."

"We're about to be married. It's not a problem."

"It is for me. I can't pee if someone's watching. Please."

He studied her a moment more and then stepped through the doorway. He pulled it partway shut, and she knew he was standing right outside, the creep. Delilah sang an old country song at the top of her lungs to disguise the sound as she quickly took care of business. She yanked up her shorts and scrambled onto the bed, determined to shimmy through the small window before he could get back into the room.

But no matter how hard she shoved, she couldn't get it open. It must have been painted shut. *Come on, come on.* Frantic, heart pounding, she shoved harder, but it was no use.

"Hurry up in there."

When she heard him move toward the door, she scrambled off the bed, so frustrated she could scream. She just needed a little more time.

With chilling efficiency, he retied her hands and feet, then took the lantern and left the room. A short while later, the cabin was plunged into darkness, then the door opened and closed, and she heard the key turn in the lock.

CHAPTER 35

THANKS TO BYTE'S COORDINATES, JOSH PEERED THROUGH THE trees at Commissioner Benson's tidy cabin. Unlike the falling-down shack they'd found earlier, this one looked fairly new and was cleverly designed to blend into its surroundings. He recognized Benson's Lexus but not the white pickup beside it.

After a quick call to Hunter, he approached the cabin from the side. He'd wait if he could, but if Delilah's life was in danger, all bets were off.

The windows were too high to see inside, but they were open and the voices carried. He pressed his back against the wall.

"Whoa. Don't get excited," he heard Benson say. "Everything is under control. The cops don't have squat. Besides, Black shouldn't have shown up when he did. If he'd just minded his own business, none of this would've been necessary."

"Yet here we are, with the cops looking for you. What happens when they find you? How long will it take before you tell them everything they want to know?"

"Give me a break. I don't plan to tell them a thing."

"Except I don't trust you not to spill your guts, so you are going to sit down right now and write a confession."

"Confession?" Benson sputtered. "What am I supposed to be confessing to? This is ridiculous."

"You will say that you killed Black, you were working alone, and you couldn't live with the guilt."

The voice was flat, completely matter-of-fact, and Josh suddenly knew who it belonged to. Aaron Atwood. Was Delilah in there, too?

"I will do no such thing," Benson retorted.

"If you write the note, your death will be quick and painless. But if you don't—" There was a pause. "It's up to you, though. I don't care either way."

When Benson started sputtering, Josh turned his radio to silent to avoid giving himself away and raced along the side of the cabin. Backup or no backup, he had to get inside.

He reached the back porch and quietly crossed to the door, relieved when the knob turned under his grip.

"I'll disappear. You'll never hear from me again. I'll never breathe a word to anyone."

There was a brief silence. "Make your choice. Now."

Josh crossed the small kitchen and burst into the living room. "FWC! Hands where I can see them!"

Benson sat at a wooden table, his back to Josh, and he swiveled around in surprise. Aaron stood opposite, knife in hand. His eyes flickered, and Josh dove for the floor milliseconds before Aaron's knife embedded itself in the wall behind him.

As Josh scrambled to his feet, Benson leaped up just as Aaron upended the wooden table and raced for the door.

"Stop," Josh shouted. He ran after him, but Benson stepped in his way, grabbed his arm.

"He's lying. Whatever you heard—"

Josh shoved him aside and barreled through the doorway. Aaron was already in the pickup.

Josh shot out two of the tires, but Aaron didn't slow, just spun the truck around and took off into the forest. Josh raced down the porch steps after him, but Benson blocked his way again.

"Look, you have to believe me—"

Josh leaped around him and took off running, but because of this bumbling idiot, he'd never catch Aaron. He radioed Hunter a description of the truck before he hurried back and handcuffed Benson. "Sit."

He checked the rest of the property, but there was no sign of

Delilah. Several minutes later, Hunter arrived and admitted they hadn't been able to intercept Aaron's truck, either. Perfect.

If his frustration wound any tighter, Josh knew he'd explode. "I've got to go," he said as he shoved past Hunter.

The minutes turned to hours and ticked away like a giant metronome in his head, but despite his best efforts, there was no sign of her. Not at Hamm's place or anywhere else. He raced around the forest in ever-widening circles, banging on doors, waking people from sound sleep, demanding someone tell him where the Atwoods' campsite was. John Henry was the only one left who could help him. But his search netted nothing. Nobody would tell him a thing.

The sun was just peeking over the horizon when he swerved so far off the road, he almost hit a tree. He pulled over and lowered his head to the steering wheel, willing his exhausted brain to come up with something, anything. He didn't know what else to do, where else to look, who else to ask.

He glanced up at the lightening sky. "If you're listening, we could sure use a miracle down here."

But he couldn't wait for that, so he put the truck in gear and got back on the road.

Stay tough, Xena. I will find you.

He'd never give up until he had her safely back in his arms.

———————————

A trickle of sweat dripped down Delilah's face as the morning sun heated the tiny cabin. Her wrists burned from fighting her bindings, but no matter what she did, she couldn't break free. There had to be another way. She couldn't let them marry her sister to that lecher.

A beam of sunlight slipped past the edge of the curtains, and it lit something halfway under the bed. What was that?

Her phone! Nate must have tossed it on the floor.

All she had to do was get there. She started rocking the chair back and forth, back and forth, sliding it across the wooden floor inch by agonizing inch. She was panting before she'd moved six inches, but that was six inches farther than before.

Hang on, Mary.

She rocked harder, trying to hurry, and yelped when the chair tipped over and she crashed into the side of the dresser. She lay there, stunned, her shoulder screaming from the impact.

Time passed as she struggled to keep moving the chair, inch by inch, but she still couldn't reach her phone. She froze when a key turned in the lock. Footsteps crept across the floor, the door eased open, and a face appeared above her.

She blinked, sure she was seeing things. "Mama? Is that really you? What are you doing here?"

Mama crouched beside her and started untying Delilah's wrists, clucking at the damage. "We don't have much time."

"How did you know I was here?" The abandoned hunting cabin hadn't been used by her family and their friends for years.

"Nate's been acting mighty strange lately. But last night, he went too far, said some things that made me worry for you." Mama untied the last binding and helped her up.

Delilah grabbed her phone as they hurried out.

Mama motioned her onto the floor of the cab of the truck. "Best if no one sees you."

Delilah was done hiding, but that was a battle for another day. "Where's Mary?"

Mama hesitated. "She's already there."

Delilah took the work-worn hands in her own. "Where, Mama? Please."

Another pause. "Mooney's Pond." She held up one end of a tarp. "We need to go. I'll take you to your truck."

Delilah checked the time on her phone. 11:55. "What time is the wedding?"

Mama swallowed hard. "One o'clock," she whispered.

Delilah climbed in and ignored the heavy weight of the tarp. "Thank you, Mama." How had she known where Delilah parked her truck? Had she been the one following her?

None of that mattered now. Against all odds, her mother had come to her rescue.

But Mary wasn't free yet.

She tossed the stifling tarp aside and called the local newspaper. "Casey Wells, please."

"Wells. How can I help you?"

"This is Delilah Paige Atwood, and if you're interested in a big scoop that will splash your byline everywhere, you need to listen closely."

After she hung up with Wells, she called the television station in Orlando that had shown the least biased reporting on the monkeys, introduced herself, and told them the same thing she'd told Wells. "I'm going to stop a sixteen-year-old girl from getting married—which is not only against the law but against her will, mind you—to a guy in his forties to cement some kind of militia alliance. Bring a chopper. Wedding is slated for 1:00 p.m." She gave the location and hoped they didn't dismiss her as a crazy person.

Thirty minutes later, Mama stopped the truck. Delilah gathered her close and froze when Mama winced. She studied the ugly bruise she had tried to hide and then cupped her shoulders. "Oh, Mama. Come stay with me."

Mama just shook her head, her voice barely a whisper. "I need to go or I'll be missed."

Delilah wanted to plead, but she bit the words back. This was as far as her mother could go. "I love you, Mama. Thank you."

"I love you, too, baby girl." She kissed Delilah's cheek and climbed back into the truck.

"Wait. Will you take the long way back? Stall for a little while, for Mary's sake?"

They looked at each other for long moments before Mama nodded. "I'll do what I can." Then she put the truck in gear and drove away.

Delilah hopped in her truck and grabbed her phone to call Josh. She hadn't wanted Mama to overhear this conversation, afraid she'd report to John Henry, who would instantly send everyone into hiding.

This ended now.

Today.

===

Exhausted, frantic, and buzzing from caffeine, Josh turned into the Corner Café, hoping maybe Liz or Donny Thomas's mother, Patty, who worked there part-time, or some other customer could help him. He didn't know what else to do. He was out of options, and desperation was making him crazy.

His phone buzzed, and he almost rear-ended another car when he saw Delilah's name. He slammed his truck in park as he fumbled to read the text.

Wedding is at Mooney's Pond. 1:00 pm. Meet me there.

He stabbed in her number, desperate to hear her voice, make sure she was really okay, but the dreaded recording came on, telling him she was out of cell range.

He checked his watch. He had just enough time to get there if he burned rubber the whole way. He called Hunter and floored the gas pedal.

CHAPTER 36

NERVES HUMMED UNDER DELILAH'S SKIN AS SHE EYED THE pickups parked in the grassy area ahead of her. There were easily twice as many as there had been at the campfire. Surely, they weren't all here for Mary's wedding. Then she noticed the targets on the far side of the pond. *Right. The militia gathering people had been talking about that night. Which meant every man present would be armed.*

As Josh had previously, she parked at the end of a row so she could make a quick exit, then grabbed her knife from the glove box and slid it into her pocket. She wished she had her Glock, but this was better than nothing.

She spotted Wells several rows away, accompanied by a long-haired guy toting a professional video camera. Wells smoothed a hand over his wrinkled dress shirt and attempted to straighten his clip-on tie as she approached.

"Thanks for coming." She didn't like the guy, but necessity made strange bedfellows. "Stay out of sight and wait for my signal. I don't want to do anything to spook the crowd. They'll all be armed."

Wells exchanged glances with the videographer, then nodded. She wanted to deliver more warnings, but movement on the platform caught her attention.

She threaded her way to where the crowd gathered in chairs and sprawled on blankets facing a makeshift platform by the pond. There had to be over a hundred people. The men wore camo gear, weapons on their hips, the women the usual long skirts, and children scampered about. She wasn't surprised to see Nate, Eli Foster, and John Henry on the platform, but where was Aaron? And what were John Henry and Nate arguing about?

She was searching for Mary when Mama suddenly appeared, slowly making her way toward the platform, eyes darting around nervously. The crowd shifted, and Delilah finally spotted her sister standing off to one side. She wore a long-sleeved, high-necked white bridal gown, a spray of cheap carnations held in shaking hands.

Everything in her wanted to burst from the tree line and spirit her away, but she took a calming breath and bided her time. She needed the element of surprise.

John Henry scowled at Mama and then at Nate, who ignored him as he walked to the portable sound system and smiled. "Ladies and gentlemen, if you'd take your seats, we'll get started."

The hellfire preacher who'd terrified Delilah as a child marched up onto the platform, Eli beside him.

Delilah scanned the area, heart rate kicking up. She still hadn't seen Aaron.

Pastor Robbins repositioned the microphone. "Marriage is a sacred institution," he began, and Delilah's palms started to sweat.

Nate motioned to John Henry, who took Mary's arm. Her sister flinched, then scanned the crowd, panic etched in her features. Delilah searched the trees behind her again, but there was still no sign of Josh or the rest of the squad.

Robbins pulled out his Bible. "In Genesis, we read…"

Delilah tuned him out and watched Wells and his videographer inch closer and then heard a telltale *thwump thwump* faintly in the distance. She spotted the chopper, closing in fast.

"…and so it shall ever be," she heard Robbins say. "With these words in mind, dearly beloved, we are gathered here today…"

Delilah couldn't wait another second.

She marched up onto the stage and faced Eli, whose eyes flashed at the sight of her.

Shocked gasps rippled through the crowd.

She glanced down and saw her mother's encouraging nod, then winked at Mary.

"What are you doing here?" Nate demanded. Dressed in camouflage gear and an ammunition vest, he looked ready to go hunting. Eli Foster was also in camo, minus the vest.

Delilah lifted her chin and raised her voice. "I'm waiting for the part where the preacher asks if anyone has any reason to object. Because I definitely do." She met Nate's furious gaze. "As does the bride."

The videographer inched closer, his camera on his shoulder.

She turned to Eli. "I warned you at the Mayor's Ball, but you wouldn't listen. Mary is sixteen years old, and she doesn't want to marry you or anyone else right now. And she's not going to."

"You can't walk in here and tell us what to do," Nate hissed.

"Oh yes, I can." The helicopter popped into view beyond the tree line, and the crowd gasped, shifting uncomfortably in their seats. "What you're trying to do is not only wrong, it's against the law. And just so we're clear"—she nodded toward the videographer, then the chopper—"cameras are rolling." Delilah speared Nate with a furious glance. "How successful will your secret militia be once everyone knows you force young girls into so-called marriages for the sake of your alliances?" She held out her hand to her sister. "Come with me, Mary. You don't have to do this."

There was a moment of stunned silence as Delilah walked toward her sister, whose eyes widened before a shy smile spread across her face. John Henry glared at the cameraman.

Two steps before she reached her sister, Mary shouted, "Behind you!"

Delilah spun around as Nate made a grab for her.

"What do you think you're doing, Wife? You should be at home, as I requested."

She sidestepped him, fury in every line. "Requested? You tied me to a chair!"

The helicopter moved closer, camera visible through the open door.

"Tell them to turn the cameras off."

"Not going to happen. Mary will get married when she decides to get married. Today is not that day."

Delilah kept her eyes on Nate's, so she was ready when he growled, "You're mine," and lunged for her again.

She waited until his hands reached for her neck, then brought her foot up and kicked him in the balls with everything she had. She landed the shot perfectly, and he dropped to the ground and whimpered, curled in on himself.

Delilah propped her hands on her hips, breath heaving as she glared down at him. "I am not your wife. I never was."

Josh approached from the trees, his weapon steady on Nate. He stepped onto the platform, deadly calm. "Get up."

Nate shot daggers at Delilah as he slowly stumbled to his feet, muttering curses. Once he was upright, Josh holstered his weapon, pulled his arm back, and punched him in the jaw with enough force to toss him back on the ground. "That's for Delilah." When Nate tried to get to his feet again, Josh growled, "This time, stay down." Then he turned to Delilah, grinned with pride. "Nice going, Xena."

She smiled back. "About time you got here, Hollywood."

As Josh issued instructions, a flash of movement caught her eye, and she spotted Aaron heading straight for Mary. "Oh hell no," she muttered and ran toward him. She intercepted him before he could grab her sister and yelled, "Run, Mary!"

That quick glance toward her sister was all it took for Aaron to wrap his arm around Delilah's neck from behind and put a gun to her temple. "I won't let you ruin everything."

He spun her around as a shield, and she saw Josh walking toward them, weapon raised, voice hard. "Drop the weapon, Aaron. It's over."

"This is an important alliance, a movement for liberty. The government has no right to intervene."

"We do when the girl is underage and you're here with a

crowd of people and piles of illegal weapons," Josh said. Until that moment, Delilah hadn't even noticed the open weapon crates in front of the platform.

Worried murmurs passed through the crowd as Hunter, Sanchez, and Fish approached from different directions, all with their weapons drawn.

"Drop your weapons or I'll shoot her. I mean it," Aaron warned.

Delilah's heart pounded, but she kept her eyes on Josh, waiting for some signal, some way to help him. She knew he couldn't fire without risking shooting her by mistake.

His gaze never wavered. "Last chance, Atwood. Let. Her. Go."

The crowd shifted nervously, several men reaching behind their backs. In the distance, they heard sirens.

Hunter raised his voice to be heard above the murmurs. "We don't want anyone hurt. Put your weapons down and stay seated. Hands behind your heads. Now."

"I'm leaving, and she's coming with me. Try to stop me and I'll shoot her!" Aaron shouted.

As he started dragging her backward, Delilah suddenly remembered an escape trick he'd taught her when they were children. She turned her head and bit down on his bicep, hard.

"Ow!" As he shifted his grip to shake her loose, she dropped straight to the ground and stayed in a crouch. She heard a shot, then Aaron stumbled backward and fell.

"Stay where you are, Atwood," Josh growled, moving closer. "You're under arrest."

"You shot me, you stupid fish cop."

Delilah saw him grip his shoulder, blood seeping through his fingers.

"Be glad it's just your shoulder. EMS is en route."

She scrambled to her feet and smiled at Josh as she ran toward her sister and wrapped her in a bone-crushing hug, her heart slamming against her ribs.

Eli Foster took off running, and over Mary's shoulder, Delilah saw Sanchez take him down in a flying tackle. John Henry was dragging Mama toward their vehicle when Fish stepped in front of them. "I don't think so, sir."

Hunter stood on the platform, eyes on the crowd as law enforcement vehicles converged on the scene. She saw FWC, sheriff's office, and even a couple of people with ATF stamped on their shirts approach the crowd.

The cameras kept rolling.

Mary sobbed against her shoulder. "Thank you, thank you! I didn't think you'd get here in time."

As Delilah rubbed Mary's back and murmured soothing words, she met Josh's eyes over Mary's shoulder. He winked, and a wave of emotion swept over her.

Mary was safe.

CHAPTER 37

IT TOOK A WHILE TO PUT ALL THE PIECES TOGETHER, AND SHE sat with Mama and Mary, keeping them from the worst of the chaos.

Nate, Aaron, and John Henry refused to say a word, but Eli Foster sang like a canary in hopes of getting a lighter sentence for his part in things. Apparently, Nate had come back to town several years earlier as a legitimate businessman while planning to start his own militia.

Aaron had gone into business with Benson, selling guns to other militias, before he decided to start his own. John Henry disagreed but hadn't tried to stop him.

Ultimately, Aaron and Nate couldn't iron out their differences, so John Henry offered Mary to Nate as a way to join the two families under one militia. When Delilah came back, Nate decided he wanted her instead and said Mary would wed Eli.

Delilah stood off to the side and listened, dazed by the lengths these men had gone to in order to get what they wanted.

She was heartsick over everything Mary and Mama had endured and utterly exhausted by the time Josh walked over and pulled her into his arms. "I'm so glad you got here in time. Thank you."

He cupped her face in his hands. "Barely. Damn, woman. You should have waited for me." His mouth came down on hers, and he kissed her like he could never get enough, and she kissed him back with equal fervor. Then he pulled her close again and held tight for several minutes, his heart thundering under her ear.

Mary was safe. Thanks to him and the FWC squad, they were all safe. Finally.

Afterward, he rested his forehead against hers. "Where are you heading? Are you okay to drive? We can come back for your truck tomorrow."

"I need to take Mary and Mama home, try to get them settled, at least for tonight."

"Will you stay with them?"

"No. I can't stay there."

Hunter called Josh's name.

"I'll meet you at home, if that's okay with you."

He raised an eyebrow. "Home?"

"Our camper. Or your parents' camper."

His slow smile spread and reached all the way into her heart. Then he picked up one of her hands and gently kissed the palm. And did the same with the other. "You were amazing today, Xena, and even though you scared the crap out of me, I couldn't be prouder."

Delilah smiled, unable to form words over the lump in her throat.

He went back to work, and she took Mama and Mary back to their camper.

Several hours later, Delilah stepped into the Tanners' camper and straight into Josh's arms.

"Have I mentioned that I love you, Delilah Paige Atwood?" He tucked a strand of hair behind her ear, love shining from his beautiful green eyes and radiating out from his heart-stopping grin.

Delilah felt her own smile widen and blinked back unexpected tears. "I don't believe you've mentioned it, no. But I'd like to hear it again. And in case you were wondering, I love you, too."

Between kisses, he repeated how much he loved her. And she told him the same. After that, he led her to the bedroom and showed her, slowly and tenderly, that he meant every word.

They borrowed kayaks from Tanner's Outpost and paddled to their favorite monkey-spotting location. Josh and Delilah rode in one, Mama had her own, and Mary and her friend Alice paddled the other. Alice had confessed that Aaron paid her and her brother, Tom, to spy on Delilah. He also had the siblings stage the kayak incident to keep FWC occupied the day the guns were to be sold. Alice told Mary she had been trying, in her own way, to help by keeping her eyes and ear open.

In the three weeks since Mary's birthday, Delilah had finished the data-gathering phase of her research project, and now the months of writing began. She was excited about taking her data and turning it into useful, accessible information. Once she completed her master's degree, all kinds of possibilities would open up.

After they beached their kayaks, Josh stepped up behind her and pulled her against him. She'd never get tired of how warm and secure he made her feel. She tucked her head under his chin as they watched Mama and Mary sitting on a log, chatting together, while Alice studied a turtle nearby. Their lives had been turned upside down, but they were handling it. Both Mama and Mary were slowly losing that haunted look, and Mama was starting to stand up straight rather than hunching into herself. Josh had arranged for them to live in a small cottage on Outpost property for as long as they wanted, and his parents had welcomed them like long-lost family.

"They're going to be okay," Josh murmured beside her.

Delilah smiled. "I know they will. They're tough."

"So are you," he whispered and nuzzled her neck.

Delilah heard chattering, and they went still as the monkeys approached, swinging from the treetops, the little ones playing and jumping. Delilah smiled as she watched the mothers and their babies, so relieved they were back together.

Suddenly, Oscar spotted her and scampered down from the

tree. He approached slowly, then stopped several yards away and sat down, waiting expectantly.

Delilah wouldn't make eye contact, didn't want to encourage him. *Go back to your mama, Oscar. It was a one-time thing. I've got nothing.* She stepped out of Josh's embrace, looking anywhere but at him. From the corner of her eye, she saw him glance from her to Oscar and back again, a grin tugging at the corner of his mouth. She knew she was busted when he said, "If didn't know better, Madam Researcher, I'd say someone fed that monkey and he's back looking for a handout."

"Really?" She felt a wash of heat stealing over her cheeks.

His eyebrows rose, and he laughed. "You fed him, didn't you?"

She looked away. "Maybe," she mumbled. "But only because it was an emergency."

He laughed and pulled her closer, kissing the top of her head. "I love you, Xena. My warrior princess with the soft heart."

Oscar watched them for a few minutes, but when no food appeared, he climbed into the trees and disappeared.

She turned to Josh. "Did I tell you that Mary and I are doing a presentation at one of the local high schools about our experiences and the dangers of child marriages? The guidance counselor said she's trying to get us into more schools in the county, too."

One side of his mouth kicked up in a smile. "Nice going, Xena. After how fiercely you've advocated for the monkeys, those girls are incredibly lucky to have you in their corner."

"I'm a little nervous about telling my story, but I'm ready. The new laws are a start, but there's a lot more to be done. I'm planning to get more involved." She paused, then said, "I got a job, too."

Josh went still, expression cautious. She'd moved into his little cottage, but they hadn't talked about the future. Not yet.

"Oh? Where will you be? What will you be doing?"

"They said I could work part-time while I finished my research project, then go to full-time."

He waited.

Unable to drag the suspense out any further, she grinned and told him the name of a local animal sanctuary.

His eyes widened before he swooped her into his arms and spun her around, laughing. He kissed her soundly. "You're staying?"

She wrapped her arms around his neck. "I'm staying if you want me to."

"If I want you to? I not only want you to, I want you to marry me and make babies with me and love me forever."

Delilah thought she could drown in the love shining from his eyes. "Even if we don't agree on the monkeys?"

"Even then." He grinned. "Marry me, Delilah."

Happy tears filled her eyes, but she blinked them back. "Yes, I'll marry you, you annoying fish cop."

He kissed her with a tenderness that made her weak in the knees.

When Mary asked what all the laughing and smooching was about, she and Alice and Mama joined their circle of laughter and joy, standing in the forest, the monkeys chattering above them.

Delilah couldn't believe how much her life had changed. Josh had uncovered all her secrets and seen who she really was—faults, insecurities, and all—and loved her anyway.

Mama had taken a job at a garden center and started seeing a counselor. She was smiling more and had started handing out opinions like they were free candy.

Mary and Alice were going to school, learning to be carefree teenagers. Alice's mother had sworn her daughter would be raised differently.

Delilah knew she and her handsome lawman would always disagree on certain things, probably a lot of things, but they'd work it out.

As the troop disappeared into the forest, Delilah looked at the people around her and laughed through her tears. She no longer had to study the monkeys to learn about families. She finally had her own, and she couldn't wait to get started.

ACKNOWLEDGMENTS

I wrote this story while my father waged his final battle against Alzheimer's. Neither caretaking nor writing would have been possible without the incredible support of so many. My thanks to Amanda Leuck, my awesome agent, and my editor, Deb Werksman, along with Susie Benton, Stefani Sloma, Jessica Smith, and the fabulous team at Sourcebooks. You all are amazing.

Eternal gratitude to Leslie Santamaria, Doris Neumann, Tammy Johnson, Jan Jackson, Lena Diaz, Judy Evans, and Scott Mitchell for their never-ending encouragement. I can never thank my husband, Harry, and my entire family enough for everything.

I am ever grateful to the Great Creator for the gift of stories, and to you, dear readers, for your support of my books. Thank you from the bottom of my heart.

If you love sultry romantic suspense, read on for a sneak peek at a hot new series from Sue Ward Drake, set in the Big Easy...

WALKING THE EDGE

Available now from Sourcebooks Casablanca

CHAPTER 1

CATHERINE HURLEY CLUTCHED HER GHOST-TOUR COSTUME close, bracing for the hit that would smash her flat as roadkill.

Nothing could be as devastating as last time.

Evening shadows darkened the sidewalks, and most of the people on the French Quarter streets this time of day were either coming home or going to work. They didn't usually hang around at the corner grocery like the guy with longish blond hair and skinny shoulders heading her way.

Lately her baby brother had been staying out of her sight, so something must be up. Cath juggled her bags and the dry cleaners' hanger, waiting for him to get close enough to read her lips. "What are you doing here?"

"I thought I'd come visit." Les hitched his backpack higher and hunched his shoulders against the cold. "I don't have any classes until next week."

O-kay. Her held breath swooshed loose. His appearance on her doorstep did not imply disaster. "I've got all the fixings for spaghetti if you want supper."

She handed him one of her grocery bags and pulled him closer to dodge a waiter in a rush to get to his shift. Her brother still flinched and stared at the guy disappearing around the corner. "What the—?"

"It's okay." Even with his hearing aids, Les did not hear sounds behind him. Cath gave him the hanger from the cleaners and pushed open the wrought iron gate.

The piano player in the upstairs rear apartment practiced some ragtime, its bouncy beat drifting down to the patio. She unlocked her back door and set her groceries on the kitchen table inside.

"Sorry," she said and also signed to make sure Les understood the most important word. "I didn't have time to warn you about the guy running down the sidewalk."

"The sidewalk?" Her brother hooked the dry cleaning on the fridge handle. "No problem."

"But you seemed—" *To overreact.* She spoke and signed her next words. "Never mind that. To what do I owe this surprise?"

"Last time I heard, there weren't any laws against surprises."

"True." She nodded and signed.

"Right now, I need a place to stay." Les raised his eyebrows in question. She held aside the bead curtain, and he followed her into the small front room. "The pipes froze this week. Then they broke when it warmed up again."

A fairly typical New Orleans problem in the city's old houses.

Les dropped his pack on the couch and stripped off his jacket. "If this is too much trouble, I'll find someplace else."

"No you won't." She punched his shoulder playfully. "Everything'll be booked now, anyway." Mardi Gras always brought hordes of tourists to town and jacked the prices sky-high. Not that either of them had the money for him to stay in a hotel.

"You don't mind?"

"Of course, I don't mind." She signed, "Doesn't matter." Her kitten, asleep in the upholstered chair, woke and stretched. Cath stroked a hand down the cat's back. "You should have texted me to pick you up after my bus tour."

Les studied the framed poster on the wall. Which he'd seen many times before. He finally looked at her again and she signed, "Did you understand? I could have come to get you."

"Yeah. I got that." He hesitated, a hand at his ear. "Wait a minute."

He reached behind one ear to pull off his hearing aid, and she carried the hanger with her dress for tonight's tour to the bedroom. When she returned a minute later, Les had replaced his battery and now cradled her pet against his chest. "I didn't call because you have a business to run. You can't be chasing all over town because your brother's got plumbers in his apartment."

"Thanks." Good to know he appreciated her situation, but Les carefully avoided mentioning the elephant in the room. She'd recently raided their rainy-day fund to bail him out. If he wanted to stay here, ground rules might be order. She glanced at his backpack and let out a pent-up breath. Her brother didn't need rules. He needed to know she would always stand by him. "When do you have to go back to court?"

"Not today." The kitten climbed to his shoulder and rubbed her chin against his neck.

"When?" She spoke and signed both, not wanting Les to misunderstand.

"Pretty soon."

"I hope your lawyer can get the charge reduced. He knows you weren't dealing, doesn't he?"

"He better." Indignation flared in her brother's eyes. "But you don't need to come this time. I'll be okay."

If he'd been okay the first time, he never would have been arrested.

fledging firm would get a black eye. Mitch couldn't afford for that to happen.

"My buddies in the marines say everyone who serves in the Middle East comes home with baggage," Hal said, continuing to be a know-it-all.

"I'm on edge is all." Mitch had been home nearly three months. Hal had been busy, sure, but they'd had plenty of time to talk. A nervous twitching in his gut flared again. "This *is* my first time."

"Understood." Hal glanced at him. "I saw your medals."

Their elderly aunt had insisted on examining them, but Mitch would just as soon have left them in the box where they belonged. "All they mean is that I can hit a target from anywhere in or out of range, and I know how to score."

"One of them has a purple ribbon." Hal raised his brows. "You could have told us you'd been wounded."

"We've all got battle scars, but yeah." Mitch ran a hand over his short hair. His throat clogged. He swallowed but the pain only strengthened. "That was a rough op."

"At least you got out alive." Hal dropped to tie a shoe beneath one of the old-style lanterns dotting the Quarter. "Remember, your skip is going to be violent. He knows he's hiding."

"That figures." His older brother took his mentoring job seriously, but he didn't need to worry. Mitch had passed the bounty hunter course and planned to make his first arrest by the book.

His brother turned at the next corner, and they entered the French Quarter's quiet residential streets.

Cold mist pushed at their backs and swirled past. Visibility would be plenty worse soon. Mitch patted his pockets, making sure he'd remembered his flashlight. "Hope we're done before this stuff gets worse."

"We'll be in and out in ten minutes, tops." Hal slicked a hand over his dark hair and waited for a car to pass before crossing the street.

Ten minutes would be the best-case scenario, but Hal wouldn't have said that if he didn't have confidence Mitch could perform. The knots tying his gut finally came undone.

Shutters covered the windows of the houses bellied up to the sidewalk. The sounds of traffic on the main arterial road faded. Hal stopped a few feet from the Creole cottage where they'd earlier located Mitch's fugitive.

A gate closed off the alley that led to a courtyard and gave street access to tenants living in the rear. A small garden filled the wedge of visible lighted patio. No one who could be collateral damage appeared to be around, and Mitch gave his brother a thumbs-up.

"There're lights behind the front shutters," his brother whispered. "He's inside."

Supposedly his bail skip holed up with a girlfriend. Mitch braced a hand on the Victorian-style porch of the neighbor's house. "What if the woman is here?"

"I'll keep her out of the way." Hal positioned himself at the bottom of the cottage steps. "You ready?"

Mitch unzipped his jacket to reveal the T-shirt identifying him as a bail recovery agent and went through his mission prep like a batter at the plate. A fist press against his upper lip. A shake to loosen his hands. He plastered his back against the front of the house and nodded.

Hal knocked.

Seconds passed. The gleam of reflected light on the knob disappeared as the door opened. Running shoes appeared on the doorjamb. Mitch tensed.

"Gas company." His brother flashed an old security badge. "We were informed of a problem at this address."

"Who is it?" A woman's warm alto voice called from inside. Mitch clenched his jaw. He'd have to watch out for her.

"Wait a minute." The door closed.

Adrenaline ebbed. Mitch whispered, "We got some wrong intel?"

FINAL HOUR

Lose yourself in a romantic thriller featuring an elite government unit and the terrifying bioterrorist outbreaks they fight to subdue

By Juno Rushdan

Every Last Breath

When a lethal bioweapon goes up for auction, Maddox Kinkade's life-or-death mission to neutralize it sends her crashing into the last person she expected—her presumed-dead fiancé, Cole Matthews.

Nothing to Fear

When Gideon Stone investigates suspected mole Willow Harper, an unlikely bond pushes limits—and forges loyalties. Every move they make counts. And the real traitor is always watching...

Until the End

Gray Box operative Castle Kinkade always comes out on top. But when he agrees to protect white-hat hacker Kit Westcott, surviving might be mission impossible...

"Tense and fulfilling. Settle back and savor this one."
—Steve Berry, *New York Times* bestselling author, for *Every Last Breath*

For more Juno Rushdan, visit:
sourcebooks.com

RUNNING THE RISK

Second in the pulse-pounding Endgame
Ops series by rising star Lea Griffith

Jude Dagan's life as he knew it ended a year ago. On a mission gone wrong,
he was forced to watch as Ella Banning, the only woman he's ever loved,
was killed. Or so he thought...

Survival is crucial. Trust is optional.

Love is unstoppable.

**"Immediately engaging... This is one
terrific tale of romantic suspense!"**
—*RT Book Reviews* for *Flash of
Fury*, 4½ Stars, TOP PICK

HELL ON WHEELS

From *New York Times* and *USA Today* bestselling author Julie Ann Walker, the men of Black Knights Inc. will ignite all your hottest fantasies...

Behind the facade of their tricked-out motorcycle shop on the North Side of Chicago is the headquarters for the world's most elite covert operatives. Deadly, dangerous, and determined, they'll steal your breath and your heart.

"Edgy, alpha, and downright HOT."
—Catherine Mann, *USA Today* bestselling author

BEYOND THE LIMIT

Team Reaper has a new mission: train the first *female* SEALs

Don't miss the Valkyrie Ops series from *New York Times* bestselling author Cindy Dees

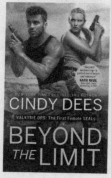

Navy SEAL Griffin Caldwell is not happy with Operation Valkyrie, his team's top-secret mission to train the first female SEALs. Griffin's determined to prove that his trainee, Sherri Tate—a former beauty queen, no less—doesn't have what it takes to join the world's most elite warriors club. But even this hard-nosed SEAL has to admit she's tough as nails. What he won't admit is the attraction sizzling between them...

When a dangerous mission lands Sherri and Griffin in the crosshairs of the world's most feared terrorist, it's going to take everything they have to come out with their lives—and hearts—intact.

"Sexy and entertaining—a perfect mix of action and romance!"
—Katie Reus, *New York Times* bestselling author

For more Cindy Dees, visit:
sourcebooks.com

TURN THE TIDE

There's breathless suspense for everyone in this free e-collection of novellas from some of the brightest new names in the genre: Katie Ruggle, Adriana Anders, Connie Mann, and Juno Rushdan

Whether you're diving into treacherous waters, racing the clock against global annihilation, or delving deep into an untamed wilderness, these thrilling tales of love and suspense will leave you breathless.

"Vivid and charming."
—Charlaine Harris, #1 *New York Times* bestselling author, for the Search & Rescue series

For more Katie Ruggle, visit:
sourcebooks.com

RISK IT ALL

Meet a band of bounty hunter sisters...and the men who steal away with their hearts, from author Katie Ruggle

Cara Pax never wanted to be a bounty hunter—she's happy to leave chasing criminals to her more adventurous sisters. But if she wants her dream of escaping the family business to come true, she's got one last job to finish. Too bad she doesn't think her latest bounty is actually guilty...

"Sexy and suspenseful, I couldn't turn the pages fast enough."
—Julie Ann Walker, *New York Times* and *USA Today* bestselling author, for *Hold Your Breath*

For more Katie Ruggle, visit:
sourcebooks.com

WHITEOUT

With a storm coming and a killer on the loose,
every step could be their last...

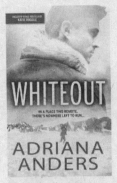

Angel Smith is finally ready to leave Antarctica for a second chance at life.
But on what was meant to be her final day, the remote research station she's
been calling home is attacked. Hunted and scared, she and irritatingly gorgeous glaciologist Ford Cooper barely make it out with their lives...only to
realize that in a place this remote, there's nowhere left to run.

Isolated with no power, no way to contact the outside world, and a
madman on their heels, Angel and Ford must fight to survive in the most
inhospitable—and beautiful—place on earth. But what starts as a partnership born of necessity quickly turns into an urgent connection that
burns bright and hot. They both know there's little chance of making
it out alive, yet they are determined to weather the coming storm—no
matter the cost.

"Scorching hot and beautifully emotional."
—Lori Foster, *New York Times* bestselling author

For more Adriana Anders, visit:
sourcebooks.com

THE COST OF HONOR

The sizzling, action-packed Black Ops Confidential
series from award-winning author Diana Muñoz
Stewart will keep you on the edge of your seat!

When an attempt to protect one of Tony Parish's vigilante sisters went
horribly wrong, he had to fake his own death to escape his fanatical family.
As "Lazarus," he disappeared to Dominica—only to awaken face-to-face
with the woman of his dreams…

When Honor Silva plunged into stormy waters to rescue a drowning
kiteboarder, she had no idea resuscitating the sexy stranger would bring
life-changing love—and life-threatening danger—crashing into her
world.

**"Poignant in places, nail-biting in others, there's plenty
of sizzle and emotional clout. An electrifying ride."**
—Steve Berry, *New York Times* bestselling
author, for *The Price of Grace*

For more Diana Muñoz Stewart, visit:
sourcebooks.com

EVERY DEEP DESIRE

First in a sultry, swampy romantic suspense
series from author Sharon Wray

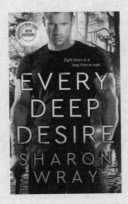

Rafe Montfort was a decorated Green Beret, the best of the best, until a
disastrous mission and an unforgivable betrayal destroyed his life. Now,
this deadly soldier has returned to the sultry Georgia swamps to reunite
with his Beret brothers—as well as the love he left behind—and take back
all he lost. But Juliet must never know the truth behind what he's done…
or the dangerous secret that threatens to take him from her forever.

**"Twisty plots, fantastic characters, and
pitch-perfect pacing. Fabulous!**
—Allison Brennan, *New York Times* bestselling author

For more Sharon Wray, visit:
sourcebooks.com

ABOUT THE AUTHOR

Connie Mann is a licensed boat captain and loves writing about Florida's small towns and unspoiled wilderness. She is the author of *Beyond Risk* (Florida Wildlife Warriors #1), the Safe Harbor series (*Tangled Lies, Hidden Threat, Deadly Melody*), *Angel Falls*, and *Trapped!*

When she's not dreaming up plotlines, you'll find "Captain Connie" on Central Florida's waterways, introducing boats full of schoolchildren to their first alligator. She is also passionate about helping women and children in developing countries break the poverty cycle and build a better future for their families. She and her husband are happiest on or near the water, spending time with their grown children and extended family, and planning their next travel adventure.

Please visit Connie online at conniemann.com and sign up for her newsletter for all her latest news.

counter and stuffed a handful of dried pasta in a clear bag. "Take all you want. Bon appétit."

Now she was quoting her hunky bounty hunter.

Her bounty hunter? Where had that come from?

He looked yummy and had set off butterflies inside. She had priorities, though, and they didn't include men like him.

Les had lied to her, yes, but her heart clenched at the way the bounty hunters had treated him. He'd managed to escape when she'd opened the door, but he wouldn't be safe for long. She pressed a fist to her lips. *Please don't let this be the last time I ever see my baby brother.*

hummed from the aftereffects of his legs pressing hers. She sought the wrist where he'd wrapped his fingers. He'd relaxed his hold immediately, but he hadn't let go because... She didn't know. The whole thing had been weird.

And she'd reacted without thinking things through first.

"Houston calling. Earth to Cath."

Rhonda tilted her head, a puzzled expression on her face, and Cath took a deep breath. "Are you talking about the one masquerading as the gas repairman?"

Her friend gaped. "There was more than one?"

"Unfortunately." What were the chances this was all a bad dream? "The guy you saw...?" Cath raised her eyebrows.

"I don't know what he wore. He whipped past me so fast I barely had time to determine his sex." Rhonda pulled keys from her wrist clutch and waggled her eyebrows. "You're not dressed. Does this mean what I think it means?"

"That I'm taking in customers and this guy couldn't wait to get away from me because I'm so inept?" Cath cinched her belt. "You know me better than that."

Though she *could* admit to a certain clumsiness in the relationship department. For which she'd already paid dearly.

"Don't you lead a tour tonight?"

"Yeah. I better get dressed." Cath held open her kitchen door. "You want some spaghetti sauce? I made enough for a crowd."

"I really shouldn't." Her friend's mouth turned down. "I'm trying to diet."

"Why?" Cath opened a cabinet to search for a storage container. Rhonda already had a great figure. More voluptuous than her on top, but a perfectly flat stomach. "You're already a smaller size than me except you know where."

"Even short people need to be in proportion." Rhonda patted her hips.

"I used ground turkey." Cath placed a plastic container on the

The thing inside clawed up his throat. Mitch raced down the block and dropped beside his brother. "What happened?"

Hal lay face up, a hand pressed to his shoulder. His eyes cracked open. "He got past the vest."

Mitch removed Hal's bloody hand and pressed his clean handkerchief to the wound. Hal inhaled with a rasp. "How...How bad is it?"

Hal needed to go to the hospital. Yesterday. Mitch switched hands on the compress and fumbled for his cell. "You'll definitely need stitches."

This was on him. Didn't matter that Hal had separated them. If Mitch had done his job in the first place, they would already have Les Hurley on his way back to jail.

Nobody would be bleeding.

The phone case bit into his palm as he raised the cell to his ear. His fugitive would not get away. He would catch Hurley and make him pay.

———————

Cath rubbed her jaw but her teeth remained locked tight. She'd always thought her brother could talk to her about any problems, but he'd lied to her. Big time. He hadn't been forced out of his apartment by broken water pipes. He'd been hiding from these bounty hunters.

"Who's the guy who charged out of here a minute ago?" Her next-door neighbor, Rhonda Owens, walked into the patio, her waitress apron dangling from one hand. "He nearly knocked me over bursting out of the gate."

"Not surprised," Cath muttered. "He was in a hurry." But he wasn't the bounty hunter inflicting the most damage. As if nearly catching himself on fire and scaring her to death wasn't enough, movie-star Handsome had to throw a stone in the equilibrium she worked so hard to maintain.

The ripples still lapped at her edges, and her nerves still

"I told you to go inside." Mitch judged the height of the barrier. A running leap took him to the top, and he hauled himself up.

"What are you doing?" The woman's pale face appeared in the shadowed shrubs below.

"Fulfilling your deepest desires." Mitch smirked. "Like the Southern gentleman I am."

A multistory masonry house faced the parallel street on the other side. A swimming pool stretched past the converted servants' quarters on one side of the patio. A soft snick drew his attention to the half-glassed door on the rear of the main house. With no side alleys here, this must serve as the street exit for the rear tenants. Or fugitives coming over this wall.

"I'm going over," Mitch said to Hal. "Meet me around the block."

Mitch dropped to the ground and raced along the pool. The doorknob turned easily, and within seconds he'd covered the inside hallway and stepped onto the street. Running footsteps faded into the night, and a flash of blond hair disappeared around a corner. Mitch reached the same intersection seconds later only to find empty sidewalks stretching in three directions.

Hal panted to a stop beside him, then pointed toward the street on the right. "I'll go this way. You go straight."

Mitch held up a hand. "We need to stick together, protect each other's back."

"Who's been a bounty hunter longer?" Hal crossed his arms. "Huh?"

"You have," Mitch said, but tightness pinched his chest.

"Let's each circle a block and meet back here." Hal moved off in his chosen direction.

Mitch crept down his deserted street, sweeping a glance along both sides. He jogged another block without any better success. He brought his gun up, rounded the corner onto Hal's street, and halted. Halfway down, a dark shape sprawled on the sidewalk.

of the banana trees at the back of the patio. He stepped forward. She didn't retreat, and his legs now pressed against hers, making certain body parts grow heavier. "Turn around and go back." *Don't make me swear like my old sergeant.*

"Not until you leave." Her hand loosened, and she accidentally flashed cleavage. "We can pretend I'm seeing you out. Southern manners and all."

That accent of hers belonged more to California than to any southern state, but his tightening groin didn't give a shit. Nor did his resolve. He lowered his voice to a purr. "You really should go back to the patio."

She frowned. "Why?"

"Nothing over there but the garbage cans," Hal called a moment before his silhouette appeared at the opposite end of the dark alley.

Mitch leaned close to her ear. "If you don't want Hal searching your house, you need to stop him."

"But, I…"

"You got him?" Hal started toward them.

"Wait." Mitch waved his brother back and raised his eyebrows at the female in his way. "We're coming out."

She huffed out a breath but spun around. In the lighted patio, Hal glanced from her to Mitch, his mouth turning down. "You missed him."

For now. The beauty crossed her arms, but Mitch shooed her away. "We're finished. Go inside."

He caught his brother's arm and jerked his head toward the shrubs and banana trees. "The skip might be lurking."

Hal waded through one side of the garden, Mitch, the other. Their twin beams hit a high brick wall without revealing a soul. Some Quarter landlords embedded broken bottles atop property walls to keep out thieves, but Mitch didn't see any here. He stowed his light and backtracked to the patio. "Hold the trees away, Hal."

"I still want an apology." The female wildcat pounced.

pretty face flushed. She stepped away, and he plunged outside after his fugitive.

A spotlight on the rear apartments cast deep shadows into the corners. A dog yipped inside a rear apartment. Big jars with cascading vines standing at either corner were too small to hide behind.

Mitch hugged the corner of the house so as not to present a target. His stupid fixation on the redhead had cost him too much time. Hurley could have already escaped. Or he could be standing only a few feet away in the black entrance alley, his knife ready. Mitch held still, but the *shush-shush* of someone breathing didn't carry back to him. *Dammit.*

He drove a fist into the vinyl siding. An old war injury spread agony across his back, and he swallowed back another curse. *Keep looking. Don't think about failure.*

Hal came up behind him. "I'll check the other side."

Mitch played his light down the alley. A clump of ferns grew in the elbow of one of the many pipes hugging the old house. Nothing else. No one else. He raced to the street gate and scanned the empty sidewalk.

"I demand an apology for barging into my house." The redhead stood close behind him, but he hadn't even heard her creeping up on him.

In the narrow confines, he barely had room to turn around without brushing her, but he managed. Producing more aggro for his shoulder. "If this is not your private alley, you have no jurisdiction. I'm the one being insulted."

"I—insulted?" She scowled. "How do you figure that?"

Light from the street fell on her pale face and flushed cheeks. He caught a powder-fresh scent. She clutched the sides of a robe together, and he admired her slender neck. Perfect for nuzzling. Not by him. Not now.

His flashlight beam shone down the alley to the swaying leaves

"What is this crap?" Hurley twisted against Mitch's thumbs, his longish blond hair flying. With more force, Mitch body-slammed the bail skip, twisting a wrist behind his back and pushing aside something heavy on the stove. He reached for the cuffs.

Flame licked at his hand. Mitch shoved the struggling fugitive in the direction of the sink. Hal needed to get over here. Now.

"Let go of him," the woman yelled. "He can't hear you."

"Stay out of the way, lady," Hal yelled. "Or else—"

"You can't just come busting in here." A female hand reached past Mitch and flipped off the burner. "This is a private home."

"Stand aside, lady." Hal held up a copy of the bail piece. "This gives us authority to arrest. Recognized by the law."

Something stung Mitch's arm. A blade glinted in Hurley's fist. "Back off."

Mitch yanked the wrist he held high behind his skip's back. His fugitive shrieked. "Give it up. I got you beat."

"You're hurting him." The woman again. "Let him go so I can sign to him."

Mitch barely heard what she said, couldn't focus—"Ouch."

Hurley had kicked out with both feet. Now he slipped from Mitch's grip and dashed outside.

Mitch lurched forward, banging his head on the open door. His boots slipped on grit spilled across the floor, and he grabbed for support.

Soft, warm skin slid under his grasp. The most spectacular blue eyes he'd ever seen glared at him, but Mitch held on to her gaze as if to a lifeline.

"Do you mind?" Her low, sultry voice whispered through him.

Mitch blinked and let go of the woman's slender arm.

"Didn't you see the skillet?" She waved a hand at the stove. "I'm making dinner."

"Bon appétit." Mitch lifted a corner of his mouth, and her

Hal shrugged and leaned forward to call through the door. "Utilities. I'm here to turn the gas back on."

The knob clicked and a sliver of light reappeared. "You have the wrong apartment," the male at the door said. "Check the mailboxes."

"Wait." Hal stowed the ID. "What's your name?"

Mitch held his breath. They needed to confirm their fugitive's identity before they entered.

"My name?" The speaker paused, and Hal nodded. "Les Hurley. Why?"

Hal stepped down and Mitch vaulted the steps. The door under his hand banged against the inside wall. Hurley staggered back before Mitch even touched him. A quick glance around the room revealed a couch against one wall. An overstuffed armchair. A cluttered coffee table. Colored beads hanging in the doorway to a back room.

A woman's pretty face flashed in his peripheral vision before disappearing. Hurley tripped over the coffee table, tumbled onto the couch.

The front door banged shut behind him. "You're under arrest, Lester M. Hurley." Hal's voice couldn't have been calmer. "Cooperate and you won't get hurt."

Hurley sprang to his feet and vaulted the overturned table. Mitch clamped a hand on his shoulder, but Hurley spun out of his grasp and sprinted into the back room.

Mitch swept aside the bead curtain and charged after his skip.

The mahogany-haired beauty huddled near the fridge on his left. The shock on her delicate face barely registered as Mitch rounded the table and caught Hurley against the counter. The guy twisted away. Lightning quick, Mitch pinned the smaller man against the stove and locked fingers around a wrist. He could kill a man with his bare hands, but lethal moves weren't allowed. Bounty hunters had to bring a fugitive in alive.

whiskey-laden breath washed over him. Slurred words tumbled from the mouth of the drunken college student staggering in front of him.

Calm down. You're not in Kansas anymore. Or Iraq. Mitch steadied the kid before pulling out his cell. "I'm calling you a taxi."

"We're fiiinnne."

And he was a horse's ass. Mitch stowed his phone and held out a couple of twenties. "I'm serious. You need to take a cab."

The kid's companion hiccupped. "We got enough."

"Don't drive. You hear?" When they nodded, Mitch stepped away and waited while Hal closed the hatch.

His brother pulled on a nondescript jacket. "What were you doing?"

"They looked in need."

"You plan on rescuing every drunk you meet?"

"You really want an answer?" Mitch flicked sweat from his temple.

"I can do without one." His usually too-serious brother cracked a smile.

They navigated around the tourists in front of an Italian grocery, then passed through the cayenne-scented steam coming from a bar serving seafood. Hal glanced at Mitch, grim lines grooving his forehead. "You sick? You've been sweating like a pig."

Was his brother looking to disqualify him before he could even get started? No, not Hal. They were closest in age and had been great buddies until the accident. Mitch shrugged. "I'm okay."

The army docs told him he'd probably have post-trauma episodes for years. Mitch had them mostly under control, the overreaction tonight his first in months. "I'm not going to let you down, Bro."

Nor Big Easy Bounty Hunters.

Every takedown counted. If he and Hal failed to return this fugitive to jail before their recovery window closed, his brothers'

They'd been circling the French Quarter for nearly an hour and hadn't even parked the car, much less made an arrest.

Mitch Guidry raised his window against the hubbub of sidewalk carousers getting a jump on Fat Tuesday. "Drop me off at the address we got. Let me grab the bail skip while you drive around the block."

"We never go in without two," Hal yelled over the roar of a passing tour bus. "Besides, you're too intimidating to be believable as a meter reader."

Mitch rubbed damp palms on his thighs, taking in the blue uniform shirt and pants his brother wore. "We're about the same size. Pull over and give me your shirt."

"No."

"You really think this ruse will work?"

"Long enough to get you through the door." Hal stopped beside a sedan and jerked a thumb over his shoulder. "Lookie what I found."

Mitch jumped out to stop the traffic behind them while Hal backed the SUV. Nighttime fog poured in off the Mississippi, fuzzing the neon signs of restaurants along the street and the headlights of oncoming vehicles. Visibility low. No wind. High humidity. *What are you doing, Guidry? You're not on duty.*

But he definitely had a job to do properly. His three older brothers had made him a conditional member of their Big Easy Bounty Hunters firm. Operative word: *conditional.*

They'd censured him before. Rightly so. If he messed up tonight, they could turn their backs on him again. Mitch couldn't let that happen. He needed his brothers and his sweet, elderly aunt more than they would ever know.

Mitch sucked in the reek of stale beer from the bars behind him and guided his brother into the parking space. Someone slammed his back. He whirled and cocked a fist, stopping only when